Ben Richards | a sweetheart deal

review

'Whiskey Girl' Words and Music by Gillian Welch and David Rawlings © 1999 Say Uncle Music/Irving Music Inc/Cracklin Music (admin by Bug Music Ltd) (70%) Rondor Music (London) Ltd, London SW6 4TW. Reproduced by permission of International Music Publications Ltd.

First published in 2000
by REVIEW

An imprint of Headline Book Publishing

10 9 8 7 6 5 4 3 2 1

ISBN 0 7472 7633 1

Typeset by Palimpsest Book Production Limited, Polmont, Stirlingshire
Printed and bound in Great Britain by Clays Ltd, St Ives plc.

Headline Book Publishing
A division of the Hodder Headline Group
338 Euston Road
London NW1 3BH

www.reviewbooks.co.uk
www.hodderheadline.com

To Vivien Bradford

ACKNOWLEDGEMENTS

Many people helped in writing this book. I would like to thank all of those from various pathology labs and trade unions who took the time to answer my questions. I would also like to particularly thank Lydia Richards.

Thanks also to Geraldine Cooke, Mary-Anne Harrington, Allan Richards, Yvonne Swain (for the eggs!), Anne Bolstridge (technical support) and Brian Denny.

The Cuban film which Pepa tells Mel about at the end of the book is *Hello Hemingway*.

Love and thanks to Rossana again.

Sometimes a man will wake up with an involuntary shudder and ask himself, 'Can I indeed be thirty . . . or forty . . . or fifty years old? How is it possible that life has passed so quickly? How is it possible that death has come so near?' But death is like a fisherman who, having caught a fish in his net, leaves it in the water for a time; the fish continues to swim about, but all the while the net is round it, and the fisherman will snatch it out in his own good time.

Ivan Turgenev, *On the Eve*

prologue

bluebells

Dusk was falling as the train came to a halt on the outskirts of London. There were some weary sighs, a few fed-up commuters pulled back their sleeves and checked their watches. They were already late and this was now the third time that their journey had been interrupted. Gordon Forrester cupped his chin in his hands and stared out from the window of his first-class carriage. He rather enjoyed these moments of stasis, absorbing the details of a place he would never see again. Beyond the back fences were the suburban kitchens whose lights could be glimpsed through the branches of the chestnut trees – people were starting to arrive home from work.

Gordon's attention was suddenly caught by a movement at the top of the embankment. At first he thought that it was a cat but then he wondered whether it might be a fox. He peered more urgently – he was sure that it was a fox. And as he stared into the strange and changing light, the animal suddenly stopped and gazed back at the lit-up train. Gordon was curious about this little urban survivor whose eyes almost appeared to be locking with his. What did it see? What impression did the bright lights of the stalled train make on its consciousness? He thought about the fox which sometimes came to the garden of his house. On cold, moonlit nights, he and his wife Lily would stand quietly at the window, watching it, her head on his shoulder, his arm around her.

People began to call on mobiles to say that the train had been delayed and that they would be late home. As they did so, the train jerked back into motion. Gordon craned his neck but he could no longer see the fox; the fences and the kitchen lights disappeared as the train began to accelerate, gathering momentum, entering the city.

A woman holding silver tea and coffee pots smiled at Gordon as she passed by. She had an attractive face, she had dimpled and giggled when he had joked flirtatiously with her as she poured his coffee. Gordon wondered where she was from – Indonesia? The Philippines? Malaysia? He recalled the documentary he had watched the night before in his hotel room. The programme had detailed the effects of *El Niño* and the extent to which its impact was compounded by man. Gordon had watched – swinging shoeless feet from the end of the bed and drinking a can of warmish lager from the mini-bar – fires crackling like a rash across the forests of Borneo. It was as if a bombing raid had just taken place. Then there were barren islands off the coast of Peru which had once sustained large bird colonies, there were coral reefs crumbling and choking in the Caribbean. What kind of world was his young son Daniel going to inhabit? What did the future hold for him?

Gordon smiled with pleasure as he thought of the son he would soon be seeing. Daniel would run laughing towards his father holding out his arms when he heard the door open. He knew nothing about burning forests, nothing about the warming of the Pacific. He was just a child kicking a ball about the book-crowded living room or chortling at the red train chugging round and round a circular yellow track. *But I will be a good father to him, I will protect him as far as I can against the horrors of the world.* Gordon smiled and closed his eyes. He thought that Lily would probably be bathing Daniel about now and . . .

When Gordon opened his eyes again he could not feel his legs at all. He could hear somebody screaming, 'My arm, my arm, oh for Christ's sake somebody help me, please help me for the love of God.' Gordon was also in pain, he was enveloped in it like the twisted metal which pinned him down, which held his limbs trapped in this bizarre swastika position. There was a lot of dust, he saw dust all over the purple tunic of the woman who had been serving the coffee, who must have been flung down the carriage by the impact. Blood trickled from her ear although her head was turned away from him and Gordon sensed the stillness of death about her. He was

4

not in a train carriage any more, there were no recognisable seats or luggage racks or sliding doors, there was no proper geometry, no order. There was just twisted metal and dust and shouting. 'Help me please, please help me, can't anybody hear me?' Gordon wanted to shout that he could hear but he could not fill his lungs with air and his mouth and eyes were clotted with dust. It was so strange not being able to move, not even to feel his legs. One arm was pinned across his chest, with the other bent back so that it was cupping his ear as if he were attempting to hear better. But the opposite was true; he could hear too well, too much.

When he looked up, able at least to move his eyes, he saw rods of light shooting through the metal. It reminded him of a film he had once watched where a killer stalked his victim and fired through a wall, causing elegant arrows of light to mark the trajectory of the bullets. He had enjoyed the film but Lily had disliked its casual cartoon approach to violence and pain. *How can torture be funny?*

Gordon noticed that above his head a wheel from the train appeared to have come to rest. Another carriage must have somehow landed on top of them. Terrifying as this was, Gordon was relieved. His limbs might be trapped but there was nothing wrong with his head. In spite of his shock, he could think clearly, he was not suffering from any kind of brain damage. He moved his eyes again to look at the head of the woman who had been serving the coffee. She had a red ribbon in her hair. She had not moved. He could see the tiny soft hairs on the nape of her neck but the beautifully smooth brown skin that he had earlier been admiring was covered in a light film of dust.

So this was it, this was disaster, he was trapped. One moment he had been thinking about his paper, about his wife bathing his child and then there had been the terrible screech and then dust and smoke and screams. He tried to think of where they might be but could not remember any stations, just the slide into the lights of London. Now the sound of screaming, the pleas for help had quietened and he felt alone. *I want to live*, he thought. *I want so much to live.* He was thirty-six years old, a university lecturer in public administration returning from a conference organised by a wealthy pro-business think-tank. Gordon had enjoyed being devil's advocate, the token left-wing academic who was also prepared to take a few swipes at some radical positions and expose their inconsistencies. He had been confident, charming, funny — he had watched heads nodding at some of his arguments. And he had also enjoyed the perks of the trip — the five-star hotel and first-class train ticket. He did not get such perks often — late last night he had lain on the double bed, eaten the complimentary chocolate left on his pillow, and murmured to Lily on the phone, told her how he wished she were with him to share this luxury. Like many people of his age, Gordon had experienced the melancholy of knowing he had not achieved the things that he had once thought he might — he had a drawer filled with poems he knew would never be read by anybody but himself. Still, he also knew that his life was filled with compensations, things that others might never have.

But now the first-class carriage had turned into a chaos of metal and crushed bodies. And Lily would not know yet, she did not know where he was. If only he could tell her where he was, not to worry.

A surge of panic filled him as he thought of his wife and child. *I cannot die. I must not die. What right do I have to die and change their lives so profoundly? To bring grief into their lives?* His son would be splashing in the bath, Lily would be shaking her curly hair and smiling, perhaps she would be singing to him in French — *Au jardin de mon père les lilas sont fleuris.* Sometimes he would go and kneel behind her, put his hands on her slender waist and laugh with pleasure at their young son. Nobody knew he was lying somewhere in the suburbs of London, unable to move and staring at a dead woman. But he was not going to die. He was thinking, his mind was working.

He was thinking but he was frightened. It was difficult to control his breathing and he remembered that crucifixion killed you through slow asphyxiation. Spartacus's slave army died like that — strung up all along the Appian Way. Who was the actor in that film? The one with the funny chin? For a while, he distracted himself by struggling with the frustration of trying to remember an all-too-familiar name. He abandoned this and tried to conjure up tunes in his head in order to calm himself. *This should not have happened.* He should have been getting off the train, he should have been phoning Lily to tell her that he had arrived and would be home shortly, that he had decided to get a cab. Now perhaps somebody else would phone her.

Dîtes-nous donc la belle, où donc est votre mari?

Why had this happened to him? These were things that you read about

— train crashes, planes plummeting, tidal waves, earthquakes, volcanic eruptions, famines, massacres, car-bombs. Yes, you read about these things, you felt horror and pity for the victims, combined with the *frisson* of relief that it had not and *would not* happen to you. This was the stuff of anxiety dreams; leaving his bag or – worse – his laptop on a train, suddenly discovering that he was walking through the street with no shoes, having to retake exams for which he had not prepared. Often he dreamed that he was on a plane and it was suddenly losing height, it was going to crash, it was too close to city buildings. He would pass through those dream-stages – *this is not a dream, this is happening at last, oh God I am not dreaming, but yes this is a dream and I can awake from it, I will open my eyes, I am not going to die.* And then wide awake, heart pounding, it was all a dream, Lily sleeping by his side, going to fetch a glass of water with soft footsteps so that he would not wake her.

All the birds in the world, all the birds in the world come to my father's garden to build their nests. Tous les oiseaux du monde . . .

Now he was drifting, now he was half dreaming. Why hold on? Because if he died, then so what? He was just a bundle of genetic information in a body, he did not believe in an immortal soul. What did it matter? The world would go on spinning as it had spun before he was born, the flowers would bloom, the pretty dove would continue to sing day and night. *Ma jolie colombe qui chante jour et nuit.* And Lily would remarry, she would grow old, she too would die. He felt a sentimental wrench at this last thought. Lily who loved opera, who had taken a sceptical Gordon on their first date to see *La Traviata.* Ah, but this was sentimentality, this was foolishness, the situation was bad enough without bringing tears to his eyes at the thought of Lily's hand reaching for his as Violetta sang of her joy in the face of hovering death. He had been there, he had been in a seat in Covent Garden, listening at first with mockery and then in delight and wonder at the melodies.

Parigi o cara noi lasceremo,
La vita uniti trascorremo . . .

He had been there but now he was here. So what? So what, Mr Gordon Forrester? The world would keep spinning, a red train would circle a yellow track, day and night the doves would sing, constituencies would change hands again, research papers would be written, others would seem dated, the trains would never run on time, day and night would be filled with the singing of *ma jolie colombe*. But now day was becoming night, the night was falling and he was sliding away with the light, he could no longer hear the dove in the burning forest, not day nor night, there was no father, no garden, the birds were not singing, there were no longer any birds on the barren islands, he could think of no more songs.

Go easy, careful now, bring it back this way a few feet!

Voices! He could hear voices! He was not dead, they were coming for him at last. He thought he could see sparks, the light was changing, there were stars, bright stars, thousands of bright blue stars in his eyes. He tried to cry out, to call for help but he could only manage a desperate moan. He was drifting in and out of consciousness, he wanted to ask if Lily were there, to tell her he was all right, he was just going to sleep for a little, he would tell her everything when he woke up, about the songs that had accompanied him in his imprisonment. And when he opened his eyes, he was staring into the face of a fireman, somebody was shouting about keeping the rain off him, he was being lifted. And he looked at the fireman and he croaked, 'My wife's name is Lily.'

'Yeah?' The fireman grinned and squeezed his hand. 'That's a pretty name. Old-fashioned though. My nan's name was Lil. What's your name, mate?'

'Gordon, Gordon Forrester. My legs are stuck.'

'OK, Gordon. We'll have you out of there soon.'

'Is she here? Does she know? Lily? I want Lily.'

He sounded like a child waking from a nightmare and demanding its mother.

'Nah, she's not here. But you'll be able to see her soon. You're going to be OK. You've had a lucky escape, mate. You're going to be all right. I promise you. Just take it easy. You're going to be all right.'

He was going to be all right. It was a promise.

Sospiro e luce tu mi sarai,
Tutto il futuro ne arridera.

And Gordon Forrester closed his eyes and almost smiled as he hummed the tune silently inside him, as he was stretchered up an embankment, passed along a human chain towards a waiting ambulance. He felt a wave of love for his rescuers, for humanity, for this collective purpose they were showing. He even wondered about making the rescue the theme of a paper – although perhaps that would be a little melodramatic, even egotistical. There were stars cascading like showers of bluebells behind his eyelids but he knew that it was just the after-image from the welders' equipment. And then he did smile to himself because a fireman had squeezed his hand and told him that he was OK, he could feel a light rain on his forehead, he was free from the twisted metal and he was going to see Lily – truly the light of his life – very soon.

part one

winter

hep cat

Melanie Holloway stood at the window of her Bethnal Green flat sipping coffee and slowly eating a banana. She was listening to Curtis Mayfield while she stared out at the street below. She always put music on in the morning before leaving for work and had chosen the record – as well as caffeine and banana – in an attempt to gather some of the energy which had been forfeited after staying up half the night as a result of Patrick's insomnia. It wasn't really working, she didn't want to move on anywhere except back to bed. Every time she had managed to drop off to sleep, he had contrived to find a way of waking her so that he would not be alone. In the end, she had got up and abandoned him. At four in the morning, she had wearily rested her forehead against this same window, watching the strange night movements of a man walking his dog as if it were the middle of the day.

Mel sighed as she suddenly remembered the couple that she had seen as she had watched from the window. They had obviously been out on an early-morning cigarette mission. At the corner of the street they had stopped and kissed each other, twisting each other's hair around in a cat's-cradle of desire. And Mel had been unable to look away, had felt both guilt and fascination as she witnessed this moment of greedy spontaneity.

Patrick and Mel had been together for twelve years now. When she met him, he had been a musician. His band, which had only ever been

13

moderately successful, had suddenly shot to super-stardom during the eighties. The only problem was that by this time Patrick had left the band after a row involving Patrick's relationship with the girlfriend of another band member. While his ex-band were exposed to general ridicule in Britain for their absurdly pretentious lyrics and dreary tunes, they found great favour among angsty teenagers in Japan, southern Europe and Latin America, where they played to packed stadia and earned large amounts of money. Meanwhile, Patrick's new band released a single and then vanished into obscurity. His only satisfaction came from following the declining fortunes of his ex-band. It was a nosedive largely caused by the rather predictable uses to which they had put their money.

Patrick may have escaped such drastic fates but he had not got away with it altogether. He had been an adventurer, an extremist when it came to seeking pleasure, was one of the most restless people Mel had ever met, with a boredom threshold that was not so much low as non-existent. Sometimes she had wondered whether he was in fact suffering from some kind of hyperactive mental disorder; an inability to find equilibrium, a minor autism. This had led him down various paths – not all of them happy ones – and somewhere along the way illness had stuck out a malevolent foot and tripped him; he had become a Hep Cat. Since then there had been blood tests and biopsies and Liver Function Tests (with ever-soaring counts) and milk thistle tea and now the latest course of treatment, which was bringing him to the edge of insanity. Last night, she had been woken by the sound of squeaky voices and had blinked into consciousness to see that he was conducting his own Sooty and Sweep show with a pair of oven-gloves.

Pain? Oh yes, Sweep, I can feel pain all right.

Perhaps you should adopt a more stoical approach, Sooty?

I'm afraid I've never been a great admirer of the Stoics, Sweep.

Mel dropped the banana skin into a carrier bag hanging from the kitchen door-handle and went to the bathroom to brush her teeth, looking disconsolately at her reflection in the mirror as she did so. She was tall with long, straight, dark hair and light hazel eyes. She often frowned when she was thinking, which made her appear stern – even moody – sometimes. Mel was unaware of this, just as she was unaware of the power of her smile which flashed out spontaneously and could make people feel privileged, funny, important. The scowl on her face this morning, however, was quite genuine. Normally, she made sure that her hair was washed and tied back in a ponytail before going to work because she could not work properly if she felt that it was greasy or smelt of cigarettes from the night before. She bunched it with her hand and tied it back. Then she threw cold water on to her face and slapped her cheeks as she had seen somebody do in a film once. It made her feel better.

When Mel returned to the kitchen, Patrick was sitting at the table drinking coffee, wearing an old *Unknown Pleasures* T-shirt, his dark hair spiked from his restless turning on the pillow. His large black eyes turned to her as she entered, appraising her mood from her body language, watching for the signs of irritation and impatience that he must know he deserved. He still had the same lithe body, all the angles he had had when she first met him, even now he had the capacity to hold his coffee elegantly, his sharp elbows on the table, cupping the mug in his hands. He nodded at the other coffee which he had prepared for her. She sat down.

'I'm sorry . . . for last night.' He looked at her, trying still to guess her mood.

She shrugged and sipped the coffee, frowned, spooned a little more sugar in.

'I'm going to go and see that consultant and tell him to get me off this treatment.'

'Then what will the point of the last months have been? You're nearly there.'

'But I felt better with the illness. I wasn't like this.'

This was true. Patrick had veered between self-pity and a fuck-the-world attitude since hepatitis C had been diagnosed, but it had been as nothing compared to this. The consultant at the Royal Free had warned them of potential side-effects but nothing had prepared them for the strength of their impact. The treatment completed his reverse metamorphosis from hedonistic butterfly to misanthropic caterpillar: depression, flu and insomnia kept him alternating between despair and hysteria.

Mel sometimes wondered why their relationship had proved so oddly durable, what it was that kept them stuck together, unable to contemplate the separation that might have seemed the obvious choice at various stages over the last twelve years. What was the nature of the love that existed between them? She wondered whether he knew, whether either of them had ever known. Why had they chosen each other in the first place? At first they had liked the seeming incompatibility of different worlds – her concerns were not his, his crowd was not hers. They had circled each other with fascination, with amused flattery, with an awareness of the eccentricity of their choice. There had been a kind of happy egotism about it. No, not really egotism but introspection. They had laughed – sometimes thumbed their noses – at the world outside and gazed at each other instead.

That could only last so long of course. Sometimes, she looked at him as if he were a complete stranger, a freak, an accident, somebody she had stumbled into and just forgotten to disentangle herself from. She sometimes felt as if there were simple questions she would like to ask him. But there were topics which were out of bounds between them, she could not see how to even raise those questions, as if to raise them were to pull at a thread which might lead to a general unravelling, to a disintegration whose consequences were too big, too terrifying to even contemplate. And yet, their relationship was not weak, perhaps it was too strong. They still functioned well together, had not degenerated into the casual infliction of pain, the ritual swapping of tired punches that she found so tiresome when she saw it in other couples. They could still make each other laugh out loud, neither of them was interested in playing either bully or victim.

The illness had also changed things. In spite of her frustration at his often selfish and childish behaviour, Mel felt protective towards Patrick. He was so scared of his illness, he couldn't come to terms with it at all. For a person who – in spite of his natural prickliness – had such a bright and lively consciousness, the possibility of this consciousness not existing, not even to be somehow conscious of non-existence, was a paralysing fear. Sometimes she would find him feeling around gingerly in the vicinity of his liver as if he should be able to find the virus that hid there like a cunning guerilla silent in the jungle. He would have the same absorbed expression that he had once had when she had caught him in front of the mirror carefully measuring his penis with a ruler. Instead of showing any signs of shame at being discovered in this way, he had glanced up at her and said, 'When they say that average penis length is six inches, they must be talking about the *erect* penis, right? Because otherwise I'm a midget.' He had given up smoking after reading an article which claimed that it made the penis shrink, taken it up again when his sacrifice appeared to make no appreciable difference.

Mel smiled at this memory, finished the bitter dregs of her coffee and stood up.

'I'm off.'

She kissed him on the top of his head and picked up her bag.

'Have a good day,' he said.

Mel worked as a regional officer for a large trade union. She had been brought in to give the organisation a good shake-up, to think the unthinkable, to break down traditional male barriers – a new broom, a breath of fresh air. This, at least, was the story peddled by John Mould – known to almost everybody as Fungus – the union's General Secretary. What Mould had really wanted when he and his team of supporters had started aggressively recruiting young regional officers (and equally aggressively waging war on anybody deemed not to fit the new image) was to bring in pliable and impressionable staff who would dance to his tune – the soulless Muzak of modernisation. Mel knew that the hierarchy felt they had chosen poorly in this respect when they had selected her.

She dumped her bag on her desk and waved at Mary, her secretary, who blew her a kiss. Then she looked through her messages. There was a brusque request for a report on her organising activities from Barry Williams, the union's pompous Assistant General Secretary. Mel frowned and threw it aside. 'Fuck you,' she murmured to herself. There was material relating to cases she was working on: a photographic assistant who had been sacked for downloading child pornography, a lab technician accused of being racist (which was true), a quality-control worker accusing his manager of racism (which wasn't), Mrs Boksic the infamous, mad Croatian who had been sacked for bullying her co-workers and who now phoned twice a day to bully Mel about what was being done on her case. Because Mel worked in a multi-sector union, her brief covered hospitals, factories, and offices. Consequently, her work was extremely varied – too varied sometimes.

She ignored most of the messages and began to sort out some of the papers and reports on her desk, sifting out old newspapers. Her eye was caught by a front page with a photograph of a mangled train which had crashed the week before. The snout of the train poked out from under a pile of carriages which appeared to have flown up into the air and landed on top of each other. Twelve people had been killed in the crash and the train driver was facing possible charges of manslaughter, while the rail union was claiming that it had been caused by inadequate safety mechanisms – something that they had been warning about for the last year. Mel slid the paper into the bin as her phone rang. She smiled as Mary placed a cup of coffee and a plate with two miniature Battenburgs on the desk, mouthing, *Thanks*, as she picked up the phone.

'Hello?'

'Mel, it's Paula.'

Mel sighed with relief. Paula was a good-natured, efficient, committed branch secretary. She had a genius for exploiting management's failure to follow their own procedures and had enough purchase on reality to know which battles were worth fighting. 'When the Trots and the Bosses hate you,' Paula had observed once, 'you know that you're doing something right.'

'Hi Paula, how was your holiday?'

Mel began to peel the thin strip of marzipan from one of her cakes and take the pink and yellow squares apart. She rolled the marzipan into a ball and ate it.

'Yeah, great. Gary moaned about the food the whole time and said it was too hot though. The kids loved it. Mel, we've got a big problem. Any chance of you getting down here tomorrow?'

'What's up?'

'It's serious. I can't tell you everything now but one of our members in the MGL lab at the Great Northern Hospital has been sacked. You remember that train crash last week?'

And Mel stopped playing with the cake and listened, appalled, as Paula told her about a young college lecturer who had been freed from the wreckage of the crashed train but then died as a result of a transfusion because the replacement blood was not his blood-group. The management of the pathology lab had discovered the source of the error and the worker responsible had been marched from the building by security guards.

'Poor love,' Paula observed. 'She's a mess. The man had a wife and child. Now, she thinks she deserves it all, that she's left some kid without his dad. There's a lot behind this, Mel. It's not such an uncommon mistake. It just doesn't usually come to this. And MGL working practices . . . Look, I'll talk to you when you come down.'

'OK.'

Mel took the paper out of the bin and straightened it so that she could see the picture of the mangled train. How strange, how fragile was the human body; Mel's hand with its two familiar rings, its intricate mechanisms of knuckles and joints, the hand that had gesticulated and clutched and caressed, the hand that was now smoothing the creases from the paper, this hand could be destroyed in an instant, could be ripped from its arm, could be torn to shreds. It was no stronger, no more durable than any other human hand. Flesh which seemed so solid, so natural, so permanent, could disappear altogether, could be scattered across a battlefield, could be scorched to a shadow on the pavement. She remembered the calcinated body of a soldier trying to climb from his tank in one of the most grotesque photos of the recent air-wars, his burned hands gripping metal in one last useless effort. He had probably smoked cigarettes, joked with his comrades, teased his little sister, ruffled her hair. And what about Patrick? He could still rely on his body, he would pad to the front door when she came in, glad to see her, they could play the intimate word games of a couple who knew each other very well. He was real, he was solid. But what if he started to decline, to melt away before her very eyes? What if his body succumbed, what if there were no Patrick any longer, just the parts of him that were seared on to her memory – the strange shadows of loss?

Mel looked at the picture of the train again. The wrong kind of blood. They had freed a man from that mess and then made a mistake and killed him – given him A instead of O or whatever it was. And his body had rebelled, it had tried to expel the scarlet fifth column that did not know the codes, the critical passwords. In so doing, it had destroyed itself, turned itself inside out, a lethal purging – *the wrong kind of blood.* And what did they say to the wife waiting in Casualty? *I'm sorry Mrs X – your husband was going to be perfectly OK but we've gone and given him the wrong kind of blood and now he's dead. So sorry.* Everybody made mistakes at work, but some mistakes had more profound consequences than others. Had the mistake been found at the last minute, it would have been a case of sighs of relief, a tale for the pub – *I nearly gave somebody the wrong blood. Can you imagine?* People would have laughed and shaken their heads. But the mistake had not been discovered and had made the crucial leap from error to tragedy. The trivialities that changed everything – a drunken car-driver, a chance meeting, an infected needle, a careless lab technician.

She tried to put the story out of her mind and started to fill out the appraisal form for a training course she had attended the week before. *Did the course meet your expectations?* Yes, Mel thought, insofar as it had been a complete waste of time. *How would you evaluate the role-playing exercises?* Fucking stupid and pointless, she thought as she wrote, *Quite useful*, in the space provided.

They had been set the task of pretending that their plane had crashed in the mountains. At least in her group there had been a few decent people and they had all agreed that the first thing that they would do would be to kill and eat their boss, Barry Williams. 'Why bother killing him?' a regional officer from Scotland had asked. 'Why not just lop bits off him as and when we need them? Then we'd have both food *and* entertainment.' The Scottish and Welsh regional officers then settled into a cheerful argument for the honour of which group was the most hated by Head Office.

Mel remembered the course-leader telling her that she would never have made it off the mountain, that she was too passive and pessimistic. While the others had squabbled about making fires, hunting rabbits and choosing a leader, Mel had drifted off. She had enjoyed the sound of their voices rising above the drone of the suburban traffic and had managed to empty her mind in a most agreeable way. 'The behaviour of somebody who would never get off the mountain,' the course-leader had pronounced (Mel was never popular with course-leaders). It was probably true, Mel acknowledged; she would never get off the mountain, although she did not think that passivity in the face of disaster necessarily indicated that she was generally passive. She would watch the others rubbing two sticks together, trapping rabbits and choosing leaders, she would gaze at the star-filled sky, she would sing quietly to herself as the cold did its job and slowly forced her into icy sleep. Why waste time trying to get off the mountain when you almost certainly couldn't? Patrick would be just as useless because although he would be able to recall every escape detail from similar incidents – Patrick was a disaster connoisseur – he wouldn't be able to do anything concrete apart from sit and bemoan his ill-fate and nag Mel about being hungry and cold and when she thought the rescue planes would arrive.

All day, she could not get the man with the wrong blood out of her mind, the carelessness of losing a recovered life, the fact that he had been reunited with his wife only to be snatched away again by a simple mistake. She wondered whether the fact that he was a young university lecturer had disturbed her more than if he had been, say, a middle-aged accountant. There was no reason why the former should be more sympathetic than the latter – he might have been an arrogant young revisionist historian who thought that it was a grave mistake to have gone to war with Hitler. But she did not imagine him like that, she imagined him as kind and liberal and humane, the sort who would be nice to his students, clever in an unassertive, almost clumsy way.

Towards the end of the afternoon, her phone rang again.

'Hey *chica*,' a familiar mocking voice murmured at her, 'you haven't forgotten we're going out tonight, you overpaid bureaucrat.'

It was Pepa.

Pepa was Spanish but had spent most of her life in London. Her family were from a small, conservative village in Galicia which still boasted statues of prominent Spanish fascists. Even though Pepa had not been back to the village for some time, mothers covered their children's ears at the sound of her name and men swallowed and looked at the ground. Because Pepa was anything but conservative – she had neither guilt nor shame, she was a sexual hooligan. She enjoyed the massive advantage of being able to look almost absurdly beguiling and innocent even when she was at her most malevolent. 'I am *rebelde*,' she would say proudly, shaking her black curls and drawing herself up to the full majesty of her five feet and three inches. 'Oh yeah?' their other friend Angela once replied. 'Is that Spanish for slut then?'

Mel had forgotten that she had arranged to meet Pepa that evening. She was torn between her tiredness and her sudden need to be away from the house and from Patrick.

'I haven't forgotten,' she said.

'What's up? You sound really flat. Don't you want to meet up?'

'Yeah, of course I do. I might even stay with you. Have you spoken to Angela?'

'Yeah, she's coming as well. She's just split up with . . . what was his name again . . . Gavin?'

'Oh, there's a surprise. OK, well I'll see you later, Pep.'

'Yeah. Mel? Are you all right?'

'I'm fine.'

Mel's colleague Graham popped his head around the door. He was carrying his copy of the *Morning Star*. Graham's politics meant that he was not popular with the union leadership and part of Mel's failure in their eyes involved not having stuck a knife in his back. But he had been kind to her when she started, had helped her to prepare for her first tribunal, he was a competent and knowledgable trade unionist. She also enjoyed sitting drinking tea and listening to some of his rants about the single currency, the Serbs as a misunderstood people, the reactionary distortions of Greek history in a recent best-selling novel. And Mel found that sitting and nodding and muttering in agreement from time to time had a certain soothing quality.

'See you tomorrow, comrade.' Graham waved the *Morning Star* cheerfully at her and laughed as Mel gave him a clenched-fist farewell.

After he had gone, Mel went to the window and leaned out so that she could smoke. She saw Mary emerging from the door at the bottom of the building, chatting to a few other workers. Across the city, thousands were doing the same. They were calling goodbye, making their way to the tube, thinking about what they were going to have for tea, what was on TV that night, nursing their hopes and frustrations as they travelled to their homes for the brief respite before work began again – to eat, to sleep, to dream. It was like the movement of the ocean pulled by the implacable logic of the moon. Or blood – the right kind of blood – travelling to and from the thumping heart, navigating the secret tunnels of the body, the one-way systems just beneath the skin. Daily life went on in this way, dictated by different but scarcely less rigid laws, people clutching scarves and gloves and bags, great flows of people engaged in the process of feeding and clothing and providing themselves with shelter.

Looking from her window on to the street, at the office-workers waving goodbye until the next day, Mel felt a similar sensation to that which she had experienced watching the couple kissing on the street corner after Patrick had wakened her with the oven-gloves. She exhaled a last sigh of smoke and flicked her cigarette away from her, watching it tumble to the pavement below.

tall grasses

Mel sat in Pepa's living room with a bottle of tequila at her feet. She was glad now that she had not cancelled the evening with her two best friends — she had picked up the phone to do so just before leaving the office but the line had been busy and she had changed her mind again while sitting watching the phone.

It was late but she was not going to catch the tube or call a cab so it no longer mattered what the time was. She was going to get drunk enough to crawl into the bed in Pepa's spare room where she would fall instantly asleep under the red duvet. She slept well in this flat with its bright colours, its endearing muddle of books, discarded clothes, empty bottles, and CDs with *For Promotional Use Only* stickers on them that Pepa brought home from her job in a large record company.

Pepa had always lived alone except for one occasion when she had been broke and rented out the spare room to Lucy — a pale, timid girl from work. Pepa had proceeded on the assumption that opposites might get on — a theory which had quickly proved to be flawed. 'A whore in sheep's clothing, a simpering trollop,' had been her verdict. 'She used to gossip about me and roll her eyes at how terrible I was but whenever I had a man here — just a friend even — it was all giggle-giggle, whisper-whisper, flutter-flutter with that little mousey voice that she obviously thought was the biggest aphrodisiac in the world.' Lucy had not paid one month's rent before she was given her marching orders and Pepa reverted to her comfortable solitude.

Mel had met her friends in a tapas bar near Pepa's flat on the Caledonian Road, where they had eaten squid, chorizos, *patatas bravas*, grilled red peppers sprinkled with basil, *gambas pil-pil*. They had drunk pitchers of icy sangria and Pepa had teased the young Spanish waiters. Mel had relaxed, revelling in the flavours and textures that she would never be able to cook – never be bothered to cook – at home. Happiness flashed through her, she forgot about work and targets and tribunals, she stamped hard on her guilt for having left Patrick on his own. She was so relieved that she had overcome her inertia and tiredness to come out, to watch Pepa and Angela teasing each other, not to be at home watching soap operas and dulling her dissatisfaction with repeated glasses of wine that had gone slightly warm because she couldn't be bothered to return the bottle to the fridge.

'How's your brother?' Pepa was now asking Angela, her coal-black eyes shining with their customary amusement, the pleasure of mischief-making and transgression.

'You leave my brother alone,' Angela retorted. 'He's happily married.'

'That's an oxymoron. Anyway, what's it got to do with anything?'

'Well, in the normal scheme of things it means that he is unavailable to scheming little Spanish punanny. And don't call me a moron.'

Pepa chuckled. 'He is lovely though. Isn't he, Mel? You've met Richard.'

Mel nodded, although Richard was not really her type. She could admire his beauty, especially as it was coupled with a genuine modesty, but it was not the kind of beauty that appealed to her. He shared many of his sister's qualities; he had the same style and elegance as Angela, the height, the cheekbones, the fastidious – almost obsessive – approach to personal appearance. His quiet modesty was OK as far as it went but it also meant that he had no spark – everything about him apart from his handsome face was dull, he had been saved by it. Mel often thought that this was very unfair.

Mel had met Angela when she had been working for the GLC after leaving college and Angela was in her first job since leaving school. Angela was not dull – she was quirky, unpredictable, her humour slyly subversive.

And she could create multiple personae just as she could affect different voices depending on her mood and her audience. It was a time when the 'loony left' councils were barely out of the news – sniggering journalists falling over themselves to report stories about Baa Baa Green Sheep, disabled lesbian whale-watchers, person-holes, compulsory Nicaraguan coffee in the Town Hall. It was strange, Mel thought, how many of the policies which had provoked these media fantasies and been held up as so outlandish and ridiculous were now treated as the norm, barely given a second thought. Mel and Angela had worked late, they had gone to parties in Jubilee Gardens, they had been young, enthusiastic and exhilarated. At the abolition farewell party, Angela had put her arms around Mel and wept. Mel had known that it was not for the loss of her job, but rather for their defeat, for their powerlessness.

It seemed so far away now that time, everything so strangely remote – the polarisations, the conflicts, the protests. The new government wanted a business leader with proven executive skills to run the city and Angela was a highly valued and well-paid PA for the owner of a smart Soho bar. She sat with her long legs stretched out in front of her, her hands behind her back, laughing as Pepa expertly slammed a tequila and passed the frothing glass to her, recoiling slightly as some of it spilt on to her skirt.

They sat drinking tequila and laughing and smoking too much. The ashtrays filled up. Angela told them about splitting up from Gavin – how his willingness to chauffeur her anywhere at any time in his BMW, and his unflagging sexual energy were ultimately no compensation for the fact that he had no sense of humour.

'I mean, I wasn't asking for a comedian or anything, sometimes they're boring as well, wanting you to laugh at them all the time and you have to do it or they sulk. But that man – you tell him a joke, right, and he just *look* at you.' Angela hiccoughed with laughter as she remembered. 'So you've got to go, "I was joking," and then he look at you again like you *mad*.'

'Gavin's a stupid name anyway,' Pepa observed as she slammed another tequila. 'I couldn't fancy anybody called Gavin.'

'Now, how shall I put this? His name wasn't . . . the most *prominent* thing about him,' Angela retorted.

'Gavin's not as bad as Barry,' said Mel, thinking of her boss.

'Oh well, who cares whether he's got a sense of humour if he's got a huge cock?' Pepa slammed another tequila.

'Technique is important as well,' Angela said.

'Technique, shmechnique,' Pepa pronounced with contempt. 'If it's three inches, it's three inches. No amount of technique can change that.'

'Or Adrian,' Mel continued.

'Mel, would you shut up about names.'

So instead of names, Mel told them about catching Patrick measuring his penis with the Ruler for London that she had got free from *Time Out* magazine.

'I thought he was going to impale himself on the ruler, he was pushing it back so far, trying to get a few more centimetres.'

Pepa and Angela howled with laughter at this image and Mel felt a sudden surge of protective affection for Patrick.

'How's your work going?' Angela asked her. 'Don't you think she works too hard, Pepa?'

'That's an understatement,' Pepa replied.

Mel told them the story that Paula had recounted that day about the man who had died in hospital after being given the wrong blood.

'What a terrible story,' Angela murmured, shaking her head. 'That's sad. His poor wife.'

'You don't think that trains will crash when you're on them but you certainly don't think a hospital will make a mistake like that.'

They sat in silence for a moment, considering the death of a man they had never met. Mel remembered a song which Patrick – ironically – was extremely fond of called 'I'm Not Afraid to Die'. What was the point of fear when something so unexpected could happen to you? You could be invaded by a virus, they could give you the wrong blood, a plane could drop out of the sky on to your house while you were eating. Fear of death could stop you from living if you tried to protect yourself too much, but there had to be something suspect about the emotions and imaginations of those who truly did not fear death.

As it grew later, the conversation returned to more predictable topics, to *the* topic which large quantities of alcohol always fuelled. Equally predictably, it was Pepa who initiated the conversation by recounting her favourite early sexual experience.

'I had just come back from Spain. We'd been away with my family and it had been horrible and I was in the dog-house as usual. It was the end of summer and it was still hot.'

'How old were you?' Mel asked.

'I was seventeen. I was feeling good about myself, I knew I looked good.'

'Like you've ever been in any doubt,' Angela said.

Pepa glanced at her and then carried on. 'I remember everything about that day. I was on the tube. I had this kind of weird mood, it's a mood I've always had – this mixture of bored and curious and reckless. It's always made me do stupid things. Well, sometimes they're stupid, sometimes they're great. Anyway, I was on the tube and I was wearing one of those silly bright eighties skirts and red espadrilles and my legs were really tanned from Spain. I felt good, 'cause I was young and I was quite enjoying getting looked at. So, I was walking down the platform and there was this guy in a suit – some businessman type – and as I walked past he just kind of glanced at my legs. I knew it, I felt it, the way he just flicked his head to look at me. Then he went back to his paper. So I stopped a little way up the platform and I checked him out. He was nothing that special, just an older guy in a suit reading the *Financial Times*.'

'But he wasn't ugly or anything?' Angela asked.

Pepa shrugged. 'He wasn't anything. He was just a suit. It wasn't because he was older than me either – I'd had quite enough of the old hypocrites in Spain. But the way he had looked at me, it made me feel . . . it was that reckless feeling again. It wasn't that I found *him* particularly sexy, I found it weird, you know, that he had just looked at me, considered my body and then gone back to reading his paper. And he had done it really fast, 'cause it would have been embarrassing for him to have been caught staring at a young girl. I started feeling almost dizzy and I started to get this feeling . . . this feeling that I could encourage him. I could do what I wanted. I could completely change that muggy afternoon if I wanted to, if I chose to. It wasn't a horrible thing, it wasn't that I wanted to fuck about with his head, I just wanted to see what happened.'

'What did you do?' Angela's face was a mixture of fascination and horror.

Pepa paused to light another cigarette.

'Oh don't worry. It wasn't that bad. Although still when I think about it it gives me the same feeling.'

She gave an exaggerated shiver and laughed.

'What did you do?' Mel knew that Pepa was teasing with this story. Whenever Patrick laughed at Pepa for talking incessantly about sex, Pepa would retort tartly that she could always tell from people's reactions whether they were genuinely bored or not.

'I got on the same carriage as him and stood next to him. I think he was surprised. He certainly noticed me again. When the train moved, his hand brushed against me . . .' Pepa paused, suddenly a little awkward with having to discuss actual details, 'but I didn't move. In fact, when the train swayed, I deliberately kept my body where it was so that his hand was pressing against me. By then it was obvious that I was doing this deliberately and I could feel that he was confused, that he didn't know why I wasn't moving. And it was *that* which was turning me on so much: his confusion, his surprise, his desire for me. I could almost feel him shaking. I wasn't moving away from his hand even when I could have done so. He must have known that. So for a while, his hand was resting against me, moving against me as the train moved and I let that happen. We went on like that for about three stops and then I got off without even looking at him.'

'What? Nothing else happened? He didn't even . . .'

'No. I think he was still scared I might turn round and shout, "What do you think you're doing, you pervert?" He didn't try and follow me. I think he didn't understand it. Also, I felt guilty as well. I knew that this wasn't normal behaviour, I knew I was crossing a line. Now when I fantasise about it, I use all the usual stranger-on-train fantasies — you know: train stops, lights go off, and he manages to fuck me without anyone noticing, that kind of nonsense. But in reality it wasn't like that. It was just his hand against me and me not moving away, allowing it to happen. But it's still the most powerful thing for me, it never fails. The fact that I let his hand stay there. The fact that I allowed it. I can always remember the pressure of him. And the other thing that I always like is thinking that that day probably changed something for him as well. That he might still remember that day. He must be out there somewhere, he must remember me, he must still imagine me sometimes.'

Mel considered Pepa's story. She knew that it was probably true, although she also suspected that Pepa would have added some detail because Pepa was a generous story-teller and had a story-teller's propensity towards embellishment if she thought that the story required it or that it was what the audience desired. Nevertheless, she had been more anxious to convey her mood than any tedious detail. This was really the essence of Pepa's character; the impulse that had led her to allow a hand to press against her was part of the same impulse that would explore the psychology behind it, that would offer access rather than construct barriers to her personality because she did not feel that she had anything to be ashamed of. Pepa might be indiscreet and even a big-mouth — accusations she had received and brushed off on more than one occasion — but she was not mean-spirited.

'When I was at school,' Angela said, 'I had this friend called Sophie. I used to go and stay with her in the school holidays . . .'

'What's this?' Pepa interrupted. 'Not your schoolgirl dyke experience?'

'Yeah, right. Anyway, shut your mouth; we've finished with your how-I-let-a-dirty-old-man-touch-me-up-on-the-tube fantasy.'

Mel laughed at Angela's sharpness. 'Yeah, shut up, Pepa. That guy's probably been hassling young girls ever since and it's all your fault.'

Pepa looked hurt which made Mel and Angela laugh even more.

'Oh she can give it out . . .'

'But she can't take it back . . .'

'All right. OK. Carry on. What happened next? Sexy young Sophie sneaked across to your bed in her flimsy white nightie and asked to get in 'cause she'd had a nightmare. You couldn't help noticing her pert young schoolgirl breasts and called over Patch the family collie . . .'

Mel spluttered and spat her tequila out. Angela scowled.

'Keep your lesbian fantasies to yourself, Pepa. Sophie's family had a massive house in Belsize Park. I always envied her that house because it was really messy. Our house was so tidy it hurt. I once asked my mum why our house couldn't be messy, why we had to come home from school and do the cleaning on Fridays. She said our house could be messy when we could pay somebody to clean it up. I didn't understand what she was talking about. Anyway, I loved going to Sophie's house — she had a massive kitchen with a big table and a noticeboard and wooden floors and everything. We used to sit at the kitchen table and drink big mugs of tea. Sometimes I'd stay to dinner and we'd get red wine. I was so envious of her. Her mum and dad worked in telly or something and I think Sophie got extra pocket money for having a black friend and bringing her home.' Angela giggled.

'Your story is so much better than mine,' Pepa said. 'The way you slip in these fascinating sociological asides about ethnicity and class.'

Mel said, 'Shut up, Pepa.'

Angela cut her eyes at Pepa and then continued, 'Sophie's family had a cottage in the country and we used to go down there in the holidays. My mum once gave me a bottle of wine to take because I told her that was what Sophie's family drank. One dinnertime I brought down my bottle of wine. Mr Falconer – Sophie's dad – he looked at the bottle of wine and he kind of smirked. He winked at his wife and said, "It's plonk, but it's perfectly drinkable plonk." I didn't even know what plonk meant but . . .' Angela looked down at her hands and twisted her ring around. 'I was really embarrassed. It's one of those things I can never forget. It still makes me cringe inside. You know what's weird though? When I went home I asked my mum what plonk was. She asked me why and when I told her what had happened I thought she was going to go round and give Mr Falconer five fingerprints on his jawbone. I never see her so vex. Apparently, 'cause she didn't know that much about wine she had asked the guy in the off-licence and he had shown her this expensive wine so she had bought that because she didn't want to show me up. So it wasn't plonk anyway.'

Angela paused, frowning, to sip her drink.

'OK, it wasn't plonk,' Pepa said. 'So what happened next?'

'Me and Sophie used to go out on these bikes. It was nice around there. We just used to cycle out and find some place and hang out there and chat. It was flat countryside, you could walk for miles down towards the sea and not pass anybody. There were channels that sometimes filled up with water and once we saw a drowned sheep that had fallen in. But further on we would get to the estuary where you could swim. It was beautiful when it was hot. Anyway, that Sophie could chat, man! She was worse than you, Pepa. Always going on about how she had lost her virginity when she was fourteen and what it was like and everything. One day we were on our way home and her bike got a puncture. So we agreed that I would ride home and get her mum or dad to come and pick her up. I was scared riding back on my own 'cause it was redneck territory. They used to stare at me and once I heard these men laughing and making stupid jokes about monkeys on bicycles. I knew I'd have to ride past them and they would have that horrible laughter, screaming and pushing each other like they had just said the funniest thing in the world.'

'Peasants,' Pepa observed. 'Where I come from they'd do the same. The worst thing is that some red-faced, cauliflower-eared, inbred pig-farmer thinks he can make comments about the way that *you* look.'

'So what happened?' Mel asked.

'When I got back to the house, I told them about the bike and Mr Falconer told me that he'd drive me back to pick up Sophie. I didn't want to go back 'cause I was shy of being on my own with him and didn't know what to say. But I had to show him where she was. So we set off in the car and we're about halfway there when suddenly he stops the car.'

'Now we're getting somewhere,' Pepa said.

'He stops the car and he's sort of gripping the steering wheel. We're in the middle of nowhere. The sky was very blue and I could hear everything like it was much louder than normal. We were in some lay-by or something and there were these tall grasses outside and the birds were singing. I just watched the tall grasses swaying and didn't say anything. Then he said to me, "I want to kiss you." That was all he said. And it was a bit like that curiosity and shame thing you was talking about, Pepa, and the fact that Sophie-the-nympho had been chatting about sex every minute of the day. I had this feeling in my stomach and it was that do it-don't do it feeling and it was like I was burning up. Plus, I liked the way he just said it direct like that – "I want to kiss you". So I let him kiss me . . .'

Angela broke off for a second and looked at her hands again.

'And?' Pepa asked more gently.

'Well, at first I was quite enjoying it. But then he started touching me and I got scared. He was changing as well. He was quite rough and it was hurting and I was scared. He was tearing at my clothes and then he started saying things. Maybe he thought I would get turned on by them but they were disgusting things like how he'd imagined me without any clothes and stuff. He was spitting in my ear and pawing at me and I was getting really scared. Then he started going on about me being so sexy 'cause I was black. I knew he thought that 'cause I was black I was sexually experienced, when I was the fucking virgin listening to his daughter going on about how she'd done half the boys in our class before her sixteenth birthday. In the end, I was struggling and this car came past and he stopped for a moment and when he stopped he saw that I was crying and suddenly he went back to being Sophie's dad again. "I'm sorry, Angela, I went too far. Let's go and pick Sophie up." So we went and picked her up and we went home. When Sophie had gone to put her bike away, he goes, "I think our little kiss had better remain just between me and you, OK?" And I felt guilty 'cause I had let him kiss me, I'd kissed him back, and so I nodded because I just wanted it to all go away.'

'You were a kid,' Mel said. 'It was natural that you would be confused by that.'

'He sounds like a right charmer,' Pepa added. 'He calls your wine plonk, he treats you like your name's Kizzy . . .'

'Have you still got his phone number?' Mel asked. 'We should phone him up and freak him out. I'll leave a weepy message on his answermachine about how he can't just get rid of me by forcing me to have an abortion.'

'The funny thing is though,' Angela mused, 'is that when I think about it now I *can* find the memory a turn-on. It was horrible and I hated it but in my mind now it's different. Like he's quite powerful and passionate and he leads me into the tall grass outside and it's like I'm looking down at our two bodies from above and my body is under his and I'm high up in that blue sky watching myself and he's not muttering all that sleazy racist shit and I can almost enjoy being frightened.'

'That is what I'm saying.' Pepa nodded. 'The imagination gets rid of a lot of unpleasant detail.'

'No, it doesn't actually get rid of it,' Angela said. 'It just kind of changes it a bit.'

Mel was uncomfortably aware that she hadn't told any kind of story. It wasn't that she couldn't – she just didn't want to. If she started talking about it, she knew that she would be brought back to the central problem, which was that she was no longer having sex with Patrick. She could not really blame the illness for this, they had stopped having sex for some time before that. She did not really know why. She still loved him, loved him more than anyone else in the world, she still found him attractive. But they had just stopped. It wasn't as if one of them were holding out or denying the other, it was just an activity that had ceased to hold much relevance for them. And yet Mel still felt desire, sometimes she felt it burning through her veins, making her hands clench and her throat constrict. She had felt it at the gym when she had been on the steps machine and she had watched a man walk past with an easy, elegant body, buttocks taut against his black track-suit, a tattoo encircling his forearm. She had felt a longing to become the object of that man's attention – of his hands, of his tongue. She had a longing to be taken to bed, to take someone to bed – for an hour, for an afternoon. Just for pleasure, just for playful lust like the couple with their hands in each other's hair at the corner of the street.

Mel knew that Patrick would not react well to any such behaviour. Not particularly because of sexual jealousy, although she expected he would have his share of that. But Patrick would be far more alarmed that somebody apart from himself was receiving Mel's attention and would become hysterical at even the remotest possibility of that attention being transferred on a permanent basis. They had, like most couples, talked about it when drunk, discussed the people with whom they could imagine having casual sex, lamented the lack of freedom imposed by monogamy, agreed that it was odd that there should be such furore about something which was about pleasure. This was all very well for a drunken conversation, but such liberalism suddenly evaporated in the cold light of day, as irrelevant and unappealing as the stuffed ashtrays and dreg-filled bottles.

Mel knew that the only possible strategy were she to satisfy some of her unfulfilled energy outside their relationship would be to prevent Patrick from knowing anything about it. Mel knew that, in the right circumstances, guilt would be an inadequate sentry, issuing a feeble challenge but accepting most passwords if they were just said in the right way. It wasn't guilt that was the problem, nor even particularly a dislike of secrets and lies. Both Mel and her sister had learned to be accomplished liars when they were growing up and Mel did not think that it would ever be possible to be a person without secrets, without hidden spaces or private territories.

The truth of the matter was that she felt a profound weariness at the idea of pursuit or prolonged flirtation or game-playing or aftermaths – it was all too messy, too much effort. The idea of either receiving or inflicting humiliation, of hysterics on either side, filled her with revulsion; she had always found people who appeared to enjoy that rather bewildering. She might not have a particular antipathy to secrets, but she had no wish to make people suffer, did not want to be responsible for their pain. And so she retreated, so she dodged the issue in a way which was dishonest only to herself. It was certainly a most miserable paradox to feel such aching desire coupled with a reluctance to take the steps to satisfy it.

She leaned back and stared out of the window. The moon flickered behind fast-moving night-clouds. It looked very cold outside.

'Listen to this,' Pepa was saying. 'It's about me.' She put on a CD of Cuban *son* and began dancing across the room, singing along to it.

'*Que bonita se ve Pepa con su camison* . . . You see, I never thought I'd find a song with my name in it.'

Mel smiled as she watched her friend dancing and laughing at the fact that she had found a song which featured her name.

'I'm going to have to crash soon,' she yawned.

'Yeah, I've got to go,' Angela agreed, reaching for her jacket. 'It's late.'

Pepa stopped dancing and put her hands on her hips.

'Well,' she pronounced, 'what a pair of lightweights you two have become. I'll call you a cab, Angela, and don't give the cheeky Kurdish bastard more than six quid. If he gets lippy tell him to come and have a word with me. Mel, the bed's made up. Why don't you go and lie down, you look knackered. I'll stay with Angela.'

That night Mel dreamed bright, intense, alcohol-influenced dreams. She was going to give blood after an accident, she was the only one who matched the victim whose life was in the balance. But she could not find the hospital, she knew she was nearby but she just could not find it. Finally, she took a taxi but the taxi driver was taking her further and further away, she knew he was planning something terrible for her. He finally stopped the car in the countryside, where another man was waiting, leaning against a stile with a sinister smile. He approached the car, put his hand to the door-handle and Mel woke with a half-cry, her heart thumping, alone in a strange room.

pathology

'Oh, you idiot!' Mel blasted her horn and stuck two fingers up at the BMW which had cut across her lane and was weaving in and out of the traffic in front of her. She was not in a good mood. Patrick was sulking because she had instructed him to clean the bathroom and Mrs Boksic had phoned to demand a meeting with her. It was a sour-milk day, can't-find-the-keys day, arrival-of-phone-bill day. London was weary from feeding on its own air which was fizzing with grey particles, the radio said that there were delays on the Central, Piccadilly and Metropolitan lines while major tailbacks were occurring at the Rotherhithe tunnel and the Hanger Lane gyratory system. None of this travel news affected Mel but it still produced a quiet desolation in her, an impotent discontent at the inadequacy of the city in which she lived. It was not the day to be crossing London to visit the MGL lab at the Great Northern Hospital.

Mel hated the inappropriately named Great Northern. It was nothing like the hospital where she had visited Paula to discuss the case of the man with the wrong blood. That hospital was like a luxury hotel or an airport. There were paintings on the walls, glass lifts humming between floors, shops which sold more than limp bunches of flowers and boxes of stale Quality Street. It was a pleasure to visit it. Outside, the streets were busy with pedestrians, there were cafés and patisseries and bars, she watched strangers drinking coffee and eating cakes through the plate-glass windows. The Great Northern, on the other hand, was a grim asylum in the middle of nowhere – the kind of building where sadists would have paid a penny to poke lunatics with sticks. It had its own micro-climate of permanent rain. The reps at the Great Northern were weak and moany, always complaining that Mel had not attended meetings to which it would later transpire they had failed to invite her. 'I'm not psychic,' Mel would protest and the reps would glower triumphantly as if they had cunningly teased out an admission of failure from their young regional officer.

Pathology at the Great Northern had been privatised and gifted to MGL – a rapidly expanding drugs company. When MGL had taken over the labs, they had either sacked union members or given management posts to those considered the most competent. MGL allowed Mel reluctant access to the remaining unionised workers because, under the terms of the privatisation deal, transferred workers were entitled to the same terms and conditions that they had enjoyed previously. Nobody had ever really tested how long this arrangement was supposed to last or what it really meant.

At first, the local MGL management had placed every obstacle in the way of Mel seeing her members until she had been forced to approach Robert Hislop, the vice-president of MGL, at the company's head office. Robert had studied PPE at Oxford, a fact which he had mentioned in conversations with Mel on more than one occasion. He was a member of Glyndebourne, he was fanatical about Shakespeare. When she had told him that they would not let her into the lab at the Great Northern, Hislop had laughed and picked up the phone. 'Of course you can visit your members,' he had grinned, 'although we both know that the TUPE regulations aren't worth the paper they're printed on.'

In spite of his studied charm, Hislop was still incapable of making any connection between his own comfort and the conditions of those who worked for his company. There was no link in his mind between the laughing party eating their picnic before a performance of *Così Fan Tutte*, and the woman waiting for a night bus on a windy night in North London. His buzzwords – flexibility, multi-skilling, rationalisation – were abstract concepts, words on reports and memos: they had no human incarnation.

When Mel had met Brenda – the worker responsible for the wrong blood – it had been at Paula's glassy, glittering hospital. Brenda had been the only person working in the lab when news of the train crash came in. Blood cross-matching was not something she felt particularly comfortable with – her background was in haemotology – but MGL had insisted that everybody should be able to do cross-matching. The first casualties were followed by more and then more until she thought that she couldn't go on any longer, until her head was spinning as fast as the machinery analysing the blood-groups.

She had also worked alone for longer than she should have done because the consultant responsible for the emergency procedure could not be located. Casualty had kept phoning to yell that they needed the blood now and not tomorrow and she had yelled back that if they left her to get on with it then they would get the blood far more quickly. The most seriously injured patients had come in last because of the time taken to free them from the wreckage and although by then she had some support, she was exhausted. She had made a mistake. Looking back on it now she could not understand how she could have made such a basic error.

'And the poor man died. And he had a little kiddie and everything. And it was all my fault.'

The mistake was confirmed the next day and management had met to consider its strategy. A head had to be seen to roll quickly and so the following day a bewildered Brenda was taken to a room by management where she was dismissed on the spot without a hearing or a chance to put her case. She was frog-marched by security, in front of amazed workmates, to her locker to collect her things and then dumped at the main gate of the hospital to wait for the bus that would carry her home. All she had been able to think about was that she was responsible for the death of a person. She could not even begin to think that the way that she had been treated was wrong.

The wind gusting through the car park whipped Mel's hair across her face and into her mouth as she walked towards the pathology lab where she was to meet Neil Evans, the lab manager. Evans had been a lab technician before the MGL takeover and had been promoted as a result of it. Mel loathed him. He had pale eyes and white eyelashes, he stared at her breasts instead of her face when he spoke to her. He also made great play of the fact that he had been a union member before the MGL takeover and that, consequently, there was nothing that Mel could tell *him* about industrial relations.

Mel escaped out of the wind and straightened her hair and clothes, buttoning her jacket to provide a further obstacle to Neil Evans's pale, unflinching stare. As she walked towards the Pathology entrance she suddenly saw Evans accompanied by a paunchy, bearded consultant who was wearing a spotted bow tie.

The two men watched her approach and Evans murmured something to the consultant who threw back his head and laughed. Then he nodded at Evans. Mel knew that she was meant to see this and so she ignored it.

'Hi, Melanie.' Evans held out his hand which she accepted reluctantly. 'Melanie's the trade-union rep,' he explained to the consultant. 'From GWA.'

'Enchanted,' said the consultant, holding out a small hand. One of his podgy fingers was adorned with an amber ring. He spoke as if only he understood that the courtesy was deliberately mannered, a self-satire only he was subtle enough to understand.

'Hello.' She returned his handshake, glancing at his brown-brogued feet.

'Does GWA still exist?' the consultant asked, half chortling as he did so. 'I rather thought we'd done away with all that nonsense.' Evans laughed. The girl behind the reception desk glanced at Mel and smiled as if apologising. She had lemur eyes and ears which stuck out through her rather lank hair. A teddy-bear badge adorned her uniform pocket. She sipped her coffee and half shrugged as she did so.

'It did when I left the office this morning,' Mel replied. 'Perhaps you know something I don't.'

'Well, it's certainly changed for the better if they're sending attractive young ladies to plead the cause of the horny-handed sons of toil. Although you won't find many of those here. Just a lot of careless buggers who can't even match a blood-group properly. Which reminds me, Neil. What time is that damn press conference this afternoon?'

'Oh.' Mel turned to Neil. 'Is there a press conference tonight?'

'You won't get much out of it,' Neil muttered. 'It's just the Trust explaining where we're at. It's at four-thirty, Gavin.'

Mel smiled as she remembered Pepa's reaction to that particular name when Angela had brought it up.

'I still might pop along. Anyway, Neil, we'd better be getting on with it if you've got a press conference to go to. I have a few other issues to discuss with you besides the Brenda Fletcher case.'

'Yes, don't let me detain you,' the consultant said. 'I shall see you at four-thirty, I hope. I'm sure that our wonderful Margaret Jowell will be able to knock the questions of any impertinent journalists to the boundary. Do you care for cricket, Melanie?'

'No,' Mel said brusquely, tired of this foolish faux-pomposity. 'Can we make a start please, Neil.'

She turned and started walking down the corridor towards Evans's office, waiting outside for him to catch her up. He opened the door and ushered her in. She sat down in front of his desk and took a pen and notepad from her bag. A photo of two anaemic, toothy children in school uniform stood on the desk. Above the chair was a sign which read, *Excellence can be achieved if . . . you dream more than others think is practical and expect more than others think is possible.*

'Right,' Mel grimaced, 'let's start with some of the grading problems in Virology, shall we?'

Nell Evans knitted his fingers and clicked his joints.

Mel sat in the hospital cafeteria stirring a cup of coffee with a white plastic stick and eating a Twix. She had decided to stay for the press conference. This was partly to annoy Neil Evans who had proved even more obstructive and unpleasant than usual in their meeting. When Mel had first raised the Brenda Fletcher case with him, he had promised to review it. But nearly two months had passed since then and his attitude was hardening.

'For God's sake, Melanie, do you know how old that man was? He was thirty-six. If killing a man of that age isn't gross misconduct I'd like to know what is!'

'She had not received adequate training in cross-matching, she was working too many late shifts, the consultant delayed activating the emergency procedure, she made a mistake. That is not gross misconduct, however appalling the consequences. Others had made similar mistakes and received no disciplinary action whatsoever – the mistake was picked up and that's the only difference. On top of that, there was no written notice, no hearing, and no chance to obtain representation.'

'But we would have sacked her anyway. We'll just use the Polkey defence.'

'I haven't said we're going to tribunal yet.'

'But you will.'

'How do you know that?'

Neil Evans leaned forward across his desk and whispered, 'Because you're a malicious little bitch. And let me tell you something. You're no more popular with the staff here than you are with management. They think you're a stuck-up little college girl and I think they're right. Do you want to know what else I think?'

'Not particularly.'

'I think you're probably not popular with your own people, with the union I mean. I hear things. So there's not much point coming here shouting the odds about Brenda Fletcher. Because hell will freeze over before she comes near a pathology lab again.'

At this point, the phone rang. Evans answered impatiently.

'What? No, Marian, I'm with the union girl at the moment. In about twenty minutes, I suppose.'

He put the phone down and stared at Mel. 'Where were we?'

'You were offering your completely unsolicited opinion of my popularity at work. I won't take up any more of your time except to say that I shall be filing for a tribunal for Brenda Fletcher. You can let me know about those Virology cases. And I shall be raising the way you spoke to me with Robert Hislop.'

Evans laughed and took a pen from the desk in front of him. He looked at it as if he were about to snap it.

'Go ahead. You think he's your friend? You're not the first young woman he's taken a shine to. Sometimes I think that's the only way to get on in this company. By wearing a skirt.'

Mel stood up, shaking her head. 'I'm sorry to see that you're letting the stress get to you.'

And yet, despite the unhinged quality of his assault, Evans had drawn blood. *I hear things*. And Mel could not be sure that he didn't. *College girl*. There were people who were supposedly on her side who would like to see her fall, who would try to undermine her.

'Don't you want that?'

'What?'

'The other half of your Twix. Don't you want it? I'll eat it if you don't want it.'

Mel stared at the man sitting opposite her. He was overweight and clumsy-looking, wearing a crumpled suit. But his eyes were laughing and there was something about his face that made her want to smile.

'Go ahead.'

'If you're sure you don't want it.'

He did not wait for her to confirm this but took the Twix and devoured it in two bites.

'I'm not particularly keen on Twixes,' he said, licking his lips. Mel raised her eyebrows.

'I prefer Fruit and Nut,' he continued.

'No,' Mel replied, 'I can't stand dried fruit. In anything. It's terrible at Christmas. I can't eat mince pies or Christmas pudding.'

'Or Christmas cake,' he observed sympathetically.

'Or Christmas cake,' she agreed. 'Although my sister and I have a ritual. She always gives me her icing and marzipan because I love that bit.'

'And she doesn't?'

'Oh yes. That's her favourite bit as well. She's just a generous person.'

A generous person who received little pay-back. Sarah was an artist who had never received the magic-wand treatment from a rich collector who had decided that she was suitable for inclusion in his new movement. Nor did she have a huge house provided by her parents in which she could hold her own private views. Nor were any members of her family connected to worlds that might activate the essential networks of attention. Sarah was cheerfully sanguine about this and joked that it allowed her to carry on painting without such vulgar distractions as money, especially contaminated money. But Mel knew that the lack of attention to her thoughtful and complex work caused her pain.

'And then she pleaded with me to cover her in raisins and sultanas and lick them off one by one.'

'What?' Mel started, guiltily aware that her new acquaintance had been talking and she had not been listening. She found herself drifting off like this more and more these days.

'Don't worry. I was just asking whether you were visiting a relative.'

'A relative?'

'Yes. You see, this is a hospital. You don't appear to be ill yourself, so I thought you might be visiting a relative.'

'Oh right. No, no, nothing like that. I'm here for a press conference.'

He nodded. 'Gordon Forrester.'

'Mel Holloway,' Mel replied.

'No.' He sighed. 'You're not exactly on the ball today, are you? *My* name is Paul Flitcroft. Gordon Forrester is the man who had the misfortune to come here after a train crash which he survived.'

Mel said, 'The man with the wrong blood?'

'You make him sound like a comic-book character but, yeah, that's what I'm here for as well. The man with the wrong blood.'

Mel picked up a sachet of sugar and began to squeeze it, until she punctured it with her nail and it spilled out on to the table.

'You're a journalist?' She began to play with the sugar on the table, pushing it to and fro with her finger.

'Yup. Aren't you? Why else . . .'

'I work for a trade union. The GWA. I'll be representing the individual who was sacked for the error.'

'You can't have much of a case. She did kill the man.'

'No, she didn't.' Mel was sick of this pious line about Brenda Fletcher, whose misery-etched face was still fresh in her mind. 'Making a mistake at work doesn't mean that you're Rosemary West. That's why I hate journalists — you don't know anything about her. You don't know anything.'

'Hey.' Paul was clearly wounded by this attack. 'What makes you think that you have the right to tell me what I know and what I don't?'

'Well . . .' Mel looked up from her hill of sugar at him. 'I'm just sick of hearing that line about her killing him. There were plenty of other factors.'

'Oh, don't worry, I know that. You could start with Dr Gavin Fitzgerald and why it took so long to page him.'

'*He*'s the consultant? The fat one with the bow tie? Where was he anyway?'

'Probably smoking crack and shagging some twelve-year-old Thai prostitute if rumours are to be believed.'

This image was so revolting that Mel swept the sugar she was playing with across the table in a gesture of repugnance.

'Something is rotten in the state of the Great Northern,' Paul said, watching a pretty nurse who was laughing with her friend.

'And they're going to try and put all the blame on to one person,' Mel replied. 'Why don't you ask that nurse whether she'd like you to cover her in sultanas?'

Paul Flitcroft laughed in acknowledgement at being caught. 'It's a funny word, isn't it? Sultana. It means the wife of a sultan as well, you know. And what about kedgeree? That's a fantastic word. What's your favourite word?'

'I don't really have one,' Mel said. He was starting to annoy her.

'Chutney is good. So is disconsolate. Come on, you must have a few words you like. We've got another half-hour till the press conference.'

'OK,' Mel said. 'Lullaby. Apricot. Forlorn. Anguish.'

Paul nodded. 'I'm not sure about apricot but lullaby is quite excellent.'

And he suddenly smiled the kind of smile that made Mel smile as well.

The press conference was being held in one of the training and education rooms of the hospital. Mel felt a shiver of discomfort at the pale raspberry-coloured walls, the flip-chart, the overhead projector and the whiteboard. She half expected there to be a round of ice-breakers before the start of proceedings – *My name is Melanie Holloway and what I hope to get out of the course is* . . . Paul Flitcroft was already seated near the front when she entered. He saluted her encouragingly. Mel smiled back at him but went to sit at the back of the room. She could see the fat consultant and Neil Evans leaning up against the wall.

As they were about to start, a woman slipped through the door and sat down in the seat beside Mel. She rummaged quickly in her bag and took out a notepad and pen, almost fizzing with nervous energy. 'Damn,' she muttered as she dropped her pen and bent to retrieve it from beneath the chair in front of her. Mel glanced at her but could not see her face, which was hidden behind soft brown curls. Then as the woman located her pen, she turned and looked up at Mel. She had clear coffee-coloured sybilline eyes and her mouth drooped at the edges. This gave her an endearingly crestfallen expression, a feature which belied the crackle of tension that

43

enveloped her. She was slight, dressed simply in a long blue skirt and black loafers – a style which suited her. There was an elegance about her, something which defied fashion or any other temporary criteria. She would not, Mel thought slightly enviously, have been out of place in a French film; she had the same quality of understated style. The woman placed her hands over the notepad on her lap as the meeting started.

There was nothing unexpected about the statement from the Great Northern NHS Trust which was read by Dr Margaret Jowell. Given that the matter might be the subject of legal proceedings and pending the official inquest they were not prepared to say a great deal other than to confirm that Gordon Forrester had died from renal failure as a result of a tragic error which had caused a transfusion mix-up. The matter had been investigated swiftly – the Trust was not interested in cover-ups – and a technician from the pathology lab had been sacked following the night of the accident. But the incident had been a case of simple human error. The woman sitting next to Mel muttered something when she heard this.

The questions from the floor were banal: whether this was the first time somebody had died as a result of inaccurate cross-matching, what new procedures had been implemented since the incident. Mel wanted to ask why, if the case were the result of simple error, it had been necessary to treat the worker involved so harshly. She decided, however, to keep quiet for now. Finally, when it appeared that no more questions were going to be asked, her new acquaintance Paul Flitcroft shuffled out of his seat like a bear ambling from its cave.

'Some might argue that Gordon Forrester's death was the result of the totally inadequate procedures operating in Pathology since privatisation. I would also like to ask you, Dr Jowell, how you would respond to the accusation that there was a connection between the Trust awarding the pathology contract to MGL and the private work which you carry out in other MGL establishments?'

He smiled genially as if he had just asked her what her favourite words were.

Dr Jowell looked at him over her half-moon glasses. She had grey streaks in her hair and reminded Mel of the head-teacher at her primary school. Mrs Beevor had looked at her pupils in much the same way.

'I would respond by saying that it is an issue which has nothing whatsoever to do with the tragic case we are dealing with. Yours is therefore an impertinent and tasteless question.' She paused to emphasise the rap across the knuckles which she had just administered. Mel frowned with distaste at the mannered bossiness. 'But I would just point out that the last person foolish enough to make that allegation had to withdraw it pretty quickly after a letter from my lawyers. I suggest that you be careful about repeating such slanders in public. Are there any more questions? No? Well, thank you very much, ladies and gentlemen.'

The meeting was breaking up when the woman who had been sitting next to her suddenly turned to Mel and said, 'Why are you here?'

'What?'

'What were you doing at the press conference? You're not a journal-ist.'

'No,' said Mel, 'I'm representing the lab technician who was sacked. I work for a trade union.'

The woman's eyes flickered and took on a peculiar far-away look although she continued to stare at Mel.

'Well, that's great,' she said. 'Everybody's got representation. Every-body's got somebody looking after them. It's nobody's fault . . .' Her voice began to rise alarmingly. 'The rail company aren't at fault, the hospital isn't at fault, the train driver isn't at fault. Now even the person who made the mistake isn't at fault.'

'I'm sorry,' Mel said, 'I don't know who . . .'

'Oh, I do apologise, did I neglect to introduce myself? My name is Lily Forrester. My husband is dead but it is apparently nobody's fault. Well, I'm not going to accept that. *He* didn't crash a train and then give himself an incorrect blood transfusion. I don't give a damn about your bloody press conferences and inquests and passing the buck. Somebody is going to accept responsibility for this. I won't stop, I won't stop . . .'

And then she began to weep. Not gracefully, not like a character from a French film, not even like the delicate provincial girl manipulated by some foppish bourgeois youth. She wept with gulping sobs that seemed to be torn from her like involuntary shouts of pain. She stood in the training room with its raspberry-coloured walls, its whiteboard and overhead projector, her bag clenched between two balled fists and her face swollen with grief. Heads began to turn expectantly.

'I'm so sorry,' Mel said uselessly, 'I'm really sorry.'

Over the weeping woman's shoulder, she saw Neil Evans, Gavin Fitzgerald and Margaret Jowell in earnest conversation at the foot of the platform. Their conversation was intense enough for them to ignore the drama developing, ignore the woman about whose husband they had been talking. Jowell was prodding her finger at Evans as she spoke. Mel shuddered. Then she put her hand on Lily Forrester's shoulder.

'Let's get out of here,' she said. And exhausted by her furious anguish, Lily Forrester allowed herself to be steered from the room.

juice

Patrick had received a penalty fare on the tube while travelling to the hospital for a check-up. He had pushed the wrong button on the ticket machine and purchased a ticket for £1.40 instead of £1.70. Despite his offer to pay the 30p difference, they had issued a penalty fare which he had refused to pay. He had also considered it beneath him to lie about his address and had started to receive demanding letters from London Underground. He sat at the kitchen table with his friend Jim, eating kebabs and composing abusive letters to Peter Nail, the Revenue Protection Officer from London Underground. They looked funny with their heads bowed together – Patrick's black hair against Jim's ruffled blond.

'Dear Mr Jobsworth, do you enjoy trying to prise a tenner from a dying man?'

'A dying and law-abiding man whose only mistake was to try and go to hospital for an appointment.' Jim tried to keep his kebab together, holding it above his head to catch a loose piece of meat in his mouth. 'What about Penpusher rather than Jobsworth?'

Mel stood in the kitchen cutting up pears and feeding them into the juice extractor, listening to the casual banter which was their principal form of communication when she was about. She sometimes wondered whether they sat and had quiet, serious conversations when she was not there, whether Patrick ever discussed their relationship with his friend. Mostly, though, they seemed to concentrate on their battles with bureaucracy and on obscure discussions about minor TV personalities – the various hairstyles of Officer Fran Belding in *Ironside*, the changing structure of golden-labrador ownership in *Neighbours*, the disturbing and unstoppable rise of identical young males on children's TV. Mel enjoyed listening to these conversations where the two men competed as to who could make her laugh the most, who could be the most shocking or irreverent. She was their audience, their fan-club.

Jim had been clean for about a year. He had been Patrick's partner in crime and Mel had hated him. He had been a selfish, opinionated, violent, thieving bully while at least Patrick was just selfish and opinionated. She knew that it was Jim who had started Patrick on some of his more crazed binging – snorting, swallowing, smoking and injecting anything they could lay their hands on, sitting for days in darkened rooms with no idea what time it was, what was going on in the world. The fact that Mel would not accompany them on their lost highway had infuriated Jim – *frigid, uptight bitch*, he had snarled at her once. Patrick had been able to slow down because he had got bored of the repetitive rhythms of excess. But Jim had lost even the highway, along with more or less everything he had: flat, possessions, girlfriend and nearly his life. They had found him in his empty flat collapsed in the fireplace with a pipe in one hand and a bottle of vodka in the other. He had wanted to die. He had come to the end.

'Clean' was an appropriate term for the person Jim had become since rehab. It was as if the dirty things had been scrubbed away and a considerate and affectionate Jim had emerged, blinking and rubbing his eyes at the light. He worked hard on his life, he concentrated on details. He had returned to his job as a carpenter, he cooked food, he went to the gym, he read books, he even brought Mel bunches of tulips because he remembered that she liked them and because she had helped him when nobody else wanted to know him owing to the value they placed on their personal property. In spite of her suspicion and dislike for him, she had told him to come round whenever he wanted, not to sit in his room scratching the walls or chewing his knuckles. Mel was not a great drinker and she enjoyed going to the supermarket with Jim to fill bags with carrots, peaches, mangoes and kiwis to make fresh juice. They compared the merits of different teas – camomile (good for the nerves) and peppermint (good for the stomach). They tried out every flavour of ice cream, argued about the relative merits of Häagen Dazs and Ben and Jerry's. In spite of this transformation, Mel knew how fragile Jim was, how sometimes he sat alone clutching his stomach and rocking with pain. Not necessarily because he wanted to drink but because he was lonely.

'I sometimes feel like one of those pigeons you see with only one leg,' he had said to Mel once.

'No,' she had replied, 'because they are worse than they were before and they are probably going to die. It's the other way round for you.'

Having Jim around now was a help to her. He took Patrick's mind off his illness by playing with him. Instead of making pictures with potatoes or blowing soap bubbles from an egg whisk, he helped him to compose outraged letters to the bank and London Underground. They moved the videos around in Blockbuster, so that *Watership Down* was in the True Stories section and *The Case of the Hillside Stranglers* with the Romantic Comedies. He ensured that Patrick did not further damage his scarred liver by drinking too much, and when Patrick went into flights of melodrama about his impending death, he reminded him that there was no evidence that he was going to die as a result of the illness. Mel sometimes thought that such reassurance irritated Patrick, who never went to the dentist, could not sleep the night before having his ears syringed, and treated every spot as if it were a tumour.

'This chilli sauce is crap. And I said no onion.'

'Well, doner go on about it.'

'You've got a really weird sense of houmus, mate.'

'Tzatziki for you to say.'

'You're both completely pitta-ful.' Mel made one of her rare incursions into their banter, handing them a glass of pear juice each. 'And they'll take you to court.'

'History will absolve me,' Patrick said. 'Right. To the task in hand. I would also like to claim several penalty fares of my own for the countless occasions you have left me suffocating in a tunnel.'

Mel drifted off while Patrick and Jim began to plan an elaborate day of protest for the day that the fares increased. She put her head back and listened to schemes to start a mass non-payment, to occupy tube stations, to paralyse the system with bomb threats. They talked excitedly as if it were all going to happen, as if the fantasies of two wounded people could make any difference, as if the London Underground system could be thrown into chaos by a recovering alcoholic and a sick insomniac barely able to get out of bed in the mornings.

From the window, the dark tree-tops of Bethnal Green Gardens shook in the wind, the moon was covered by cloud, yellow light shone from behind the net curtains of other flats. Trains tracked out of Liverpool Street towards the badlands of Essex, the flatlands of Suffolk, the wind-blown dunes of the Norfolk coast. And beneath the railway bridge, gaggles of Bengali boys were eating fried chicken and shouting at their friends across the road. In other parts of the city it was different, there were all the strange histories and geographies of power. There were dances and dinners and ceremonies, there were uniforms and disguises. There were secret places where decisions were taken which might not be known now but which somehow, someday, might bring terrible consequences for the people talking in their living rooms, or laughing beneath the railway bridge or sleeping in far-off places of the world. Somebody somewhere was lighting a cigarette, ruffling the hair of their little sister.

Mel held up her glass and looked at the brownish liquid which would, perhaps, appear off-putting if she did not know that it came from fresh conference pears. Somewhere too in this city which was so carefully shambolic and unostentatious about its unequal distributions of pleasure and power, was Lily Forrester. In fact, Mel knew where Lily was likely to be because she had driven her to her house in Crouch End after steering her out of the press conference.

'I'm going that way anyway,' Mel had lied. She knew that what she was doing was not entirely correct. She was representing Brenda Fletcher in a case which involved this woman's husband. But there was something about her that aroused a mixture of both pity and curiosity. And perhaps it was more than either pity or curiosity, perhaps Mel felt a strange fascination for this woman who was struggling against her misery and grief.

Her first instinct had been to look for a pub and buy Lily a large brandy. But there was nowhere around the Great Northern and even if there had been, Mel would not have been too enthusiastic to try out their hospitality. Besides, Lily wanted to get home to her young son.

'Why don't I just take you home?' Mel had asked. 'It's a horrible journey from here.'

'I must learn to drive,' Lily said, aware of the truth of Mel's comment and peering at the dreary rain outside. Her anger had abated – at least towards Mel. She did not appear to be a person who found aggression very easy. Mel suspected that she was naturally rather gentle and tolerant.

They sat in the car, avoiding conversation about the press conference or Brenda Fletcher. Lily studied some of the tapes scattered about in the car.

'Do you want to put something on?' Mel asked.

'I don't know. It's not really my type of music. I'm sure it's very good though,'

Mel smiled and switched on the radio to GLR. There were hold-ups at the Hanger Lane gyratory system and delays on the Hammersmith and City line. Somebody started talking about their new book which was an account of Women in Rock. Listening to GLR always cheered Mel up; there was something soothing about the music, the amiable chat with authors and film-makers, especially as the rain began to fall, streaking the car windows. Mel turned on the windscreen wipers.

'What is your type of music?' she asked Lily.

'I like opera mainly. I quite like Simon and Garfunkel as well,' she added with a worried look on her face that made Mel want to tease her. She decided, however, that it might not be the best time.

'So do I,' Mel said. 'Well, the Greatest Hits anyway. "Mrs Robinson", "The Boxer".'

'I know which the Greatest Hits are,' Lily said.

Mel laughed at her companion's return to sharpness. She switched off the radio and put a Dusty Springfield tape on.

'These are the Greatest Hits of Dusty Springfield,' she said.

'What, you mean like "I Only Want to Be With You," and "If You Go Away". That sort of song?'

'Exactly.'

They glanced at each other and they both laughed this time.

Mel said, 'I don't know much about opera really. There was a song we learned at school once. It was about a man who catches birds.'

'Papageno,' murmured Lily, '*The Magic Flute*,' and suddenly she began to cry again, but quietly this time, fat tears dropping on to her lap. Mel handed her a tissue. Excessive displays of emotion often got on Mel's nerves, just as crying babies or somebody else's coughing made her clench her fists with annoyance. And yet she could also be quite sentimental on occasions, could be moved suddenly to tears of sympathy.

'I like the way you drive,' Lily said after a while. 'Which is strange because I don't drive and I normally can't stand cars.'

'What I can never understand,' Mel said as she flashed her lights to let somebody out, 'is when people get in their cars to go for a drive. I don't like driving unless I'm going somewhere. Then I quite enjoy it.'

Lily laughed and wiped her eyes. 'Gordon's parents live in Shropshire. They used to make us go for drives. We would drive out into the countryside for about two hours, stop for ten minutes, then drive back another two hours. I hated it. Especially when I was pregnant because I needed to go to the toilet every half an hour and it was such agony. His dad always drove and I started to detest him for it, watching how pleased he was with the car, loving the feeling of being in control, pointing things out as he drove. Self-satisfied. I thought I might scream with boredom and frustration. Gordon always said I was a snob.'

She broke off and Mel glanced at her quickly, afraid she might be about to weep, but Lily was smiling.

'I am a snob I suppose,' she said, 'but not in the way that they were snobs, which was ten times worse. Gordon's dad always used to tease me about opera. He had this favourite joke about it just being a bunch of fat ladies wailing and I had to smile all the time.'

She grimaced painfully like a halloween pumpkin.

'You don't like him much,' Mel said.

'No. I don't. Although I never told Gordon that.'

'Some things are better left unsaid,' Mel replied.

'This is my street. If you pull in just there.'

Mel parked beside an end terraced house. The lights were on behind net curtains, a Japanese lantern glowing like a huge moon. Mel could see shelves of books through the window – it was the kind of house she might have expected, the house of decent, progressive, North Londoners. It was easy to criticise such people but Mel could think of far worse types, far more corrupt values, far more worthy targets.

'Will you come in and have a cup of tea? Or a drink?' Lily asked.

'Oh no, thanks anyway. I should be getting home.'

'Please,' Lily said. 'I've brought you out of your way. Just have a cup of tea. You can meet Daniel.'

'Who's Daniel?'

'Our son.'

The child shrieked as he heard his mother coming through the door. She bent down and scooped him into her arms. A young girl followed him out, smiling. She was pretty, rosy-cheeked, her skin smooth.

'He's ready for his bath, Mrs Forrester.'

'Thank you, Claudia. You can go now if you want. Here . . .' She took out her purse. The girl blushed.

'Oh, Mrs Forrester, it's OK, really. It makes no difference if I do my schoolwork here or across the road.'

'Don't be silly.' Lily pulled out a note. The girl's face was tense with embarrassment.

'The thing is . . . my mum said . . .'

Lily's hand paused. She frowned. Mel watched her to see how she would play this, could see that she did not like being the topic of compassionate tongues.

'Oh, I see. Well, look, I can't let you babysit and not pay you. Especially when you look after him so well. So take this and don't tell your mum. Go on, take it, Claudia.'

The girl held out her hand hesitantly and then snatched the note, still blushing. Mel stepped through into the living room. The child's toys were scattered about – a red train on a circular yellow track in the middle of the room. On the bookshelf, there was a photograph of Lily with a man Mel assumed to be Gordon. They were on a boat. Lily was pretty and laughing up at the sky, Gordon seemed to be shading his eyes from the sun, looked as if he might just have made a joke.

'Venice,' Lily said as she saw what Mel was looking at. 'We took a boat from the airport. Gordon asked a man to take the photograph of us. Isn't that great – to arrive in a city by boat?'

She picked up the photo and looked at it for a moment without expression before replacing it on the shelf.

Mel nodded. She felt pleasure at being in this house, as if she had been removed from the normal patterns of her life and had had all her responsibilities lifted from her. She was curious about this unusual woman whose softly cocooned world had suffered such violent disruption. She took in quickly the stuff of Lily's life — the Matisse poster, the rows of classical CDs arranged by composer, the Guatemalan cushions on the sofa.

'Listen,' Mel said, 'if you need to bath Daniel, why don't you do that and I'll make some tea. Just show me where it is.'

'Would you? That would be great. I shan't be long.'

The kitchen was down a flight of four stairs at the back of the living room and faced on to a small garden. Lily showed Mel the tea bags and cups and disappeared upstairs. While Mel was waiting for the kettle to boil, she gazed out into the darkened garden. A path of light fell across the gloom from the garden next door and she was startled to see a pair of eyes gleaming back at her. At first she thought that it was a cat but then she realised that it was a fox standing as if in a spotlight.

'Oh,' she said. The creature stood absolutely still in its small urban domain, one paw raised, staring with fierce concentration. Then it trotted away — confident, self-contained.

Mel went to tell Lily about the fox but paused as she climbed the stairs. Lily was kneeling by the bath and singing to her son in French as she washed him. *Que donneriez-vous belle, pour avoir votre mari?* The song sounded familiar, they had sung it at school — *au près de ma blonde qu'il fait bon, fait bon, fait bon*. The little boy laughed and waved his arms as she playfully pulled an ear with each *fait bon*.

Mel watched this moment of intimacy and then turned and went back down the stairs. She would tell her later.

'Oh yes, the fox,' Lily said when they were sitting at the kitchen table drinking their tea. 'She comes every now and again. I haven't seen her for ages.'

'I went to tell you but I didn't want to disturb you. You were singing in French.'

'My mother is French,' Lily said. 'Her family are from Lyons. Very staunch Catholics.' She wrinkled her nose. 'Do you have children?'

Mel shook her head.

'Do you not want them?'

Normally, Mel found this question irritating but somehow she didn't mind it in these circumstances.

'You know, the strange thing is that I don't really know. I don't dislike them. Well, sometimes they can be a real pain. I'm just not sure that I'm prepared to make the sacrifices required. And I'm certainly not going to do it just because other people want me to.'

She could hear the familiar chorus in the back of her head. *You're not getting any younger, you'll regret it later, you're too selfish sometimes.*

Lily nodded. 'I used to think that it would be a kind of surrender. Daniel wasn't planned. But he has brought me such happiness.'

'I'm sure,' Mel said. 'It's a personal thing. I suppose I just don't have that biological drive. I think I would find the constant demands irritating.'

Lily nodded absent-mindedly as if she had already forgotten what they were talking about.

'This woman,' she suddenly said. 'What's she like?'

For a moment Mel was puzzled and thought that Lily might be referring to somebody from her world who was linked to the vexed decision on childbirth. Then, as Lily gazed at her, she realised to whom the question referred.

'I'm not sure I should go into that,' she said, 'I have to respect her confidentiality. But I can tell you that she's going through hell. That won't be much comfort to you . . .'

'Oh, I don't know,' Lily said and then she shook her head. 'No, no, that's not right. I don't mean that. You can understand though? If she had only been a little more careful, Gordon would be alive. I can't get rid of that thought. I can't say that nobody is to blame because I think that somebody is. I just feel so powerless.'

'I'm not saying that nobody is to blame,' Mel murmured. She did not think it would be particularly helpful to start talking about MGL's cost-cutting and lack of training – all things she would raise at the tribunal. Bad publicity, something to shake up that smooth bastard Robert Hislop.

'I saw him at the hospital. He was conscious. He held my hand so tightly. He told me that he had thought about me all the time that he was trapped. He told me that he had thought about songs. He never used to like opera, he had all his dad's prejudices. But I took him and he loved it.'

Mel smiled, unable to know what to say to this.

'Actually, you know what the last thing he said to me was? It was very strange. He suddenly said, "What's that actor called – the one from *Spartacus* with the funny chin?"'

'Kirk Douglas?' Mel asked.

'Yes. I told him that and he smiled as if it had been really bothering him and he could relax now. Then they wheeled him away and I waved at him. Kirk Douglas.'

'It's frustrating when you can't remember a name,' Mel said.

'A funny thing to be thinking about though. And funny to think that my last words to him were "Kirk Douglas".' She shook her head in wonder.

It was certainly strange, Mel thought. What had been her last words to Patrick that morning? *I'm going to make a Waldorf salad so don't eat all the cheese*. And Patrick had repeated the joke from *Fawlty Towers* about being fresh out of Waldorfs. Hardly very profound. Kirk Douglas, Waldorf salads, but why should it be any different? You couldn't go about from day to day assuming that your partner might be dead by the evening. Mel half smiled as she remembered her dad when they argued. *You'd better say sorry for that because if I die and that's the last thing you said to me you'll feel guilty for the rest of your life*. This always succeeded in making Mel laugh. There were certainly worse things one could say than *Kirk Douglas* or *Don't eat all the cheese. You are stupid, ignorant and retarded, I don't know why I ever thought I loved you*. She had said that once in an argument with Patrick and he had thrown a plate at her. But at least it wasn't the last thing she ever said to him and she wouldn't want it to be.

'You remember I said my family are Catholics?' Lily switched subjects. 'I guess I kind of lapsed. But now I think that even if there were a God I would just hate him.'

'That's never been a particularly strong argument for me. If you accept the concept of God it seems to me that you have to accept that he might move in mysterious ways.'

'I'm sorry. I didn't mean to offend . . .'

'Oh no, you haven't. I've never had that problem because I have no concept of God.'

Mel – who had an active and restless imagination – had sometimes found this absence quite troublesome. Absence of comprehension? Absence of faith? She could not even say what was lacking because she did not understand what it was she was supposed to comprehend or have faith in. Arguments with religious people were pointless because she simply had no idea what they were talking about, they had no shared terms of reference. She could much more easily discuss agreeable fictions like the tooth fairy or Father Christmas than the existence of God. Her sister Sarah had once embraced a kind of customised Catholicism but Mel suspected that this was posing – an attempt to appear singular and cerebral. They had had an unusually sharp exchange about it when Sarah had patronisingly told Mel that she pitied her. Mel had deliberately responded with the kind of argument about religious wars, bigotry and persecution that she knew Sarah considered low-level and vulgar. In fact, Mel still thought that there was a case to answer on this point.

'When I was a little girl, I broke my leg playing netball,' Lily said suddenly.

'Right,' Mel said, puzzled.

'I fainted from the pain. I thought I would never feel such agony again. Then I gave birth which was another level of pain altogether.'

Mel understood where Lily was going. 'And this is another level again?'

Lily bowed her head to look at the hands she was twisting on her lap and then looked up at Mel. 'I wouldn't wish this pain on anybody,' she said. 'No matter what they had done.'

There was silence and they both turned to the glass door leading out to the garden. There standing, looking in at the two women with piercing eyes, was the fox again.

'It's so strange,' Lily murmured. Then she shook herself as if from a trance and smiled at Mel.

'I'm sorry for earlier.' She brushed a strand of hair from her face. 'You're just doing your job. But I meant what I said. Somebody is going to accept responsibility for this. People can't just get away with things.'

'When do you want me to come and fix those shelves, Melanoid?' Jim asked her as he got up and put on his jacket. They had agreed a strategy whereby Patrick would send Herr Penpusher von Jobsworth a letter containing a penny as the first instalment on his fine and a promise to continue doing so for the next nine hundred and ninety-nine weeks. Even if this were rejected, they calculated that they could then enter an argument as to whether they now owed London Underground £9.99 rather than £10.

'Oh.' Mel cleared the glasses and an ashtray from the table. 'Any time, you know, whenever's convenient for you.'

'Maybe next weekend then.' He ruffled her hair. 'I'll be off then.'

Later that night in bed, Mel told Patrick about Lily and their conversation. He maintained a polite interest for a short while but paid little attention. His banter with Jim sometimes exhausted the small quantities of energy and good-nature which remained to him. Mel began to feel a sense of dejection at not being listened to.

'Can you imagine how she must feel?' she asked.

'No,' Patrick replied. His head was turned away from her on the pillow.

Mel regarded him, irritated by his perfunctory response when she had so often to listen to his interminable rants. 'No,' she said. 'Because I sometimes wonder whether you have any imagination at all. Apart, of course, from things which concern your health where your imagination is highly advanced.'

'You don't know what it's like,' he said in a whiny, self-pitying voice.

Mel told him to change the record.

She lay in bed staring up at the ceiling. She had half wanted to ask Lily if she wished to meet up again but it had been awkward. Why should they meet again? What could she say? And yet she had enjoyed the time she had spent in her house – listening to Lily singing in French to her son, the pair of glittering fox-eyes staring through the garden door. She was restless, did not like the thought that she might never see her again but knew that this was foolish – it had just been a chance meeting.

How many lives had been changed by that train crash? As it sped towards its destruction, Lily had been waiting for her husband – she might have greeted him with a glass of wine. They might have gone to bed and laughed at the TV the way that Mel and Patrick did, they might have made love. Brenda Fletcher had been on her way to another late shift which she could not have anticipated would be any different from all the others. Mel had been chatting on the phone to Pepa. But the train had raced on through the night, the passengers grateful to be arriving in London, glimpsing the first lights of the city. And Lily was not the only grieving person; eleven other people had been lost, eleven other families bereaved, eleven sets of friends devastated – as if a stone had been hurled into a calm pond, sending ripples out in all directions.

In the living room, the telephone rang. She waited for the answerphone to take it. After hearing her voice give the message, there was a short pause and then, 'Whore. Fucking silly whore.'

The phone clicked down again. That was it.

She got up and went into the living room, played the message back. *Whore. Fucking silly whore.* She frowned and repeated the message, trying to see whether she could recognise the voice. It had a genuine edge of hostility to it but it was nobody that she knew.

Whorefuckingsillywhore. Whorefuckingsillywhore. Whorefuckingsillywhore.

It must be a wrong number. Or a stranger who had selected the number at random.

Out there in the great immensity of London, there were people who would do this sort of thing, they would mumble obscenities down phone lines, they would give free rein to their bored, lonely and twisted yearnings, their deviant passions, their unhealthy imaginations. They too spent time at the window, they wove predictable fantasies as they watched people in the street, they felt their blood running hot and heavy. She imagined the mouth close to the receiver, the hand clenching the phone, the insult spat out. Was there relief in that? No more so probably than after the sticky response to distant and inaccessible images; afterwards the living room would be just as empty, the silence just as oppressive, the tinnitus of frustration just as humiliating.

'Who was that?' Patrick called from the bedroom.

'Some pervert,' she answered as she walked back into the room.

'I wish I had answered,' he said.

'Well, it's best not to,' Mel replied.

When she slept she dreamed that hideous red-faced, red-coated huntsmen were chasing a fox through London. Horses with flaring nostrils and clattering hooves, huntsmen with the brute faces of upper-class thugs, whirling truncheons like mounted police, the fox hurled into the air, fresh wet red blood on the streets. She woke from the furious images of the dream breathing fast as if she had been running.

chlorinated

Light rippled across the bright blue of the swimming pool at York Hall as Mel swam. From the corner of her eye, through misty goggles, she glimpsed the passing forms of other swimmers, the sudden slope of the pool floor into the deep end.

She loved it here, the faces that she recognised but didn't have to speak to, the trophy cabinet of the Bethnal Green Sharks, the small rituals of the changing room. People came to use the gym, to have Turkish baths, to swim, to play badminton. They came in the early morning, during their lunch hour, on their way home. She liked both the collectivity of the pool and its diversity. There were pairs of fat-bottomed women waggling stubby legs as they chatted, blocking two lanes, there were graceful long-legged girls flashing up and down. There were paunchy, clumsy, splashing men and there were flat-stomached athletes. A pregnant woman floated on her back, her stomach a serene dome. And, when the adults-only session was finishing, spindly kids with orange armbands splashed out frantic widths under the eye of the young teacher who laughed and flirted with the attendants.

When Mel was swimming, she did not think about work or about Patrick or about anything other than the number of lengths she had completed. It was not a time for reflection or meditation, it was a time for emptying her mind of everything apart from counting lengths. Sixteen and then four more is twenty. Ten more and then a pause. Last ten lengths makes forty.

Wrapped in her towel, sitting on the bench in the open cubicle of the changing room, Mel glanced at other women. A girl walked past drying her hair and Mel envied the easy grace of her body; the resolute breasts, long legs, taut stomach and buttocks. In the cubicle opposite, a middle-aged woman with frizzy greying hair was getting dressed and laughing with her neighbour about the horrors of half-term. Rolls of fat bulged under her arms and her skin was mottled. Mel looked down and wriggled her own toes with their chipped nail varnish. She was not especially unhappy with her body, although she might have preferred it to be a little more like that of the girl so thoughtlessly drying her hair. She might also like it to be paid more attention. She did not want it to change any further though, she did not want all the inevitable folds and creases of age, she just wanted to stay as she was for ever.

When she arrived at work, head clear and skin smelling pleasantly of chlorine, Graham was drinking a cup of coffee and teasing Mary, who had a large bundle of files under her arm but who never missed the opportunity to squabble with Graham. They were arguing about Mary's fervent mish-mash of beliefs in astrology, faith-healing, reincarnation, tarot, and spiritualism. Mary also kept hens and supplied the office with a steady flow of fresh eggs – something Graham did not appear to mind so much.

'Hi, Mel,' Graham greeted her. 'Mary's just explaining how her chiropractor has advised her to run three times widdershins around a dock leaf when Aries is in the ascendant. It might help cure her varicose veins apparently.'

Mary whacked Graham with the files.

'Oh no, she's putting a curse on me with her magic wand,' Graham shrieked. 'Bad karma. The wicked witch of the filing cabinet. We must have a laying on of hands – get the ouija board out, Mel.'

'I never said any of that, you cheeky monkey. You must open your mind a bit, that's all.'

'Why must I? It's backwardness.'

Mel dumped her bag on the desk. 'Ask him about the AGM of the Stalin Society which he went to this weekend, Mary. Followed by a short film on the natural resources of Siberia. That must have been a bundle of laughs, Graham. Not at all backward.'

The meeting had been advertised in Graham's *Morning Star* which he had left lying about. Mel had been reading it at lunchtime and had noticed that Graham had circled the meeting.

'Stalin saved the world from Nazism,' Graham said. 'I happen to think that's quite an accomplishment.'

'It would have been some accomplishment if he had achieved it single-handedly . . .' a voice from behind him chipped in. 'But I think the Red Army might have played a small part. Not to mention the weather.'

The voice belonged to Mark Thompson, the second of the union's Assistant General Secretaries. Thompson was a younger, more popular – albeit less powerful – figure than Barry Williams and the two men detested each other. They were also locked in a battle for succession, given the impending retirement of the GWA's General Secretary. Rumour had it that Mould had delayed his retirement for some time, simply because the union hierarchy suspected that Williams might not beat his arch-enemy.

Unlike many senior union figures, Thompson had not had to jettison any ideological baggage or allegiance in his voyage up the ranks. He had never been associated with a party or faction, although he always gave the impression of an energetic radicalism. Given that Barry Williams was the choice of the 'modernising' New Outlook caucus within the union, Thompson also needed a less orthodox and more populist image in order to appeal to the rank-and-file. Mel had noticed that his face was appearing more frequently in union publications and knew that this was part of his undeclared campaign.

'Why don't you ask your spiritual adviser whether Mark will ever become General Secretary, Mary,' Graham mocked in retaliation for Thompson's slur on the Generalissimo. 'Or perhaps he'll just come back as one in another life.'

'Perhaps,' Mark said mildly. 'Anyway, I'm not here to debate such remote possibilities, fascinating as I find myself as a topic of conversation. I want you!' He pointed at Mel as if he were General Kitchener.

Mel tried not to blush. When she had first started working for the union, she had been given the privilege of attending the annual conference. In the bar of the hotel at one of the evening drinking sessions, Mark Thompson had attached himself to her, he had been by her side for most of the evening. She had been aware of a few raised eyebrows, some whispered comments and it had been this that had caused her to detach herself and retire to her room alone. Under no circumstances was she going to provide spectator sport for a group of drunken, red-faced men. Mark himself had done nothing to make her feel uncomfortable, she had no evidence that he had been encouraging the observation or conniving in any way.

Mel did not want to think about what might have happened had she not witnessed the distasteful sniggering. There was something about Mark. He had a bright, purposeful, vulpine quality that she had found attractive and – if she were going to be really honest – still did. She had thought – on more than one occasion – about what it would have been like if she had gone back to his hotel room that night. He was good at what he did. He possessed the seductive confidence of the salesman who truly believes both in his product and his ability to charm the prospective buyer. But this was not the fake appeal of the skilful conman, nor the bluff of the poker player who in reality holds a weak hand. He was neither bombastic nor interested in the sound of his voice alone. He asked questions and gave people time to speak, betraying impatience only when they began to digress from the essential point under discussion. This was perhaps Mel's one criticism of him – he sometimes defined the essential point rather narrowly.

Thompson sat on the end of the desk and glanced at the postcards and notices pinned on the board. He mock-grimaced at a picture of the West Ham squad. 'They'll win fuck all again,' he said.

'Well, winning isn't everything,' Mel replied, uncomfortably aware that her mock-primness was sliding into flirtation again.

'Not a philosophy that will get you very far as we approach the millennium. I suppose you've got an excuse for supporting them, being an East End girl and all that.'

'I don't need an excuse. At least we're not bankrupt and heading for oblivion like Crystal Palace. But you're not here just to betray your ignorance of football?'

Thompson laughed. 'No. I was going to talk to you about MGL. I heard you wanted to go to tribunal over the MLSO they sacked.'

'I think we've got a good chance. And I wanted to use it as well to expose the problems of privatising Pathology.'

'Yes, although the word is that the government's not going to permit any further privatisations.'

Mel raised her eyebrows. 'We'll see. Anyway, they'll renew the contracts of those which have already been privatised. Plus, they're not going to rule out private involvement altogether. I'm sure MGL will be pressing for a favourable deal.'

'Probably,' Mark conceded. 'Anyway, it's always good to take them on. But you might not be too popular with Fungus. Or Barry Williams.'

'I don't think I'm so popular with them anyway.'

'Well, you're more popular than Graham,' Mark said and stood up. He went to the window and looked down at the street-scene below. Mel glanced at his back. He was a slender man who wore well-fitting suits. There was something a little suburban about his style but he carried this off to his advantage. She could imagine him playing squash, emerging from the leisure centre in Thornton Heath where he lived, throwing his gym bag into the back seat of his Rover.

'So what are you trying to tell me?' she asked.

'It's just that Robert Hislop, the MGL vice-president . . .'

'I know Robert Hislop.'

'Well, he's kind of tight with a few ministers at the moment. And there's word that he might be seconded as an adviser for some health project the government's running.'

'And?'

Thompson sighed and knitted his hands. 'It's just a bit more complicated than it appears. Hislop's also quite friendly with Fungus. When Fungus retires he might want a directorship. He certainly wants a seat in the Lords so he doesn't want to upset the government. The People's Peer. And Hislop's been suggesting to Fungus that he might concede union recognition in MGL's other factories. Regardless of percentages. Which has got Barry Williams very excited of course.'

'Organisation, organisation, organisation.'

'Exactly.'

'So you're telling me that I shouldn't go ahead?' Mel met his gaze.

Thompson twisted the ring on his finger and frowned.

'Not at all. I think you should.' He turned away from the window. 'I'll back you up. I just wanted you to be aware of the dangers, that's all. You don't want to cross Lord Mould of Dulwich. And Barry Williams will want an invitation to Glyndebourne when he becomes our new General Secretary.'

'I thought you were the next General Secretary.'

Thompson rubbed his eyes. 'It's pretty hard if you've got those bastards of New Outlook against you. Especially Leo Young. Last I heard he was plotting to have me seconded to a European confederation of unions.'

Mel couldn't help laughing. Leo Young was the union's media relations officer as well as a machine politician with access to high levels of government. Politics for Leo Young was about power and defeating enemies – real or imaginary. As an apparatchik he was a master craftsman. He was amiable, amoral and knew everybody. He lunched with politicians, journalists, spin doctors, lobbyists, businessmen, anybody who might be important – now or one day. The double bluff was far too simple a stratagem for Young – he was like a child with a puzzle that everybody else found baffling but he had to discover ever-more complex ways of solving in order to keep himself entertained. Young had nothing but contempt for the General Secretary but his was the job of protecting Mould's interests and he applied himself to the task with a vigour which suggested that nothing else in life really mattered. It amused him even more that Mould was stupid and drank too much and pawed women, it made his skill at manipulation even more entertaining. At the moment, his task involved preventing Mark Thompson from becoming General Secretary and he was devising increasingly ingenious methods of blocking Thompson's access to the membership.

'If you want me to come down and talk to your branch on this MGL thing just let me know,' Mark said.

Mel liked Mark but knew that his motive here was ambiguous so she asked him whether that particular offer had been prompted by a real desire to speak to the branch or a shrewd recognition of the electioneering possibilities involved.

Thompson grinned cheekily and put his hands up. 'You've got me bang to rights, Ms Holloway. A bit of both, I suppose.'

'Well . . .' Mel reached for her diary. 'We've got a branch meeting at the beginning of the month.'

'Book me in then, Scotty.'

'Will you be a fire-brand? A rabble-rouser?'

'Oh no. I shall be very moderate and restrained. I shall treat it like the organising opportunity that it is. Can we take a helicopter view of this, people?'

They laughed again at the passable impression of Barry Williams. Then there was an awkward pause and Mark Thompson said, 'We should have a drink after work sometime.'

Before Mel could answer, her telephone rang. She lifted the phone and put her hand up to wave goodbye to Mark, who slipped away.

'Hello, you whore. I'm going to get you, you fucking silly whore. I know where you live and I know where you work. I know everything about you.'

Across the office, Mark Thompson was holding a box of eggs from Mary's hens and aiming a mock-punch at Graham. They were both laughing. Mary glanced across and mimed a cup of tea at Mel.

'Did you hear me, you cunt? I'm going to hurt you. You're going to suck my cock.'

'Oh, fuck off,' Mel said and slammed the phone down. She knew that you were not supposed to answer back but it was really starting to get on her nerves.

'Somebody doesn't like me very much,' Mel said to Pepa. 'They keep phoning up and calling me a whore.'

The two friends were sitting in a pub on Upper Street. The bar-staff were Australian, they were wearing polo shirts with the name of the pub on them. A bright, flashing computer game was distracting Mel with repeated images of cars turning over and a cartoon woman with a huge cleavage in a leather jacket. This was the only place they had been able to find where they could sit down. They were drinking beers with tequila chasers.

'You?' Pepa said. 'What on earth put that idea in their head?'

'I dunno. Maybe they've mistaken my number for yours. Seriously, though, it's a bit freaky. They've got my home and my work number. Although that's not very difficult to find out, I've given them both out enough times.'

'That's bad.' Pepa raised her eyebrows. 'You should get on to British

Telecom. It's probably just some arsehole manager you've pissed off trying to wind you up.'

'Yeah.' Mel shifted uncomfortably. She was remembering Neil Evans and his 'malicious little bitch' outburst at the Great Northern. It was the kind of thing that Evans was quite capable of, although the voice didn't sound like him at all.

A man wandered over and asked if he could join them for a chat. He had a Scouse accent and there was a tell-tale red dash across the bridge of his nose where somebody had recently hit him.

'No,' said Pepa.

'Come on, girls. Just for a chat like. I'm all on my own.'

'No,' Pepa repeated.

'Give us a fag then.'

Pepa looked at him over the top of her glass. 'My mum has always said to me that the two most important qualities in life are good manners and cleanliness.' She looked him up and down disparagingly. 'It's one of the few things I agree with her about.'

The man glowered at her and muttered something unintelligible as he rocked on his heels. Mel sighed and reached in her packet and gave the man a cigarette. He wandered away without a word of thanks.

'What did you do that for?' Pepa asked, astonished, when the man had gone.

Mel shrugged. 'What does it matter? It got rid of him.'

The city did this, it threw these people across your path, with their sudden entrances and walk-on parts, their aggression and vulnerability, all the inarticulacies of powerlessness. They came out of the shadows and stood blinking in the spotlight. For some unlucky or weak people such encounters could be dangerous or even fatal. When the fine nerve-endings ached from the dull decay of loneliness, a chance encounter in a pub could result in a fatal invitation to proximity. Kindness or compassion might be rewarded with a blunt instrument and an empty purse hurled over a garden fence. And perhaps such acts of kindness and compassion also contained their own predatory instincts, their own gentle menace. Sometimes you just had to sidestep, you had to know the tricks, you had to know when to pull a rabbit from a hat, when it was time to engage – *Now you see me!* – and when it was time to slip quietly away – *Now you don't!*

Mel thought about Lily Forrester and tried vainly to imagine her faced with this situation. And yet Lily was neither feeble nor pathetic, she was certainly not foolish. Mel had taken pleasure from their conversation, she had felt relief that it did not have to be constantly laced with jokes and banter. It was not that Mel disliked either jokes or banter but it could get tiring, repetitive. Sometimes she also thought that it was lazy. Mel had enjoyed being able to talk without having to rush for a response, to have time in which to consider her words. Lily's cleverness seemed thoughtful and reflective, her humour gentle. Not that these were qualities in particularly good currency, they were too easily confused with weakness and passivity, the person possessing them highly susceptible to the brute elbow in the eye. A vicious blow had certainly landed upon the unsuspecting Lily – her life with her academic husband, their trips to Venice and to the opera, their book-lined living room, their child, all of their songbird strategies had been reduced to nothing when a train shot through a red signal and when a tired and under-trained worker sent down bags of the wrong blood.

Mel felt a pang as she remembered Lily singing to her young son, the child's laughter.

Je donnerai Versailles, Paris et Saint Denis.

'Opera's rubbish,' Pepa said when Mel told her about Lily.

Pepa's deliberate black-and-white approach to the world pissed Mel off sometimes. She had experienced it before when she had invited Pepa to go with her to films which her friend would dismiss as 'arty shite'. Pepa would then make a virtue out of her enjoyment of populist entertainment as if Mel were the stupid one, as if she failed to understand that this made Pepa more subtle, more complex than the subtitle-watching poseur.

'I'm afraid I really don't know enough about it to say that,' Mel retorted a little frostily.

'Well, you don't need to,' Pepa said. 'You want reasons why opera's rubbish? OK. The three fat bastards for a start. Then there's the fact that they charge the earth but still need gigantic subsidies. TV channels clogged up with four-hour productions of *Die Liebfraumilch* and *Der Lederhosen*, idiots standing like sheep in the rain in Hyde Park for Pavarotti, boring documentaries about Covent Garden that set the trend for ten million similar programmes, "Nessun fucking Dorma" . . .'

In spite of herself Mel laughed. 'Yeah, like football's just twenty-two grown men running around after a bag of wind,' she retorted.

Her mum used to repeat this when Mel and her sister went to Upton Park with their dad. Sarah and Mel sat one on either side of him with a bag of peanuts each. *Peanuts, peanuts, getcha roasted peanuts.* The fat man in front of them would show them his glass eye and they would squeal and wriggle with delight. Afterwards, they would walk each side of their dad, both holding a hand as they followed the crowd down Green Street. Her dad had dragged them along very fast once when there was fighting with Manchester United in the market behind the tube station. Mel remembered the mixture of fear and excited curiosity, just as she remembered the mighty tower-block there, the great monstrous slab of a building. She had always stared up at it in wonder and terror, imagining it leaning forward and toppling on top of her, squashing her into a paper-thin Mel. Now the council had pulled it down; it had vanished along with the peanut sellers.

Her mum and dad were arguing once and she had heard her mum shouting about the football, about the way in which her dad dished out treats while she had to administer punishments. At the time, Mel had simply thought that this was true – her mum was always doling out restrictions and then punishments for breaking them. If she didn't like doing it, why didn't she just stop? Then everyone would be happy. Her dad bought them sweets and said, 'Don't tell your mum' and they loved him for it. Then there was no more football for a while because their dad had gone to live with Jenny from work. Even now, Mel couldn't hear the name Jenny without clenching her fists. When he had taken them to the football again, it hadn't been the same at all. He had been distracted and had snapped at them for swinging their feet.

'How's Patrick?' Pepa changed the subject.

'He's . . . well, you know . . . he's OK. Jim comes round quite a lot. They sit around talking about how they're going to assassinate London Transport managers, kidnap Carol Vorderman as a celebrity hostage, deprive her of sleep and make her do mental arithmetic until she has a nervous breakdown.'

'Jim the monster?'

'He's OK now. I like him. He's putting up some shelves for me.'

'Mmmm, well watch him all the same. So Patrick's just sitting about feeling sorry for himself still.'

'It is one of the side-effects. Some people get suicidal. I looked it all up on the Internet. I can't really blame him for it.'

'When you're working all the hours of the day, getting perverts calling you a whore, and then going home to look after him. Does he ask you how your day was? Does he even make you a cup of tea?'

Pepa was growing quite angry as she spoke. Mel was surprised as she knew that – deep down – Pepa liked Patrick.

'It's not that bad,' Mel said. She did not want to explore this issue. And it really wasn't that bad, at least it would be better when Patrick's treatment was finished.

'I haven't seen you have a laugh for ages,' Pepa said. 'You always look exhausted or you drift off into your own little world. I watch your eyes go vacant. You never used to be like that. He's dragging you down, Mel.'

'And what do you suggest? I still love him you know.'

'I don't know,' replied Pepa unhappily. She had clearly wanted this meeting with Mel so that she could raise these concerns with her. 'But if you live your whole life around that bloody union and your sick boyfriend, there's not going to be anything left of you.'

'I love my job.'

'You love your boyfriend, you love your job. And yet you don't look very happy. It seems to me you'd be better off working for some evil capitalist. *My* manager would never dream of treating me like they treat you in that union.'

Mel had to concede that this was probably true. She had received memos from Barry Williams which – had they been received by one of her members – would have led her to initiate grievance proceedings against the employer. It was as if those who ran the union had made a note of all the bullying management techniques they had come across in their careers and decided that it was legitimate to use them against the people who worked for them.

'Anyway, I do have a practical proposal. I was going to ask whether you want to come on holiday. Sicily. I'm going with Claire from work. She's a laugh. We'll lie on a beach, read books, drink wine, eat seafood, find some local sex-toys.' Pepa tilted her head endearingly from side to side with each of these proposals. 'Come on, Mel, you have to say yes.'

Mel contemplated with longing the vision which Pepa was offering. Then she thought about the mountains of work in her office, about the battle with MGL, about Patrick and the despair he would feel if she went. Strangely, she also thought about Lily Forrester but it was not as if she represented a reason not to go to Sicily.

'I can't,' Mel said. 'I know you'll be mad with me, Pep, but please don't nag me. I've got responsibilities here, I can't just go away, even if I would love to.'

Pepa almost hissed with irritation and disappointment. She bowed her head so that Mel could not see her face through her dark curls.

'Responsibilities? You've got responsibilities to yourself as well . . .'

'I know. And if it was any other time . . .'

'Don't give me that. There is no other time for you. There's always something. Maybe you just like playing the victim.'

'That's not fair.'

'Or maybe you'd prefer to go to the opera with your posh new friend?'

'Oh, don't be so fucking childish.'

There was silence and they both stared at their drinks. Mel picked up a beer mat and began to tear pieces off it. Pepa reached for her jacket.

'I'd better go.'

'Yeah? See you.'

No one spoke. Mel threw the little strips of paper at her empty glass.

'I will go you know,' Pepa insisted.

'Good. Hurry up and fuck off.'

'Right, I'm definitely going.'

'Go then. I'm not stopping you.'

Mel couldn't look at Pepa. She knew that she would laugh first. Pepa got up and pulled her jacket on. Their eyes met and Mel spluttered with laughter.

'You owe me a fat tequila,' Pepa said. 'But let's get out of this pub first. We're far too good for it. I want one of those soups from that Latin-American place.'

*   *   *

Mel lay in bed that night watching Patrick who was, thankfully, sleeping by her side. His hand was gripping the top of the bedstead as if for security. He had slept like that for as long as she had known him.

They had been together for a long time. They had met when Mel had been working at the GLC. While Patrick's old band were playing in Tokyo and Rio de Janeiro, Patrick was doing Jubilee Gardens. At a dinner party, somewhere in south London, the conversation had turned to the debate on rape between Susan Brownmiller and Angela Davis. One of the guests had said that rape was nothing to do with sex, it was all about power and everybody – including Mel – had nodded at the reiteration of this orthodoxy. Suddenly, Patrick – who was sitting next to Mel – had dropped his fork laden with vegetarian lasagne and squawked, 'Pieces of eight. Who's a pretty boy?'

The girl who had made the original comment had turned on him angrily. 'What do you mean?'

'Well, do you really believe that it has *nothing* to do with sex? And who says you can disentangle sex and power anyway? Why do rapists choose a sexual act to express their power? What are you going to say next? Black people can't be racist. It's all about *power*.' He had affected a middle-class social-worker twang.

'That's so unbelievably *arrogant*,' a man sitting next to the woman had retorted in the accent which Patrick had just mimicked.

Patrick had put his hands behind his head and leaned back on his chair, grinning arrogantly. 'And what's wrong with arrogance? Arrogance is greatly under-rated. I'd rather be arrogant than a parrot with spectacles. You'll never have an original thought in your life, you middle-class prick.'

At that piece of gratuitous rudeness, the conversation had exploded. Mel could tell that Patrick was pleased for having provoked the uproar. After it had subsided, nobody would talk to him apart from her. He had flirted outrageously with her, making her cackle with laughter so that she also began to earn sideways glances of disapproval. At the end of the evening, when they were leaving, he had suddenly turned to her and invited her to his flat. And Mel had been so surprised she had said yes.

'Aren't you afraid I might be a rapist?' he had said as they sat on the top of a 38 bus, their knees touching. 'It'll be nothing to do with sex though. I just want to express my power over you.'

'Stop showing off,' she had said. 'Or I'll go straight home.'

'You don't want to go home,' he had said, taking her hand and kissing her for the first time there in the front seat at the top of the bus.

She had not gone home. Her heart had been drumming with anticipation, her mind fluttering with the excitement of flirtation pursued to its conclusion, at the thought of what was going to happen next. And now, he was lying beside her and she knew so much about him – his addictive personality, the way he gripped the bed when he was sleeping as if he might fall out of it. At the foot of the bed was his guitar which he had not played for some time. She missed watching his face as he picked out the language of chord changes, the seductiveness of the expert, the person who does something well. She knew his likes and dislikes, his favourite food, and his obsessional, multitudinous hatreds. She knew that underneath most of his noise and bluster, he was a sensitive and insecure person, a mid-thirties misfit who owned very little apart from his sickness.

She knew so much about him, she had told Pepa that she loved him and she did. But would she *never again* feel that beat of impatient yearning, that percussion of lust, that moment of mouths meeting for the first time? Would she *never again* in the whole of her life experience the sensation of the couple on their way to buy cigarettes who suddenly stopped and kissed each other on the corner of the street, their hands in each other's hair? It was a cruel tension, a bitter conflict; her unquestionable loyalty and love, her dislike of trauma and upheaval, all of this struggling with the pervasive and universal messages – the secret, shameful, insistent exigencies of desire.

Never again in her whole life?

And if she were to give into such urges, how could she stop it from degenerating into the dreary and the sordid? How could she prevent the lies and hysterics that she both despised and feared, all the banal side-effects of submission to the wearisome nagging and tantrums of the body? And wasn't such submission also a form of laziness? What did she say to the small girl at the football game reproachfully swinging her feet, silently grieving for the father who would never return?

Never again, never again.

Patrick stirred and turned round. His eyes blinked open and he smiled at her, the smile of recognition of somebody emerging from a dream.

'You're not asleep,' he mumbled.

'No,' she said, stroking his hair. 'I'm watching you sleep. Like a good angel.'

'Have I been asleep? Oh good.'

'Yeah, you've been asleep. Go back to sleep now.'

'I love you,' he said, 'I like it when you watch over me.' He smiled and gripped the bedstead again. Mel heard his murmurs and twitches like a dog dreaming of rabbits.

She lay awake, staring at the ceiling, waiting for his breathing to deepen. When she finally slept, she dreamed about the fat man at the football grinning obscenely and rolling a glass eye in the palm of his hand, holding it out to her like an offering, inviting her to disgrace, to transgression.

hunchback

The evening was clear and cold, an early moon low in a sky that ran its display of various blues towards the pale west. Mel sat in her car, hands gripping the steering wheel. She felt stupid. Why had she come here? What purpose could it serve? She looked across the road at a room which was lit behind net curtains. Somebody was in. She could start the car and drive home but that would make her feel even more foolish, that would confirm that what she had done was strange. No, it was not strange, it was perfectly normal – an act of generosity, a follow-up call.

Still, she found it hard to get out of the car. A pair of Hassidic Jews walked past, white-faced with soft corkscrews of hair, dressed in the old uniform of the Polish ghetto. On the other side of the road, tapping a stick in the opposite direction, was an elderly Muslim. A young couple arguing furiously stopped almost by the car. The woman was gesticulating, the man running his hands through his hair in impatient exasperation. Mel slouched down in her seat, not wanting to witness this private scene but still half fascinated by the evident fury of the protagonists, the misery they were inflicting on each other. The woman turned away from her partner and saw Mel. She glared at the spy, the intruder. Then she strode swiftly away, brushing dismissively past the man. Mel sighed and opened the car door, gulping cold air.

Lily Forrester did not seem at all surprised to see Mel.

'Hello,' she said. 'Come in, you must be absolutely freezing.'

She was dressed in a white T-shirt and jeans. Her hair was tied back from her face and her face showed the flickering distress of the sleepless. But she smiled at Mel and there was welcome in her smile.

'I was passing nearby,' Mel lied. 'I suddenly remembered that you lived here. I thought I'd see how you are.'

'That's lovely,' Lily said. 'I always like it when people just drop by. The English are very bad at that, don't you think? Everything has to be arranged. Would you like some tea? Or a whisky?'

'Whisky sounds great,' Mel said. She still felt awkward. Lily's tone was not false but it was high and brittle, it was as if a faint shadow of pain followed her. It might be true that people didn't just drop in enough but you would expect those that did to be people you knew and not a stranger who had driven you home once. She got the impression that, much as Lily might like people dropping in, it was not a regular occurrence.

'I'll just get some ice,' Lily murmured.

While Lily went to the fridge, Mel stepped over the circular train set and inspected the books. The shelf seemed to be carefully ordered into themes – theories of public administration, economics, sociology, feminism, post-modernism. Mel commented on the latter section to Lily as she returned with the glasses of whisky.

'Ah yes, Gordon hated post-modernism. He said it was a terrible con. But he still read all that stuff. It was as if it fascinated him as well, he became obsessed with hating post-modernists. Especially if they were French. He hated most French theory, not just the post-modernists. Sometimes, when he was reading late I'd hear him muttering away down here, "Oh fuck off, Deleuze, you pretentious French bastard," every now and again. It was quite funny, especially when I heard a thud, which meant he'd thrown the book across the room. Sometimes, I think he got into it because his own area was rather practical – regulation of public services, the consequences of privatisation, all that sort of stuff. So he took refuge in the most abstract theory. Cheers.'

They clinked glasses.

'What's the opera?' Mel asked as she sipped at her single-malt whisky, watching the little lights flickering green and red on the CD player.

'Oh, I'm sorry. I'll switch it off.'

'No, no, it's fine. It's only low anyway. It's nice.'

'Do you like it? It's *Rigoletto*.'

'I don't know . . .'

'Rigoletto is a jester, a hunchback. He must have done something pretty bad in a previous life because he has terrible karma. He tries to arrange for the murder of the aristocrat who . . . ahem . . . "seduced" his only daughter. But there's a bit of a mix-up and what he thinks is the Duke's body in a sack is in fact his daughter, Gilda.'

Mel said, 'That must have come as a bit of a shock to him.'

'Yes. The Duke has a kind of signature tune and Rigoletto hears him singing it while he's gloating over the body. But even though the story is rather silly, just listen to the last duet between Rigoletto and Gilda as she is dying.'

'What are they saying?'

Lily sat next to her on the sofa and opened the libretto to almost the last page.

'Look, here we are . . .' Her finger moved down the page. 'Rigoletto is saying, "Do not die, my dove . . . if you fly away I shall be completely alone . . . please do not leave me or let me die with you".'

Mel glanced at Lily's face but she was dry-eyed. She watched Lily's finger tracing the words on the page, the light glinting on her silver ring. And then a soft plaintive soprano wound around the male voice as if they were embracing, a farewell duet, and it was Mel who suddenly and rather embarrassingly felt a shiver in her spine and tears prick at her eyes. She was almost dizzy; the music, the whisky, a faint perfume of soap from the person sitting next to her. The opera crescendoed to its dramatic conclusion.

'Now Gilda's dead,' Lily said. 'And Rigoletto remembers a curse that was placed upon him and sees that it has come true and . . . that's it.'

That's it. Mel imagined Lily and her husband smiling at each other, fetching their coats and making their way into a crowded West End street, the night clear and cold like tonight, descending into Leicester Square tube, talking about the performance as they made their way companionably home. Probably neither of them had heard of MGL at that time, certainly not of Brenda Fletcher, doing puzzles in a pathology lab on another uneventful night-shift. Neither of them had read the report that Mel had obtained from the research department that afternoon on Serious Hazards of Transfusion. The heart was a tenacious and miraculous muscle, beating out the stubborn tempo of life, reified in song and poetry – cheating hearts, aching hearts, foolish hearts, weary hearts. But no kind of heart was capable of resisting when it could not understand the codes, when it was fed the wrong blood. *We're losing him. What's going on here? This shouldn't be happening.*

'Are you OK?' Lily asked.

'What?'

'You just drifted away. It was as if you weren't here. Shall I get you some water?'

Mel laughed. 'No, it's OK. I keep doing that. It's such a bad habit. My friend Pepa – it drives her mad. She hates opera by the way – she says it's just the three fat bastards.'

It was Lily's turn to laugh. 'Well, actually she might have a point about them.'

'Why was Rigoletto cursed?' Mel asked as Lily poured more whisky.

'Because when he was the court jester he cruelly ridiculed a man whose daughter the Duke had seduced.'

'But he paid the price while the Duke got off scot-free?'

'I'm afraid so. Are you surprised?'

'I suppose not.'

There was a pause and then Lily asked, 'How is your case going?'

Mel had met Brenda Fletcher again when Brenda had tried to pull out of the tribunal. Mel had had to point out the vulnerable position she was in. She had been sacked for a fatal error with no chance of getting a reference. Brenda had also been working towards the end of her post-graduate qualification when she was dismissed. All of that work was going to waste. And with no new job, she was struggling to keep up her mortgage payments.

'I just can't face it,' she had said. 'I keep thinking about his wife and child. I can't argue that I was right. That I deserve money.'

'That's not the point,' Mel had answered. 'You made a mistake, Brenda. But the problem was much deeper than that and MGL have made you a scapegoat. That's not fair. We're not trying to get you reinstated but we might be able to sort out something with regard to a reference, getting you out of your mortgage difficulties, at least making it possible for you to get another job.'

'I keep going back to it over and over again. I keep thinking, what if . . . and if only . . . I look at everything in terms of whether it was before or after the accident.'

And Brenda had wept. Quietly, as if she were ashamed of herself. She had rummaged through her handbag, scattering car-keys, a packet of Murray Mints, and a kidney donor card on to the table before finally producing a hankie which had MUM stitched clumsily into the corner.

Mel had taken Brenda's hand. 'That always happens with accidents. If only. What if? It's a terrible feeling but you'll destroy yourself if you go over it so much. I'll help you. I promise. It's not your fault. Brenda? Listen to me. It's not your fault.'

'Not my fault?' Brenda had stared at Mel with genuine incomprehension. 'Well, whose fault is it if it's not mine?'

Now, Mel looked at Lily and wondered how much she should tell her. She couldn't break confidentiality but she wanted Lily to know that Brenda's agony was real. She was about to say something when upstairs the child began to cry. Lily's eyes flickered. She is exhausted, Mel thought, wondering whether – in spite of the child – Lily was actually younger than her. The child's whining rose and fell like an air-raid siren. He was not going to stop until he received attention. Mel gritted her teeth. People said it was different when it was your own child but she doubted it. She didn't mind children and often found them amusing and entertaining, but she knew that their perpetual interruptions, their needs and demands would drive her crazy. Lily looked into her whisky as if she wished she could jump in there, then placed her glass carefully on the table.

'He wakes up every night now. He misses his dad.' She rubbed her eyes. 'So do I. I'd better go . . . I won't be a minute.'

Mel picked up the glasses and took them down to the kitchen. She stared out into the dark, cold garden. There was no moon high in the sky, no gleaming-eyed fox, nothing but the distant shudder of a train passing nearby. What was she doing here? She was in no way competent to deal with this woman and her sorrow for her recently dead husband. Why had she come? Something had fascinated her, something had opened a trapdoor and cast light into the dusty attic of her imagination. In the days following her first visit, she had thought about Lily on more than one occasion. It was as if she were reaching toward her in some way, as if Lily somehow exposed a lack in her and Mel had to keep checking Lily to see what that lack was.

Returning to the living room, she picked up the photo of Gordon and Lily in Venice. He looked as she had imagined him when she had first heard about the case. She was glad that he had not been a revisionist historian or a drab lecturer in Business Studies. They were a nice-looking couple, they appeared comfortable with each other. Mel felt a little stab of envy at the obvious companionship, she imagined them arriving in their hotel, wandering around the narrow streets of Venice looking for somewhere to get a drink, crossing the dark canals. Then she frowned and replaced the photo. This was ridiculous, feeling envy for somebody who was dead, reinventing a scenario she knew nothing about. She vaulted down the steps to the kitchen, gazing out once again into the dark, empty garden.

'Are you looking for the fox?' Lily had reappeared. She stood beside Mel and once again Mel detected the faint scent of soap and cotton.

'No, I was just thinking. Is your son OK?'

Lily sighed. 'He keeps asking for Gordon. Especially at night. It drives me crazy sometimes. What can I say? What can I say? I want to ask that question as well. Who do I ask?'

Her voice was plaintive, desolate, and Mel instinctively put an arm around her, hugging the slight and unfamiliar frame. Lily did not seem surprised by this and rested her head on Mel's shoulder. They stood in that strange posture for a second, looking into the garden in silence as if the fox would appear at any moment. Mel could feel Lily's soft hair on her cheek, she could see their reflections in the glass, sense the beat of a pulse.

The doorbell rang.

'Oh God, I forgot that journalist . . .' Lily pulled away and clasped her hand to her mouth. 'He wanted to talk to me about Gordon. I wanted him to come this afternoon but he has been getting some reports.'

Mel was startled, when Lily opened the door, to see that she recognised the figure stamping his feet and exhaling air like smoke. It was Paul Flitcroft, the journalist from the press conference; big, bright-eyed and cheerful like a Newfoundland dog. He was also surprised to see Mel.

'The trade unionist? With the Twix?'

Lily looked puzzled.

'We met before the press conference,' Mel explained. 'He stole my Twix.'

'You *gave* me your Twix,' Flitcroft corrected her. 'I did ask. How are you, Mrs Forrester?'

'Please call me Lily,' said Lily, smiling her crease-eyed smile, the smile that transformed her face utterly, that gave it almost an ecstatic look.

'I've brought you the reports, Lily. From the Health and Safety Executive's investigations into other rail accidents. I've also got some rather interesting information about MGL. Did you know they're conducting clinical trials on a new drug that's sent their share price rocketing? It's some kind of wonder drug for people with hepatitis. Anyway, the last thing they want at the moment is bad publicity.'

'What type of hepatitis?' Mel asked quietly.

'God knows. Hepatitis Q? Hepatitis Z? I don't know. By the way, I came up with some great new words. Indigo, velvet, umbrella, confectionery. Fantastic. Eh? What do you think?'

'Yeah, fantastic,' said Mel. Lily glanced at her.

'The other thing I found out,' Flitcroft patted his stomach contentedly, either unaware of or immune to Mel's faint hostility, 'is that Robert Hislop is about to be seconded on to a government health task-force as a special adviser.'

'I knew that,' Mel said.

'Did you? Did you know that his brother-in-law is Malcolm Dodds the lobbyist?'

'No, I didn't know that,' Mel conceded. She knew that Dodds was a good friend of Leo Young, that they belonged to a drinking club which also served as an information exchange. Mel hated everybody she had met who worked for Dodds. They were usually boastful, brash graduates who were quick to manifest their contempt for anybody who did not belong to their club. Mel disliked their vulgarity and their casual misogyny – she also thought that, in spite of their financial success, they were disturbingly stupid.

'Dodds has done a lot of work for MGL. They've been lobbying the government on all sorts of things: privatisation, clinical trials, regulation of drug spending.'

'Would you like a whisky?' Lily asked.

'Oh, thank you. I'm pretty partial to a single malt.'

I bet you are, you fat bastard, thought Mel sourly. She did not know why she had suddenly developed such an antipathy to this jovial journalist. He had something of the know-all about him, he was self-satisfied. Neither did she like the way that he appeared to be appropriating Lily, spreading papers on the table, pointing things out to her, turning his big back to Mel. They talked about the solicitor Lily had been seeing who was a specialist in medical negligence, the problem of suing the Trust or MGL or both.

'Or even the individual who made the mistake?' Flitcroft speculated.

Lily shook her head. 'I wouldn't want to do that anyway. It's not about vengeance. That's what I wanted to say to you earlier.'

'Are you still trying to get her her job back?' Flitcroft asked Mel as he refilled his own glass with whisky.

'The point about Pathology at the Great Northern is that it was a disaster waiting to happen.' Mel felt Lily's eyes upon her as she spoke. She chose her words carefully. 'Their procedures were totally inadequate, their training negligible. The woman who made the mistake had been working far too many night-shifts, the consultant who was supposed to initiate the emergency procedure could not be located. I want to use the tribunal to show all of this. I want to show that heaping all the blame on one individual and trying to settle the case out of court is an inadequate response. How did it happen that one person was able to make such a catastrophic mistake? And if it gives anybody any satisfaction, she is a broken woman now. She knows that she was the final terrible link in the whole episode, although unfortunately she thinks that she bears sole responsibility.'

Lily nodded slowly at Mel's words. 'You must understand as well that we get a bit tired of hearing about the suffering of those who we still feel are responsible. The train driver went through warning lights and she gave Gordon the wrong blood. But I do know that it's much more than that and if you say that she is suffering then I believe you and I don't want her to suffer any more. But there has to be a hearing and people have to answer for their actions. Not just them but the private companies who failed us. We're having a meeting next week of families of the crash victims. You might want to come to that, Paul.'

Flitcroft nodded and made a note in his diary. Mel noticed that he was left-handed and clenched his pen in a strange grip. For some reason, this softened her attitude towards him; she often found clumsiness touching. She was relieved that her irritation was diminishing, she could feel it sliding away. The irrational contempt had reminded her uncomfortably of school and a plump, bespectacled girl called Jane Rowlands whom she had bullied for no particular reason, whom she could not stop bullying even though it sickened her, even though she felt as much disgust for herself as for the puppy-faced, bespectacled girl whose hair she pulled and whose possessions she stole. She was so ashamed, looking back on it, of the misery that she must have caused. Once, the girl had had a new fountain pen – it must have been a gift from a relative who could never imagine or understand how their precious niece or granddaughter could inspire such ferocity. Mel had bent the nib while Jane watched helplessly. She had felt terrible self-loathing and contempt and pity as she had done it. Even now, hot shame pounded in her head at the pointless cruelty of it, at the memory of the girl's desperate face.

'What are the other families like?' Flitcroft asked.

Lily sighed. 'Well, they're a pretty disparate lot, as you might imagine. Some of them are terrified of doing anything in case it messes up their compensation. And then they're from all over the place so it's hard to organise anything. What we really need is one totally dedicated person . . .'

'You seem quite dedicated,' said Flitcroft.

Lily hugged her knees and ignored this last comment. Mel could feel the tension gathering around her. Lily was staring intently at a spot on the floor as if some old adversary were slouching on its stomach towards her.

'Do you know there's a man who lost an arm in the crash? He had just finished learning sign language – he wanted to go abroad and teach deaf children.' Lily spluttered with laughter. 'I'm sorry but it's almost as stupid as rescuing somebody and then taking them to hospital and giving them the wrong blood.' She laughed again, shrill and artificial, and then looked at the floor again.

Flitcroft chewed his pen and glanced at Mel, who made a quick gesture with her eyes towards the door.

'OK,' Lily said. 'I don't mean to be rude but I'm rather tired now. And Daniel will probably wake up again soon.'

'I must be going,' Mel said. 'Can I give you a lift somewhere, Paul?'

'Hackney?'

'Hackney's on my way.'

She turned to Lily.

'Goodbye.'

'Thanks for coming to see me,' Lily replied, taking her hands. 'I'm sorry if . . . well, please come again anyway. We can listen to another opera. I think you would like *La Traviata*. That's actually my favourite. Favourite Verdi at least.'

Paul Flitcroft furrowed his brow. 'I can't stand opera. It's just a lot of fat ladies wailing as far as I'm concerned.'

And Lily and Mel exchanged a glance and laughed.

'Come again,' Lily repeated to Mel and Mel nodded.

'You're sure you want to be alone?' She felt the foolishness of the question as soon as she had said it. 'I didn't mean . . . I meant . . .'

'I know what you meant,' Lily said. 'Yes, I'm sure. But please come again.'

'This is a big car,' Flitcroft said as he settled down into the passenger seat. He opened a tin of travel sweets which had been in the car for as long as Mel could remember and popped two-stuck-together into his mouth.

'Mm-hm,' Mel replied.

'I wonder how many of your members' subs went to buy this car,' he added.

'Don't start,' Mel retorted, 'or you can take the bus.'

Flitcroft seemed unperturbed by this threat. He appeared to remain in a state of permanent affability, something which Mel found both irritating and endearing.

He said, 'You're pretty touchy, aren't you?'

'Not normally, no.'

'You don't seem very happy. You should relax. Nothing's worth it.'

'Is that right?'

'I think so. We could all die tomorrow.'

Mel recalled Lily's tale of the hospital, holding her husband by the hand as he spoke about his ordeal. She thought of Patrick and his liver, the battle to save himself from cirrhosis or cancer by submitting to this treatment that had transformed him from a lively and complicated person into somebody who could barely strum his guitar any longer. Boredom had driven him to excess, he had been like a trapped bee bouncing against a windowpane, he had pushed and pushed in frustration, wanting more and always more: more out of life, more out of people, falling disappointed when they inevitably failed him, refused his entreaties, played safe.

We could all die tomorrow, we are all in the process of dying. These things meant nothing, they were the emptiest of words. Too petty, too trite in the dying days of this century, ending with both a bang and a whimper – furrowed brows over computer screens, bright white lights flaring and curving away from dark seas, an orange glow somewhere on the edge of a foreign city, charred bodies in the morgue, a dusty hand in the ruins. A miscoding, a virus, the arc of a rocket – frightened, suffering people on hospital wards or in air-raid shelters – so many possibilities, so many endings, such morbid symptoms. How could you possibly know what lay in store for you, what was planned for you?

'You know that you shouldn't really be driving if you're a narcoleptic,' Paul remarked. 'The light's gone green. We have authority to proceed. And I think the person behind is getting a little impatient.'

They drove to Dalston, where Paul lived on St Mark's Rise behind Ridley Road market. When Mel had first met Patrick, he had also been living in a large, shambling Hackney house, on Graham Road. His flat was at the top of the tall building which was being managed by a short-life housing co-op. His bed was a double mattress on the floor beneath a window brushed by the branches of a great tree. The first time that she had gone into that room they had started undressing each other without saying a word, shedding clothes as they moved slowly to the mattress by the window, high up and close to the branches as if they were in a tree-house. After that, she had come to his room at different times – in the afternoon, late at night. Sometimes, he had called her when she was asleep and told her to come round straightaway, to take a taxi. And she had gone, had loved the slightly ridiculous feeling of dressing quickly but carefully, sitting in the back of the cab and shivering with anticipation.

There were things that Patrick had had in that room that were his: posters on the wall, coffee cups, a bedside lamp, books, lots of music. He had had a string of fairy lights hanging over his bed, a collage of tickets from old gigs. He had played her records she had never heard before and she remembered lying in the dark, listening to Eno's *Another Green World* – still Patrick's favourite album. In the very early days of their relationship, she knew that he probably continued to entertain other women in that room but she didn't really mind. In fact, she quite liked the idea of the sound of other women's pleasure, as if she could hear their faint audacious echoes, high up there among the branches of the trees, the moon shining through the sash window. It seemed to add an extra dimension of freedom to their own abandonment. She had enjoyed staying in somebody else's territory, sliding into another person's space, being the invitee, nothing taken for granted. She remembered Patrick making tea and toast in the morning, kneeling down and brushing the hair from her eyes as she lay on the floor wound in strange sheets, blinking at the morning light, still drowsy with love-making.

'I can get out here,' Paul said. 'Look out for my article on Lily Forrester. I'm thinking of calling it "Blood on the Tracks".'

'Yes, that's very tasteful,' Mel answered. 'Why don't you call it "The Wrong Blood on the Tracks"?'

'Bit clumsy. Anyway, drive carefully. This car represents the sweat and toil of honest trade unionists like myself.'

'It'll certainly go a lot faster without you in it.'

'Actually, most women love large men, you know.'

Mel laughed. 'Yes, but you may have misunderstood what they meant by large. Seeing as you're such an expert, why don't you write a book about it? *Women: A Complete Guide* by Paul Flitcroft.'

He swung out on to the pavement and straightened his suit.

'That's not such a bad idea,' he said. 'Won't need to be very long. Oh, and by the way. Disdainful. Fantastic word.'

He gave her a cheery thumbs up and she watched him climb the steps from the pavement to his front door. He stood clutching the paint-peeling balustrade, fumbling in each pocket for his keys. When he found them, he held them up like a prize and jiggled them at her triumphantly. As he opened the door, a cat sped past his ankles into the night. Again, she felt almost tender towards him, half regretted her rude banter which was rather out of character. She suspected that he lived alone and that he was probably lonely. She imagined him eating unhealthy food, drinking beers on his own in front of the football.

Mel drove down Mare Street towards the Cambridge Heath Road, watching for the familiar sights of the car showroom forecourt packed with Mercedes, the dark railway arches, St John's on Bethnal Green opposite Paradise Row where the dossers sat with their cans, the Museum of Childhood, the trees above the basketball hoops. This was where she lived, this was what she knew, had known for ages. It was so long since she had left here for anything other than work. A sudden image of Pepa's offer flashed in front of her: the warm Mediterranean, seafood and cold beer, necklaces of lights from fishing villages at night, the sea, the plash of the sea in the warm darkness, wriggling toes in the foam at the edge of the world. She was suddenly filled with longing, a longing to be away from these urinous streets with their dossers and their chip shops, away from the estates which stretched all around, the estate on which she lived, the impatient sound of horns from waiting cars summoning boys down from their flats. Her heart was hungry with longing for different sensations: for the sea softly slapping the shore, for the smell of acacia or pine, for station announcements in strange languages, for cool grass under bare feet, for the sun on her ankles.

Mel pulled up beside their block and sat for a while in the car just as she had done before knocking on Lily's door. *Something is happening, something is happening*, a voice was singing inside her. She was not happy and neither was she sad, it was a feeling of restless agitation. *Please come again*, Lily had said to her and had sounded as if she meant it. And Mel wanted to see Lily again. There had always been people who had made her miss them almost as soon as they had parted, whose presence was strong enough to make her hear and see them in her mind. It was harsh but Mel could usually divide the people she knew and had known into those capable of making the pulse race faster at the thought of meeting them and those whose presence or absence really did not make too great a difference. Mel was not certain why Lily should have been able to create this feeling in so short a space of time and found it unsettling. But it mattered to her whether or not she saw Lily again.

'Hi, Mellifluous. You've been a long time,' Patrick greeted her as she entered the flat and threw her coat down. He was sitting on the living-room floor playing with his record collection, listening to Ian Drury. There were LPs and old singles scattered on the floor all around him.

'I love this track,' he said, shaking his head happily from side to side. 'Listen, it's about his dad.'

'I thought Jim was coming round.'

'He went to one of those bloody stupid meetings. He's going to need to join a group to wean himself off them. My name is Jim and I'm addicted to meetings.'

'He must have been quite down if he went there.'

'Selfish bastard. Only ever thinks of himself.'

They both laughed. Mel went and kneeled behind him, put her hands on his shoulders. There were punk records and two-tone records and reggae records. Some of them were quite valuable. He still had the Joy Division *Ideal for Living* EP, most early singles by The Clash and The Buzzcocks. She picked up 'Ever Fallen in Love with Someone', turned it round in her hand and gave a mock-sigh.

'Ah, now there was a single,' she said.

'A lot of these records still sound good,' he replied. '"Atmosphere" is a brilliant track. I was in love with this girl once and I used to play it over and over again. Especially that tinkling bit. It was a really cold winter and it kept snowing. Remember the early eighties, how it used to snow?'

Mel nodded. 'I remember coming back from a party and I was so drunk and the pavements were all icy and I kept falling over. My mum and Sarah were watching me from the window, killing themselves laughing. In the end they had to come out and get me, lift me into the house.'

'It's nearly twenty years ago,' Patrick said almost wistfully. 'Doesn't feel like it. Where are some of those people now? Speaking of which, remember this?'

He held up the only single made by his last band. There was a picture of a youthful Patrick trying to look sultry on the back, pouting in a white shirt with rolled-up sleeves.

'I always liked that record,' Mel said. 'It was quite funky in its own way.'

He turned it around in his hand and smiled up at her sadly. 'Yeah, but what did I get?'

She put her arms around his neck. 'Well, you got a lover unlike any other.'

'True, but I never got rich.'

'No. Do you regret that?'

'Course I fucking do.'

Mel laughed and held out her hands to pull him up. 'Yeah, so do I. I'm not living the life to which I'm entitled. And it's all your fault for shagging the lead vocalist's girlfriend. Was it worth it?'

Patrick considered this as he hung from her hands, refusing to get up. 'Not really, although she did give good head.'

Mel let go of him so that he fell on his arse. She cuffed him round the ears. 'Yeah? How good?'

'Not as good as you, darling.'

'That's OK then. Let's go and watch TV in bed.'

She pulled him up off the floor and they went to the bedroom where they lay watching TV, relaxed in each other's company. When they could no longer be bothered to watch TV, Patrick took up his guitar and sang to her – something which Mel loved but which had not happened that often recently.

> *I'd take you down*
> *Honey if I could*
> *We'd find a place*
> *In the sunshine*
> *We'd be feeling good*

'That's lovely,' Mel murmured drowsily. 'Keep singing.'

Soothed by the simple melody, she remembered Lily's hair on her cheek, the smell of soap and cotton, the dark foxless garden. Private worlds, caged birds singing gentle lullabies, these were such beguiling dreams. To sing in spite of everything, to turn inwards, away from the world outside, the charred bodies in the morgue. But they were flawed dreams, they were the dreams of poor fools and crippled jesters. Because there was always the approaching hangman's brute step on a cold stone floor, there was always the Duke's triumphant song of impunity in the distant air. Still, she felt her earlier anxious longing soothed by the sound of the guitar, by the smell of clean sheets, by her gathering sleep. *Nowhere man*, sang Patrick. *Nowhere man and whiskey girl.* And Mel smiled dreamily, still able to taste the golden spirit warm at the back of her throat. When he put down his guitar, he got into bed beside her and held her in his arms and Mel did not know who fell asleep first.

mrs goatfucker

Mrs Boksic's workmates had thrown a two-day party when management had finally summoned up the courage to sack her, one of the reasons why Mel found it impossible to represent her. But Mel was also nervous of Mrs Boksic; her violent rage was legendary, and Mel was not going to change her mind on representation, especially since management had taken ostentatious care to observe the correct procedure. Curiously, Mrs Boksic was silver-haired and greeted Mel with a warm and sympathetic smile. The only giveaway to her true personality was the small jabbing motion of her head as she spoke – like a red-beaked bird of prey plucking at the innards of its victim.

'I want to be reinstated,' Mrs Boksic announced when Mary had brought them both a cup of coffee. Mary was down in the dumps because she had just found out that the man she had met – and rather liked – at the weekend was a Taurean.

'OK,' Mel said. 'My problem is this. Several of your colleagues actually requested management to take action.'

'Turks!' Mrs Boksic spat.

'I beg your pardon?'

'Turks. Muslims. Of course they say these things about me.'

Mrs Boksic had worked in a small company supplying parts for photo-copiers. A large proportion of her work colleagues were Asian and being referred to as Turks by Mrs Boksic had formed part of their complaint.

'I am a union member. I pay my money. Now you have to help me. I want my job back. Why won't you help me?'

Mel leaned back in her chair and studied Mrs Boksic. What if she said what she really thought? What if she used Graham and Mary's name for her — Mrs Goatfucker? I'm so sorry, Mrs Goatfucker, but I'm not going to be demanding your reinstatement. In fact the only tribunal you're ever likely to be attending is for war-crimes.

'I think the way you refer to your colleagues rather sums up the problem.' Mel placed her hands on the desk and tried to appear brisk but not unfriendly.

'You get me my fucking job back. I paid for my membership. You take the word of these Turks before you take my word.'

'Actually, they're not Turkish — not that it makes any difference.'

Mrs Boksic fingered a heavy cross hanging round her neck. 'I want industrial tribunal. I know my rights. I work there for six years. I have rights. I pay my membership.'

'Mrs Boksic, we're going round in circles. I explained in my letter why I felt unable to pursue your case. I'm not here to defend the indefensible and I have also got responsibilities to other union members who claim that they were subject to intimidation and bullying by you.'

'I did not bully nobody. You listen to me, you filthy whore, you fucking bitch, you suck the cocks of the Turkish man.'

Mrs Boksic was working her way into a frenzy now, her eyes gleamed with hatred and anger. Her crescendoing voice could be heard outside the office and Mel could see that Graham was itching to intervene. Graham was stubbornly pro-Serb and blamed the Croats and the Germans for the violent disintegration of Yugoslavia.

'Mrs Boksic—'

'I pay your wages but you are not better than dirty prostitute, you should be out walking the street, not sitting in comfortable chair, in comfortable office with all your nice pictures on the wall.'

'Mrs Boksic—'

'How much you charge Turkish man to suck his cock?'

Unfortunately, Mel laughed out loud at this point. This had the effect of transforming Mrs Boksic into a Catherine wheel of wrath, firing out incoherent obscenities which all seemed to involve Mel performing oral sex on Turkish men. Graham and Mary both left their desks and hurried over.

'Right, Mrs Boksic, that's quite enough . . .' Graham swung into battle.

'And you! You dirty homosexual, you queer, you too suck the cocks of the Turkish man.'

'Call Security, Mary,' Graham snapped. 'We're going to have to throw Mrs Boksic out again.'

'I kill you, you faggot.'

'Well, I've got news for you, Mrs Boksic. We are a democracy. We respect things called Human Rights in Britain. We have laws here that stop you from just killing somebody because you don't like their ethnic origin or because they won't do what you want.'

Mel was rather taken aback by Graham's sudden discovery of the virtues of bourgeois democracy.

'My son, he will kill you for this! He will come down and then you will be sorry. My son he is a Catholic, he is proud, he will deal with you, you cock-sucker, you communist faggot.'

'Mrs Boksic, I'm not frightened of you or your Ustashe son. You clearly have a dirty and an unpleasant mind for which I suggest you seek help. Now, I am asking you to go before Security gets here.'

'Oh yes, I go. I go now. But I come back. I come back with my son. I tell him what you call him. You will see me again. Especially you, you cow, you bitch.' She pointed dramatically at Mel. 'You are so ugly even Turkish man would not let you suck his cock. YOU WOULD HAVE TO PAY HIM!'

'OK, well, I'll bear that in mind if the situation ever arises. Goodbye, Mrs Boksic.'

And Mrs Boksic stormed towards the lift, sweeping a half-full mug of coffee on to the floor as she left.

'It said in my stars that today would present me with a difficult challenge at work,' Mary said as she picked up the mug.

'What about her son?' Mel asked Graham.

'Young Master Goatfucker? Oh, he's a horror all right. Quite mad.

She brought him down to the office once when there was some problem with her regrading. People blame the Serbs for everything but it's much more complicated than that. And at least they fought on our side against the Nazis.'

'I don't think that what they did in a war fifty years ago entitles them to do what they want now,' Mel observed mildly.

'I went to Croatia once,' Mary said. 'When it was still part of Yugoslavia. Holiday. It was lovely. And the people were ever so friendly. But that woman is horrible.'

'She's got one big obsession about oral sex and Turkish men.'

They began to laugh.

'Frustration,' Graham said. 'She lies at home stroking her crucifix and fantasising about enormous Turkish cocks.'

'Oh, she's terrible,' Mary said. 'Why are people like that? Why can't people just be, you know, normal?'

'Why can't people just be nice to each other?' Graham mocked her.

'Well, I don't think that's so unreasonable a question,' Mel said. 'Why are there some people who want to torture and hurt others? Who enjoy giving pain? There was a girl at school I used to pick on. Oh, I was so horrible to her. But I stopped . . .'

'Why?' Graham asked.

Mel paused. What was it? Why had she suddenly found that pain-filled face so distressing? 'I suppose because in the end I could imagine being her.'

'So, it's a kind of self-interest,' Graham said. 'You stopped because you wouldn't want what was happening to her to happen to you.'

'I suppose . . .' Mel said. 'But not just self-interest. The pain I was causing her caused pain to me. It was like I *was* her. In the end at least. Some people just don't have that . . . that . . .'

'Imagination,' Mary said suddenly. 'That's what it is. Are you OK, Mel? That must have been a bit of an ordeal.'

Mel shrugged. 'I'm fine. Although I never knew I was so ugly I'd have to pay for it. That's a real blow.'

'Bad choice of word in the circumstances,' Graham muttered.

'Anyway, you're not ugly, you're lovely,' Mary protested. 'Isn't she, Graham? She's lovely, isn't she?'

Graham started to rummage about on his desk for an imaginary pen. His ears were red.

'I'd love to have a figure like yours. Hasn't she got lovely legs, Graham? Come on, say something nice, you old misery-guts.'

'I do not spend my time looking at the legs of female members of staff,' Graham announced sternly without looking up.

'Yes, you do. Remember that young Asian girl we had temping? Tasmeena? Was that her name? Such a pretty girl but completely useless. Tasmania we used to call her, 'cause she was a bit detached from the mainland so to speak. Anyway, you were always looking at her legs.'

'I was not! That's an outrageous accusation. I don't engage in sex-ist behaviour like that.' Graham was growing more pompous in his embarrassment.

'What's sexist about that? It's just appreciating somebody's good points. And you certainly spent a lot of time appreciating them. I saw you peeking over the top of the *Morning Star* every time she reached up to put something on the shelf. You blushed every time she spoke to you. Of course, we never did find out who left that Valentine card on her desk. There were some who had their suspicions given that it was a picture of the first female Soviet astronaut. Not very romantic I thought but . . .'

'Oh get back to your tarot cards and your horoscopes, you old witch. See if you're going to meet a tall, dark stranger.'

Mary cackled with laughter. 'At least I'd know what to do with him if I did. Cup of tea, Mel? Oh and your friend phoned while you were with Mrs Goatfucker. Pepa? She said to call her back.'

Mel scanned through her e-mails while she called Pepa. There was a funny one from one of the reps, teasing her about West Ham crashing out of the FA Cup, there was the usual hit-the-delete-button-instantly trash and there was one from Barry Williams. Mel's heart sank as she read that he wanted to see her for an informal discussion on her workload. Whenever a message from Barry Williams was headed, 'Re: Your Workload,' it meant that he was unhappy about something. He wanted her to bring her diary with her and he wanted to see her that afternoon. Mel had not had time to read her messages recently – it must have been sitting there for a couple of days, she couldn't cancel now. Goodbye afternoon of catching up on paperwork.

'Pepa? It's Mel.'

'Hi, sweetheart. How's life?'

'It's great actually. I've just been told that I'm so ugly that I would have to pay Turkish men for the privilege of giving them a blowjob. And my manager wants to see me this afternoon to discuss my workload.'

'Well, firstly, nobody's *that* ugly that they'd have to pay a man. Turkish or otherwise. Least of all you. And if your manager gives you any grief tell him to stick his job up his arse. Anyway, cheer up 'cause I'm coming to see you tonight. If you'll have me.'

'Sure, what's up?'

'Well, I wanted to see you and I haven't seen that idiot boyfriend of yours for some time. Strangely, I quite miss him every now and again. I'm sure an hour in his company will cure me of that. Also, I wanted to ask you about maternity leave.'

'Pepa! You're not . . .'

'Do me a favour. No, it's this girl at work. I'll come over about eight if that's OK.'

Mel was glad that Pepa was coming to see her that evening. She had a hunch that she would need some drunken conversation after her meeting with Barry Williams.

'The problem is, Mel, that I just can't see the organising opportunity in this case.'

Barry Williams put both hands flat on the desk as he said this, as if he were about to push himself up into a standing position. He had asked Mel to go through her caseload and had plucked the example of Brenda Fletcher at MGL from her diary to demonstrate that Mel was spending too much time on individual cases, not enough time organising.

'It's not even as if she's a private-sector worker. We're established in the public sector and it's not one of our recruiting priorities.'

Mel said, 'Well, she is a private-sector worker, actually. She works for MGL. Worked for MGL.'

'Oh yes, I take your point. But she's still part of the health-service branch. Look here. This case, Mrs Boksic, is it? You saw her this morning. At least she works at Jansens and that's a company where there's still a lot of important work to be done.'

'I'm not representing her. It's a case of bullying at work . . .'

'But Mel! That's a critical issue at the moment. That's the kind of case I want to see you taking up. Private-sector worker being bullied. Excellent organising opportunity.'

'Barry, *she's* the bully. She refers to her Asian colleagues as Turks. Four of them – including the steward – said they would leave the union if we took up her case.'

'Oh. Oh, I see. Well, perhaps that's not the best example then. But you see what I'm getting at?'

Mel sighed. She knew exactly what Barry Williams was getting at.

'I mean, let's take a helicopter view of this,' Barry beamed. 'Let's try and stand back a little in order to see the overall picture. I'm not entirely happy with the organising approach you've been showing in the IT sector. You'll remember that we agreed that this was an organising priority for you? Now the question I want to ask you is whether you think that pursuing individual cases like this pathology thing, whether you think that it takes you away from the bigger challenge.'

'I think that it's an important case.'

'All cases are important, Mel. But is it the *most* important thing for you at the moment?'

Outside the office, Mel saw Mark Thompson. He did a mock double-take when he recognised Mel and took aim with an imaginary pistol at Barry Williams. She looked away quickly.

'I'm asking you to prioritise, Mel. That's what is lacking in your work at the moment.'

'OK,' Mel said, remembering that one of Barry's pet themes was the importance of not responding negatively to his constructive criticism. 'I find that a helpful suggestion, Barry. You're probably right that I could prioritise more.'

Barry grinned happily and leaned forward. His voice became earnest, approving. 'Nobody's questioning your workrate, Mel. You know that we hold a very high opinion of you. That's why I just feel that things need a little fine-tuning. Don't spend your time on this Brenda Fletcher case, pay attention to your organising projects.'

Mel gritted her teeth. What was the point of having so many members if you could not represent them when they needed it? When she made this point to Barry Williams, however, he sighed, ran his hands through his receding hair and told her that MGL was a rather sensitive area.

'Robert Hislop has a very high opinion of you. He's exactly the type of person we should be seeking a partnership with. He's not anti-union and he has a very good relationship with several ministers.'

'But what are you saying, Barry? That I can't represent MGL workers because their vice-president enjoys a good relationship with several ministers?'

'Of course I'm not saying that!' Barry snapped. 'Don't be so stupid. I've . . . you know I've been around for years. Don't talk to me like a fool, Mel. That's a very big mistake.'

Mel stared at him. He *was* a fool. He was an unbearable fool. Everything about him was repellent to her: his self-importance, his turncoat nature, his enjoyment of his authority, his lack of self-awareness.

'I don't think that I was talking to you like a fool,' Mel said carefully. 'I was asking whether you meant what it sounded like you were saying, that's all.'

'Well, I wasn't bloody saying that. I'm disappointed that you've responded in this way, Mel. I am trying to help you prioritise your workload and I'm hurt that you've come back in such a negative way, basically suggesting that I'm some kind of sell-out.'

Mel half laughed and shook her head. 'I'm not saying anything of the sort.'

'I'm sorry, Mel, but I think we should adjourn this meeting. I want you to think about what I've said. I want . . . no, I instruct you to reorder your workload so that organising projects comes before everything else. We will meet again in a month's time to discuss how you are implementing my instructions. You will write a report analysing each of your work areas in terms of success rate. Do I make myself absolutely clear?'

There were times when Mel regretted her inability to unleash the abuse bouncing about in her head. She imagined spitting on to the desk in front of her or picking up the clay elephant that had been made by Barry's young daughter, tossing it to the floor and stamping on it.

'Yes, that's perfectly clear. But unless I see a good reason to do so or unless I'm specifically instructed to do so, I'm not dropping the Brenda Fletcher case. I wanted *you* to be clear on that.'

'We will discuss this in a month's time. Make sure that you keep a whole afternoon free for a month today.'

For somebody who insisted on the importance of prioritising workloads, Barry Williams certainly liked filling diaries with useless meetings.

make love, not war

'Oh no, what are you doing here?' Patrick said as Pepa sashayed through the front door with a bottle of wine in each hand, pushing it shut with her backside. She was wearing new Acupuncture trainers and a T-shirt advertising the hip-hop compilation that her record company was currently promoting. While Angela's style was always elegant, Pepa's was bright and cheerful but equally carefully put together.

'I'm visiting. What are *you* still doing here? I thought they might have carted you off to the hospital for people with terminal self-obsession,' Pepa retorted. 'I keep telling Mel she should kick you out but she won't listen.'

'*Nobody* listens to you, Pepa. I thought you might have noticed that by now. Especially when you talk for twenty-four hours solidly about sex.'

'Oh . . . excuse me, Patrick, but the last time I was here you were telling me how you fantasised about taking me to a pub filled with sex-starved men, standing me on a table and auctioning me off to the highest bidder. I didn't notice you holding back.'

'Yeah, but don't get too excited about it. It was just a fantasy. You've probably been checking out the local boozers already.'

'OK, you two, stop flirting,' Mel said. 'Here, give me one of those bottles, Pepa. I'll stick it in the freezer.'

'Take these as well.' Pepa always brought gifts whenever she visited. She handed Mel some roasted red peppers in olive oil, and a box of quince jam. 'They're from the area I come from. About the only good things to come from there. Apart from wine.'

'And you,' Mel said.

'And me of course,' Pepa agreed.

They sat in the living room drinking wine and laughing at the local news on the TV. There were reports on a campaign to save a fire-station from closure, on a ten-year-old who had been caught with crack at school, and an item on overcrowding among Bengali families in Tower Hamlets council properties.

'They shouldn't have such big families then,' Patrick said grumpily. 'It's not the council's fault if they don't have flats big enough for ten children and all the fucking aunts and uncles.'

Mel glanced at him and then raised her eyebrows at Pepa. 'Come on, Pepa, Patrick's in a bad mood. We must be outraged in a liberal way by his lack of political correctness.'

'Patrick, how dare you?' Pepa mocked. 'I find your comments just totally racist and just totally offensive.'

'Thanks for pointing that out, Pepa,' Mel added. 'Patrick, I'm thoroughly ashamed of you. What you said was just totally racist and insensitive to Pepa who is after all a woman of colour.'

'What are you talking about, woman of colour? She's a fucking Spaniard. Her relatives invaded Latin America, and forced them all to become Catholics.'

Pepa laughed. 'Well, as a Catholic I find that last statement just totally offensive.'

'You're a Catholic? How many priests does it take to hear your confession? They'd have to work in shifts.'

'At least I've got something to confess. By the way, are you sure the doctors didn't say hypochondria C? I've got a friend with hepatitis C and she manages to go to work.'

Patrick spat his olive stone out at her.

But Mel wasn't listening to them any longer. The item on the news had changed to a campaign by a group of families to prosecute the rail company involved in the accident in North London. Her pulse quickened as she saw that the person being interviewed outside the headquarters of the Department of Transport was Lily Forrester. She stood amid a small group of protestors, their homemade placards bent back around the flimsy sticks by the wind. In the background, Mel was sure that she caught a glimpse of Paul Flitcroft.

Patrick and Pepa were giggling and spitting olive stones at each other. 'Shut up!' Mel snapped, turning up the volume.

They turned to look at her, puzzled by her sudden vehemence. She gestured at the TV.

Understandable as your grief is, what do you hope to gain from this campaign? Do you think that it might appear as simply a desire for vengeance?

Lily brushed wind-blown hair from her eyes.

Over and over again in this country, ordinary people have been killed and nobody has taken responsibility. People have drowned on ferries and river-boats, been crushed and burned in football grounds, been smashed up in train crashes. Of course, we are aware that accidents happen but it is not acceptable that those at the top always escape from their responsibilities, never have to answer for their deficiencies, make profit at the expense of human lives . . .

Well, Lily Forrester, thank you very much. Back to you in the studio, John.

Thank you, Luke. And now here's Katy to tell us about the weather.

'I know her,' Mel said. 'She's the wife of the guy who died in the hospital. They gave him the wrong blood. He would have survived otherwise.'

'Oh yes. Your friend who likes opera,' Pepa said neutrally.

Mel nodded. Seeing Lily on the TV was disturbing. She almost felt troubled that she had not been there with her, that she had only caught the broadcast by accident. Paul Flitcroft had been there, she was sure that it had been his face that she had seen. Perhaps they had all gone for a drink afterwards, perhaps they were laughing together right now. But if they were then so what? Neither of them were part of Mel's world. Since the evening at Lily's she had not made an effort to see her again. She had let time slide past and the agitation that she had felt when she had last left Lily had more or less gone away. She could choose not to see her again.

But she wouldn't choose that.

Mel knew what she was up to, what her mind was doing, the dangerous processes underway. It had happened to her before when she was younger —

a sudden transformation, an agitation, a craving. Humiliation and heartache were never deterrents. Yet it was not sexual, or not just sexual, this internal theatre, this piece of dumb masochism. *Where are they now? What are they doing now?* Almost envy as much as desire, wanting to be that person, and not even the real person but the person already idealised by the imagination; a person who, in reality, might be foolish or banal. One might, later in life, meet these people and wonder that they once had the ability to make the blood race and the heart pound, to inflict torment with their absence. She had some power, some control over this; she could decide not to invent this situation. She did not have to give into such folly, such juvenilia. It had not yet gone too far.

There was a difference though, there was a big difference, there was something that she was not facing up to properly, something that was unavoidable. In the past, the people who had had the capacity to make Mel long for them, to give them a place in her imagination, to promote them above the rest, these people had all been men. And Lily wasn't. So how did she feel about that? She didn't have much desire for women. The feelings that Lily provoked in her bore no resemblance to those produced when Mark Thompson made one of his visits to her office, when he suggested they meet for a drink. It was not that she had never considered the idea before – sometimes she had thought vaguely that it might be worth trying out; more to say that she had done it than for any other reason. There had been odd moments of drunken possibility which she had usually dealt with by ignoring the obvious messages. She knew that any stirrings came from the excitement of being desired and not so much from the act itself. But now she was agitated again. She didn't know what she felt although she knew that it was Lily's presence that she was beginning to crave and not particularly her body. But it wasn't even that simple – her presence covered such a wide range of possibilities, her presence included the feeling that Mel had experienced when she instinctively put her arm around her and they looked out together into the dark garden. *Poor me*, Mel thought to herself indulgently, *I don't even know what I think about anything any more.* And she thought suddenly of the icy mountain, of waiting amid the wreckage for the delirious dreams which preceded the annihilation of time, of her body with all its tedious limitations and shameful urges, frozen stiff in the snow.

'You've slept with women, haven't you?' she asked Pepa when Patrick had retreated to the bedroom, spitting a final olive stone at his old adversary as he departed.

Pepa raised an eyebrow in mock-alarm. 'I hope this isn't a belated attempt to come on to me, Mel. We've gone past that stage.'

'I'm not into women,' Mel said, curling her legs under her on the sofa. 'I'm just curious. Somebody was talking about it at work today.'

'Yeah, I've slept with women. Threesomes sometimes as well. Although with a woman I usually like it to be just me and her.'

'Do you like it more?'

'More than what?'

'More than skateboarding. What do you think?'

'Do I prefer women to men? I couldn't really say. I've got this mate, Fran, who always gives me a hard time about it 'cause she says there's no such thing as a bisexual, just straight girls playing silly games or dykes in denial. "OK," I said, "there's no such thing as a bisexual, in which case I'm completely straight and I won't go to bed with you." That made her revise her opinion pretty quickly.'

'I'm sure it did.'

Mel thought that Pepa was living proof that an early exposure to Catholicism did not automatically involve subsequent trauma and guilt over matters relating to sex. Pepa would be utterly dismissive of such an idea. This was one of the reasons why Mel loved Pepa so much – she never sought to blame anybody or to justify her own behaviour by reference to anything outside her own personality. If there were problems in Pepa's life then she never wasted time blaming her parents or her upbringing, she just got on with removing the problems. She rarely moaned and despised self-pity.

'They both have their places . . .' Pepa continued. 'It's like a glass of champagne or a pint of beer. Sometimes you're in the mood for one, sometimes the other. Sometimes, believe it or not, I don't want either. The other day, for example, I had this guy back at my flat and when he started undressing me I suddenly got so bored that I had to tell him to stop. I just couldn't be bothered. How terrible is that? He went mental so I threw him out, which was what I wanted to do anyway. I just didn't want this man in my flat and I certainly didn't want him fumbling around trying to get my bra off.'

Mel giggled at this image of Pepa suddenly growing bored and throwing out her conquest.

'If he'd been a bit quicker he might just have made it.' Pepa was laughing as well now. 'You should have seen his face when I went, "Stop!" He was going, "What, what, what's the matter, what have I done wrong?" He sounded so stupid that it sealed his fate. He was handsome as well. Media boy. I don't think that had ever happened to him before. God, the things he called me. Whore, pricktease. He said I was lucky I didn't get raped. "Raped?" I said. "At the rate you were going? I'd have died of boredom first."'

Pepa suddenly frowned and gazed at her hands. 'He said I would never be happy.'

Mel studied her friend. Although Pepa rarely moaned, Mel knew that, deep down, she was hurt by her family's rejection of her, by the way that – because she chose to live differently from them – they had turned their backs on her so vehemently, never defended her against spiteful tongues, punished her with sustained sulking for slights invented by minds corroded by boredom. Pepa was far too proud, far too contemptuous of such low strategies, to give into their pressure, to forfeit her independence for their acceptance. She laughed, shrugged it off, called them peasants and fascists, revelled in her black-sheep status. But once when she was very drunk she had wept a little and said to Mel, 'I may not be perfect but I think, you know, I'm basically a good person. I just can't stand being represented as such a bitch all the time. I'd like to have a mum to talk to like you do.'

Mel had suddenly felt a wave of indignation on her friend's behalf. 'They're stupid morons,' she had said. 'They must be very bored if they've got the time to worry about you so much. Fuck them. They don't deserve you.'

Pepa had laughed through a glistening of tears and raised a glass. 'Yeah, fuck 'em.'

'But you are happy?' Mel half asked, half affirmed now.

'Sure. I mean, I'm not unhappy. I get the Bank Holiday blues like every other single person.'

'Not just single people,' Mel said. 'Anyway, you love being single. You're not unhappy being single?'

Pepa paused. 'Well, you know, it's a tricky thing. I wouldn't mind a relationship . . .'

Mel smiled at the less-than-convincing tone with which Pepa said this.

'But then I also know I can't answer to anyone, they always end up trying to control what you do, even small things like the washing-up. And I want to be able to sleep with whoever I want, whenever I want. And supposing . . .' Pepa suddenly shuddered, 'supposing they wanted to have children?'

'So you still haven't reached that broody stage?'

'Have I fuck.'

'At least you've chosen,' Mel said. 'You accept that there are negative sides to your choice.'

'Sometimes I think nobody's really happy whatever they choose. Look at the TV schedules. It's all about sex, horrible programmes about sex. Sex, sex, sex — this society is obsessed with it. Patrick says that I'm obsessed with it but I'm obsessed with why it's a problem. I'm not particularly interested in people's preferred sexual positions.'

'So. Vy is it such a problem, Doctor?' Mel asked, pouring more wine.

'Vell, liebchen, zie reason is because we're so boring about it. We could do a lot more than either total monogamy or Ibiza promiscuity. But it's like people are stuck on that either/or thing. I was listening to this girl at work — she's always seemed quite sensible. Anyway, she'd found out her boyfriend had slept with somebody else and she was saying that, although she had been very angry and punished him, it was OK because he was so drunk he didn't even know what he was doing.'

'And?'

'She was being treated like she was incredibly broadminded, some kind of sexual radical. I said I thought that was pathetic. I would much rather my partner — if I had one — liked the girl he slept with, had enjoyed it, chose to do it, could tell me why he had enjoyed it. And they all started shouting at me, like they were really angry. "That's bullshit, Pepa. You don't really mean that, Pepa. It's all very well in theory, Pepa. How would you know anyway, Pepa." They were so rude just because I didn't think the excuse of being unable to tell the difference between a girl and a pair of socks was a particularly good one.'

Mel laughed at the idea of Pepa corralled by a group of outraged workmates. They were making a great mistake if they thought that Pepa did not mean exactly what she said. Lack of honesty was definitely not one of Pepa's faults. In fact, part of Pepa's problem was that she rarely considered the option of concealing her opinions or emotions. Feelings were to be spoken about, analysed, offered up for inspection. This was all very well if everybody had the same degree of openness but, of course, they didn't. Poor Pepa the big-mouth often looked a little baffled when people responded in the wrong way to her good-natured and unashamed frankness. Mel could imagine her frustration at being told that she didn't really believe in what she was saying, could imagine her friend furiously spitting back outrageous defiance.

'The worst thing was, I could see in their eyes that they half pitied me. Not only did I not have a boyfriend, I was this swinger wannabe, this rampant, frustrated nympho who would almost certainly try and drag their men into bed . . .'

'But you *are* a rampant, frustrated nympho.' Patrick had emerged from the bedroom to get some toast.

'I'm a rampant, *satisfied* nympho,' Pepa said quickly, putting an olive in her mouth. 'There is a difference. Not that you'd know anything about it. I hope you're not hiding there with the door open by the way.'

'You would have heard me snoring, I think.'

Patrick's toast popped out of the toaster.

'Give us a bite,' Pepa demanded.

'OK, but don't spit that stone at me.'

Mel watched amused as Patrick and Pepa played, Patrick holding the toast to her mouth and then snatching it away. She never minded the way that they flirted, it was just repetitive play. She also knew that it was partly to entertain her, that her mediation was critical and that if she got bored they would stop. They reminded her of two polar bear cubs she had once seen in the zoo. They had played a game over and over again where they took it in turns to sneak up and nudge each other off a rock into the pool. Mel had liked the way one cub would sit on the end of the rock as if it were whistling nonchalantly, pretending it did not know that the other was creeping up behind it to send it, paws splayed, splashing into the pool.

In the end, Pepa grabbed the piece of toast and crammed the whole slice in her mouth, opening it to show Patrick the half-masticated food. Patrick ignored her, walked over and kissed Mel on the forehead before disappearing back into the bedroom.

'What about love, though?' Mel asked. 'What if you fall in love?'

'Ah, love, love, careless love . . .' Pepa half sang and then fixed her friend with a quizzical stare. 'What about it?'

'It doesn't make much sense when you think about it. Maybe it's just a sort of hyper-attraction. Maybe there's no such thing as love.'

'It depends. There's different kinds of love,' Pepa said. 'I love you and Angela. That's easy. The thought of anything bad happening to you makes me almost crazy. But there was somebody . . . a little while back . . . I nearly made myself sick. He hurt me badly. But if I'm honest he didn't do anything, he wasn't a bastard even though I called him one. He got hurt as well. In these matters, apart from the odd case of really damaged goods, people rarely are bastards even if they behave like idiots.'

'Why didn't you tell me about it?' Mel was both astonished and a little hurt.

Pepa shrugged. 'What would be the point? It would have sounded too cliched when in fact it wasn't at all, it was rather complicated. Pepa and a married man – you can imagine what people would have made of that. Yawn, yawn. And I didn't want advice, I wanted him. Some things you just have to deal with. I took myself away for a bit and when I came back I was fine, I was . . . cured. I still miss him though. Not just the sex but the way we had such a laugh together.'

'He went back to his wife?'

'Yeah. He loved misbehaving but he loved her as well.'

'Did she know?'

'Who knows,' Pepa said thoughtfully, 'what anybody really knows?' She suddenly grinned. 'The one great thing about getting myself a long-term partner I suppose would be that I would be able to have lots of illicit sex.'

'You'd get caught,' Mel replied. 'You're such a big-mouth you'd find it far too interesting not to discuss it.'

'I suppose so. I'll have to rein myself in and become one of those silent people who never make fools of themselves but are probably nursing the darkest, cruellest fantasies. Never trust people who are too quiet.'

'I don't know any,' Mel said.

'Good. Silent people are often seen as possessing gravitas but in my experience they're either sneaky, stupid or mad. Often a combination of all three.'

Mel smiled at her friend's familiar habit of cheerful polemicising. Then Pepa said in a more subdued way, 'I do sometimes miss that friendship that couples have. Like you and Patrick. The way he knows when to leave us alone. The way you can be tender with each other. Little things.'

Little things. Soft conversations at night on the motorway, slow-starting Saturday mornings, the first nervy day in a foreign city, seeking Patrick's arms after a nightmare, cradling him in her own when he was desperate with insomnia. It might not be fierce lust or frenzied passion but it was certainly not trivial, not inferior either, not something to be treated lightly. In her head she heard familiar refrains about cake – wanting to have and eat it – bowls of cherries and rose gardens – life's not, didn't promise you. The faint echoes of cries from a room among the tree-tops, the young lovers on a boat crossing the lagoon to a floating dream-city, the companions in soft, late-night conversation – these were perhaps moments, points on a line, stages in a life-cycle. One might resent this process and rail against it but perhaps it was better to accept it with grace and dignity? Should you admire or pity the people who were able to do that? *Never again, never again* – was there really a mind unbroken by that thought? Helpless, foolish love with all its humiliations – was there really a person immune to its siren call? Just as life might not be a bowl of cherries, whatever that might mean, it was too bleak to see it as a straight line leading to inevitable conclusions and minor compensations. There should at least be some optimism of the will, some baring of teeth, some digging in of heels.

'That woman on the TV that I know,' Mel said to Pepa, 'she really misses her husband. I think they did most things together.'

'Mmmm . . .' Pepa studied her friend carefully. 'She must still be in shock. People like that are quite insecure, quite vulnerable.'

'I like her actually,' Mel said. 'She's sort of . . . different.'

'Yes,' Pepa said. 'Well, I guess it takes a long time to get over something like that.'

Mel said, 'But she's getting out and doing stuff. Pulling the families together. I admire her.'

'You have to watch people like that though. They can seem as if they're getting back to normal and then boom! It's total breakdown again.'

'Well, I don't think that's very likely, actually.' Mel felt uncomfortable with Pepa's insistence on Lily's psychological frailty.

'You never know,' Pepa murmured. 'Anyway, Mel H. Phone me a cab, sugar. I'm going to go home and get into my lovely solitary double bed. Oh and Angela's got a new boyfriend. Did she tell you? He's called Michael, he drives a Mercedes, he looks like Lennox Lewis.'

'I give him a fortnight then,' Mel replied.

'That long?'

Mel woke with a start that night. She had been dreaming about a lion, its muzzle obscenely stained with blood, an image from a Goya nightmare. Helplessly, she had watched it devouring its cubs one by one, grinding and crunching, its power overwhelming, irresistible. Then it had turned towards her, grinning, scarlet-mouthed and she had been unable to run as it advanced upon her. When she awoke, she remembered that she had once seen a wildlife programme where a lion had eaten its cubs – the image must have lodged in her mind like a sliver of shrapnel, a fragment of horror for the subconscious.

Patrick was not in bed beside her. He sometimes went to the living room or the spare room when he could not sleep because he felt less abnormal and frustrated; there was always the possibility that he might drift off. She might find him in the morning on the sofa, the TV remote control at his feet.

She tried to rid her mind of the grinning lion, allowing other images to creep and then cascade through her mind, images that she might have resisted in daytime, that might have no resonance except for here at night, with the darkness all around her, the breeze clinking the fish-chimes that hung in the bathroom by the window. Now she gratefully gave into these images, soothed and seduced by both their absurdity and their boldness, their shameless diversity. More images; sometimes subtle, sometimes cheap, pictures of abandonment, widening pupils, laughs and whispers, hands in hair, heads thrown back, turning and twisting, memory and imagination, her eye to the kaleidoscope, the invisible and solitary spectator looking in at her own windowpane – only such a frenzy, such a flood of images powerful enough to drive the nightmares away.

part two

spring

ethics girl

Ten times now, for the last ten springs, Mel had seen the tree in the courtyard beneath their flat encrusted with soft white blossom. She paused to admire it at the kitchen window as she made herself a coffee, feeling the transition, the lighter evenings, jets trailing across skies pale with promise, children playing outside again, a city collectively relaxing, people outside pubs, the weather suffering bouts of adolescent hysteria – whipping hailstones against the bare legs of the over-optimistic who had already donned shorts, followed by thunder and lightning and then sunshine – all within the space of an hour.

Mel was surprised one of these early-spring mornings to receive a call from Paul Flitcroft.

'How's your car?' he asked.

'My car's fine.'

'Saturnine.'

'Yeah, that's OK. Sibilant?'

'Nice, but I don't know what it means.'

'Consonants pronounced with a hissing sound. In fact, that last sentence was a good example.' Mel felt rather pleased with herself for this.

'Clever clogs. Anyway, the reason I was phoning was to invite you for dinner.'

How could she get out of this one? She had overcome her irrational distaste for Paul but did not particularly relish the thought of dinner on her own with him. He couldn't possibly think that anything could happen between them?

'Even if I do say so myself, I'm an excellent cook. I love cooking, so any excuse. Do you eat seafood?'

'Yes, but . . .'

'Scallops? I would have thought that saucy trade unionists would savour sibilant scallops.'

'I love scallops but I'm very busy at the moment.'

'That's a shame. I thought I'd invite you and Lily Forrester. It's such an interesting case this one and you have different perspectives. Besides, I owe her some favours. It would have given you a chance to meet Miranda as well.'

Mel was so confused by this sudden development in the conversation, her desire to retract her refusal, that her mind froze up like a locked computer screen and she blurted out, 'Ah yes, your cat.'

'I beg your pardon?'

'I thought . . . well, I saw your cat when I dropped you off . . . I assumed you were talking about . . .'

Mel was aware of what a stupid and thoughtless assumption she had just made.

She could hear barely suppressed laughter at the other end of the line.

'That's not my cat. I fucking hate cats, especially that one. They're vermin, they kill birds. Anyway, the animal in question belongs to the upstairs neighbour. Miranda's my girlfriend. Hold on, you thought I was some sad bastard who lived alone with his cat, didn't you?'

'No!' Mel protested. 'It's just somebody was handing me a file and I got kind of distracted and I had this image of your cat in my head.'

'But I don't have a cat.'

'No, of course not. I just thought it was your cat – I assumed because it came out of your front door . . .'

'. . . that I would now be inviting you to dinner to meet it?' Flitcroft laughed again.

Mel's humiliation was complete.

'I must remember to ask it if it likes scallops,' Paul continued with gleeful

malice. 'Ice and lemon with your G and T, Felix? Rudely, I've never asked
its real name. Before I realised what an excellent dinner guest it would
make I just casually booted it up the arse whenever I saw it.'

'OK, OK, it was a stupid thing to say. I wasn't thinking. You don't have
to rub it in.'

'And this from the girl who knows the definition of sibilant. Anyway,
I'm sorry that you're too busy.'

'Well, hold on a moment. When were you thinking of? I've got my
diary here.'

'I thought next Friday.'

'Friday, Friday, Friday. The fifth? Oh, that's the one day I've got free.'

'Well, that's excellent. We like white wine but bring whatever you
want. A can of Whiskas should suffice for the cat. Look forward to
seeing you.'

When she had replaced the receiver, Mel put her head in her hands. Then
she started to laugh. Both at her mistake and at her cynical *volte-face*.

Patrick refused to go to the dinner party, which was neither surprise nor
disappointment. He would not have gone anyway but Mel guaranteed his
absence by telling him that Paul was a journalist. Journalists were third on
the 'Year Zero' list drawn up by Patrick and Jim of groups who would be
herded out of the city and set to work in the fields after the revolution.
First was, of course, the royal family for whom various humiliations were
planned and whose continued existence furnished proof – if any were
needed – of the bovine nature and collective stupidity of the British people.
Mel had noticed that Edward in particular seemed to arouse Patrick and
Jim's ire; most of the worst punishments were reserved for him. Second
on the list were cabbies, especially since one of their rare excursions into
town to see *The Exorcist* had ended in a fight with a cabbie who had wanted
to charge them fifteen pounds to Bethnal Green.

'I might have let it go if I'd been spannered,' Jim had mused.

'So there were some advantages when you were like that,' Mel had
muttered sourly. She had had to go down and broker a peace after half
the estate had heard Patrick telling the Nigerian cabbie to go and fill out
a housing benefit form if he wanted to rip somebody off. Understandably,
the cabbie had taken exception to this, pulling out an iron bar from under

his seat and chasing Patrick — who had always been a coward when it came to fighting — in and out of the blocks, finally cornering him in the bin-sheds before Mel came to save him.

Patrick had been suffering for the last few days. He had been sore all over, his sleep patterns were shot to pieces, he had stumbled into a depression which gripped him in strong, corpulent arms, like a sinister and unrelenting circus strongman. There was no mistaking Patrick's symptoms for self-pity or attention-seeking. He sat and watched the news — weeping refugees, burning cities, laser-guided bombs, bodies torn apart — with an expression of dumb helplessness, images of misery compounding misery. And Mel had to deal with this, this was what she came home to after an afternoon stuck in the traffic of London, after meetings spent discussing grievances, disciplinaries and pay-claims. She felt sorry for Patrick, she knew that it was not his fault, but she also felt that her own part in the drama went unrecognised. It would never occur to anybody that life was not so great for her either.

She was grateful that Jim had noticed Patrick's increased suffering and came round more often. They played Frustration, phoned TV stations to complain about bias in news coverage, watched videos, argued about whether Phish food was better than Chunky Monkey ice cream, whether Gwyneth Paltrow was or was not a dog. The only problem was that sometimes Patrick would take these debates a little too seriously and start ranting, accusing Mel of always siding with Jim if she used her casting vote against him. 'Call yourself a feminist!' he had snorted angrily when she had lined up with Jim in the anti-Gwyneth Paltrow camp. He had then grown furious when Jim and Mel had laughed at this and turned it into a catchphrase. 'Call yourself a feminist!' Jim would say if Mel was putting on nail varnish or when she asked him if he could do something about the bathroom door which was always sticking.

One morning at work, she was surprised to see Leo Young, the media relations officer, waiting for her in her office. He was sitting in her chair, spinning from side to side, his hands under his chin, contemplating the pictures on her noticeboard.

'Ah, Mel,' Leo said, his face lighting up when he saw her. 'I've come to take you for lunch. It's been ages since I've had a chat with you.

We've almost become complete strangers. I checked with Mary, you've got nothing important on this afternoon.'

Mel did not like surprises, she had been looking forward to a sandwich and some minor paperwork. But she knew that there was no point in arguing. Leo never acted without a reason and he never did anything which he considered a waste of time.

'Shall we go to that pasta place across the road?' Mel asked as she pulled on her jacket.

'Oh no,' Leo said. 'Let's go somewhere a little more up-market than that. We'll take a cab.'

Mel did not like eating in restaurants at lunchtime, especially when it was a working lunch. She disliked drinking during the day but also found it frustrating not having a drink with a meal. And everything seemed more circumscribed by time, so that even if it were a leisurely lunch it was still disorientating to wander out at four in the afternoon with the beginnings of a headache. She also knew exactly the kind of place that Leo was going to take her to, what his conception of up-market would be. It would be full of chrome, the menu would be fussy, ostentatious and sound more impressive than the food tasted.

'The duck here is delicious,' said Leo as they sat in the large, chrome restaurant in Farringdon.

'I think I might just have a salad,' Mel replied. 'I'm not that hungry. And a mineral water, please.'

'So . . .' Leo folded his hands under his chin as they awaited their food. 'How are you, Mel?'

'I'm fine. Too much work. Plenty of organising.'

'I gather you saw Barry Williams. He can be rather neurotic.'

Mel shrugged and smiled. She certainly wasn't going to commit herself to any comment about Barry Williams in front of Leo Young.

'Quite honestly, he can be a fool. God knows how we're going to get him elected as General Secretary. He certainly seems to want to make it as difficult as possible.'

Mel sipped her water. 'Mmmm,' she said.

'It's going to be close, this election,' Leo said. 'It's going to get quite bitter.' He looked carefully at Mel. 'So of course it's important not to nail your colours to the wrong mast.'

'I haven't nailed my colours to any mast,' Mel replied.

'No, of course not. You're far too shrewd for that.' Leo beckoned the waitress. 'That's what's puzzling me. You're clever, you're not a big-mouth like some. You could go a long way. At the moment though I see you as slightly rudderless. I doubt if we would disagree about much politically and yet you don't want anything to do with New Outlook. But you're rather identified with Mark Thompson, if you don't mind me saying so.'

'I can't see why,' Mel replied. 'We don't have so much to do with each other. We get on OK, that's all.'

'Fellow mavericks,' Leo observed almost fondly. 'To be honest, I don't have a problem with Mark. Off the record, I could work with him. Of course, I would prefer the next General Secretary to be Barry Williams but I think that Mark and I would be able to accommodate each other.'

Mel was confused. Was Leo trying to build some kind of bridge to Mark Thompson and use her as a messenger? If so, it was a strange choice. There were people closer to Mark than she was. Or did he really think that she knew something about Mark's plans that he could coax out of her with a fussy restaurant and some cheap flattery?

'Are you making the assumption that I will be supporting Mark in the election?' Mel asked.

'Oh well.' Leo patted the corners of his mouth with his napkin. The gesture was self-consciously delicate. 'That's your business of course.'

'It is . . .' Mel agreed. 'But your assumption wouldn't necessarily be correct.'

'As I say, you have the right to support whichever candidate you please. Please don't think that I took you to lunch to ask you to do anything so crude as to switch allegiances. Do you think I could have a glass of wine?' He beckoned the waitress again.

Mel watched Leo carefully. She could not really imagine him doing anything but scheming. He was fastidious when it came to his appearance – polished shoes, crisp white shirts, silk ties. But she could not imagine him outside this environment, could not imagine him doing the sort of ordinary things that were the basic ingredients of day-to-day living. At least Barry Williams had his daughter's clay elephant on his desk. True, Mel sometimes contemplated picking it up and smashing it, but at least the thing was there to smash, at least it hinted at something human. The presence of a child meant that Barry had had sex at some point, even if the thought was truly appalling and even though Mel felt that nobody deserved the fate of being the offspring of Barry Williams.

She played with her salad which was filled with irritatingly bitter bits of foreign lettuce and had a sudden yearning for the kind of salad her mum used to make, with proper lettuce leaves, cucumber and tomato. Her mum also used to make them cakes: gingerbread, chocolate cake, meringues stuck together with cream. Mel could remember watching chocolate melt in the glass bowl placed inside a saucepan of boiling water, being given the white spatula to lick or the metal attachment from the Kenwood mixer clogged with the sweet remains from the bowl after the cake had been put in the oven. At that time, her mum had only been a few years older than Mel was now. The thought made her slightly uncomfortable.

'So what's all this about nailing my colours to the wrong mast?' she asked Leo.

'Ah well, some people in this union – as I'm sure you know – can be terrible backstabbers. It was a mistake to put it like that because it might give the impression that I thought you capable of shifting allegiances just for personal advantage.' Leo's shrill laugh suggested that he suspected that everybody was really capable of such a sensible strategy. 'The thing is, Mel, you do potentially have an exciting future. And I think that in spite of appearances you're ambitious. Most of the time I have to work with idiots. If they had half your ability and dedication I wouldn't have so much of a problem.'

Leo sighed at the inadequacy of the material with which he was forced to work. Mel looked down at her food. She was beginning to find this irritating. In particular, she did not like it when people implied that they had a special grasp on her character, that they understood what made her tick. *I know that you like to present a certain face to the world but I am perceptive enough to know that there is a different you.*

'I understand that you are fighting your own battle with MGL at the moment.' Leo switched subjects, taking Mel aback.

'Well, I don't know what you mean by my "own" battle. I've got a tribunal for the woman who was sacked for the error that killed Gordon Forrester.'

Leo nodded and began to orbit the salt cellar around the pepper mill. 'Tragic and bizarre. Imagine surviving a train crash to be killed by a hospital error.'

'It's a very interesting case because you've got the train driver and the lab technician being scapegoated,' Mel continued.

'Yes,' Leo said. 'I've seen the guy's wife on the TV. Seemed a little unhinged actually. It's always the way with these cases. Somebody gets killed and they won't or can't accept that it was an accident and unfortunately these things happen. They've got to have a public inquiry, somebody has to be prosecuted.'

'I don't think "unhinged" is quite how I'd describe her.'

Leo frowned, stuck on a track of thought which meant that he was not particularly interested in his companion's opinion.

'I would also just mention in passing that I don't want you talking to that journalist Flitcroft who's writing a lot on this case. He's a slippery bastard and he's not on our side. Anything he wants just send him to me. I noticed that he mentioned "a GWA officer" in his last piece. I don't want that to happen again.'

'OK,' Mel said. She wasn't prepared to make an issue over Paul Flitcroft.

Leo leaned forward as if what he was going to say next was especially important.

'Let me put a hypothetical case to you, Mel. Hijackers take a plane with hundreds of passengers. They say that they will kill all the passengers unless one of their opponents is delivered to them. You know that they will kill this innocent person if you hand him over but you also know that they will certainly kill all the innocent passengers if you don't. Shouldn't you at least explore the possibility that the morally right position is to hand over the individual, thus saving hundreds of other innocent lives?'

Leo sat back and stared at Mel. She was annoyed by the stare, which she knew was supposed to imply that he had just said something rather profound and serious. Mel thought for a moment of Brenda Fletcher and the wreck of a woman that she had become: ashen-faced, shaking, impoverished. She remembered how she had fumbled with the contents of her handbag as she searched for a hankie to dry her tears.

'OK, yes, I would consider it. I don't, however, see the analogy as particularly appropriate since it is an example of a moral dilemma and I'm not sure ethics are playing a large part in what is going on here. Should Brenda Fletcher be sacrificed for the interests of Robert Hislop? I certainly don't think so. If you give into hijackers all the time, just as if you submit for opportunist reasons to the pressures of big business, then you lose any power or authority you had. And each time they threaten or blackmail you again, you'll be in an even weaker position. Supping with the devil and long spoons – you know the score.'

Leo waved away the waitress who was approaching with the dessert menu. Mel waved her back because she wanted an ice cream.

'I know that you would like to see this as union sell-outs colluding with corporate interests. I'm just trying to say that it's far more complex than that.'

'I don't see how you can possibly know how I see it. All I know is that I am doing my job, which is defending the interests of one of my members and exposing poor working practices in a large and wealthy company. But if you want my personal opinion, then I do think that the relationship between Robert Hislop, this union and the government is too cosy. Hislop's going to be on a taskforce, he picnics at Glyndebourne with the Minister. And Brenda Fletcher gets her house repossessed because she can't pay her mortgage.'

Leo Young's mouth twitched and Mel suspected that in spite of his patient, unruffled tone he was starting to find her irritating. She knew that if she showed the faintest sign of weakness she was finished, he would move in for the kill. She could not drop this case, she had to go on with it. When it came to absolute moral principles, Mel preferred to travel lightly but those she did have she would not violate. She would not drop the case unless instructed to.

As if reading her mind, Young said, 'You know, we could stop this case at any time if we wanted to.'

'Why don't you then? Because it's a bit of a sensitive time for you?'

'Ah, don't challenge me, Mel. That would be very foolish.'

They both stared at each other. Then Leo laughed. Confrontation was not his style, certainly not direct confrontation with his opponent present.

'The world has changed.'

'Really? I hadn't noticed,' Mel replied bitterly, stirring listlessly at her ice cream so that it began to melt into liquid. It wasn't very nice, had a slightly sour taste to it.

Leo held out his hand with a placatory hear-me-out gesture.

'The world has changed. Power has changed. If you are outside certain circuits you are lost. We may not like it but that's all there is to it. Maybe it's not about saving hundreds of lives but it is about remaining relevant as a union and I happen to think that's quite important. This government is not anti-union but it's not particularly pro-union either. So we have to make sure we don't get marginalised, we have to build partnerships. That's my job and obviously my contacts within the government help.'

'Yes,' Mel murmured, suddenly thinking of her sister. *If you are outside certain circuits you are lost.* It was true, undoubtedly true. It still didn't mean that getting inside those circuits was the appropriate strategy. Sometimes it might just be better to be lost.

Mel rubbed her eyes. Once again she saw the icy mountain, the falling snow. Once again she imagined the feeble lullaby, the love-song she would sing to herself through blue lips and chattering teeth. All this vulgarity, all this nonsense fading to nothing – a black-out amid the white glare, the final refusal, a refusal to even contemplate the question of whether it would be worth killing one person to save a hundred, to even engage with such trashy ethics. Only to float incoherently away up there in the thin air, far from illness and corruption and frustrated love and hopeless longing.

'Do you mind if I'm frank with you?' Leo Young was asking her. He had not noticed that she had drifted away. She shook her head slowly and smiled, feeling strangely calm.

'When you joined the union both myself and John Mould saw you as a potential General Secretary . . .' He paused and nodded to emphasise the seriousness of what he was saying. Mel was filled with a desire to giggle or blow a raspberry. 'I still think you have that capacity. Which is why I want you to know that the little things that trip you up now could have quite profound consequences in the future. Don't underestimate the impact these things can have. I don't want you to make mistakes that will ruin things for you.'

'Thanks for the advice,' Mel said, trying as hard as possible not to sound wooden. 'I do understand what you're saying and I appreciate it . . .'

But Leo Young was not interested in unnecessary platitudes. He had said what he had come to say, he had delivered his compliment-wrapped warning.

'Everything is in your hands. Everything. Now where's that waitress? Let's get the bill.'

under my skin

Patrick and Jim whistled as Mel walked into the living room. She was wearing a light, clinging red skirt, a short cardigan, her long dark hair fell around her shoulders and she was dabbing perfume on her wrists. She smiled at her audience, pleased also with the effect of the effort she had made. It had been some time since she had last dressed up to go out.

'Pretty as a peach,' Jim said.

'A peach melba,' Patrick added. 'Who is this journalist? I'm getting an uneasy feeling. Of course I understand that there's an in-built conflict between monogamy and desire which you must feel free to explore – as long as I can watch.'

'Yeah, in your dreams,' said Jim.

'Never mind,' Patrick said. 'I've always found jealousy something of an aphrodisiac. I remember the first thing I did when one of my early long-term girlfriends told me that she'd been unfaithful with her boss was to go and have a wank. I found it a real turn-on. I was gutted as well of course. I was crying and wanking at the same time.'

Mel and Jim stared at each other with mock-incredulity.

'Thank you, Patrick,' Mel finally said. 'I really needed to know that.'

'Weird though, eh?'

'Astonishing.'

'Shut up, Patrick,' Jim snapped. 'You look really beautiful, Mel.' He glared at Patrick.

'You look really beautiful, Mel,' Patrick mimicked his friend with a nerdy nasal voice. 'Since when did you become Mr Chivalrous?'

'Since I noticed what a lazy, undeserving, spoiled cunt you were, actually.'

'I'd like to see you put up with what I have to put up with.'

'Yeah, yeah.'

'It's OK, really,' Mel said. 'Thanks anyway, Jim. Look outside. Isn't the sky lovely?'

They all looked out at the high, blue spring sky and for a second there was no arch humour or facetious commentary. It was such a challenge, such a taunt for the lonely. *Come out, come out*, it called into dusky living rooms. And for a second, both men glanced at Mel with envy; dressed up, smelling fresh, and with the sun in her face.

'Come here, darling,' Patrick said and pretended to spit on his finger and polish her forehead. 'There. Now you're ready. How are you getting there?'

'Cab.'

'Call yourself a feminist,' Jim muttered.

'Don't feminists get cabs then?'

'Certainly not. It's tantamount to shaving your armpits.'

'A feminist in a cab is like a fish on a bicycle,' said Patrick sternly. 'Surely you knew that?'

'Silly me,' Mel said, picking up the phone for the cab company. 'Thank goodness I have you two about to keep me on my toes.'

'OK, Jeem my leetle fren'', which video shall we watch first?' Patrick asked.

'I don't know,' Jim replied. 'Maybe the one about the dwarf serial killer?'

'No, no, no. "My leetle fren", was a hint. Cocker-roaches? I ate Colombians?'

'I can't believe you can watch that again,' Mel said, peering from the window for her cab.

'What? You mean the best fucking film ever made?'

'God I want a drink,' Jim said plaintively.

'There's carrots in the kitchen,' Mel said. 'And apples. There's lots of ice cream in the freezer. And a trifle in the fridge.'

Patrick gazed at her and pulled a wry face. 'Go to your ball, Cinders. I think that's your pumpkin sounding its horn out there.'

As she was leaving, the telephone rang and she stopped to pick it up.

'You're dead, you whore. I'm going to—'

She replaced the receiver straightaway.

'Wrong number,' she said to Jim and Patrick. 'See you.'

Every assumption that Mel had made about Paul Flitcroft turned out to be mistaken. His flat was far from a depressing shrine to male loneliness; there were no Pot Noodle cartons or empty beer cans on the floor, no porno magazines half kicked under an unmade bed. There was no Lily either and Mel felt a little rush of butterflies at this absence. Paul guided her into the flat where a sustained battle between minimalism and kitsch appeared to be taking place. He was waving a ladle cheerfully and also, to Mel's contempt, sporting an Arsenal FC apron.

'I suppose it makes sense,' she said. 'You do work in the media after all.'

'Ah, but West Ham are, of course, my second team,' he retorted mischievously after ascertaining her own loyalty. 'How can you not love them? Trevor Brooking, what a gent, attractive passing game, proud old East End club, jellied eels, I make you right as it goes bruv, Bobby Moore, another true gent, come on you Irons, no silverware, triffic fans though, dodgy Romanian fly-by-nights, vanishing Chilean centre-backs, where's your famous ICF?'

Mel put her hand on her hip, glad that Paul supported such a risible team, so easy to pull apart.

'Highbury the Library, pass the Aqua Libre, sing when you're winning, boo your own players when they're struggling, don't know your history, allez les rouges, I'm in Cannes darling but I simply must find out how the Arsenal are doing. And exactly how long have you supported *the* Arsenal? You might remember one piece of silverware we won in nineteen eighty.'

'Oh darling, only since they signed that wonderful Dennis Bergkamp of course. It's pure theatre you know.'

He twirled his ladle with a camp flourish and gave Mel his beguiling smile — the mixture of self-confidence and self-deprecation — that made her feel a rush of affection for him. She sank into a large white sofa and accepted a glass of wine in a long-stemmed glass. A tall woman emerged from the bathroom fixing her earrings. She was wearing an expensive, figure-flattering dress, her long blonde hair reached almost to her waist. Her face was oddly angled, could almost have been ugly, but there was something striking about her.

'Hi, I'm Miranda.'

'I liked the way you made your entrance there, Miranda,' Flitcroft said, glancing at Mel. 'If you don't mind me saying so, it was very . . . feline.'

Mel looked at her feet. Miranda mock-frowned at him. 'Are you taking the piss again?' Her voice was husky, upper-class, the voice of someone who had spent her trust fund on things of which her parents might not approve, and who had chosen a boyfriend of whom they would definitely not approve. No straight-backed, fag-beating, officer-class, polo-playing aristo for Miranda. Paul did not look as if he had ever hunted anything down in his life apart from the frying-pan or the TV remote control.

Paul slapped his knee and glanced at Mel. 'Absolutely. It was just one of those stupid cat-and-mouse games.'

Miranda flapped him away and sat down next to Mel who glared at Paul. Paul pretended not to notice, humming the tune from *Top Cat* to himself. Mel made a mental note to cause him physical pain at some point in the evening. Her sister had taught her this trick — to pretend that everything was normal but to exact revenge when the person was least expecting it. *I'll get you back when you're least expecting it.* It was Sarah's direst warning and the worst thing was that she was always true to her word — she never forgot anything and always caught Mel when she was least expecting it. Asleep, for example.

'You're the trade unionist?' Miranda asked.

'That's right. What do you do?'

'Interior design. Nowhere near as interesting as your job. It's a strange thing, isn't it? Paul's told me about the case you're working on. Actually, he's rather obsessed with it.'

'Well, I think he's had more to do with the other side of it. The woman who's coming tonight . . .'

'Oh, but I don't think she is any more, is she, Paul? Didn't you say she couldn't get a babysitter at the last minute?'

A hoof-kick in the stomach? A hand at the throat? Perhaps Mel felt these things but she also felt a curious depressed calm. This was the way things were in real life. It was nothing anyway, it was nothing. It was a foolish emotional crush she had invented for herself, schoolgirl antics from somebody who should find better things to do with her time, with her mind. She would be fine, it did not really matter, in a sense she was glad. Get real, Mel.

'Well, I'm not sure . . .' Paul refilled their glasses. 'There was some problem with the babysitter. She said she'd phone if she could get one at the last moment . . . Oh, that'll be Ellen and Gerry.' He levered himself up to answer the front door.

'Come on, Fatty, you can do it,' Miranda said affectionately, patting him on the stomach.

Ellen and Gerry turned out to be two genial Americans. Ellen was working on a PhD thesis at the college where Paul's mother lectured in feminist literary theory.

'And she should know all about mad women in the attic,' Paul announced. 'She did have her office in the top of the house.'

'I think she's great,' Ellen said defensively.

'Well you're not related to her. I'm telling you – she's a bully, a psychological terrorist. My brother became a trans-sexual because of her.'

'That's a lie,' Miranda said. 'Robert is not a trans-sexual. And you adore your mother.'

'We used to catch him dressing up in my sister's knickers.' Paul ignored her. 'And putting lipstick on.'

'When he was five,' Miranda said. 'And stop saying that about him – you know it upsets him. Everyone does weird things when they're kids.'

'That's true,' Gerry assented. 'I used to get really turned on by the girl in *Scooby Doo*, the one with the short purple skirt. Especially when she was getting chased by monsters. I used to wish they would catch her.'

'And I wonder what *that* says about you,' Ellen remarked.

'Yes, we don't need my mother to deconstruct that one,' Paul said.

'Hey!' Gerry spread his hands and grinned. 'I was only ten. It doesn't make me Ted Bundy.'

Mel went to the bathroom and as she did so she clunked Paul's ear with her elbow.

'Ow!' He rubbed his ear, looking genuinely confused. 'That hurt. What was that for?'

'Take a wild guess.'

As Mel clicked the bathroom door behind her, she noticed that somebody — it could only be Paul — had turned the bathroom into a shrine to Sinatra. There were framed covers of albums, film stills, photos: Frank with the rest of the rat-pack — sharp suits, black ties — in front of the Sands; benign Frank looking down on two swinging lovers; cheeky, cuff-linked Frank thumbing us aboard a TWA jet — to Paris, Capri, Brazil, Hawaii, Mandalay. *It's nice to go trav'ling. Let's get away from it all.* She thought suddenly of Pepa, who always went away when she got bored. What would she make of this evening? It wasn't unpleasant, she just felt a little numb, immune to the people present however nice they were. Mel splashed cold water on her face, pushed her hair behind her shoulders and winked goodbye to Frank.

But when she returned to the living room, Lily was standing there wearing a jade crushed-velvet dress, a slight cardigan about her shoulders, an emerald necklace around her throat. She turned and flashed a smile at Mel.

'I thought you weren't here,' she said. 'I was so disappointed. Look at you, you look lovely. Really summery. Isn't it a beautiful evening? The sky over to the west is all pink.'

'I thought you couldn't get a babysitter,' Mel mumbled.

'Oh, I thought I might not be able to. Thanks.' She took a glass of wine. 'Claudia had a date or something but he let her down. I'm afraid I was pleased, although she was distraught. You know how it is when you're her age. Anyway, it isn't exactly an evening for sitting in and I was quite desperate. Poor Daniel, I would probably have kept him up so as not to be on my own.'

Mel knew perfectly well what that feeling was like. Lily seemed far more composed than the last time they had met. Mel guessed that there was something about dressing up to come out that had had a benign and soothing effect on her. She must have suddenly become very alarmed by her solitude.

Lily asked, 'How's it going anyway? Your work?'

Mel knew that she was referring to the MGL case. She could feel Paul listening and remembered Leo Young's warning.

'Further and better particulars,' she said. 'It's a matter of getting more information for the tribunal. And they haven't even given me a date yet. But I've found somebody who is prepared to say that these mistakes had happened before at MGL and that management knew about it. That's totally off the record by the way, Paul. I've already had my collar felt about "a GWA officer."'

'So-rry,' Paul sang insincerely.

One of the things that Mel had discovered while investigating this case was that Brenda Fletcher had been popular and that people were angry over the way she had been treated. She had been given the name of a woman who no longer worked for MGL by a non-union member and had arranged to meet her at the branch meeting. She was going to the meeting with Mark Thompson. Mel doubted he would face any problems in getting the branch to nominate him for General Secretary. For all their obsession with winning elections, the New Outlook caucus had made themselves unpopular by the contempt they showed for members and their arrogant dismissal of even the mildest criticism of their tactics. Even Leo Young seemed to be realising this, but contempt and arrogance had been so programmed into them that trying to rid themselves of these unappealing faults was as tricky as turning around a very large ship to rescue somebody who had fallen overboard in mid-ocean. Mel found it satisfying to think that those who justified their tactics principally in terms of winning elections might be on the point of losing one.

'Shall we eat now?' Paul said and they all made their way to the table on which he had placed plates of scallops balancing on nests of rocket and topped with a sweet chilli sauce.

'So who's the Sinatra fan?' Ellen asked. 'I mean the guy was, like, a crook – right? And he treated women really badly.'

'That's probably why Paul likes him,' Miranda said.

'I find him fascinating.' Paul ignored her. 'Especially the thing with the Kennedys. It was so fucked up. They had that whole bright, young idealist image, all that Camelot crap. All those figures – Marilyn Monroe addled with drugs and getting fucked by the whole lot of them – it was so twisted and corrupt. But they still had talent and style. Who are the icons from our Camelot?'

There was a collective silence as everybody contemplated the possible candidates.

'I know everybody's meant to like Sinatra but I think he's rather a grotesque figure, just like Kennedy was a repulsive politician,' Lily said. 'Even the way Sinatra sings. I find something almost grotesque about it.'

'The greatest singer of our century! Grotesque? Oh, but I forgot, you like all that operatic stuff, don't you? *Il testerone, Vorsprung dürch technik.*'

Mel could see that Lily had entered this aggressive banter unprepared. She blinked at Paul's onslaught. Lily might seem relatively composed but she was still fragile. And Mel – for reasons which were not entirely unselfish – did not want to tip Lily towards the kind of mood they had seen when they were last with her, did not want her to start staring at the floor at that invisible, slouching enemy.

'My dad loves Sinatra,' Mel intervened. 'Maybe that's why I can't really be bothered with him.'

'So does Gordon's.' Lily's voice was quiet.

'Who's Gordon?' Ellen asked with bright nonchalance.

'He was my husband,' Lily replied. 'He died in a freak double accident. First there was a train crash. Then he was taken to hospital and they gave him the wrong blood.'

'Oh yeah, yeah. God, I'm sorry. Paul mentioned . . . well you know . . .' Ellen looked with anguished apology at Paul. 'He said you'd recently been bereaved. I'm sorry, I should have remembered . . .'

'It's OK. Don't feel uncomfortable.' Lily suddenly smiled at her. 'I sat through the inquest last month. After that . . .' She shrugged and sipped her wine.

'The inquest into the rail crash?' Miranda asked.

'No,' Lily said. 'They can't have that until after the court case.'

'I saw you on TV,' Mel said. 'It was strange. I was sitting around at home and suddenly you just popped up. It looked quite windy.'

'Yes,' Lily said, meditating over the top of her wine glass. 'It was very windy that day.'

It was strange, Mel thought, how she had resigned herself to Lily's absence and now she was here in her jade dress and the whole evening had changed. Somewhere in Crouch End, a miserable, rosy-cheeked teenager whose heart felt like a pin-cushion was lamenting the absence of her love, her not-so-obscure object of desire, and perhaps it seemed like the end of the world to her. *You know how it is at her age.* But the boy who had abandoned Claudia to her lonely evening with the TV, that unknown boy had changed other lives without any awareness of having done so. Such mystery, such exquisite chances, such intricate patterns – perhaps it was not so surprising that people like Mary took to their numerology, horoscopes, tarot cards and all the pseudo-gibberish of the esoteric because they could not embrace and accept this uncertainty.

There was uncertainty also in what Mel felt for the woman sitting beside her, who would not have been there that evening if Claudia had not had her hopes dashed, who would not have been there at all if a train rushing through the night had not ignored the signal telling it to stop. Green lights and red lights everywhere across the world, giving such simple instructions. Stop. Go. Mel's own signalling system was a mess, as confused as that of any adolescent: Stop what? Go where? What did she want from Lily? Did she just need to be with her? Did she want to go to bed with her? Did she envy Lily's dead husband for what he had seen, what he had heard? Would she like to undress her, to slide her hands around the crushed velvet, to take the zip between her fingers, to feel the curve of her back, to touch a woman's body for the first time, to touch that particular body? She could both imagine it and not imagine it. Would she like to kiss her? Yes, she thought – clutching at a piece of certainty – yes, I know I would like to kiss her. She rocked slightly on her chair as the image presented itself vividly in her mind. What would they think, these people around her, what would they make of her thoughts right now? What would Paul Flitcroft and blonde, feline Miranda and the two friendly Americans think of all of this? What would Lily think? Lily who had so casually tossed her the compliment – *Look at you, you look lovely*. When Lily had said that, Mel had almost shuddered. Had she fallen in love? Was that what was happening to her? What kind of love was it? What would Lily think about these thoughts that Mel was patting about like a cat with a ball on a string? Was it even remotely possible that she harboured such thoughts herself?

'What do you think, Mel?'

'I'm sorry, I didn't quite . . .'

They all laughed at her startled face.

'You looked as if you were praying,' Miranda said, but not unkindly. 'So self-absorbed.'

'Floating downstream . . .' Lily laughed, 'looking up at the stars. You have a knack of doing that without seeming to be rude. In fact, I always feel crass interrupting you.'

'I think it must seem very rude,' Mel said. 'I don't mean it.'

'Well, I agree with you,' Paul said. 'I think it is rude.'

'Oh, you don't count,' Mel said. 'I don't care if you think it's rude. You're so rude yourself.'

'No I'm not,' Paul protested. 'I place a high premium on good manners. My problem is that I just can't help saying something if I think it's funny. I always seem to be offending people.'

'That's true,' Miranda said. 'The problem is that when you think something's funny you don't only say it once, you repeat it *ad infinitum*. Especially when you're drunk. My brother will punch your lights out one of these days, you know. Laughing at his name all the time.'

'Well, I'm afraid if I were called Prospero I'd just change my name,' Paul retorted.

Lily put her napkin to her mouth. Mel noticed that her shoulders were shaking slightly. Watching Lily try to smother her laughter made her snigger as well.

'I'm sorry . . .' Lily hiccoughed at last when it became quite obvious that she was laughing. 'I know I shouldn't.'

'It's OK,' Miranda responded wearily. 'I'm kind of used to it. I guess I escaped lightly from my father's obsession. Anyway, Mel, what we were saying when you were engaged in your reverie was that my family have got this place in Kent. They don't use it, it belonged to my grandmother. And we sometimes go down there on a Sunday if it's warm. Paul gets drunk and pretends to mow the lawn. I was just saying that you'd all be welcome if you wanted to come for the day.'

'It's very nice,' Paul said in a conciliatory tone. 'You should both come. I could do a barbecue.'

'I don't think so,' Miranda said. 'Last time he set a tree on fire.'

Mel thought about Patrick and the contempt he would undoubtedly express at the idea of her spending a day in a country house. For the first time she felt guilty. He would probably grumpily enjoy it if she managed to persuade him to come. But she wanted to be selfish, she wanted to be herself, not to have to worry about the observations he was making, his endless judging and categorising, the exacting quality control that he seemed to apply towards anyone to whom she was close. It wore her down sometimes, it was too tiring. She wanted to have responsibility only for herself. This was an oasis she had stumbled upon, it did not have anything to do with either office or home. Outside the desert heat might be scorching but she did not want to offer her shade and water to anybody else.

Lily had to leave early to get back for the babysitter. Mel had noticed that she was already growing slightly restless about her child, as if she had been irresponsible for coming out. She had phoned Claudia once but the girl had told her that Daniel was fine and that they were watching a video of *ToyStory*.

'Poor Claudia,' Lily said. 'She was so excited about this boy. She went red every time she talked about him.'

'Well it could be worse,' Miranda said. 'I quite like the idea of sitting with a child and watching *ToyStory*.'

She gave Paul a meaningful stare.

'Yeah, but it's not all sitting watching videos, is it?' Paul muttered. 'It's not getting any sleep and changing nappies as well.'

'I could live with that,' Miranda said.

'Well, I couldn't.'

Lily pulled a funny panic-stricken face at Mel and they both moved aside slightly.

'I nearly forgot,' Lily said. 'I got you a present. I hope you don't mind but I remembered that you liked that bit from *Rigoletto*. And I have these tickets for the opera. It's not for a while. You can always say no if you want. For some reason, people seem to find it utterly ridiculous, so I'll understand.'

'It's just the stereotype,' Mel said. 'Most people would admit that what you played me that time was beautiful. I'd love to come. You'll have to tell me the full story though. All I remember is that he was a hunchback.'

'Oh no,' Lily said. 'It's not *Rigoletto*. It's *La Traviata*.' She laughed. 'The fallen woman.'

'OK,' Mel said. 'You can tell me what that's about then.'

'All you need to know really –' Lily peered out of the window at the sound of a car horn – 'is that it's about sex and death.' She paused and then said, 'I want to go, it will be horrible if I don't go. I need someone . . . I need someone . . . someone like you,' she concluded.

'Someone like me,' Mel said in a tone of wonder. It was half a question, but she did not have the courage to ask Lily what she meant.

'Don't forget about coming to the country,' Miranda said as Lily put on a light, cotton jacket.

'May I bring my son?' Lily asked.

'Of course.'

'Well, he'll love that. OK . . .' She smiled around the room. 'Good-bye.'

And she slipped away, out alone into the dark, warm night.

2.8%

'Bad news I'm afraid, Mel.' Graham sat down on the edge of her desk. 'Goatfucker's bringing in the CRE. She says we're discriminating against her for being Croatian. They've written to Fungus about it.'

'Well I suppose you have let your feelings slip from time to time. But I've done nothing. And I'm the one who took the decision. Oh shit, that means I'm going to have to do one of those stupid reports.'

'She says that both you and I made slurs on her nationality. And I have nothing against Croats as such. Tito was a Croat. But I do have something against Franco Tudjman and his neo-Nazi followers. Anyway, she also says we insulted her religion as well, that we're anti-Catholic, the whole works. You see, Mel, there's loads that people don't know about the Balkans. It's all very well . . .'

'Yeah, Graham? I'm just getting ready to go to a branch meeting.'

'Really? I was going to ask if you wanted to come to our meeting against a federal Europe this evening.'

'I'll come.' Mary pushed past him with a cup of tea and a strawberry tart for Mel.

'Really?' Graham was both surprised and pleased.

'No, will I fuck,' Mary answered. 'Mel, Mark Thompson phoned to say he'd be a bit late. He's leaving his car at Head Office and getting a cab here. You're giving him a lift to the branch meeting?'

Mel nodded.

'Are you meeting the rest of the coven tonight then?' Graham asked Mary, still stung by the fact that he had walked right into her trap.

'Listen, Graham, I'd rather watch paint dry than listen to you and a room of six people going on about the Germans and the Bundesbank and how the Fourth Reich are taking us over. What was that last meeting you dragged me to? The campaign to save manufacturing industry. I've never been so bored in my life.'

'It probably went over your head. These things change our lives you know. Stop reading your stars and look at what's going on around you if you want to know the future.'

'Can you take this discussion somewhere else,' Mel said. 'I've got to prepare for the branch meeting tonight.'

They both rolled their eyes indignantly and returned to their desks still arguing. Mel knew that the branch meeting was going to be difficult. There was fury among the members that the nurses with their own pay review body had agreed a no-strike clause in return for a generous settlement, while those who had remained within the Whitley structure had been offered an insulting 2.8 per cent. The porters, the clerical staff, the therapists and radiographers, the pathology workers – they were not worth any more than that, the work they did was valued no higher than that, these was nothing angelic about them.

Before the meeting, she also had to meet Brenda Fletcher and the ex-MLSO who was prepared to say that mistakes had been made in the transfusion process by both nurses and pathology workers and that these were mistakes which had come to management's attention. There had been the case of the two Reeves patients where each had received the blood destined for the other – fortunately without lethal consequences. There had been incorrect telephone requests, there had been mislabellings and simple cross-matching errors. It was this type of information that she wanted to use at the tribunal to expose MGL, to bring Hislop the bad publicity his company so deserved. Especially since her eye had been caught by a headline in the business section of the paper: MGL SHARE PRICE SOARS IN ANTICIPATION OF NEW WONDER DRUG.

She knew though that, just out of sight, forces were being mustered against her. Three senior members of the union had now approached her on the subject: Mark Thompson had warned her, Barry Williams had threatened her, and Leo Young had taken her for lunch and suggested what might be in her best interests. If they wanted to, of course, they could stop her – simply instruct her not to pursue the case. But Mel suspected that what she had said to Leo Young was true, that they did not want to do this at the present time. Most of all, they wanted Mel to take the hint, to choose the squeeze over the guillotine, to understand that this behaviour was not only inconvenient *for all concerned*, but also raised further issues about her reliability and trustworthiness. *Don't make us have to spell it out for you.* Hislop must be waving the stick and dangling the carrot and Mel was spoiling everything for them by forcing everybody to the brink of confrontation when confrontation was part of an old order.

And who was making the phone calls? It wasn't Hislop's style, although she could imagine Neil Evans relishing the task. He had, after all, leaned across his desk and called her a malicious little bitch, a stuck-up college girl; he had warned her to watch her back. There was no doubt that he was a breast-staring creep. But that was still different from the kind of insult she was receiving over the telephone. Although Mel did not like the phone calls, she was not as worried about them as she knew those close to her would be. It was clear that they were linked in some way to the MGL case. Therefore she did not think that it was likely to proceed beyond insults.

Mel yelped in terror as a hand suddenly covered her eyes from behind. The hand instantly released her.

'I'm sorry,' Mark Thompson said. 'I was just messing about. I didn't mean to scare you.'

'Didn't mean to scare me, you fucking idiot! I've been getting threatening phone calls and you come creeping up behind me like a kid. For God's sake.' Mel was trembling with tension and anger.

'I'm really sorry, Mel. Honestly, I was only playing.' Mark looked genuinely contrite, scared by her wrath.

'OK, it's all right. You did scare me, that's all. Come on, we'll be late.'

'So what's all this about threatening phone calls?' Mark frowned as Mel flashed several times at the driver in front who was crawling along in the outside lane.

'Move over, you prick. Oh, I don't know, nothing I suppose. Just since this battle with MGL, some idiot keeps calling. They're more obscene than threatening really.'

'I hope you're logging all of this.'

'Yeah, yeah.'

'Do you think it's something to do with MGL?'

'I don't know. Neil Evans at the Great Northern. I wouldn't put it past him.'

'Remember horror films though. It's never who you think it is.'

'This is real life, Mark. It's always who you think it is.'

The lecture theatre where the branch meeting was being held was already beginning to fill up when they arrived. Paula had collared Yolanda Munro who was relishing the opportunity to give evidence against her former employers. Yolanda was a dark, bright-eyed, wiry woman with a fierce energy. Mel wanted to ask where she was from originally but knew that the question always sounded stupid and gauche. Yolanda also had the curious habit of peppering her conversation with the name of the person she was talking to — as if they had been friends for years.

'You see, Mel, Casualty was always phoning us up and screaming at us and telling us to hurry up. I swear, Mel, it got impossible sometimes, you just couldn't think straight. And I'm like Brenda, Mel, I never wanted to do cross-matching in the first place, it wasn't what I was trained in, Mel. Do you know what I mean, Mel?'

Mel nodded. She didn't want to catch Paula's eye because she had already seen the corners of her mouth begin to twitch.

'And you're sure this had been brought to management's attention?' Mark Thompson asked.

'Oh yes, Mark. Most definitely. Neil Evans knew all about my mistake, Mark, there's no doubt about it 'cause he said something to me about it. And, Mark, a couple of us said to him that there were going to be problems if there was a big incident at night. You get someone in there with a massive bleed and you're low on O Neg. then it's obvious you're going to have problems, isn't it?'

'Why that blood-group in particular?' Mark asked. Mel admired him for this question. He was demonstrating that he was listening and not just mumbling politely because all he cared about was her evidence.

'O Negative blood can be given when you don't know the blood-group,' Brenda said quietly. 'That's why it's in very short supply.'

'And if you've got somebody who's not had much training, who's been doing a lot of nights, who gets a big incident, quite a few massive bleeds . . . Well, it's obvious, isn't it, Mark?'

'I suppose it is, Yolanda.' Mark smiled at her.

A massive bleed. Mel thought again of the figure in the photo, the young, pleasant-faced man on a boat crossing the lagoon to Venice.

'It's such a shame,' Yolanda continued. 'Brenda wouldn't hurt a fly. She always made us do collections for Comic Relief and the starving children and that. We all sponsored her daughter when she done the marathon. Well, most of us did – that tight cow Marian wouldn't put her hand in her purse. Anyway, why should Brenda take the blame for this all on her own?'

'It was my fault,' Brenda murmured. 'I made the mistake. Nobody else did.'

'No, Brenda, that's not right. And you put me in a room with that Neil Evans and see what I've got to say to him. Anybody could have made that mistake, Brenda. They treated us like slaves, they paid us nothing and then when you make a mistake they throw you into the street. When Pam told me I couldn't believe it. "Not Brenda," I said. "They never took poor Brenda and just marched her out and left her in the street. Tell me it wasn't Brenda, Pam." That's what I said. I swear on my son's life. Ask her if you don't believe me, Mel. You bring me that Neil Evans and that Dr Fitzgerald. Oh, you'll see what I say to them.'

'There was a case in another hospital where they mixed up the blood of two patients,' Mark said. 'One of the men died and they found out it was because two nurses had made a mistake. Anyway, they didn't sack the nurses. They reviewed their training programmes and brought in new procedures.'

Yolanda Munro wrinkled her nose. 'Yeah, but the thing is, Mark, they was nurses. That's the difference. That and the fact they didn't work for MGL. Sometimes, those nurses get right on my tits . . . pardon my French, Mark. The way they talk to us sometimes . . .' She shook her head almost sorrowfully. Then she looked up. 'The thing is, what most people don't realise is that blood is a drug. Just like mistakes can be made with drug dosages so you can make mistakes with blood. The difference is that doctors can protect themselves against their mistakes. We can't.'

'Well, we'll do our best,' Mark said.

'I think we'd better get things underway,' Paula said. 'Ready, guys?'

Mark turned to Brenda. 'It sounds like you have an excellent case,' he said. 'I know Mel is one hundred per cent committed to winning it.'

And for the first time since Mel had met her, Brenda Fletcher smiled.

They drove back into the city, where bored cops still stood at road-blocks, either cursing the distant war that had reawakened security fears or welcoming the overtime. The branch meeting had gone well and Mark Thompson had secured their nomination for General Secretary. He had made a good, short speech attacking the injustice of qualified staff on such pitiful salaries. 'Without you, there would be no health service,' he had said. 'You *are* the health service.' He had dealt wittily with the standard abuse directed at full-time officials from the floor. When he was accused of being a sell-out to the government for not promising immediate, indefinite strike action with full pay, he had simply laughed.

'I'll buy you a pint if you'll come and repeat that at Head Office. Then they might stop trying so hard to prevent me from winning this election. But –' and here he had fixed his questioner with a direct and taunting gaze – 'we're not talking about occupying a refectory any more. This isn't student politics. We're talking about major industrial action in the National Health Service. Which might of course be necessary. I would rule nothing out. I hope that those who feel such justified anger will attend the lobby of Parliament on Tuesday.'

The debate had then degenerated somewhat because one of Graham's favourite reps had shouted at the questioner, 'Yeah, so fuck off, Nigel, you middle-class Trot bastard.' This had caused an immediate uproar as insults flew across the floor and one of Nigel's hangers-on had jumped up and down waving her arms and screaming, 'Stalinists! Stalinists! State capitalism has collapsed. You can't put us in psychiatric hospitals any more,' in a voice so high-pitched that it might have shattered light-bulbs. Somebody had shouted back, 'Don't you believe it!' Nigel – when he wasn't deluding himself that he was directing military operations from a train in the Russian Civil War — was an effective and amenable rep with whom Mel sometimes chatted about their mutual fondness for Steve Earle. Even in his current incarnation as Lev Nigelovich, he had become alarmed at this eccentric behaviour from one of his foot-soldiers and had tugged her arm and motioned her to shut up.

'What are we like?' Mark said to Mel. 'Still arguing about a dispute in Russia over seventy years ago. It's pathetic really. Stalinist! Trot! Aren't we ever going to get beyond that?'

'I doubt it,' Mel said. 'My dad still describes the invasion of Czechoslovakia as friendly assistance from one socialist government to another.'

'Do you want a drink?' Mark asked her as they approached Head Office.

Mel did want a drink. It had been a good branch meeting, she was tired but still buzzing slightly, the night air was mild and beguiling. She glanced at her watch. 'Where's a good pub around here?'

'Not in a pub.' Mark grinned and took a key from his pocket. 'In Fungus's office. He's got a fantastic drinks cabinet.'

'That's outrageous,' but Mel was laughing. 'Come on then. I've never been in his office when he's not there.'

'It's the only time to go,' Mark said.

The building was dim and strange — abandoned desks covered with the clutter of the day, all the cheery paraphernalia of postcards and calendars, coffee mugs, angle-poise lights, little expressions of personality, but no people. Only a middle-aged, grey-haired cleaner moved between the desks, emptying bins into black plastic bags. Mark waved at him across the office and the man smiled back.

Mel still felt alarmed as they entered Mould's office and Mark shut the door carefully behind him and switched on the light. She looked at the leather sofa on which she had sat doodling while Mould bored her senseless with his combination of tedious anecdotes and self-satisfied aphorisms.

'Brandy? Whisky? Vodka?' Mark opened a small cupboard with a magician's flourish to reveal a selection of bottles and several glasses on a silver tray.

'A large whisky,' Mel said. 'I assume that you will be dispensing with this unnecessary self-indulgence if you become General Secretary?'

'*When* I become General Secretary,' Mark retorted, pushing ice out of its plastic container and obviously more confident about his election prospects than the last time he had spoken to Mel. 'Of course I won't. This is one of the reasons I want the job so much. Cheers.'

They clinked glasses. There was silence and Mel felt the shiver of tension building between them. She sipped quickly at her whisky to prevent herself from trembling. Stop? Go? Red? Green?

'Look at that.' Mel pointed to a photo of their General Secretary grinning foolishly as he shook hands with Nelson Mandela. 'What an arrogant . . .'

But she paused mid-sentence because Mark Thompson was not looking at the photo, he was looking at her. And she knew that he was going to kiss her and that she was going to let him because her sentry – who she had always suspected might be a lazy good-for-nothing when actually put to the test – had simply downed rifle and ambled off. There was nobody else in her head now, absolutely nobody, just this moment, just the fizz of energy between two people suddenly alone, where what was known but unacknowledged had suddenly become unavoidable and the air heavy with the transition.

Mark stepped forward and put his hand on the back of her head, stroking her hair gently. She thought he was going to kiss her then but he took her by the hand and led her to the sofa, the same sofa on which she had tried not to yawn while Mould droned on about recruitment targets. At last, at last, cried a voice in her head as their arms encircled each other, as their mouths and tongues met, as their hands moved quickly and impatiently, hardly bothering with zips, clips or buttons but pushing clothes up, aside, out of the way. His hands were on her breasts, she unhooked his belt, took him in her hand. He knew what he wanted, knew what he wanted to do and she was glad that he did, welcoming his audacity as he turned her so that she was, in fact, looking up at a photo of a legendary African leader rather than the face of the man who was bunching her hair with one hand and steadying her hips with the other. She rested her forearms on the back of the sofa and closed her eyes as he pushed aside rather than removed her underwear and she was pleased because that was exactly what she had wanted him to do.

Don't come inside me. But she didn't want him to stop.

Don't come inside me. But she couldn't tell him that.

Because, as the sound of their pleasure began to crescendo on the leather sofa of the office of the General Secretary of the GWA, all of her signals had suddenly switched to green.

'I'd better get another tissue,' murmured Mark and they both laughed.

'Don't come inside me,' she had gasped once secure of her own pleasure and he had managed to come both out of her and over her. Mel knew that she should still be worried but wasn't particularly. She felt light-headed and cheerful.

'Watch out for the cleaner,' she said.

'Don't worry. He'll probably just think we're working late,' he replied.

'Very likely,' Mel muttered.

She got up and straightened her clothes, pulled her bra back over her breasts, fastened the buttons on her shirt. Suddenly something on Mould's desk caught her eye. It was a memo from Leo Young.

Re: Situation with MGL

She frowned and pulled it out from the pile and began to read.

I am worried about the situation we discussed. May need to act swiftly on this. RH stroppy. Talking about pulling out. Can't rely on MH at all. This needs urgent attention. No more Mr Nice Guy??

She carefully replaced the memo. It was not so surprising really, although she still felt uncomfortable – as if she had overheard her name in an unfriendly corridor conversation. She knew that they had always considered her to be unreliable. She also knew that Leo Young's transition from Mr Nice Guy – not that he had ever truly been that – would not be comfortable for her.

Mark came back into the office and Mel was suddenly filled with an urgent wish to leave.

'I had better go,' she said.

'Now?'

'Yeah, Mark, I'm sorry, I have to get home.'

'OK. Look, Mel, I hope you don't mind me asking. Where do we go from here?'

Mel felt a flash of impatience. It was the kind of question that she dreaded. 'Nowhere,' she said. A little Pepa sprang defensively on to her shoulder, hands on hips, glaring at Mark.

'Nowhere?' Mark looked astonished and hurt.

'Nowhere. That was great. We both knew, I think, that it might happen. Maybe, sometime, it might happen again if the circumstances are right. That may sound harsh but that's the way it is. I don't want an office romance. We both have long-term partners and you have children. I don't feel at all guilty about it and nor should you. It was sex, Mark, and you know it.'

The little Pepa on her shoulder performed a celebratory cartwheel.

'OK,' Mark said, frowning. 'It seems a bit cold to me but if that's the way you see it . . .'

'I'm afraid I do. I really like you. What's happened has been great . . . spontaneous. I really enjoyed it.' She grinned at him. 'But we should just leave it at that.'

Mark shrugged. 'At least wait and I'll come down with you.'

Mel laughed. He had become a little boy. She walked over to him, put her hands on his shoulders and gave him a light kiss on the lips. He held her to him for a moment, pulling her against him, and she felt another rush of desire. But she knew that she had to go.

'Of course I'll wait. Stop feeling sorry for yourself. You know I'm right. We'll always know this has happened and that will be kind of funny and nice as well.'

And they made their way through the building, nodding at the cleaner who was drinking a coffee at the reception desk. '*Hasta luego*,' said Mark in an atrocious accent, obviously engaging in a familiar routine which he believed demonstrated his cheerful accessibility. Overdoing it, Mel thought. The silver-haired cleaner raised his hand and grinned a little cheekily but not unpleasantly at Mel. '*Portanse bien*,' he replied. She did not know what it meant but she blushed anyway.

Mel walked into the flat, closed the door behind her, paused for a moment, and then went to face Patrick. He was lying on the bed in T-shirt and boxer shorts, one leg crossed over the other, watching a programme about air disasters. He waved at her.

'Hello, Melamine. You should watch this, it's mental. They recreated Tenerife with computer graphics. Two jumbos heading straight for each other on a foggy runway. BAM! The KLM jet slices the top off the PanAm plane like a boiled egg.'

Mel felt as if she had SLUT tattooed on her forehead.

'Your meeting go OK?' Patrick asked. 'I made a pie.'

'A what?' The evening was taking on a dream-like quality.

'A pie. It was fantastic. Really therapeutic. I suddenly got this urge to make something.' He mimed a pie with his hands and pulled a Bisto kid face. 'So I got out this recipe and I made a chicken pie. Go and have a look at it. It's fucking brilliant. I thought pastry would be hard but it's piss-easy. I got hungry so I ate a slice. There's plenty left though.'

'That's great, Patrick. I might have some when I've had a bath.'

EVIL SLUT.

Lying in the bath, though, Mel couldn't help giggling as she imagined telling Pepa this story – her first infidelity on the sofa of her boss's office and then coming home to find that Patrick had made her – of all things – a chicken pie. She splashed water over her stomach and breasts, closed her eyes and remembered his mouth on her, the first feel of him inside her, warm semen on her back, the way that she had cried out. She was detached, floating away, cold-hearted Mel, a selfish bitch, washing away the sins of the flesh, utterly oblivious to the chicken pie going cold, its gravy congealing, in the oven.

But after her bath, she went to the kitchen and made herself a cup of tea. She took the pie out of the oven to put in the fridge and noticed that he had carefully embossed her name on the pie crust with pastry letters, surrounded by four little pastry love-hearts. Clumsy gestures, oh what a fool she was for clumsy gestures – the M had obviously posed him a serious challenge. For a second, tears stung her eyes and all her scarlet-woman bravado evaporated. What was she doing? What on earth was the matter with her? Where the fuck would this sort of behaviour get her?

'Did you try it?' Patrick asked her drowsily as she came into the bedroom wrapped in her dressing-gown.

'No, sugar, if you don't mind I'll leave it until tomorrow. It'll be nice cold. I might take some to work.'

'OK. By the way, there were a couple of messages for you. That journalist you're having an affair with. And some woman called Lily Forrester. She's the one whose husband died, right?'

'Yeah.'

'Nice voice.' Patrick turned round and clutched the bedstead. 'Kind of sexy. She says she's taking you to the opera. Rather you than me, mate.'

Mel lay on the bed, staring at the ceiling. *Can't rely on MH.* Perhaps they were right. She was bad at her job and unfaithful to her sick boyfriend. And Lily? Who was Mel kidding getting all wound up about her? What did tonight say about the depth of her feelings? At this point, however, the little Pepa popped out again, wagging her finger. 'It says fuck all,' she admonished sternly. 'You did what you did because you wanted to, so just grow up, accept responsibility, and have a little pride in yourself.' Mel yawned, leaned over to kiss Patrick and then switched off the light. At least she had something to feel guilty about and she smiled suddenly to herself in the darkness as she began remembering again. She had this secret now, she would have to make sure she knew how to care for it properly.

what was I thinking of?

'Fantastic! Oh, that is so brilliant! Let me get this straight. There was a little me
dancing on your shoulder. And then you come home and Patrick's made
a chicken pie with your name on it. That's too much.'

Mel knew that telling Pepa would cheer her up. She had hesitated
about including the chicken pie as part of the humour of the story but
in the end it had proved irresistible. She also knew that although Pepa
liked Patrick she would understand completely why Mel had needed that
particular escape.

'And did you take the pie to work the next day and eat it?' Pepa asked.

'I'm afraid I did. It was pretty good actually. Although the pastry
was weird.'

'So you had your pie and ate it. Oh, Mel, I was beginning to worry about
you. Not just *that*, you know, you seemed so distant from everything. I'm
so glad that you told the guy where he stood. "Where do we go from
here?"' Pepa impersonated a pleading male voice. 'Nowhere. Exactly. He
doesn't know how lucky he is.'

She raised her glass to Mel. They were sitting in Pepa's flat after work,
drinking rosé wine from an unlabelled bottle – a gift from Spain. Mel
sometimes wondered why, if Pepa were so unpopular at home, she
continued to receive so many gifts: homemade wine, roasted peppers,

chorizo and ham, boxes of *dulce de membrillo* from her village. It had been a tiring day and Mel was grateful for the wine. She had had a working lunch with the Information Technology team, she had harassed MGL about the information they were still not sending, she had attended a reps meeting at the Great Northern.

At the hospital, she had also met Neil Evans. He seemed to have forgotten his earlier aggression; in fact he was behaving most strangely, staring over Mel's head and laughing for no reason. When his phone had rung, he had been snappy with the person on the line. 'Tough. It'll have to wait then. Not my problem I'm afraid. Ask somebody more senior than me. Somebody with BREASTS.' He had then started a long and almost nostalgic story about his time in the GWA – in the good old days, of course, when it was a proper union. Mel was rather puzzled as this was not the behaviour of a person who was responsible for the obscene phone calls.

'What is the matter with Neil Evans?' she had asked one of the reps from Cytology, dunking a ring doughnut into a cup of miserably weak coffee.

'Haven't you heard? We think he's losing it. He got passed over for promotion. They gave it to some Oxbridge graduate. And a woman at that. If anyone asks him anything he just says, "Have I got breasts?" Or, "Pop upstairs through the glass ceiling and ask somebody with breasts!" He's flipped. He thinks he's the victim of a giant female conspiracy. People have been getting away with murder, he just doesn't care any more.'

'Right,' Mel had said, chewing her doughnut while she contemplated this strange behaviour.

Angela arrived at Pepa's, she had also come straight from work. She looked so elegant, so classy, so in control of her appearance, that Mel felt shabby and envious in her dull and mediocre work clothes.

'How's your new boyfriend?' Mel asked. 'The one who looks like Lennox Lewis.'

'Lodged.' Angela flopped down on the sofa and waved her hand for a glass. Mel and Pepa both laughed.

'What did he do?' Pepa asked.

Angela said that she didn't want to talk about it so Pepa poured her a glass of wine and set down some plates of olives, fresh anchovies, and almonds. Mel adored Pepa for her natural hospitality. It would simply never occur to her not to offer something – in fact she never did offer, she just put things out without fuss as she was doing now, as if it were the most natural thing in the world. This was a grace, Mel thought, an elegant thing to do.

'I saw that woman you know on the TV,' Pepa said to Mel as she sucked an olive stone. 'The one whose husband died. Something to do with the court case against the rail company. Corporate manslaughter.'

'Oh, that was the horrible story you were telling us,' Angela said. 'You met the woman then?'

'Yes.' Mel glanced at Pepa who was watching her without any obvious emotion in her face. For some reason, Mel was uncomfortable discussing this with Pepa. She also, however, felt irritated at the idea that there was anything she had to feel uncomfortable about.

'They've become mates,' Pepa said, still just at the borderpost of sarcasm.

'Yeah? That's nice,' Angela said, reaching for the almonds. 'What's she like then?'

'Yeah, what's she like?' Pepa asked and Mel could hear the tone hardening, the sneer. 'Aren't we allowed to meet her or something? I suppose we might betray our ignorance of opera, we might be a little too loud . . .'

'Fuck off, Pepa.'

'What? What's wrong with—'

'Just fuck off. I'm not in the mood.'

Angela looked confused. 'Hey, what's the matter with you two?'

'Nothing's the matter with me,' Pepa retorted icily. 'I was just joking. What's the matter with you, Mel?'

Mel knew that there was little point in arguing with Pepa as she fought mean and also resorted to childish blocking tactics. Her favourite technique was to be provocative – as indeed she had just been – and then adopt an air of wounded innocence if a voice were raised in irritation or retaliation. Mel was annoyed with Pepa because she had been thinking warm thoughts about her when her friend had launched her surprise offensive. *Why do you have to do that?* she wanted to ask. *Why do you have to resort to such childish aggression?* On the whole, however, it was easier to coax Pepa out of tantrums than prove that she had been unreasonable. And coaxing Pepa out of tantrums was never hard because try as she might Pepa could not sulk for long.

'Give it up.' Mel started tugging at Pepa's foot, trying to take her sock off, to bite her toes.

'Get off me, you mad bitch.'

'Oh, Pepita, don't get all moody. It doesn't suit you. I can understand that you're jealous but you know I love you the most. You're my shoulder-elf. I'll always love you the most, you spoiled cow.'

Pepa tried to look lofty and dismissive but Mel could tell that she was pleased.

'Well, thanks very much,' Angela said. 'Not that I've ever been in any doubt.'

'Mel's known me for longer,' Pepa said. 'And it's natural that I should be the most loved.'

'Also, you don't need the same level of love and reassurance as Pepa does because you're a well-balanced, independent woman,' Mel said.

'Excuse me, but when it comes to independence . . .' Pepa started.

'I'm not talking about living on your own.'

'Well, how independent are *you* then?'

Mel said, 'I'm not making any claims for myself.'

'I think I'm independent,' Angela said.

Pepa studied her for a second. The phone had started to ring. 'Yes . . .' she said to Angela. 'I think you are.'

'What do *you* want?' she asked rudely when she picked up the phone. 'We've got Mel for the evening . . . OK, OK, I'll just get her.' She pulled a face as she passed Mel the phone. 'It's your ball and chain. It's *really* important and I've got to stop messing about.'

Patrick was unusually sombre. Jim's wagon, which had been trundling along as normal, had suddenly suffered a derailment, plunged down an embankment and exploded spectacularly. He had been on a binge and was currently in his flat – angry, paranoid and talking about throwing himself from the balcony. Mel knew that this was not empty melodrama. She said she would meet Patrick at the flat.

'I've got to go,' she announced when she had replaced the receiver. 'Can you call me a cab, Pepa, please?'

'Very independent,' Pepa grumbled.

'It's not Patrick, it's Jim. He's got a bit of a problem. I have to go.'

'Fallen off his wagon, has he?'

'How do you know?'

Pepa shrugged and reached for the phone. 'Just a wild guess,' she said.

It was another mild, sweet night as Mel made her way to the Bow Quarter where Jim lived. The day had been muggy but this had given way to a warm, almost continental feel, the promise of summer. Couples were sitting around the fountain by the security-lodge, or on the edge of the pond, watching the shoals of carp which reminded Mel of swimming bananas. Some people were drinking bottles of beer and sending clouds of cigarette smoke into the air.

Mel took the lift to the top floor of Jim's building. She could never make up her mind whether she liked the hotel atmosphere of this middle-class ghetto, although she approved of the attempt to create a sense of communal living, however artificial. She liked the rows of balconies with their mountain bikes, tea-towels drying, plants purchased from Columbia Road. She liked coming here in the early evening when people were returning from work, the men with loosened ties and the top buttons of their shirts undone, carrying food from the supermarket, bottles of wine, brown takeaway bags. Most of all, she liked the view from Jim's flat, perched above all the arteries and veins of the city: trains rushing down the railway lines, the planes climbing from and descending to the City Airport, cars crossing lanes on the busy motorway with its signs to Newmarket, Chelmsford, the Blackwall Tunnel.

Patrick opened the door to her. He rolled his eyes. Jim was on the sofa with a bottle of vodka in his hand. To slow his racing pulse, he said.

'What happened?' Mel asked him.

Jim had been sitting on his balcony, happy on a spring evening, when he had caught the smell of a foreign cigarette on the warm air. It had been so delicious, so evocative, that he had been filled with melancholy. On another balcony, he had watched a couple laughing and drinking a bottle of cold white wine. Why couldn't he have those simple pleasures? Why couldn't he just relax with a bottle of wine? Why was he defined by this even when he was clean? Was his whole life going to revolve around denying himself things? He didn't want carrot juice or iced coffee or a blueberry muffin, he wanted a glass of cold wine and a cigarette.

The couple drinking wine on the balcony had invited him over for a glass. He had accepted it, then a cigarette, then more wine, then more cigarettes.

The conversation had got lively, somebody made a joke about wanting some drugs, Jim had said nothing, a few minutes later the conversation had returned to drugs, glances were exchanged, wallets checked, Jim had offered to get some. And so on and so on and so on. Twenty-four hours later – with the self-reproach orchestra tuning up and just waiting for the appearance of the conductor – he was wearing the same clothes and sitting in a different flat with some of his old crew who were so glad to have him back – *Don't worry about it, mate. You've got to let yourself go every now and again. The best-laid plans of mice and men. We're having a laugh, aren't we? Etc. etc. etc.*

'At least I got to experience time travel,' Jim slurred as a finger of ash dropped on to his chest. He had brown nicotine stains around the corner of his mouth. ''Cause nothing had changed from a year ago. They might as well have been in that living room for the last twelve months. I swear to God they were having exactly the same conversation as when I was last there.'

He got up and staggered on to the balcony with his bottle of vodka. Mel followed him out. They stood looking out at the city, at the Millennium Dome, at the tree-lined ridge which marked the distant horizon, far-off territories.

'I've got to start all over again,' he said. 'Mel, what the fuck was I thinking of? Why have I done this to myself?'

'Look out there,' Mel said. 'Look at all those windows, all those cars, look at it all. Not everyone's got the same story, Jim, but there are sadder stories than yours out there. It's a set-back but you've got to deal with it, try and get back on course. And at least you're not calling me a frigid, uptight bitch.'

'I never meant that you know, Mel. Truly, I never fucking meant that.'

Patrick wandered on to the balcony with a black coffee in a glass. He had been listening to the conversation.

'What was I thinking of?' he said. 'Story of my life. They'll put that on my gravestone. And how many times do I have to tell you – sobriety is the new rock and roll. We were in the middle of making an important fashion statement until you went and blew it. I shall enjoy holding the moral high ground for a few days.'

Jim glanced at the coffee which smelled sweet and strong on the evening air and Mel knew that he was envying Patrick his ability to drink and savour it right now. The temptation was no longer the heavenly smell of a foreign cigarette in the early evening, the false promise of a pot of gold at the end of the rainbow, it was the pleasure of the clear-headed, of being able to think straight, to perform small but satisfying routines, to notice things. Jim hawked the phlegm of two nights' smoking out of his lungs and spat over the balcony. The three of them stood in silence as the dusk gathered around them. They gazed over the lights of their city, at the familiar landscape which could still produce a feeling of vertigo. You might miss London if you were removed from it, it might speak in beguiling tones with all the power of its histories, but it would not let you feel completely at ease within it — it was brutal, atomised, stratified. It was small wonder, Mel thought, that so many drugs were consumed here. Jim lit another cigarette and swigged at the bottle of vodka. Then he threw the cigarette away in disgust.

'You should get some sleep,' Mel said. 'You can come to ours if you want.'

'You know what, Mel, I would. But I can't. I want to get up in my house. I won't be able to sleep at yours, and you sleeping will drive me crazy.'

'Join the club,' Patrick said. 'It's worse when she snores — it's like a reminder that you're awake.'

'It's more than you deserve,' Jim snapped, lighting another cigarette.

'Well,' Mel said to Jim. 'You might find these useful.' And she passed him three valium wrapped up in tissue paper.

'Oh, you angel. You treasure. Where did these come from? This is just what I need.'

'My friend Pepa gave them to me.'

Pepa had handed them to Mel as she was leaving. 'At least get the stupid bastard to sleep,' she had said.

'Pepa? The cute Spanish bird?'

'She's as cute as a mouth ulcer,' Patrick muttered.

'Well, she's saved my life this time. Go on, you two Samaritans, get home.'

'You know where we are,' Mel said.

They walked from Bow to Bethnal Green, up on to the Roman Road, past the dark shadows of the trees and locked gates of Mile End Park. They did not make much conversation, just occasional interrogations, quiet observations, benign murmurs. It was the understanding generated by their years together, this comfortable familiarity. Mel was not foolish, she did not underestimate this, nor was she unaware of how much she would miss it if it were not there. They must have presented an enviable sight to Jim, alone on his balcony, contemplating his solitude. Perhaps Pepa had been right, nobody was happy. There was certainly no blueprint, no easy answer. Why should there be? Mel was walking down the Roman Road to her house, she was not fleeing a burning village. She had more than food and shelter, she had a job which – in spite of its drawbacks – engaged her intellect and emotions. She had friends. Yet suffering – like poverty – was still better understood as a relative rather than an absolute concept. She did not believe in a fixed line above which one could be considered to be out of the danger zone. There were people who appeared to be well out of that zone who still carried an open razor at their throat.

Mel and Patrick arrived back at their flat, at the home they shared, turning on lights, opening doors, reoccupying their space. They flopped exhausted on to the bed to watch TV. A woman who was having her breasts enlarged grew indignant when the consultant timidly suggested that she should lower her sights and opt for a C- rather than a D-cup. *If I'm paying £1,500 for each one then I want a D-cup*, the woman said.

'Quite right.' Patrick turned on to his belly and waggled his bare feet. 'Accept absolutely nothing less than a D-cup in life.'

They both started to laugh, shaking with laughter on the bed. When the woman came round from her anaesthetic she cried but later she said that her life had changed entirely and that it was the best investment she had ever made. *I never thought it would make me this happy*, she said. *I'm a new woman.*

'Well, fair enough,' Patrick said. 'If that's what it takes.'

Mel went to the living room to check the messages on the answerphone. From the bedroom she could still hear Patrick making comments at the TV. 'Oh no, get off my TV, you horror.' Mel smiled but then she heard Lily's voice. Lily sounded forlorn, she had left a couple of messages but Mel hadn't answered. Lily hoped that Mel hadn't reconsidered the opera and could she ring her the next day. There was a pause as if she were still hoping that Mel might pick up the phone and then *click*.

Mel sat on the sofa and looked at the phone. She tended to make the assumption that it was only her who worried about other people, that she did not have the quality that caused people to crave her presence, to agonise over her absence. She could not imagine somebody worrying about her not calling, or longing to hear her voice at the end of a phone. She had not called Lily simply because she was waiting for a quiet moment and that moment had not arrived.

Skipping hearts, missed beats, racing pulses — Mel was always surprised if people grew obsessive about her and, much as she disliked those who blamed their parents for everything, she knew that this did have something to do with assigned childhood roles. Sarah — pretty, flighty, sensitive; Mel — clever, anxious to please, Daddy's girl. He had not only taken her to the football, they had gone to political meetings together. While Sarah was out partying and bringing boys home, Mel was reading about the Spanish Civil War and working her way through *The Ragged Trousered Philanthropists*. But then he had gone away and Mel had had to reverse her heroes and villains. Her mother weeping, howling in the hallway, holding on to his leg, half dragged along the floor. *Don't go, Michael, don't go, please don't go.* Her father looking down at this demented creature, this sobbing woman with whom he had shared so much. *For Christ's sake, Kath, have some self-respect. Don't humiliate yourself like this.* Mel bending down to lift her mother from the floor, holding her like a stringless puppet, looking up at her father, her eyes gleaming with hatred. *I hate you. I never want to see you again. You are dead as far as I am concerned.* Mortal blows, venomous darts aimed at the interstices of the ribcage, straight at that tender, thumping muscle — mythical home to all our emotions and passions. The pain flickering in the eyes of the one we love, the shout of despair. *Go then, go to your slut, you cruel, heartless bastard.*

Mel went to the window, pushed her face against it. She could smell the old, sour enamel paint on the metal frame. She could hear the TV next door, a stand-up comedian making a series of banal observational gags. 'You're fucking useless!' Patrick shouted. Mel smiled again. She felt a sudden urge to listen to music, hunting through her records until she found what she wanted, exactly what she wanted for that moment, the most reductive, seductive song.

That night, she had another nightmare. She dreamed that she was in a small house by the beach, glimpsing through a crack in the curtain a tremendous tsunami, a great salty sneer, curling and angry with foam. The little house withstood the force of the wave crashing over it but she went outside to a scene of dark desolation. Wandering waist-deep through the flood, under a sky of flickering stars, pushing aside splintered wood and broken toys, she realised with horror that there was a shark in the water, a dark torpedo of finned menace. She tried to run for the shore but there was no shore and she couldn't, anyway, run in water. When she awoke and had calmed herself, she resolved to ask Mary the significance of wave dreams. She had a nasty feeling that she knew what the answer might be.

deep throat

An anonymous letter arrived on Mel's desk – the first such letter she had ever received.

> *Dear Miss Holloway,*
>   *If you really want to upset MGL, why don't you start asking some questions about clinical trials on new drugs?*
>   *I could help you.*
>   *Yours,*
>   *A Wellwisher*

Mel suspected that A Wellwisher might be the breast-obsessed Neil Evans. He was fed up with MGL and this cloak-and-dagger performance was in keeping with his personality – if that wasn't a rather generous term to use for the mentally disturbed Pathology manager. But she doubted whether Evans would be making obscene phone-calls *and* hinting at skeletons in MGL's cupboard.

'Very interesting,' Paul Flitcroft said when she called him to solicit his opinion on the anonymous letter. 'I haven't heard anything along those lines. They would have a good reason not to publish the results of dodgy clinical trials.'

'Reasons not unconnected with share price.'

'Exactly. They've been rather bullish about this drug.'

'What's so good about this new treatment?'

'It attacks hepatitis without causing side-effects. Something like that. Anyway, it sounds as if you'll be hearing again from A Wellwisher. I'll dig around and see what I can find out. Did you enjoy yourself the other night?'

Mel said that she had, told him the food was delicious, complimented his friends.

'Miranda liked you. And Lily. Lily's great, don't you think? She's got this quality about her. It's quite unusual, I can't put my finger on it. Anyway, Miranda wants you both to come to the country with us. By the way, have you noticed how the names for birds are really excellent? Lark, swallow, linnet, goldfinch.'

'Mmmm, what about crow, rook, vulture, bald eagle?'

'Exceptions. Terns, gulls, plovers, finches, puffins . . .' He immediately began to laugh. 'Puffin! Isn't that a fantastic word? Who made that up, do you think? It's so spot-on as well. You can just imagine it. "See that weird-looking one over there? Let's call it a puffin."'

Mel began to laugh as well. 'Poor puffins. Look, see what you can find out about this MGL thing, yeah?'

'Are you trying to get rid of me now?'

'Yes.'

'OK then. Well, don't forget about coming with us to Miranda's dacha. We can beat a few serfs if we get bored. Or go searching for puffins to tease.'

Mel saw Brenda Fletcher and Yolanda Munro coming out of the lift. They were both giggling.

'I've got to go,' she said to Paul. 'I'll call you.'

'I've got to go as well. I'm a bit scared. I've been ordered to the gym. Miranda's said she'll leave me if I don't lose two stone. It's an empty threat I know but . . .'

'It'll be very good for you. You'll feel better.'

'Do you think so? What about all those muscle-bound chubby-chasers who'll probably try and gang-rape me in the showers?'

'A risk you'll just have to run if you want to keep your girlfriend. See you later, Paul.'

'Am I being paranoid . . .' Mel asked Brenda and Yolanda as they sat in the café across the road from the office, 'or does that man by the window keep staring at me?'

'Maybe he fancies you, Mel,' said Yolanda.

'I don't think so,' Mel said. 'He looks like he wants to kill me.'

The man was intimidating enough; bullet-headed, crop-haired, refusing to avert his gaze when Mel attempted to stare back.

'Poor soul,' said Brenda Fletcher. 'He's not going to win any beauty competitions, is he?'

'Not like that Mark Thompson?' Yolanda nudged her friend and they both laughed.

'But I think we are a little old for him, Yolanda, not like Mel here. I think he has his eye on her. "Mel is one hundred per cent committed to your case."' She mimicked Mark at the branch meeting. 'He's a smooth one all right.'

'If I was twenty years younger I would give him a run for his money,' Yolanda said. 'Look, Mel, your boyfriend's leaving. Tata, gorgeous.' She gave him a cheeky wave.

'Yolanda!'

The man walked over to their table.

'What?' he said. His fists were clenching and unclenching. He was wearing dirty white Reeboks and his body appeared to strain against his clothes.

'I was just waving goodbye,' Yolanda said, her chin jutting in defiance. 'You seemed so interested in our table. Didn't anybody ever tell you it's rude to stare?'

The man looked at her. His eyes were watery blue, his hair very blond. Then he leaned down, his hands on the table so that his face was very close to hers.

'One more word, you stupid old cow, and I'll break your fucking scrawny neck.'

The three women stared at him dumbfounded.

'Stupid whores,' he said and turned and walked away. At the door he looked back again as if he were committing them to memory.

'Compliments pass when the quality meet,' murmured Brenda after a short stunned silence. 'Don't worry, Yolly, there are lots of lunatics about.'

'I'm not worried,' Yolanda said. 'I just sometimes wish I owned a gun. Here's our food.'

But Mel noticed that she blinked and touched her neck.

Yolanda and Brenda mocked Mel for her tuna sandwich as they attacked plates of spaghetti bolognese and kept telling the waiter to shovel more Parmesan on. They were becoming quite a double-act. Brenda did not have the same defeated, downtrodden look about her, she even said that she was glad that she was going to have an opportunity to put her case. Mel was coaching them on their witness statements and trying to curb Yolanda's tendency towards the theatrical. Yolanda was treating the tribunal rather like a murder trial in which her innocent friend Brenda was facing the gallows. *Your Honour, Brenda Fletcher is innocent. I swear on my son's life. She must not hang, Your Honour!*

Yolanda was originally from Caracas, her husband a Scottish sailor from Aberdeen. Brenda Fletcher was from Galway, she had come here when she was nineteen. Exiles, migrants, and refugees – the life-blood of this great, shabby, beating heart. Distant voices, crazy alphabets, songs of loss and longing, oranges in Southampton Street, coquettish folk dances stamped out on the floors of community centres, curly-haired, dark-eyed kids holding paper cups of Coca-Cola.

Yassasin! Venceremos! Joi Bangla! Tiocfaidh ár lá!

A tree blossoming in a drab courtyard, firemen picking through a mangled train, a fanatic treading the infamously thin line between love and hate and clutching a nail-bomb to his . . .

'What about you, Mel?' Yolanda asked. 'Are you a born-and-bred Londoner?'

Mel was. Her uncle and aunt had once done a family tree for their grandmother on her eightieth birthday. Uncle Joe and Aunty Rose were snobs who were desperate to find a drop of blue blood, at the very least a tenuous link with somebody famous. Instead, they found washerwomen, domestic servants, gardeners and labourers. To their horror it got worse the further back they went. Job descriptions such as traveller started to appear. Aunty Rose gave up in disgust when it turned out that more than one Holloway had ended life prematurely dangling from a hangman's rope. Mel's dad had laughed at his *arriviste* sister. 'I always wondered why we had so many distant relatives in Australia. Tinkers and thieves, that's all we are, Rose. Pure bloody lumpen.'

Mel told Yolanda that she had been born within the sound of Bow Bells.

'It's not where you're from. It's who you are,' Brenda said firmly.

'I'm one hundred per cent English, I'm afraid,' Mel said. She was thinking, strangely, of her grandfather who had been a firewatcher during the Blitz. Walking in the East End after a raid, he had found a human eye staring up at him from the gutter.

'There's no afraid about it.' Brenda looked at Mel over her cappuccino, wiping away a foam coffee moustache. 'You're a lovely girl. A really good person. Isn't she, Yolanda?'

'She's a sweetheart,' Yolanda grinned, 'a little jewel.'

'Oh, stop it,' Mel mock-protested but she blushed with pleasure.

'Voted yet, Mel?' Graham was putting on his coat to leave the office.

'Yup.' Mel was playing Hearts on her computer. Most people she knew played Solitaire but she liked the more competitive edge of this game – working out strategies to avoid receiving bad cards or making daring attempts to receive all the bad cards which then turned them into good cards and forced her opponents to pick up twenty-six penalty points. There was sadistic pleasure to be gained from outwitting and punishing three computer-invented characters: Michelle, Pauline and Ben. Of the three, she hated Pauline the most because Pauline seemed to take malevolent delight in handing Mel the Queen of Spades. Pauline was definitely thin, spiteful and frigid. Sometimes, she wondered whether Pauline even lost deliberately to prevent her from winning. Michelle she imagined as pretty, sluttish and not especially talented, while she almost felt sorry for Ben who was a gullible fool and only won clumsily through luck rather than skill.

'You voted for Mark, of course?' Graham snapped his briefcase shut. It was covered with decades of stickers. *Jobs not Bombs! Coal not Dole! People's March for Jobs! Brent – a nuclear-free zone! I support Wealdstone FC! Campaign for Real Ale!*

'I'm afraid not.' Mel swivelled round after hitting all her opponents with twenty-six penalty points. 'You see, I believe that we need a flexible and realistic approach to trade unionism. It's not beer and sandwiches any more. The key to this is our organising activities, without forgetting, of course, the need for partnerships. Furthermore, I want to go on lots of training courses and learn about the benefits of taking a helicopter view of a topic. I want a New Outlook.'

'Is it too late to change my vote? You're frighteningly convincing as a social-fascist, Mel . . . Oh hello, Mary, how's the ether tonight? My birthday is the fourth of May. Four and five is nine – does that make me a bubbling cauldron of sexual passion or does it all depend on whether the Fool is on top of the Priestess?'

'It wouldn't matter when your birthday was, mate. You've got more chance of scoring the winning goal for England in the World Cup final than you have of being described as a bubbling cauldron of sexual passion. Mel, Peter Wright has cancelled the meeting for tomorrow. He has to go into hospital to have his piles done. Don't work too hard.'

'Hold on, I'll come down with you,' Graham said and they disappeared bickering towards the lift.

After they had gone, Mel sat and stared into space. Then she called Lily. Lily was anxious about the court case, which now involved both the train company and the driver facing charges. The CPS had been reluctant to include Fastline Trains in the manslaughter charges but had bowed to pressure from the families and the case would at last be coming to court.

'You haven't forgotten the opera?' Lily said.

'No. How could I have forgotten?'

There was a pause.

'I'm really looking forward to it,' Mel said.

'Yes. So am I. Come and see me soon, Mel.'

When Mel had put the phone down, she wrote Lily's name on the pad in front of her as she had done with boys' names when she was at school. Then she scribbled it out.

The lift door clunked and Mel wondered whether it was Mary or Graham coming back to pick up something they had forgotten. But when the lift door opened, she saw a crop-haired, bullet-headed man, the same man that had abused them in the café earlier. For a second, she foolishly thought that he was connected in some way with the building. Perhaps he was doing some maintenance work, in which case she was going to make a complaint. As he looked at her, she knew that he was nothing to do with the building.

'I've come to have a little word with you,' he said as he opened the glass door to her office.

Mel tried to control the wobble in her voice. She stood up. 'You can't just come walking in here like that—'

'Sit down, you silly fucking whore.'

Mel recognised the insult immediately. She sat down and pushed her chair back on its wheels so that she was as far away from him as possible.

'It's about the tribunal, isn't it?' she said doubtfully. He didn't look like the type that a private company might be using to intimidate her. He looked mad.

He perched on the edge of the desk. 'That's right. And I ain't leaving here until we get it sorted out.' He looked around and leered. 'You should be careful, working alone up here. Especially dangerous for a woman. Anybody could walk in when there's nobody about.'

One moment she had been planning to destroy a trio of computer characters at Hearts. Now some MGL-sponsored thug was making threats edged with sexual menace to her.

'They can't possibly think I'm going to back down by sending you to threaten me . . .' Mel asserted.

At this, however, Bullet-Head went crazy.

'They? They? You think you can get away with that? Eh? Do you? Do you fucking think I'm going to let you sit there and get away with that?'

'Well, they must be paying you to come down here or—'

A fist slammed on to the desk beside her. His face leaned into hers as it had earlier gone face-to-face with Yolanda Munro. He had blond stubble on his chin.

'Now I'm warning you. Don't wind me up. I'll break your neck. Do you understand me?' He brought his fist up until it was just touching her nose. 'I'll smash your face in.'

Mel was trying hard to control her fear. The office was so empty. There was no way she could get past him.

'I'm sorry,' she said. 'I just can't understand why you're so sensitive on this issue. It's not like it's personal.'

'Can't understand . . .' Curiously, the man was beginning to sound like an enraged teenager. He was almost groaning with self-righteous fury, his face red with rage. 'You won't help my old dear, she comes to see you to ask politely for help and all she gets is abuse, an old woman as well, and YOU SAY IT'S NOT FUCKING PERSONAL, YOU COCKSUCKER!'

Cocksucker? An old woman asking for help? A penny was wobbling towards the edge of a sharp and horrible precipice in Mel's mind.

'You're not from MGL, are you?' she said. 'But you said it was about the tribunal . . .'

'MGL? MGL? Who the fuck are MGL? What the fuck are you talking about? Don't try and mess me about, you whore. Don't try and confuse me. I'll break your neck. I'm that –' his finger and thumb were pushed into her face – 'fucking close to doing you some serious damage.'

A knight of Croatia had arrived to avenge his mother's treatment at the hands of communist faggots and Turkish cocksuckers.

Mel rubbed her eyes. Suddenly, the idea of receiving a visit from the ambassador of a pharmaceutical company did not seem so unattractive. Cold and professional, he would have warned her off and left. Now she was being held captive by a Croatian Orlick. Somehow she did not think that a promise to review his mother's case was going to persuade him to put down the cudgels he was flailing about on her behalf.

'Why don't you take a seat, Mr Boksic,' she said. 'There's no way that we'll sort this out with you shouting threats at me, is there? I'm sorry that there was a misunderstanding for a moment. Now I'm prepared to talk to you rationally about your mother's case but if you just start shouting at me we're not going to get anywhere. Yes, that chair's fine.'

The voice of officialdom succeeded in calming Boksic down briefly.

'We're gonna get this sorted,' he mumbled.

'Yes, well, it doesn't help sort things out making obscene phone-calls,' Mel said in an attempt to be stern and press home an advantage which she knew could only be temporary.

'Dunno what you're talking about,' he said, clenching and unclenching his fist.

Mel realised that any period of calm was simply an eye in the Boksic hurricane and that the next instalment of furious, foul-mouthed rage was not far away. Somehow, she had to get out of the office.

'Nobody knows I'm here,' he hissed as if reading her thoughts. 'Nobody knows you're here either.'

'Of course they do,' Mel said. 'My secretary knows I'm here. I'm also meeting somebody in half an hour.'

He ignored her.

'I've been watching this place for a while. I know where you live. I could keep you here all night if I wanted to.'

He was working himself up again, rubbing his thighs as he went up through the gears of obscenity. Mel knew that it was hopeless to expect the return of Mary or Graham. She also knew that she would rather leap from the sixth-floor window than spend the night in her office with Son of Boksic.

'Look,' she said, 'let me just get your mother's file so that we can try and work out a solution that's satisfactory to everybody.'

The clenching and unclenching of his fist grew even more rapid. He was starting to sweat, fixing her with watery blue eyes.

'You're gonna suck my cock,' he said. 'Whore!'

'Don't be ridiculous, Mr Boksic. Now where's that file.'

She stood up.

'Sit down!'

Mel ran, taking advantage of the fact that he was still seated to propel herself past him. She zigzagged in and out of desks, heading for the stairs, the obstacles negating his speed advantage. She knew that he was following her but adrenalin was giving her a single-minded dedication to flight which meant that she could not decipher the noises coming from behind her, did not care what he was saying anyway. She slammed through the swing doors, nearly stumbled as she hit the stairs, and began to leap down them. She had often had nightmares about being pursued down stairs and it was, of course, the stuff of many thrillers. But she did not think about any of that now, she only had one thought in her head – to get down the stairs as quickly as possible.

Had it been two flights of stairs, she would probably have made it to the ground floor but it was six. Boksic was also leaping down flights of stairs, she could hear the thump of his landings, knew that he was gaining on her, and this increased her panic and her fear of slipping. He reached her on the stairs just below the landing of the third floor, catching her hair, swinging her round and slamming her against the wall. She screamed and he slapped her across the face and tore at her shirt. She was filled with such rage by this that she spat in his face. He drew back his fist and she closed her eyes. It was at precisely this point that somebody emerged through the swing doors on to the landing above them, speaking with customary pomposity on his mobile.

'Yes, I'm coming back to Head Office now. Frankly, disappointing but I'm sure you know that already. What tone? Well, taking a helicopter view. What in God's name is going on here? Mel? Don't you dare push me! Who the hell are— UMPH!'

A mobile clattered down the steps, followed by heavier footsteps, the footsteps of her pursuer. Mel sank to the ground, clutching the banister and facing Barry Williams. He in turn was clutching what was left of his nose after it had felt the full force of the Boksic head. Mel decided that now was not the best time to ask Barry whether he still thought she should pursue Mrs Boksic's case given the fantastic organising opportunity that it represented. It was, after all, the first time in her life that she had been pleased to see him.

Mel staggered down the steps to the mobile. Her head was ringing from the slap she had received. She picked up the phone and was about to dial 999 when she heard squawking from the other end.

'Barry? Barry? What's going on? Can you hear me? You have to face facts. Don't just throw a tantrum about it . . .'

It was Leo Young.

'Leo, it's Mel.'

'What on earth is going on there, Mel? Where's Barry?'

'Call the police, Leo. Somebody's hit Barry.'

'Who? Who's hit him? Was it a Trot?'

Mel almost laughed. 'No, it was a maniac who was attacking me. Barry arrived just in time. Call the police. The guy might come back. We're on the third floor. I'll take Barry to the research department.'

She went back up the stairs to Barry Williams, who was still sitting hunched up like a small bird hiding under its wings and refusing point-blank to leave the nest. The concrete steps were splashed with his blood, he was holding a hankie to his nose. He was a pitiful figure but Mel could not help thinking that people would pay money to visit the site where somebody had headbutted him. It might well become a place of pilgrimage. Mel reached in her pocket and handed him another tissue.

'Come on,' she said. 'Let's get you inside.'

She helped him to his feet and took him through to the research department where she sat him down.

'Hold the bridge of your nose,' she suggested, as he rested his elbow on a stack of leaflets explaining the union's opposition to the Private Finance Initiative in the NHS.

'Bel?' Barry said through blood, hand and tissue.

'Yes, Barry?'

'Why does dobody like be?' He sounded almost desperate. The fatal question at last.

'Pardon?' Mel played for time.

'Dobody likes be id this office. Why?'

Mel did not think that, 'Because you're a cunt,' represented an appropriate answer in the circumstances.

'That's not true,' she murmured, replacing his bloody tissue with a clean one. 'Plenty of people like you.'

'Dabe wud!'

'Name one? Well, it's difficult to say just like that.' She prepared herself for one of the greatest lies she had ever told in her life. '*I* like you,' she said brightly, closing her eyes and wincing as she did so.

There was a contemptuous snort from behind the tissue, followed by an instant squeal of pain. Mel suspected that he had just sent what remained of his septum into the hankie.

'It's true . . .' Mel cast around desperately for something positive to say. 'One knows where one stands with you, Barry.'

'But I bet you still voted for Bark Thobsod.'

And astonishingly a big fat tear rolled out and splashed by his feet among the blood splatters. Then another one. He was weeping. Mel noticed that above his black slip-on shoes, Barry's socks were adorned with sleeping cats. She wondered who had bought them for him, maybe his daughter, a daughter who would have been horrified and distraught to see the violence inflicted on her father. Barry rubbed his eyes with his hankie-free hand.

'By dose is broked.'

Understatement of the year, Mel thought, glad that there were no mirrors about. 'Mmmm . . . you'll need it seeing to in hospital.' She tried to sound breezy. 'Do you want another tissue?'

'Doh thags. I've lost this electiod. Leo dows I've lost it. So do I.'

'You can't tell. It's very close, I've heard. Here, you've got blood all over your hand.'

Barry shook his head. 'It's over,' he said. 'Ad Leo's a fuckig bastard.' Before Mel could ask him anything else, especially on the fascinating topic of why he had fallen out with Leo, she heard the sound of a police walkie-talkie. She reached for Barry's hand and squeezed it — something which until half an hour ago she would have contemplated with the same enthusiasm as a gazelle facing a crocodile-infested river.

'At least with be you dow where you stad,' Barry replied. 'You're right there.'

Which is precisely why you're not going to be General Secretary, Mel thought as three police officers emerged through the swing doors.

under the lime tree

'You tell that story as if it were funny but it must have been absolutely terrifying.'
Lily was still half laughing, holding her hand to her mouth.

They were sitting in Lily's small back garden and drinking Kir Royales
while Daniel kicked a football about. Mel had brought a bottle of Cava and
Lily had produced cassis to mix it with. It was a perfect evening for the
drink, the day had been hot without humidity, there were no clouds in the
sky. Lily had brought a rocking chair into the garden, with an old blanket
draped over the back. She was wearing a yellow-striped thin-strapped vest,
her hair tumbled around her shoulders, she had scrunched up her skirt
to rest her bare legs on another chair to catch what remained of the
sun. On her feet were simple leather sandals. As usual, she produced a
pleasing impression, a sensation of unstrived-for coolness, and Mel felt
uncomfortable and sweaty in her white shirt and long black work skirt.

'I can't believe you were actually being chased down some stairs. I'm
sure I would have just given up.'

'I've always thought that I didn't have much of a survival instinct –'
Mel tried vainly to imagine Lily hurtling down a flight of stairs with
Boksic in pursuit – 'but I definitely did. He would have had to knock
me unconscious.'

'It sounds as if that was exactly what he was about to do.' Lily refilled their glasses and they clinked them together. 'To your survival . . . anyway, they've got the man?'

'Oh yes. They've put him back on his medication, tucked him into his strait-jacket.'

'And your boss?' Lily giggled again.

'Totally back to normal apart from his nose, which might never recover its earlier aquiline grace. He sent off loads of furious memos about office security. We've all got to go on a security-awareness training afternoon. It's become a bit of an obsession with him now. Women can't work alone etc. etc.'

'Well it is dangerous,' Lily said. 'You're vulnerable if there's an intruder.'

'He might not be around for too much longer. He was right about losing the election.'

The result had been announced one afternoon to the general jubilation of a tense office. Mark Thompson had defeated his arch-opponent by a small margin – a result which the newspapers claimed would send shock waves to the heart of a government which had made no secret about its preferred outcome. It was as if Mark Thompson had been impudent to stand and even more outrageous to win, as if he were only standing in the election to annoy the government. The irritation did not seem to stem from any real fear of what Mark Thompson might do, just from the fact that he was called Mark Thompson and not Barry Williams. The government had wanted Barry Williams and that should have been enough to secure his election. GOVERNMENT FURY AS LEADING UNION MODERNISER NARROWLY DEFEATED, ran one headline, as if it were perfectly legitimate for the government to be furious rather than disappointed with the decision of an electorate. One eager-to-impress MP went too far by referring to the vote as a sign of the union's immaturity, something which he would later have to grumpily retract.

On the night of the victory, Mel, Mary and Graham had gone to join the others in a celebratory drink in a pub near to Head Office.

'What's he doing here?' Graham had hissed to Mel as Leo Young appeared with a tray of drinks and an expression of benign satisfaction on his face. 'What will it take to get rid of that guy?'

'A stake through the heart,' Mel said. 'What are you drinking, Graham?'

Graham frowned. 'The beer in this pub is horrible.'

'Oh, not this bloody performance again. You're not with your Communists for Real Ale mates now. I'll have a Drambuie please, Mel. Let him get his own,' Mary snapped.

When Mel went to congratulate Mark he displayed an obvious reserve towards her. He was not unfriendly or unpleasant but it was as if he would prefer her to be on the other side of the pub. Mel did not really mind this – she suspected that it was wounded pride, and that he had obviously hoped that if anybody was going to do the brushing off it would be him. He was chatting up Stephanie from the research department. Mel usually tried not to speak to Stephanie as she was quite mad and had exclaimed shrilly, 'But what's wrong with privatisation? We're in favour of that now actually, Mel!' when Mel had explained about the MGL case. Stephanie had spent too much time in the National Organisation of Labour Students – it showed in her poor dress-sense, in the way that she got embarrassingly drunk at public events and in the fact that she saw nothing abnormal about sticking hundreds of pictures of the Prime Minister on the wall of her office. She liked shouting, 'Oh, grow up!' or, 'Don't be so childish!' if anybody disagreed with her. Mel wondered whether Stephanie would get a nocturnal invitation to the General Secretary's office or whether Mark would find it less of a buzz now that the office was to be his.

'And how does this affect your industrial tribunal?' Lily turned her face upwards to catch the sun, closing her eyes almost ecstatically.

'Well, it shouldn't really. Although it might take the pressure off me a bit. There was something I was going to ask you actually . . .'

Mel hesitated. Brenda Fletcher had asked her if she would pass a letter to Lily. Mel had said that she would have to ask Lily first.

'No, I don't mind.' Lily rolled her head towards Mel, shading her eyes with her hand. 'I saw her at the inquest anyway. Not quite what I had imagined. You're right. It's the companies who should take responsibility. That's what Gordon would have said as well. At least soon we'll have the rail company in court. That's the big one. With the hospital, they've admitted liability, it's just a question of establishing compensation. But I'll go to court with them as well. Lawyers and journalists – that's all I seem to deal with at the moment.'

A greenfinch flitted over their heads, skeering in the spring air. It landed on the delicate branch of a larch at the bottom of the garden. The branch swayed but the bird clung on bravely like a tight-rope walker. They both looked at it for an instant as if expecting it to fall.

'Paul's OK though,' Mel said as the bird took flight again.

'I thought you didn't like him.'

'I do. He irritates me sometimes.'

'Yes, he can be irritating. I like him though. He gets quite passionate about things. That's a good quality. Even his Frank Sinatra thing is quite appealing because it's genuine. He really likes birds as well.'

'Yes, I've noticed,' Mel said, raising an eyebrow.

Lily giggled. 'I meant the feathered type.'

'I know,' Mel said. She had met Paul for a coffee and he had talked to her about birds. She had enjoyed the way he had passed on information, tiny pleasing facts about robins being the only birds to have a winter song, male linnets having red foreheads in summer, the acrobatic flight of the swallow. It was like listening to Graham talk about the Battle of Stalingrad, how the Germans were terrified of dogs trained to run under tanks with mines strapped under their bellies. It wasn't just that these men wanted a captive audience, they actively enjoyed their story-telling, they wanted to share the fascinating information they had accumulated. Some people found this irritating but Mel thought that it was endearing. As Graham had told her about the dog-bombs, he had drawn a little picture of a tank with a swastika on it, a few trees where the Red Army might be hiding and an arrow pointing out where the dog would have to run. And Mel had nodded as if she had not understood the concept without this important piece of graphic assistance.

Mel lit a cigarette and told Lily about what had happened with Jim, the way in which the smell had lured him into doing something that had brought him disastrous consequences. Sadly, Jim's lapse had been followed by others. He had not been in touch for a while and nor had he returned their calls. Mel worried about Jim and also about Patrick, who was sulky and morose without his playmate. She found half-finished letters to the Penalty Fares Appeals Office and to the bank – it was clear that Patrick's heart was no longer in it. Mel had an image of Jim being carried away by a strong current; he had stopped struggling, his head bouncing in the foam. She felt as if she should rush downstream and hold out a branch for him but was not even sure if he would see her on the bank. One night, out of the blue, she had been battered by memories of him: the trips to the supermarket to buy fruit and ice cream, their attempts to make such a perfect Virgin Mary that it would not matter that it contained no vodka, watching him with his tools putting up shelves, handling drill and spirit-level with the self-assured grin of somebody competent and fluent in what they do – like Patrick with his guitar, like Pepa chattering in Spanish on the phone. And as she had thought of Jim, her eyes brimming with tears, she had been filled with pain and pity – the kind of pity that would probably now make him snarl with dismissive contempt.

'My brother's a bit like that,' Lily observed. 'He's lucky though because he doesn't have a conscience. Or self-doubt.'

'Your brother?' Mel was surprised. She realised – rather to her shame – that she didn't ask many questions about Lily. It was as if when Mel were not there, Lily was alone, she only came to life when Mel appeared, in spite of the very real small child who watched Mel as his ball rolled to her feet, waiting for her to pass it back to him.

'He lives in Paris. He wants me to go and stay with him, forget all this stuff about lawyers and court cases.'

'Ah,' Mel said, trying to sound neutral.

'Anyway, he was quite wild. Still is in his own way. He took a lot of drugs, always had thousands of girlfriends, never settled down anywhere. He had jobs in LA, Japan, Indonesia. He's rich now.'

'He should be in a film,' Mel said. 'Handsome and unpredictable.'

'He thinks he is in a film,' Lily said. 'The itinerant rogue. Sadly, he regularly has his ego boosted by women with poor judgement. We argue a lot actually. Last time we met I told him that he was a callous, superficial little snob.'

'It's a shame how one always has to pull punches with siblings,' Mel said.

'Well, he had just described me as a self-absorbed freak married to a suburban nerd. He could be very contemptuous of Gordon, he was terrible to him sometimes . . . Darling, don't bounce the ball against the window . . . No, bring it back over here . . . that's right.'

'Why?'

'Oh, because he used all the wrong indicators to judge him. Gordon didn't take drugs, had no interest in having sex with sixteen-year-old Indonesian girls – well, as far as I know. He certainly neither knew nor cared about fashion although he had his own style. Laurence thought that made him boring when, in fact, he was anything but that. He was far more creative and imaginative with his life than Laurence with his drearily predictable vices.'

'Didn't Gordon get angry?'

Lily laughed. 'He didn't care at all. He knew that he was far cleverer than Laurence. Benign indifference. That made Laurence even angrier, even more provocative because Gordon did not bother to conceal that he just wasn't interested in the things that Laurence takes so seriously. The only thing that hurt Gordon was when Laurence laughed at his name because he was rather sensitive about that. Laurence always put on a nasal, suburban twang when he said it. You know, like a Mike Leigh character. "Hello, Gaw-dern." But even that didn't bother him so much – he had other things, things Laurence would never have.'

Perhaps this was the elusive factor which Paul Flitcroft had tried to identify about Lily. She seemed to construct her life around a different set of principles, a different aesthetic from most people. Mel imagined that she and Gordon must have made a powerful combination in this respect, easily arousing hostility and jealousy. They had not led a self-satisfied or a lazy life – it was as if they had seen themselves as engaged in a complex project which involved care and judgement, subtle touches. Walking together in the cool of Venetian churches, listening to the haunting song of a dying girl, hurling abuse at post-modernist charlatans – it was certainly a different strategy from most, a more elegant strategy than crack-cocaine or Indonesian teenage prostitutes, but a strategy nonetheless. And how had it ended? In twisted metal, in a stupid mix-up over bags of blood, a young woman in a side-room watched by a young doctor helpless to ease her pain. Whose voice is that singing in the distance? Is it the Duke?

Que donneriez-vous belle, pour avoir votre mari?

'It sounds as if he was jealous,' Mel said, holding out her glass to receive more wine.

'Perhaps. I've made him sound horrible. He can be funny and charming and generous as well. He gives good presents, which I always think is an important test of character. And he was very upset by Gordon's death.

Underneath it all, he loved him. It was hard to dislike Gordon. He was a kind and funny person . . .'

Mel knew instinctively that Lily suddenly wanted to talk about Gordon so she just nodded and allowed her to continue.

'It's such a shame you couldn't have met him. He would have liked you.'

Mel flushed. 'How do you know?'

'Well, for one, although he might not have gone for Indonesian prostitutes he would certainly have flirted with you. He was a terrible flirt. Shameless. He flirted with women at check-out desks, with waitresses, with all his friends. He liked making them laugh. He just found women irresistible.'

'That must have annoyed you sometimes though?'

Lily shrugged. 'As long as he found me the most irresistible I didn't really mind. Actually, I find jealousy very off-putting, almost vulgar. It shows low self-esteem.'

'I see.' Mel contemplated teasing Lily for this rather pompous last statement but decided not to.

'God, what a ridiculous thing to say.' Lily laughed suddenly. 'But I do kind of believe it. You lose all your freedom when you're jealous.'

'Hey, move over Simone de Beauvoir.' Mel did tease her now.

'Well, everyone laughs at existentialism but at least they made an effort to address an issue. I think it's sad to hear people ridiculing something that was quite brave and experimental. What have we got to be so proud about? Where is our avant-garde?'

Mel said, 'Where is our Camelot? Where is our avant-garde?'

'Ask where our self-serving elites are. That's an easier question to answer. Anyway, he would also have liked what you do. He would have been fascinated by the fact that you are a trade unionist. I think he rather despised his armchair involvement with politics. His dad always teased him about that. "Well, you shout about changing the system but what do you actually do about it?" God, he was so pompous. *Is* so pompous. You know what he did at the funeral? I had made brie and avocado sandwiches and he lifted the top from one and sneered and said to one of the relatives, "Careful you don't choke on a frog's leg." Ignorant petty-bourgeois pig. He would probably have preferred Spam.'

Mel tried not to laugh at Lily's haute-bourgeois contempt for her father-in-law. 'Who would have thought that brie and avocado sandwiches would cause tension at a funeral?' she murmured.

'I'm surprised he didn't make us all go for a drive afterwards,' Lily muttered. 'And that's the local paper-clip factory, and over there is the museum of steam, if you went down that road there you'd come to the golf club, come on, come on, I'm letting you pull out – bloody women drivers, oh you can't need the toilet again, you've only just been.' She mimicked him with brutal dislike.

'Mummy, can I have a drink?' Daniel rocked the arm of the chair.

'Of course you can, sweetheart. What would you like?'

'Ribena.'

'Come on then, let's go and get it. Excuse me for a moment, Mel . . .'

As Lily guided her child into the kitchen, the boy turned and rather disarmingly waved goodbye to Mel, so Lily laughed and did the same. Suddenly Mel felt as if her heart were performing pirouettes; she could stay in this garden for ever, drinking Kir Royales, talking to Lily, watching the hot day slide away. And suddenly she felt the tragedy of Gordon Forrester's death so acutely it almost took her breath away – he might have been sitting here now watching his son play but the boy would never see his father again, would only have the dimmest memories of him. Small wonder that Lily felt that somebody should be held to account for this outrageous inversion of justice. Why should Robert Hislop be laughing and opening the picnic hamper, distributing champagne to his guests? Perhaps one of the party was a man who had made millions out of the acquisition of Fastline Trains? *Oh, I'm not worried about the court case. They've never been able to make charges of corporate manslaughter stick. Wonderful picnic, Robert.* Gordon Forrester would have seen the irony, she was sure of that, and he might have lamented the fact that his only recourse was to write articles in journals read by a few thousand academics and post-graduate students of public administration. If he had envied Mel – as Lily had suggested – then it would have been a misplaced envy because she sure as hell couldn't do much more about it.

'What are you dreaming about now?' Lily had returned with another bottle of wine. Daniel followed her, clutching a large glass of Ribena.

'Oh, nothing. I was just getting the sun on my face.'

'I thought you might like to read this before we go to *La Traviata*.' Lily handed her a slim paperback. It was *On the Eve* by Ivan Turgenev.

'What does it have to do with the opera?'

'Wait and see.'

'I've never read anything by him,' Mel murmured.

'Well, you must read this. You'll see why . . . oh, it's so sad.' And Lily's eyes suddenly filled with tears.

'Are you OK?' Mel asked anxiously.

'I'm fine.' She brushed a tear away and smiled. 'Sad things are good for the soul. They're not depressing.'

'You're right,' Mel said. 'TV depresses me. *Countdown*, *Catchphrase*, Australian soaps, cookery competitions, snooker; any programme involving cars, Brits on holiday or the paranormal. My boyfriend watches TV all the time. Sometimes I just want to throw it out of the window.'

Lily arched an eyebrow. 'Ah yes, your boyfriend. How come you never talk about him? I was beginning to wonder whether he existed.'

Mel told her a little about Patrick, about his days of hedonistic abandon, about the illness and about the treatment. There was more that she wanted to say but she could not bring herself to do so — it felt disloyal and inappropriate.

'He sounds funny,' Lily said.

'Funny ha-ha or funny peculiar?'

'A bit of both I guess.'

'I suppose he is.'

Daniel arrived at Mel's side with the picture he had been drawing. He proffered it shyly.

'That's lovely,' Mel said. 'Who's that?' She pointed to a figure with long dark hair.

'That's you.'

'Right,' said Mel. 'So this one with the curly hair is your mum?'

The child nodded. He was a solemn, quite imaginative boy who played intensely, could amuse himself alone for hours. Mel would sometimes hear him muttering to his toys, constructing stories, disappearing into his own private narratives, his small invented worlds.

'And this is?' Mel pointed to a smiling winged figure hovering above the two principal characters, who appeared to be sprinkling something on to them.

'That's my daddy,' said Daniel simply.

'Oh.' Mel glanced at Lily. 'And what's he dropping on us?'

'Wine,' Daniel said. 'He's giving you wine because he knows you like it.'

And Lily put her head back and looked up at the sky as if she really might see her husband there, a benign angel making it rain wine on to a small garden in North London.

Patrick was lying on his stomach watching TV when Mel got in.

'Can you believe that somebody would go on a cookery programme and take a jar of Chicken Tonight sauce as one of their ingredients?' he said, shaking his head in disbelief.

'No,' Mel said but then she laughed. She sat on the edge of the bed with him and ruffled his hair. He rolled over on to his back and held out his arms, allowing her to fall on top of him. They lay with their faces pressed together, watching news footage of a laser-guided bomb hitting its target and sending an oily black stain across the screen.

Patrick snorted with disgust. 'You know that they say that they can't afford to give most men Viagra on the NHS? Well that little show, that one bomb represents millions of Viagra exploding. Makes you fink dunnit?'

Viagra not Bombs! Mel thought of a new sticker for Graham's case.

'The worst thing is that people will have forgotten all about this in six months' time. Where have you been anyway?'

'Lily's.'

'Ah, the mysterious Lily.'

'Why do you say that?'

'Well, we never meet her. I'm beginning to think you're like one of those kids that talks to imaginary mates or has a dog that they only see when they close their eyes.'

'Don't be so stupid. You sound like Pepa.'

'Do I? Well, maybe Pepa has a point.'

'And what point would that be?' Mel regarded him coldly.

He stared at her for a moment and then shook his head. 'It doesn't matter. You're the clever one, aren't you. I must be wrong.'

'Oh, I haven't got time for this.'

Yet when she looked at him she saw not anger but sorrow in his eyes. She was about to say something conciliatory when the doorbell rang.

It was Jim.

Or somebody who looked exactly like Jim.

'I've got to borrow some cash,' he said, slumping into the sofa.

'You can fuck off,' Patrick said.

'It's OK.' Mel shook her head at him. 'How much do you want?'

'Two hundred. I'll give it back.' He turned to Patrick. 'What the fuck are you looking at me like that for?'

'Do you want a mirror?' Patrick sneered. 'Or is that a bad question?'

'Are you all right?' Mel asked him. *What have you done to yourself? Why do you do this to yourself?*

'Of course I'm all right. Are *you* all right? Haven't died of boredom with each other yet?'

'No. But we might if you hang around much longer,' Patrick said.

'How's your sex life then?' Jim grinned at Patrick who blushed and shot an anguished look at Mel.

'That wasn't fair,' Mel said.

'I didn't say . . .' Patrick started.

'I'm not talking to you, Patrick. Whatever you said was private. You have the right to talk to your friend and expect him to keep your confidence.' She stared at Jim whose blue eyes flickered helplessly. But he only seemed to have renewed aggression as an option.

'Fair? Fair? Who gives a fuck about fair?'

'I do actually.'

'You're always looking down on people, aren't you, Mel? Even when you make out you're being nice you're just feeling superior to them. It must make you feel good in yourself to see me like this.'

Mel stared at him. 'Like what? I thought you were fine. And if you think that, then you're even more pathetic than the weak-willed, self-pitying junky you've proved yourself to be up until now.'

'Yeah, let it all out,' Jim said.

'I will. The worst thing about it is that you know you're in trouble and what you really want, right now, is for us to be down there with you, down at your level. Which doesn't make you a very good friend.'

'Bollocks,' said Jim.

'Is that the best you can come up with then? Bollocks. I take it all back then.'

'Are you going to give me the money or not?'

'I don't have two hundred quid spare actually. I could get you fifty,' Mel said. Her tone was cold, contemptuous.

'Don't give him anything,' Patrick said.

'Don't worry, I don't want anything from you anyway. Some fucking mates you are.' And he got up and walked out of the front door, slamming it angrily behind him.

They sat deflated and depressed in the living room. Neither wanted to talk about what had just happened, there was nothing really to say.

Later that evening the phone rang. It was Jim, jabbering incoherently about the misunderstanding and how important they were to him and how he did not want there to be any bad feeling between them. He had clearly got hold of the money from somewhere. Mel listened to a stream of over-emotional, self-justifying drug-nonsense for about thirty seconds and then just dropped the phone and switched off the ringer.

She sat on the sofa and started reading from the book Lily had given her – two young friends on a hot day under the lime tree, talking about love and beauty and happiness.

A living soul, that will respond to you – above all a woman's soul. And so, my dear sir, I recommend you to get yourself a soulmate, then all your melancholy will vanish.

Mel read these lines and rolled her head back and stared at the ceiling. She let the book slip from her hand. A soulmate. Wasn't that ultimately what everybody wanted? She remembered Lily's words about the existentialists and a photo of an old woman staring into the grave of a man she had known for almost all of her life, a man with whom she had travelled across continents, with whom she had shared the great events of the twentieth century. It had ended there at the grave-side as if the old woman was gazing at her own death, at the death of memory and dreams, at the cruellest nothingness. Even if you had a soulmate there was always the speeding train, the tired pathology worker, the everyday treachery of the body. There were nail-bombers, pipe-bombers, Stealth bombers. There were fragments of love-letters, intimate pages from teenage diaries blowing around the remains of bombed-out hospitals. And Mel shivered, she suddenly felt bewildered and insignificant and utterly alone. The feeling was so uncomfortable, so troubling that she picked up her book again. As she read, as her eyes moved up and down, she slowly felt her anxiety subsiding, she felt the calming power of the text, a young English woman turning the pages of a work by an author whose remains lay thousands of miles away beneath the Russian soil, buried deeper than the roots of the lime tree by the side of the Moscow river.

puffin chutney

Dear Miss Holloway,

You might ask why MGL have not released the results of 2,000 trials on their new hepatitis drug. Could it be that they do not want this information released until the time is right?

It might be worth your while to investigate this matter. I shall be contacting you shortly with some more concrete information.

Yours sincerely,

A Wellwisher

'Interesting,' said Paul Flitcroft when she called him to tell him about the latest letter. 'I've been sniffing about and there is definitely paranoia about this drug. They're not releasing all their data at the moment and they're not being very convincing about the reason for that. Especially when all their propaganda is suggesting that this is a miracle drug. Some hard evidence about what's going on would be good.'

He sounded tired and depressed, there were no new words, no chortling about puffins or chutney.

'Trampoline, giddy, rotund,' Mel said to cheer him up but he did not respond.

'What's up?' she asked.

'Oh nothing. It's just this newspaper gets me down sometimes. It makes out it's all liberal and everything but I've been given a subtle warning to tone some of my stuff down. Apparently, somebody high up is getting upset and putting the normal pressure on about not giving us access to information.'

'Which is just another type of censorship.'

'Yup. Do you know the name of the ruling party in Mexico?'

'Nope.'

'It's the Institutional Revolutionary Party. Fantastic name. Anyway, they control everything through the party machine. That's what this government is trying to do. You will only choose from these candidates, you will only publish this information, we don't want factionalism so we'll have no debate at all.'

'Oh dear, you're not a happy bunny are you?' Mel said, lighting a cigarette.

'I'm not. At least it sounds like Leo Young was a bit more cunning in the case of Mark Thompson.'

'What are you talking about?'

'Well, the hot rumour is that Leo Young realised that Mark Thompson was a far more attractive package than Barry Williams. There was a big debate because some diehards would try and sell Hannibal Lecter to the electorate if they thought it was what Number Ten wanted. They saw it as a climb-down.'

'Saw what as a climb-down?'

'Leo Young allowing Mark Thompson to win a knife-edge contest right at the death in return for certain assurances. It wouldn't take that many votes to tilt the balance.'

'Do you think that's really true?' Mel remembered Leo with his tray of drinks in the pub. She had assumed that it was just his desire to stay on at least amicable terms with Mark.

'I don't know. But there was an article in the paper on Sunday where Mark Thompson praised the government for its legislation on union recognition and stated his desire to create genuine partnerships with the private sector.'

'Well, the union recognition stuff *is* a massive improvement. I would say that as well. It's hardly proof of some shady deal.'

'Funny timing though.'

'Not really. He's just become General Secretary. He's obviously going to say something like that. Especially with all the bad press he's had. He's no raving lefty and has never pretended to be. You know that just having an independent mind is threat enough for this lot.'

'Well, we'll see. It's a pretty strong rumour. And you know, of course, who'll be spreading that rumour – true or not. Who always wants to appear as if he's in control? Who sees himself as the power behind the throne?'

'He might be the power behind the throne with or without a deal . . .'

Mel remembered Barry Williams weeping and nursing his broken nose, the sleeping black cats on his socks. She remembered Mark Thompson opening Mould's drinks cabinet with all the confidence of the heir-apparent. She remembered Leo Young dabbing his prissy mouth with his napkin and announcing his ability to work with Mark Thompson. If it were true, Mel was not particularly shocked. You didn't become General Secretary of a major trade union without certain manipulative skills or the ability to make compromises and concessions. Mark would have to come to terms with the powerful forces that Leo Young represented one way or another and writing a few articles saying that the architect of the new union legislation should receive a Nobel Prize was harmless enough. She was a little surprised, however, at Leo's willingness to dump his protégé. She would have imagined that he might have been one of those diehards who would see it as vitally important to impose their political will regardless of the popularity or charisma of their preferred candidate. In fact, Hannibal Lecter had far too much personality to be the favoured type of the New Outlook modernisers. The more dreary, boring or just plain stupid they were, the more they seemed to fit the bill. Perhaps the simple truth was that Leo had known that Barry Williams was going to lose with or without his intervention.

'Don't forget about Sunday,' Paul reminded her.

'Oh yes. Miranda's cottage.'

'Cottage?' Paul snorted. 'Wait until you see it. Anyway, you're taking Lily in the car and you'll bring me back?'

'Yes. What about Miranda?'

'She's staying down there for a few days. Perhaps she's having an affair with the gamekeeper or the gardener. Perhaps both. I like to think so anyway.'

'I bet you do. I'll see you on Sunday.'

'Cricketers' names,' Paul said suddenly. 'Heath Streak, Nixon McLean, Herschelle Gibbs, Curtly Ambrose.'

He was obviously cheering up a little.

'I don't like cricket,' Mel said, 'but they're great names.'

And she remembered the fat consultant in the bow tie asking her about the topic on the day that she met Paul Flitcroft, on the day that she had driven Lily Forrester through the rainy streets to her home.

'Cricket's the new football,' Flitcroft said. 'Football's just for kids and wannabes now. But you can learn to love cricket. I may have to take your education in hand.'

'Better still, write a book about it,' Mel said. 'You never know, it might just make you a millionaire.'

'Hey, I was in Norfolk over the weekend and guess what bird I saw?' Paul was back to normal again.

'A sparrow?' Mel said.

He laughed. 'No. A golden oriole. They're very rare and it's still quite early for them.'

'I'm very pleased for you,' Mel said. 'Did you put its number in your special notebook?'

'No, I killed it and stuck it on my wall.'

It was Mel's turn to laugh.

After the phone call, she sat organising her papers for Brenda's tribunal. The case she was putting together was thorough and impressive. Apart from Brenda and Yolanda's witness statements she was calling expert witnesses who would give their opinion of procedure in the Great Northern pathology lab. MGL were having problems responding to her requests for documentation on their training procedure. They were probably in the process of writing it up. Mel felt happy organising her papers, checking and double-checking her witness statements; she felt the contentment of work, she felt balanced. She expected to win and, at the very least, get the building society off Brenda's back with a decent settlement.

'Don't work too hard.' Mary popped her head around the door as she left the office. 'Here.' She passed Mel a KitKat Chunky. 'Now that they've got these I know I'll never ever lose weight.'

'You don't need to,' Mel said. 'Actually, I think I'll come down with you.'

When she returned home, she opened the door to the sound of familiar voices in the living room.

'It's a bloody marriage of convenience,' Jim was shouting at the TV.

'How could you marry somebody who showed her tits to Chris Tarrant anyway?'

'Get back to the Marines you wimp!'

Patrick was drinking a bottle of beer. Jim was drinking a Diet Coke. They both looked up when Mel appeared. Guilt and worry flashed across their faces.

'Hi, Mel,' Jim said quietly. Mel wanted to laugh out loud at their nervousness.

'We did the washing-up,' Patrick said. 'I was going to put the washing on but I thought that I might make a mistake with the settings or the colours so it wasn't worth it.'

'Very wise,' Mel said and stalked into the kitchen determined to make them sweat. She began to bang a few cupboard doors in order to ratchet up their anxiety.

'Are you OK, Mel?' Patrick called.

'Yeah. Why shouldn't I be?'

'Don't worry about the beer. I'm only having the one.'

'It's true,' Jim shouted. 'He's only had the one.'

'Is there one left for me?'

'Yes, of course. There were four. And I had one so there should be three left.'

Mel opened the fridge door.

'Oh, for God's sake!' she roared. They both came scampering like frightened rabbits.

Mel smiled and held up a brown, soggy iceberg lettuce. 'I meant to throw this away this morning,' she said. Patrick gave her a reproachful look and returned to the TV. Jim paused in the doorway.

'Listen, Mel, I'm really sorry about the other night,' he said. 'You probably weren't expecting to see me again and if you want me to go I will. I've been back to my counsellor and we've been through it all and I'm really back on top of things.'

Mel decided that enough was enough. She put her arms around him.

'Don't be stupid, I'm really glad that you're here. And if you need to stay for a bit then that's fine. But don't ever say that I like seeing you in that condition.'

'It doesn't matter anyway,' Jim said. 'You'll never see me like that again. I've fucked up. I don't know why all that stuff comes out when I'm like that. It scares me as well. Like, maybe that is the real me?'

'I don't know if there's such a thing as the real anybody,' Mel said.

'I sit there sweating and talking bollocks and boring people and I can't stop.'

'Which makes you just like everybody else who's consumed large quantities of drugs.'

'But I hate it so much afterwards. I can hear and see myself and I'm just wincing. And I think about how if I were somebody else listening to me I would just think, What a complete wanker.'

'If you truly were like that then why would you be striving for something different, why would you prefer the other version?'

'But if I can't be that other version . . .'

'You can. You'll learn from what has just happened. You've just said that I'll never see you like that again.'

'I hope not. Just one thing . . . Why do you think I attack you so much when I'm in that state?'

Mel was uncomfortable. He held her gaze. His eyes were very blue, unblinking.

'I don't know,' she said, looking at the floor.

'Think about it.' He turned away now.

She shook her head. 'Some things are better . . . better just left, aren't they?'

She wanted to say, Keep it for your counsellor, but knew that that would sound cruel and she did not mean it that way. Jim frowned for a moment. He might have said something else, but she willed him not to, she did not want unanswerable words spilling out, words she would be forced to give answer to.

'Maybe you're right,' he said and took a coin from his pocket and balanced it on the shelf he had put up a few months ago. He smiled as it stood motionless. 'That's a fucking good job I did there, even if I do say so myself.'

'And if your shelves can be straight . . .' Mel grinned at him.

'. . . there's hope for me yet. Jesus Christ was a carpenter you know.'

'Yeah, and look what happened to him,' Patrick said, coming up behind Mel and putting his hands on her shoulders. 'By the way, Jim, I hate to tell you this but counselling is not broadly different from any drug that makes you talk about yourself incessantly. Me, me, me. I, I, I. Me, I, me, I.'

'You're right,' Jim grinned. 'One of the things I've always admired about you, Patrick, is that you manage to do it without any kind of external stimulus.'

They ordered a Chinese and settled in front of the TV eating sesame prawn toast, scallops with Chinese mushrooms and baby sweetcorn, chicken with cashew nuts and yellow bean sauce. The government announced a reconstruction programme for the area it had just helped to bomb to smithereens. Somebody, somewhere was rubbing their hands and thinking of their signature on a dotted line. Somebody, somewhere was still grieving for a dead lover, relative or friend. And the spotlight would move off this place, leaving behind the shattered lives, seeking new arenas, a giant sparkling lottery finger – *it could be you* – circling the globe like a grotesque Puck, arriving in a blaze of fury from the dark night sky.

'Too fucking depressing,' Patrick muttered, switching channels.

Mel looked about her flat, at the books and records, at the poster of *Scarface* on the wall, at all the little things that made this her home, at the coffee mugs, at the telephone, at the papers on her desk, Patrick's huge record collection. She glanced at Patrick and Jim eating Chinese takeaway and laughing now at the television, imitating Jeremy Paxman on *Newsnight*. It was stable, it was reassuring, it was unbearably fragile, disturbing her like handwritten dates in old books or black-and-white photographs of long-ago holidays. She thought about her grandfather as a young man walking through the smouldering East End and bending down in wonder and horror to gaze at an eye as soft and squidgy and sightless as one of the Chinese mushrooms left on her plate. Mel sighed, put her head back and thought about Lily, her face turned ecstatically to the sun, the way she had rolled her head on to her shoulder and shaded her eyes with her hand when she was talking to her. She would have come in from the garden now, she would have bathed Daniel, sung to him, perhaps made some phone calls about the court case. She might be sitting drinking a whisky, feet tucked under her on the sofa, while outside the fox stood alone in the garden, one paw raised in the darkness, looking in through the glass door with emerald-gleaming eyes.

the orchard

Lily's son would not, after all, accompany them to the country. Gordon Forrester's parents were visiting London and had decided to take Daniel to the aquarium. Lily had not been happy about this but when Gordon's dad had told him that he might see sharks and rays at the aquarium, the matter was settled.

'Oh, stop moaning,' Mel had said to Lily on the phone. 'It's not such a big deal. They just want to take their grandson out.'

She was happy and energetic, felt fresh and comfortable in her rose-patterned skirt that reminded her of the sleeping bag she had slept in on family holidays, white sleeveless shirt and leather flip-flops, her washed-that-morning hair pulled back with a red hair scrunch. She had got up early, painted her nails, made fresh coffee, bought and read the paper, watched the sun begin to warm the day, silently applauded the bright, blue cloudless sky.

'Wait until you meet him,' Lily had said after registering a little surprise at being spoken to so briskly by Mel.

Mel had the chance to meet Bill Forrester when she arrived to pick Lily up. Mel did not find him hard to deal with. He was a powerful, cantankerous, bullying man who exaggerated these defects as if half hoping that some equally no-nonsense and strong-minded person would pull him up for them. His head was a shiny bald dome, his hands liver-spotted, a pen stuck rather self-importantly from the breast-pocket of his jacket. On the table in front of him was the *Daily Mail*.

Bill Forrester obviously found his daughter-in-law infuriating. Because he was not a very discerning man he could only see her as precious and weak. At the same time there was something obsessive, almost sexual, in the way that he would not let her be, had to keep needling, contradicting and interrupting her. His own wife, Maureen, was quiet and her dark eyes were heavy with her loss. She was a long way from everybody else. Maureen asked Mel whether she had known Gordon and when Mel replied in the negative she turned listlessly as if there were nothing left to say.

'What sort of car have you got, Mel?' Bill asked her and nodded approvingly when she told him.

'Bit greedy on the fuel though,' he said.

Mel replied that she didn't pay for most of it.

'Can't understand how anybody can get by without having a driving licence.' He looked straight at his daughter-in-law.

'I hate cars,' Lily said. 'I think they're the most boring things in the world.'

Mel wanted to put her arms around Lily, to tease her for her petulance, to murmur to her to take no notice.

'You don't mind them when somebody else is doing the driving. You don't mind Mel here being your chauffeur.'

'Well, that's good because I don't mind being the chauffeur,' Mel said cheerfully. 'So everybody's happy.'

The whole day with Lily stretched in front of her.

'Some people are more agreeable to be in a car with than others,' Lily scowled. She was beginning to behave like a teenager.

'Beggars can't be choosers,' Bill retorted with mock-affability.

Lily balled her fists. Mel wanted to giggle. Bill reminded her of some of her uncles; there seemed little point in getting worked up by him.

'Anyway, perhaps I'd better take a look at that car of yours before you head off into the countryside,' Bill beamed at her. Lily looked as if she were about to explode.

'Would you?' Mel smiled at him.

Lily stared at her. She muttered with grim disapproval as Mel followed

Bill on to the sunny street outside and leaned languidly – posing – with her forearms on the warm bonnet while he kicked the tyres. She was enjoying flirting with him a little, caught him glancing at her legs.

'Excuse me, young lady,' Bill said as he came round to open the bonnet.

After he had ascertained what she already knew, that the car was more than capable of making the trip to the wilds of Kent, they leaned on the car and chatted for a while, reluctant to leave the sunshine now they were immersed in it.

Bill said, 'She's not the only one who misses him.' Mel did not know whether he was referring to his wife or daughter-in-law. She made a vague non-committal noise.

'I wasn't always a perfect father. I know that. When he was a teenager we had some terrible fights. But I think . . .' He sighed and rubbed his eyes. 'I do think we might have been understanding each other a bit better lately.'

Mel could feel the inarticulate pain behind the words. She looked at the leather patches on the elbows of his jacket, thought how mysterious it was that she was talking to the father of a man she had never met but who had assumed such importance in her life. She felt a sudden ache of sympathy for this lonely, clumsy man who would never see his son again.

'I took him to an airshow when he was little.' Bill Forrester removed his glasses and wiped them with his sleeve. 'The Red Devils were performing. You know the Red Devils?'

Mel nodded.

'Quite amazing really. Such incredible coordination. They let out red, white and blue smoke and when they all peel apart it's quite a spectacle.'

He made a gesture with his hands to demonstrate the jets crossing paths.

'He got lost. I ran around looking for him. I was really very worried. I found him in the tent for lost children. Somebody had kindly taken him there. He was quite OK though. I was more worried than he was. Yes, I was more anxious. They'd given him toys and he was happy as Larry.'

And he told her how clever his son was, the prizes he had won at school, the fact that he had been the first from either side of the family to go to university. Then he frowned suddenly as if a cloud had unexpectedly appeared on this horizon of achievement.

'Do you know, he didn't go to any of his graduation ceremonies – he said they were a waste of time and money.'

'Well, I think they usually are,' Mel said.

'It was inconsiderate of him. His mother would have enjoyed it. So would I. We had to make sacrifices to put him through college.'

He looked up at the sky as if expecting to see jets trailing their coloured smoke coming in from all four corners, as if he were suddenly surrounded again by other fathers buying ice creams for their sons and pointing out Spitfires and Comets and Tiger Moths, as if he could push his way through again to the tent for lost children.

'Yes,' he said. 'It would have given me and his mother great pleasure. She would have liked a photograph with the gown and hat and everything. He was her pride and joy. But he wouldn't even put Dr on his cheque book.'

'Well, that's a good quality. He was obviously modest.'

'Oh no,' Bill Forrester laughed and shook his head. 'He was never modest. Chip off the old block. In fact, I think his refusal to do the things that everybody else does was just showing off.'

Mel suddenly imagined Gordon Forrester laughing and rolling his eyes in exasperation. *Oh, not this one again, Dad.*

'He and Lily loved each other very much,' Mel said and squinted sideways to see how he would respond to this.

Bill Forrester did not speak for a moment and then he looked up at the sky. 'I always wondered how those planes never crashed into each other,' he murmured.

Oh you fool, Mel thought. You poor stubborn fool. If you just opened your eyes it is right there in front of you. Why do you so wilfully make yourself bitter and unhappy? Why do you choose this graceless path? You will drive home tonight clutching your misery and contempt as tightly as the steering wheel and it is all so unnecessary. Just the smallest act of generosity rather than pride and you might begin to relax that painful grip.

Those things that had only a moment earlier seemed oddly benign, almost endearing to Mel – the patches on the elbows, the pomposity about the car, the liver-spotted hands – now seemed rather despicable;

the marks of a mean-spirited self-regard that Lily was right to hold in disdain.

'Are you nearly ready?' Mel called to Lily as she appeared at the front door clutching a bag and bending down to kiss goodbye to her son. She held him to her and Mel realised that she was scared to leave him. Bill Forrester watched the farewell with a blank face and Mel wondered whether he realised as well. He gave no sign of it, perhaps he would think it weak and girlish. It was only for the day after all. It wasn't as if they didn't have plenty of experience in bringing up children. They would take Daniel to the aquarium and show him the sharks and the rays, they would buy him ice cream, he would not end up in the tent for lost children.

'Thank God, thank God,' Lily sang, drumming her hands on the dashboard as they drove away. 'This is like Thelma and Louise. That bastard has been driving me crazy. Why were you so nice to him?'

'I guess I felt sorry for him. He seems a lonely old man.'

'He should pay more attention to his wife. Then he might not be so lonely.'

'She seemed like she was on another planet.'

'Maureen? He's always treated her like she's stupid. But she isn't, she's much cleverer than him. I like watching you drive.' She laughed out loud; she was excited, jittery, coltish. 'I'll never learn to drive just to spite him. I'll just have you for my chauffeur like the selfish, spoiled, half-foreign GIRL that I am!'

'He said he misses Gordon.'

Lily brushed her hair from her eyes and put on some shades. She was wearing a faded denim dress. Silver bangles tinkled on her slender wrist, flashed in the sun.

'I'm sure he does. Perhaps he regrets the fact that he sent him into exile for so long and missed out on seeing him in some of the best years of his life.'

'Why did he do that . . . Oh get in lane you stupid tart and stop looking at yourself in the fucking mirror!'

Lily laughed. 'My God, you're a monster behind the wheel of a car! Why did he exile him? Who knows. Some imagined insult, some perceived slight. Probably something to do with me as well. He never even tried to sort it out by telling him, which was for me the most unforgivable thing. He just fell into this protracted sulk and went about telling everybody what a bad son Gordon was. Things only got a little better just before Gordon died. It's funny because although I was really quite pleased when Bill wasn't talking to us, it upset Gordon. He hated the thought that one day he might get a phone call to say that his father was dying and he would not have seen him for all that time. But in the end it happened the other way round.'

'Well, that must cause him great anguish.'

'One would think so. But that would demand a degree of self-examination from Bill that I'm not sure he is capable of. He doesn't know the meaning of the word doubt. If he's ever questioned himself he's kept pretty quiet about the results. He's probably even angrier now, even more self-righteous, thinks Gordon was inconsiderate for dying.'

'That couldn't happen in my family,' Mel said, glancing in her mirror at the car that was tail-gating her. 'I mean, I can't imagine it. My dad's done some bad things, I've been very angry with him. But I love him. I can't imagine just pretending that he doesn't exist. Or him pretending that I don't exist.'

'Count yourself lucky. It caused Gordon a lot of pain even though he knew that his father was being a fool. He didn't like being labelled a deviant. He didn't deserve it either. We watched a programme once about a woman whose only daughter had been disappeared in Latin America. What that mother would give to see her child again! It made everything else seem so trivial, so petty. People don't know how lucky they are.'

'Yes,' Mel agreed, thinking affectionately of Pepa and her contempt for moaners and sulkers.

Lily opened a tube of sun cream and rubbed some on her arms. Mel inhaled the unmistakable odour of holidays: sandy towels, arms salted from the sea, humid hotel rooms, white sheets.

'I think he was suffering,' Mel said. 'It might be self-inflicted suffering but it was still there. Perhaps that makes it worse.'

'I guess he exhausted my patience a long time ago. I'm not the best judge.'

They swung out on to the motorway and Mel put her foot down and felt the pleasure of speed. If Jim had been watching from his balcony, he might have seen their car racing out of the city, where the motorway dipped and rose again, under the signs for Newmarket and the Blackwall Tunnel. He might have seen Lily's arm on the open window, her silver bracelets flashing in the sun. It was unlikely that Jim would be watching, however, because he had more or less moved into their flat. He and Patrick were planning a big celebration for the day Patrick finished his Interferon treatment, they wanted to light fireworks from the balcony. In the meantime, they kept up their complaints to TV companies, the bank and London Underground. They were planning to set up an agency which complained on behalf of people who didn't have the time or couldn't be bothered. It was going to be called 'Give me your name please'.

They stopped for petrol on the motorway and Mel sat in the car waiting for Lily to come out of the shop. She emerged triumphantly waving a bag of drinks and ice creams. Mel watched her and suddenly gripped the steering wheel tightly. They were playing old Abba songs on the radio and there was something about the bright, foolish lyrics, the poppy melodies on this sunny day that made Mel's heart beat even faster, made her catch her breath.

'What's your favourite Abba song?' Lily asked as she swung into the car and took the paper off an ice cream before passing it to Mel.

'None of them really. No, wait, I do quite like "Fernando". I like the chorus and I used to think it was about revolutionaries for some reason. I suppose because they go on about fighting for freedom and stars shining for liberty. What's yours?'

Lily unwrapped her own ice cream and cupped her hand under it to prevent it from dripping.

'"Take a Chance on Me". I like the background vocals. The way the woman kind of pleads. Not very right-on, I suppose. There's always something rather melancholic about Abba lyrics. Have you noticed that?'

Mel was about to tease her but when she paused to think about it she realised that it was true.

'I suppose you're right. I like trashy sentiment. For ages one of my favourite disco songs, one of my favourite songs really, was "Black is Black". Partly because of the lyrics. Wanting someone to come back so much, that terrible ache . . .'

Mel felt a sudden rush of dismay at what she had just said, which Lily noticed. She laughed and touched Mel's shoulder.

'Don't panic,' she said. 'You don't have to walk on egg-shells. I like those lyrics as well. Remember, I'm a Verdi fan. A lot of that is pure sentimentality.'

'I like songs that I can imagine playing in the background of half-empty bars,' Mel said. 'Cheap places in the middle of nowhere where somebody who has been crossed in love sits gazing into their whisky.'

'Ah, but it always looks poignant and elegant in films,' Lily said. 'In real life you just feel like you're going to throw up and you never really have a song playing behind you and you're not actually enjoying the whisky.'

At that moment, Mel felt such a desire to tell Lily that she loved her that instead she laughed out loud and shook her head.

'What's the matter?' Lily asked.

'Nothing, nothing, it's too stupid.' Mel threw her ice-cream stick from the window.

'Do you know that swallows are arriving earlier and earlier because of global warming?'

Paul Flitcroft sipped his long glass of vodka and tonic and looked up at two swallows perched on a wire high above them.

'How do you know they're swallows? Don't swifts look almost identical?' Lily asked. It was the type of question which Paul loved.

'Well, because of the angled wings, but then swifts and martins also have those wings. Swallows have longer tails – see as it flies, it's like streamers – and they have different colouring. You can't see so well from here but I'll get the binoculars out later. Swifts are black but swallows have red faces and a blue upper body.'

He looked rather comic in bright red shorts and a floppy West Indies cricket hat. Miranda handed gin and tonics to Lily and Mel. She was wearing a white dress and a straw hat which suited her role as hostess in the large elegant house with its gardens and orchard. Mel kicked off her flip-flops and wriggled her toes in the soft grass under her bare feet. She looked up at the blue Kent sky and imagined planes dog-fighting as they had done over fifty years earlier – frightened men, blazing cockpits, small children watching from the ground. When she was very young, her dad had taken her to the cinema to see *The Battle of Britain* as a birthday treat. Her mum had muttered something sarcastic, which Mel had not understood at the time, about whether he had ever noticed that Mel was a girl. She had loved it though, and had squealed in delighted horror when the goggles of one of the pilots had filled with blood.

'Any more information on MGL?' Paul turned to Mel.

Mel shook her head.

'They've put out more material on this hepatitis drug. How it's going to transform treatment. And guess what? The share price shot up again.'

Mel thought of Patrick, his desire to let off fireworks when his treatment was finished, some of the nights he had spent tormented by misery and pain.

She said that she thought that she might hear from her informant again. A Wellwisher.

'Do you have any idea who it is?' Lily asked.

Mel shook her head. 'I thought that I might. But now I'm not so sure. After all, I thought that the same person was making the obscene phone-calls and it turned out to be that madman who wanted to avenge his mother. Also, I think Neil Evans is too obsessed with the imminent world takeover by women to pay much attention to hepatitis drugs.'

'Poor guy. It is a terrifying thought if you let it get to you,' Paul said. 'Most of us just try and pretend it's not happening. Like global warming.'

'If women *did* run the world we might actually do something about global warming,' Miranda said.

'Rubbish,' said Paul affably. 'Sentimental drivel. You sound like one of those horrible postcards that say things like, "Women fly when men aren't looking." The only things women do when men aren't looking are moan incessantly about their partners and overspend on the credit card.'

Mel was glad that Patrick wasn't around to agree with Paul and outline his plan to open an institute which would dedicate itself to the study of female tantrums and sulks. He and Jim had sat around sniggering and making up degree courses – applied recrimination (with double-standards as an optional module), advanced door-slamming, strategic bath-running, as well as a Master's in *Nothing's the matter with me, what's the matter with you?* And a PhD in *Tell me honestly whether this looks OK on me.* She laughed as she remembered and looked up at the swallows on the wire, wondering if they realised that they had been fooled, whether they found the temperature change utterly confusing.

'And what do men do when women aren't looking, Paul?' Miranda asked mock-innocently. 'Or rather when they *think* women aren't looking.'

'I doubt if our guests want to hear about your sneaky and voyeuristic tendencies,' Paul said, although he looked embarrassed.

'Oh, I don't know,' Mel said and Miranda laughed her husky cigarette-laugh.

'I'm trying to make a serious point,' Paul said. 'Men aren't responsible for global warming and nuclear weapons any more than white people are responsible for slavery or non-Jews for the Holocaust. Collective guilt is nonsense. That would make the unemployed man as guilty as the Duke of Westminster.'

Lily fished the lemon from her glass and sucked on it, screwing up her face in pain-pleasure. Miranda poured her another drink.

'There are some things we tolerate as a society that we shouldn't,' Lily said. 'So I think there is some collective responsibility. I'm not interested in guilt.'

Mel looked around the garden at the great oriental poppies, pinky-white shrub-roses, peonies and irises. There was a long elegant lawn which stretched back to the orchard and she could imagine parties on mid-summer evenings, the gentle trill of conversation, laughter echoing in the summer breeze, swallows winging above, chasing each other across the sky, bats fluttering out at dusk. At the entrance to the kitchen was a herb garden with mint, rosemary, thyme, sage, basil and coriander. She imagined the luxury of being able to cut herbs as and when you wanted them. Once she had bought pots of coriander and basil from Sainsbury's and tried to grow them on the walkway to their flats with a predictable lack of success.

It was hardly a surprise, she thought, that the British country house had been used with such success to seduce radical or potentially radical politicians down the ages, these charming and privileged worlds far from the slums and the factories and impoverished constituencies – an aesthetic and political onslaught that might tempt a passionate, imaginative, weak-willed man as much as the mediocrity to the sell-out born. *Oh now you are ours, now you are ours and how charming it is to meet you, you see this isn't so disagreeable, aren't the roses lovely, my dear I simply must introduce you to Mr Ramsay MacDonald . . .*

Mel went to help Miranda bring out salmon, potato salad, plates and napkins. She liked the fact that Miranda took no refuge in self-justification or self-mockery, sought neither approval nor condemnation for her surroundings. Neither did she seek attention – there was an amused detachment about her. In contrast to Paul's volume and brashness, her humour was understated, even subdued.

'Paul's depressed,' she said to Mel. 'I'm worried about him. He says that even if you turned up some stuff on MGL there is no guarantee that the papers would do much with it . . . There's fresh mayonnaise in the fridge if you wouldn't mind just taking that through as well.'

'You're staying down here on your own?' Mel said as she opened the fridge door and reached for the mayonnaise. 'Won't you get a bit lonely? It's so big.'

'Lonely?' Miranda looked puzzled. 'I've been coming here since I was a little girl. My grandmother lived here. I know it so well I could never feel uncomfortable in it. I like doing the garden, reading, just pottering about. I've tried to persuade Paul to stay as well, at least while the weather holds, but he gets so restless.'

'It's a lovely house,' Mel said. 'It's got stairs.'

'Um . . . yes.' Miranda cocked her head. 'We find them quite useful for getting up to the bedrooms.'

Mel laughed. 'I live in a flat. I'd forgotten how nice stairs were. Having an upstairs. All this space. And I like the smell of old houses.'

Miranda smiled and poured dressing on to a salad.

'What about your boyfriend? Did he not want to come?'

'He's not so well at the moment,' Mel said. 'He more or less doesn't leave the house if he can help it.'

'What is it – depression?' Miranda asked as she cut lemons into quarters.

'Partly,' Mel replied.

'My brother also suffered from depression. Really badly,' Miranda said.

'Prospero?' Mel asked, thinking that she would also be depressed with a name like that.

'No. My younger brother. Ferdy. People used to think that he couldn't be depressed because his family was rich. They just saw it as self-indulgence.'

'Mmmm . . .' Mel picked up the plates and tried to ignore the side of her that couldn't help agreeing with Ferdy's critics.

'I think I'll leave the raspberries in the fridge for now,' Miranda said. 'Otherwise we'll just get loads of wasps. Do you think Lily's OK?'

'Yes,' Mel said, puzzled. 'She seems fine to me.'

'Good. It must be so difficult for her sometimes. Especially with all this debate about the court case.'

But she's with me, Mel wanted to say. I'm looking after her. She's OK while I'm with her.

They both looked out of the kitchen window to where Lily was sitting laughing at something Paul had just said. Above their heads, a lone swallow looped and plunged, flashing its curved wings in the warm air before a long effortless glide across the empty sky.

'No, I'm sure she's all right,' Mel said.

'She seems so fragile sometimes,' Miranda said. 'But she can be quite tough as well. I've seen her laying into one of those interviewers who suggested that she was just after revenge.'

At that point, Lily jumped up and pretended to beat Paul around the head while he fended off her blows. They were both laughing. Then Lily stood breathless, hands on hips, and Mel felt a shudder pass through her like the sweet hit of a drug.

After lunch they lay on the lawn. Mel took her book out but felt too lazy to read. Paul and Lily talked for a bit about the case against Fastline Trains and the pressure on the CPS. Then Lily said she didn't want to talk about it any longer. There was a peanut feeder hanging from a cherry tree and Lily lay on her back watching the birds through binoculars while Paul told her what they were and made vulgar jokes about watching out for a pair of great tits that reduced them both to helpless giggles. Miranda took a photo of the three of them – Mel lying on her belly, Paul with his floppy hat and Lily sitting with binoculars around her neck.

Mel smiled and drifted into a half-dream state. She remembered a long-ago time when she had been on a family holiday. Somehow she and Sarah had ended up wandering through the countryside with a group of children who had an air-rifle. The boys had shot at some cows across a river and they had all laughed as the cows appeared to jump with the impact of the pellets. Then one of the boys had aimed at a bird in a tree and had brought it down to earth. He must have only hit its wing because Mel remembered it fluttering in circles on the ground. She had been scared and almost disgusted by its sudden crippled proximity, by its crazed and impotent flapping. She tried to remember what they had finally done – even at that age, even after what they had already done, they had known they couldn't just leave the injured bird. The boys had tried to shoot it again but they were also agitated and the bird was moving too much. Finally, she knew that they had managed a brutal end to its frenzied movements. She had led a crying Sarah home by the hand – her sister had had nightmares about it afterwards.

In the late afternoon, they began to make lazy preparations for their return. They washed the plates, cleaned away the mayonnaise that had gone yellow and translucent in the hot sun, threw out a drowned wasp from the dregs of a glass of beer. Miranda gave Mel and Lily plastic bags and told them that they should fill them with apples from the orchard.

'Otherwise they just go to waste,' she said.

They wandered barefoot through the soft grass by the apple trees, turning the fruit over in their hands to check for the tell-tale holes of insect invasion. In truth, Mel was deeply suspicious of natural fruit with its bumps, tunnels and cavities, would prefer her apples to be carefully selected by supermarkets and rendered free of worms and grubs. She wasn't particularly interested in the dubious methods which had been used to make them big, bright, shiny, smooth-skinned and creepy-crawly free. It was preferable to biting into a worm, the idea of which filled her with horror.

Lily must have been thinking along similar lines because she laughed and said, 'I don't think I'll pick any more. I doubt if I'll even eat these. Look at this one. That's not just a worm, it's a fully fledged serpent.'

'Yeah, I'm not tempted by them at all.'

'Look.' Lily held out an apple to Mel. 'This one is unblemished. A gift.'

'Thank you. I'll save it for later.'

They wandered down the rows of apple trees, barely bothering to pick any more. The sky was beginning to cloud over and a breeze was shaking the leaves as if there might be a storm on the way.

'Ow . . . Christ!' Lily suddenly yelped with pain.

'What's up?' Mel said, alarmed.

Lily sank to the ground like a collapsing ballerina, holding her foot.

'Ay, that really hurts. I think I've stepped on some glass. Ow, fucking hell, that's sore.' She was half laughing, half crying.

'Let's see.'

Mel went down on to her knees and took Lily's foot in her hand, placing it on her lap. It was bleeding quite heavily.

'It hurts,' Lily wailed.

Mel tried not to laugh. 'It's just a cut,' she said.

She had nothing to staunch the flow of blood so she took the scrunch out of her hair and held it to the wound. Her hair fell forward across her face and she brushed it impatiently behind her ears, then tucked it back into her shirt. Lily watched Mel silently as she held her foot gently and dabbed at the cut with her hair scrunch.

'You've got tiny feet,' Mel murmured. Lily did not answer.

'We'll have to get you inside.' Her hands were red with blood.

'Yes,' Lily said strangely. She was pale and Mel wondered if she might faint. She held the heel of Lily's foot in her hand as if reluctant to let go of it, feeling the soft skin beneath the arch, and just for a second their eyes locked and they stared at each other, frozen for an instant beneath the apple trees.

'Hey, come on you two. What's up?' Paul Flitcroft had appeared.

Mel said, 'Lily's cut her foot.'

'I should have warned you not to come in here barefoot. There's glass about.'

'Well, we know that now. Here, Lily, you'll have to hop.'

They each gave her a shoulder and she laughed as she hopped along, supported by them.

'I'm afraid I have a very low pain threshold,' she said. 'I become an absolute baby. My dentist won't treat me without sedation.'

'That's OK,' Paul said. 'I always demand sedation. It's extremely pleasant.

'They gave it to me after Gordon died,' Lily said. 'I don't know how I would have coped without it.'

They manoeuvred Lily into the house and set her down on a chaise longue while Miranda went to look for antiseptic cream and plasters. Lily joked that Mel looked like Lady Macbeth so she went into the bathroom to clean her blood-stained hands. She looked at herself in the mirror above the sink and held her hands up. This was the blood that pumped around Lily's body, that sustained it with oxygen, that allowed her to talk and laugh and sing to her child, to go on living. This was the rapid response unit that rushed to the remotest territories of the body, the most delicate capillaries. This was what made Lily real, made her lungs fill and limbs move, a different flesh-and-blood Lily perhaps from the one, or the ones, moving in Mel's imagination.

Mel put her blood-stained fingers to her lips, touched the end of her tongue with three fingertips. And as she did so she suddenly saw Miranda behind her watching through the door which she had left open. Mel felt as if all of her own blood must be rushing to her face. Perhaps Miranda had not seen anything, however, because she simply told Mel that Paul and Lily were ready and that Lily appeared anxious to return to her son whom she had just phoned. Daniel had arrived safely back from the aquarium and was eating cheese on toast with his grandparents.

Mel glanced at Miranda while they were loading the car but she was unchanged. Mel also knew that Miranda's discretion would mean that whatever she had seen and however she had interpreted it, it would be kept to herself. In which case, there was little point in dwelling on it any longer.

'Bye-bye, darling,' Miranda said, embracing Paul as they parted. 'Phone me when you get in and remember to video that programme about Eltham Palace for me. I'll be really annoyed if you forget.'

'I won't forget,' Paul said. 'Come home soon.'

They watched her waving at the gate and then turn and enter her large, empty house with its chaise longue, its loudly ticking grandfather clock, its stairs, its garden of herbs and cherry trees and swallows.

Paul Flitcroft stretched out in the back seat and put his hands behind his head. Mel turned the radio on, flipping across stations.

'Oh, put it back there!' Lily exclaimed suddenly. 'That was *La Traviata*. The opera we're going to see.'

Mel went back to the classical station. A woman was singing. She was agitated, alarmed. Gradually this built into a passionate outpouring of song.

'So what was going on there?' Mel asked finally when the audience began to applaud at the end of the act.

'The bit at the beginning was when Violetta is about to leave Alfredo. He comes back just before she leaves and she tells him that she will always love him and he must always love her. Then she goes away.'

'Why does she leave him if she loves him?' Paul asked from the back of the car.

'To ensure another person's happiness,' Lily said. 'She makes a sacrifice. Alfredo's father – a typically meddling old man – prevails on her to leave his son because her bad reputation will jeopardise his daughter's plans to marry in respectable society. Alfredo doesn't know the reason so he insults her and calls her a whore.'

'But he finds out the truth?' Mel asked.

'Yes, but it's too late. Violetta is dying when Alfredo comes to see her. She sings of her joy, she imagines that she is returning to life and then . . .'

'Kaput,' Paul said.

'Exactly. Kaput,' Lily replied and turned to look out of the window.

They were silent for most of the journey home. Paul fell asleep in the back of the car, Lily continued to stare out of the window, chin in hand. Mel remembered her excitement when they had left London, buying ice cream at the service station as their outing was just beginning. The weather had changed and it was beginning to spit with rain; grey clouds formed a dreary ceiling over London. Things had not exactly gone sour but there was an emptiness now.

Mel was exhausted but dropped Paul in Hackney and then Lily in Crouch End. Bill Forrester opened the door as Mel was parking and Daniel ran around the back of his legs to greet his mother who swung him up into her arms and told him how much she had missed him, covered his face in kisses. Mel accepted the offer of a cup of tea and then wished she hadn't because Lily went to put Daniel to bed and she had to sit impatiently listening to Bill as he outlined the route they would be taking back to Shropshire and his conviction that bus lanes were just the first step on the road to totalitarianism. He was cheered by his conviction that the government would almost certainly back down on this issue. 'Otherwise we might just as well hand over the keys of 10 Downing Street to that Reclaim the Streets mob,' he said darkly.

Mel drank half her tea and went upstairs to say goodbye to Lily. The door was open, her son was lying in bed beneath a mobile of stripy, felt hot-air balloons and she was talking to him in a soft voice while she stroked his face.

'Sing me to sleep,' he pleaded.

'What do you want? "Alouette"?'

He shook his head in an exaggerated manner and giggled. 'No, we've had that before. Another one.'

So Lily began another song as she stroked his hair. Mel tried to distinguish the words.

Il n'était qu'un petit navire . . .

She turned away from mother and child, a lump in her throat.

Qui n'avait ja ja jamais navigué . . .

She tiptoed back down the stairs.

'Say goodbye to Lily for me,' she waved at Bill and Maureen, 'I didn't want to disturb her.'

'Oh, I'm sure she'll want to say goodbye anyway,' Maureen said. Then she gave Mel a kind, generous smile, her face transformed from its aching sorrow.

Mel was so startled that Maureen had not only smiled but offered an opinion that she almost turned to go back up the stairs.

'No, Mel's right.' Bill nodded in appreciation of Mel's original thoughtfulness. 'Let Lily put the child to bed.'

And that settled it.

Patrick and Jim were playing Frustration when Mel arrived home; she heard the familiar clicking of the plastic bubble, the rattle of the dice, and Jim cursing because Patrick had just landed on him and sent him home. They were listening to the Lauryn Hill CD that Angela had given Mel for her last birthday, joining in by clicking their fingers and emitting the odd Unh! and UhUh!

'Nah, if the dice is on its side you gotta click again. Don't matter if it is a six.'

'I think you mean the die, don't you? Dice is the plural of die and there's only one die as far as I can see . . .'

'Unh! Call it what you want, just stop cheating. Hiya, Melanoma, how was your day in the country? Worry any sheep?'

It was an old joke.

'Yeah, I told them that demand for lamb chops was booming and that they were all alone in a Godless universe.'

She bent down and kissed him. There was a vase of freesias on the mantelpiece.

'Who bought these?' she asked, sniffing them. 'They're lovely.'

'I did,' Patrick said. 'There's chicken pie in there as well.'

'Oh right, you made another one.'

'Yeah, I'm really perfecting it now. Even moany cunt here had to admit it was nice. I put mushrooms in it this time. So it's not another one, as such. It's a chicken *and mushroom* pie,' Patrick said.

'I see,' Mel said. 'Well, I'm going to have a bath before I have any chicken *and mushroom* pie.'

'Are you sure, Mel?' Jim looked up, his blue eyes glinting mischievously. 'You might want your chicken *and mushroom* pie before you have a bath. Unless you're worried about developing stomach cramps and drowning. You could armour-plate a tank with the pastry from that . . .'

He paused for a fraction of a second. '. . . chicken *and mushroom* pie,' they both chorused and began to laugh.

'You'll be getting nishman's pie, mate, if you carry on taking the piss,' Patrick said.

'Why don't you try a steak and kidney pie next time?' Jim asked him. 'Or will you just carry on with your variations on a chicken pie? Chicken *and sweetcorn* pie? Chicken *and profiteroles* pie?'

'How about chicken *and a smack in the face* pie?' Patrick said.

'Now, now boys,' Mel said, patting Patrick's head. 'Where did the flowers come from?'

'Columbia Road. We took a walk down there this morning.'

'Columbia Road? Why did you go down there?'

'To buy some flowers and laugh at the caners. It was aversion therapy for Jim. Show him the sorry state people were in and then go and have a massive breakfast, read the paper and feel smug.'

'And did you have a massive breakfast?'

'No, we got bored and bought some drugs instead.'

'Yeah, very funny,' Mel said. 'Right, I'm off for my bath.'

'Unh!' said Patrick, moving his piece.

'One time!' Jim added, watching Patrick's hand intently. 'Think again, buster, that's one, two, three, FOUR.' He moved the piece back one. 'You're not safe yet.'

a fox in the henhouse

a) Training – inadequate for cross-matching.
b) Events on night – delay in activating emergency procedures.
c) Management had had clear warnings – Yolanda Munro.
d) Expert witnesses – Professors Blake and Lovett.
e) No opportunity to put case – scapegoating.

Mel looked down at the notes that she had jotted quickly in her notebook. She was still confident that they would win Brenda Fletcher's tribunal and was going through her paperwork again to check for any unexpected pitfalls. There was little that she could check for in terms of the documentation that had arrived from MGL because it was so inadequate.

'Don't forget your meeting with Mark Thompson this afternoon.' Mary arrived with a cup of coffee and a slice of her son's birthday cake. It had been a football pitch and had green icing. 'He met Graham yesterday and they just spent the whole afternoon in the pub patting each other on the back.'

'I can imagine,' Mel said.

'Oh, and by the way, there was a rather strange message for you. Somebody who wouldn't give their name. Said that you would know what it was about . . . clinical trials at MGL. Does that ring any bells?'

'What did they say?'

'They said that they wanted to organise a lunch-date with you for next Thursday. I thought they were rather rude actually. When I said I would check with you, they said to tell you that it had to be then and that they would meet you in the café across the road.'

'If they do phone back, tell them that I said that it's OK. I doubt whether I'll come back after my meeting with Mark so just page me if there's anything important.'

'OK. I've left you six eggs in the fridge. Yours are marked MH because that idiot Maggie took the last lot that were meant for you. There's a bloody fox getting into the henhouse at the moment.' Mary clucked anxiously as if she were the mother hen.

The fox in the night – silent at the door, paw raised, glittering eyes. Swirling feathers, the henhouse shaken like a crazed snowstorm of fear amid the snapping jaws. Who would be unlucky? Mel thought about Lily's garden, about Miranda watching her at the bathroom door.

'Sit down, Mel.' Mark Thompson gestured to the leather sofa. The smile with which he did this showed that it was a piece of calculated cheekiness rather than outrageous insensitivity. Mel half smiled back and took a seat on one of the armchairs instead. Mark had placed a picture of Che Guevara on the wall where there had once been a photo of John Mould meeting Nelson Mandela. Everybody loved Che, Mel thought. He could mean anything you wanted – an ironic nod towards revolutionary chic, a self-conscious reference to a previously radical past on the part of those who had long abandoned any belief in the overall transformation of society. Che was glamour, he was eternal youth, he was the badge of incorruptibility worn sometimes by those who wished to see their transformation as something other than corruption. And yet this was also the man who would put a bullet in the heads of subordinates if they betrayed signs of intolerable weakness, who had unromantically preferred the idea of nuclear war to capitulation to the Americans during the missile crisis. It was odd that he was so popular among liberals when he had been anything but liberal himself. Perhaps it was the beret. Even the iconic photo was misleading because Che had been seething with anger when it was taken, not gazing soulfully towards some benign revolutionary sunset. Whenever Mel had read about Guevara she had always suspected that he might have been slightly mad.

'So how are you?' Mark asked.

'Yeah, I'm OK. How's your new job?'

'It's good.'

'I hear you've been praising the new legislation in the papers, making yourself popular.'

'If we don't praise it they'll tear it to pieces in the Lords.'

'Some people say that's what the government wanted all along.'

'Maybe. Maybe.'

Mark Thompson appeared agitated. He busied himself with some papers.

'I see you're booked on the Personal Development and Leadership Skills training course up in Yorkshire.'

Mel grimaced. 'Four wasted days. I don't want to go.'

'Well, Leo Young mentioned us seconding some officers to Birmingham for the by-election. Apparently the local party workers objected to having a candidate imposed on them so there's a shortage of campaigners. The constituency has some lovely estates, I'm told. I'll just phone and let them know you'd like to do that instead.'

'Put that phone down!'

They both laughed but Mark was still uneasy. He suddenly blurted out, 'Listen, Mel, about this MGL case you've been working on. They've offered to settle. You're going to get a call from ACAS.'

Mel felt a shudder run through her. She knew what was coming.

'And the terms are?'

Mark Thompson turned his face to the ceiling.

'Two and a half grand.'

'Two and a half grand! They must think we're fucking stupid.'

'Mel, we've got to accept it.'

'I don't believe this. I've got expert witnesses lined up. We can use this to show the dangers of private involvement in the health service. I bet they want a confidentiality clause as well. They do, don't they? Oh, fuck this.'

Mark did not say anything.

'So that's it. Two and a half grand. No reference, no agreed reason for dismissal, a confidentiality clause. And you say we've got to accept it. Why do we, Mark? Just be honest with me. You at least owe me that. What was it you said? "I'll back you on this"? What was it you said to Brenda Fletcher at the branch meeting? "Mel's one hundred percent behind you"? Doesn't it make you feel just a little bit embarrassed? I'm going to have to tell some woman who didn't want to go to tribunal in the first place but now at least feels that there's a glimmer of hope that we're dropping her?'

'You might not have won, Mel. Two and a half grand will help her with the mortgage arrears at least.'

'But that's not it. That's not why. Why do I have to drop it? Why have I had virtually the whole of the leadership of the union trying to undermine me on this from day one?'

Mark ran his hands through his hair. He fiddled with his tie. Mel could tell that he was finding this painful. She did not intend to spare him though.

'OK,' he said finally. 'We're about to sign a partnership deal with MGL. It's a good deal, Mel. Lots of work-based training opportunities, family-friendly policies, facility time, recognition across MGL factories. It will dramatically increase our membership. You can see that there is at least an argument not to jeopardise all of this over one contentious tribunal.'

He looked at her almost imploringly. Mel remembered his energy and humour when he had been addressing the branch meeting, his careful manner with Brenda Fletcher and Yolanda Munro. His touch had seemed so light, his manner so fresh.

'There is an argument. You're right. I've already had it forcefully put to me by your new friend Leo Young. It's about hijackers, isn't it? Look, Mark, you know me well enough. You know that I'm no nutter who wants to launch us into action which we could never win and which could only weaken the union. You know that I've stood up to some of the real fruitcakes and taken a lot of abuse for it. But this sweetheart deal you're talking about, it already means that we've got to drop a tribunal on behalf of one of our members. What happens when the going really gets rough?'

She saw him wince as she used the term 'sweetheart deal' and looked at him challengingly, daring him to contradict her.

'I don't know what you're trying to imply about "my new friend, Leo Young".' Mark's tone became harder.

'It looks a bit cold and calculating to me,' she said.

'Well, *you* would know all about cold and calculating,' he said.

For a moment she had no idea what he was talking about.

'What . . . Oh no, Mark, don't stoop to that.'

'Why not? You insulted me. You implied that all I wanted was a quick shag in the office. You never asked how I felt about you. You assumed that I had no feelings for you whatsoever. If a man had done what you did, nobody would be applauding him. They would be calling him a sleaze. You hurt me.'

Mel was astonished. She stared at him incredulously, remembering his celebration drink.

'You seemed to have recovered from your grief when you were wearing Stephanie at your party,' she snapped.

Mark blushed. 'Well, what was I supposed to do? Anyway, nothing happened there.'

'I don't care.'

'Exactly, you don't care, you're thoughtless.'

'Mark, if you wanted to talk to me about this you could have done so. And just for the moment we're not talking about what happened between us. We're talking about Brenda Fletcher and the sweetheart deal with MGL.'

'Would you stop calling it that, please. It's a *partnership* deal.'

'Oh, sure. Family-friendly policies! Facility time! You think Hislop cares about union rights? He's sucking up to government and making sure that he looks suitably modern. But it's just icing sugar, Mark.'

'Thousands of new members? A voice on the board? That's not icing sugar.'

'And how do we represent our new members?'

'We've given MGL no assurances. There isn't a no-strike clause.'

'But there won't be any strikes, I bet. And we have to drop the Brenda Fletcher case.'

'We've agreed to *settle* the Brenda Fletcher case.'

'You know she had nearly finished her post-graduate qualification when they sacked her? Now what does she do?'

'Sometimes we have to make hard choices.'

'Oh no, Mark, please. Please don't use that horrible language.'

Mark laughed disarmingly and raised his hands. It was difficult to hate him.

'OK, OK, that was accidental as a matter of fact. Honestly! I'm not trying to sound like that. Look, Mel, I understand what you're saying. I'm not stupid and I'm not a complete sell-out. But you have to see things from my point of view as well. These negotiations were quite advanced when I took over. I couldn't turn round to Hislop and say that it was all off because of one industrial tribunal which we might not have won and which they have agreed to settle for a sum which is not massive but is not so far off the average either.'

'That's not the point. This was about much more than that.'

'Mel, if there was any other way I would take it. But there isn't.'

'So you are instructing me to drop the Brenda Fletcher case?'

'I'm telling you that this union considers the terms which have been offered to be acceptable. If Brenda Fletcher wants to pursue . . .'

'Don't be ridiculous. How can she pursue it on her own when she's about to have her fucking house repossessed?'

Once again, Mark's eyes hardened. He clearly did not like being called ridiculous. Mel was aware that this would be the last time that they spoke as two colleagues on equal terms.

'Well, at least that might not happen now. Who knows if she would have even got this much if you had continued with your moral crusade. Maybe we should look at your own motives. It could be seen as a little egotistical. One individual case being given more attention than the interests of the union as a whole.'

Mel shook her head disbelievingly. Above them on the wall, Che Guevara gazed into the distance through black eyes.

'Was this part of the deal?' she asked suddenly.

'What deal?'

'For you to become General Secretary. Did Leo tell you to sort this one out? "You have a better relationship with Mel, Mark. You'll have to get her to drop the Brenda Fletcher tribunal."'

Mark was obviously stung by this.

'Contrary to what appears to be general opinion, there was no deal between myself and Leo. Sweetheart or otherwise.'

'But you discussed it with him.'

'Of course I did. I've discussed a lot of things with Leo. This was a problem that had to be resolved for the partnership deal with MGL to go ahead.'

'And now it has been resolved. Congratulations everybody. I just have to inform Brenda Fletcher.'

'I'm sorry about that, but you are the one who has to do it. Frankly, I think she'll take it better than you have.'

'You're probably right. But that's irrelevant. She's used to being trampled on. She's paid heavily for MGL's inadequate procedures. There are people who bear far heavier responsibility who have all kinds of access, all kinds of ways of getting what they want. Robert Hislop will be meeting government ministers in country houses and discussing his position as a special adviser on health task-forces.'

At the door, Mark's secretary held up a piece of paper which obviously needed signing and he mimed ten minutes with both hands and smiled. Then he turned back to Mel.

'I agree with you. But as Lenin said, you should never mix up what you want to be the case with how things actually are. We have to work within this context. For the time being at least.'

But the time for flippant references to Lenin had long gone. He looked uncomfortable as he said it, as if he realised this.

'How convenient,' Mel said. 'Well, you can tell Leo that it's all sorted at last. You used the personal touch.'

Mark said, 'Don't, Mel.'

'What else do you discuss with Leo? Is it all nudge-nudge down the pub? "Oh, Mark should be able to bring Mel to her senses. He's got a bit of a way with the ladies."'

'It's never been like that.'

Mark half-rose from his seat. There was genuine distress in his eyes.

'I'm sorry you think that of me.'

'I don't think anything of you,' Mel said with a composed brutality. 'You're my boss and you have given me an instruction which I will have to carry out. That's it.'

She stared at him. She did not hate him, nor even particularly despise him. He was doing what everybody always did — accommodating himself to the logic of power. He was not her enemy, she could even remember the way she had felt just before he kissed her, although she knew that she would never let it happen again. There was certainly no aphrodisiac in his authority and office – he appeared to have lost his power of attraction, all his charisma.

There was nothing left to say. They both knew it.

Mel stood smoking in her office, looking out at the street below. On her desk lay the now redundant papers relating to the tribunal, the report on Serious Hazards of Transfusion. Outside, people ate ice creams and intrusive, show-off beats pounded from cars. Mel felt hot and lonely and troubled.

'Hello, comrade.' Graham's head popped around her office door. 'Don't jump.'

'Why not?' Mel replied bitterly.

'Well, for one because we'd all miss you. Secondly, you escaped from Goatfucker and it would seem such a waste if you then hurled yourself from a window. What's up?'

'Everything. MGL have just fucked me over on this tribunal. We're going into partnership so it's been "settled". We can call ourselves the MGL staff association now.'

'It's a cruel world, Mel. I'm growing old and learning to take disappointment in my stride. We must sabotage from the margins. We are Partizans. We strike when the enemy least expects it.'

'Great . . .' Mel angrily wiped a tear from her eye. She was not going to weep for those bastards.

'Hey,' Graham said gently. 'Don't let it get to you. Mary and I are going for a drink. Why don't you join us?'

'No, I'm not in the mood.'

'Oh, come on.' Mary's head appeared in the doorway. 'We can sit outside. Graham can moan about the beer and explain that all your problems are caused by capitalism . . .'

'Rather than by the position of the planets,' Graham added. 'Seriously, Mel. Get your bag. I've been hearing rumours about some deal in the offing. Let's go and get pissed and bitch about our new General Secretary. I told him yesterday that I would be watching him for any signs of selling out.'

'I bet that put the fear of God into him,' Mary muttered. 'Come on,

Mel, I'll buy you an ice cream on the way. Don't forget your eggs. I gave you the speckled ones because you said that Patrick liked them.'

Mel smiled although her chest was still tight with anger and pain.

'Let me just switch my computer off,' she said.

They walked to the lift while Graham berated Mary for having given his name and address to some Scientologists she had encountered in the street. Mel smiled sadly as she listened to their cheerful bickering. There was a sour taste in her throat.

a roman candle

Oh God! thought Elena, why must we die, why must we suffer separation and illness and tears? And if we must, then why all this beauty, why this sweet feeling of hope . . .

Good question, Mel thought as she laid down her copy of *On the Eve*, having understood as she approached the end why Lily had given it to her to read before going to see *La Traviata*. Before Lily's gift, it had been some time since she had read a book. She wasn't really sure why — at one point she had read with a hunger that had almost made her indiscriminate. Tired, she had said. Too tired. The most foolish of excuses. No time. Too tired. Now, the subtle, humane prose had wakened something in her again, had made her realise that when she was bored, lonely, or frustrated there was another option besides staring from the window. She had gone to a bookshop again, and among the pile of books she had bought was *Mary Barton*, which she had chosen as a gift for Lily. 'It's about unions,' Mel had said shyly when she gave it to her. 'I was given it once for a birthday. My mum always made sure that we were given books on our birthdays.'

'Then you have a lot to thank her for,' Lily had said.

Lily had been sympathetic about the collapse of the industrial tribunal. She said that she had always known that Mel had been doing it for the right reasons and that it must have been hard to see her work undermined by such a shabby compromise. Lily herself was in a state of high nervous energy because the case against both driver and train company was about to come to court. There was some division among the families over the driver — the hawks considered him more responsible than the company because he had ignored the lights. The dovish faction, which included Lily, considered that the overall responsibility lay with the company and that the driver — who had also been injured in the crash — had suffered enough.

Lily had also written a response to Brenda Fletcher. Mel had caught just the smallest glimpse of it when Lily had folded it to put it in an envelope. *Dear Brenda Fletcher, Thank you so much for your kind . . .*

Mark Thompson had been right about Brenda Fletcher's response to the settlement. She had shrugged resignedly.

'It will get the building society off our backs,' she sighed, staring at the doughnut sprinkled with hundreds and thousands that Mel had bought for her. She had found work as a part-time clerical assistant in her local authority. She missed her old workmates and was sad about the studies which she had nearly completed.

'I won't get a chance to study like that again,' she said.

'I'm so sorry,' Mel said. 'I wanted you to have a chance to put your case. There's a confidentiality clause as well. If you accept the money you can't talk to anybody about it.'

'Who would I talk to about it?' Brenda Fletcher replied. 'Oh, by the way, I got such a nice letter from Lily Forrester. She seems a lovely woman.'

'Oh yes,' Mel said. 'Yes, she is.'

'I dream . . .' Brenda Fletcher murmured. 'I dream about it sometimes. I wish that it was all a dream.'

Mel felt a surge of compassion for the wounded woman before her. She would never be offered counselling, could join no support group. All the foundations of her life had been removed; she had collected money for famine victims, enjoyed her studies, belonged to her trade union. Now all that was gone. Mel imagined that the letter she had written to Lily would have been kind, she remembered Brenda smiling over her cappuccino and telling Mel that she was lovely.

'I know you put a lot of work into this,' Brenda said.

'Ah well,' Mel shrugged. 'That's my job.'

'All the same. It's nice to know that there are people who still care. You can only do your best.'

And she reached across and squeezed Mel's hand as if it were she who needed comforting.

Mel called Pepa and asked if she wanted to go shopping with her. She wanted to buy a new dress but didn't tell Pepa that it was for the opera.

'Where shall we go?' Pepa asked. 'Lakeside or Blue Water?'

Mel laughed. 'Let's just go into town,' she said. 'We have to be back for the evening because Patrick's celebrating the end of his treatment. We're having fireworks.'

'Fireworks?' Pepa said. 'Where are you going to get fireworks at this time of year?'

'Don't ask. Jim's supposed to be getting them. We have to go to Jim's as well 'cause he's on the top floor and can fire them from his balcony. We were going to do it at ours but there's a balcony right above. Are you going to come?'

'Might as well. Nothing better to do.'

'You're too kind.'

They took the number 8 bus to Oxford Street and wandered about getting irritated by the crowds. Mel couldn't find anything she wanted so they went to Selfridges food hall instead and bought different types of olives, smoked salmon, tortelloni with porcini mushrooms, rollmops. They chose some expensive Riojas and then went to the cigar counter and purchased four Cohibas, laughing at the fat American who was arrogantly informing a bored assistant that he could not possibly smoke a Cuban cigar until the restoration of democracy.

'Yeah, but say what you want,' the handsome young male assistant said as he glanced with appreciation at Pepa who was batting her eyelids at him, 'you can't beat a Cuban cigar.'

'I greatly admire Fidel Castro,' Pepa said loudly. 'He is a *Gallego* and we have fire in our veins. We can't be pushed about by anybody.'

'His days are numbered,' the American said without looking at her as he rolled a cigar from the Dominican Republic in a pudgy hand.

'He'll outlast you, you fat cunt,' Pepa said and the assistant spluttered and turned away, feigning a coughing fit.

'There are moments,' Mel said as they swung out laughing on to the crowded, hot street, 'when nothing but gratuitous abuse will do.'

'What's this dress for?' Pepa asked as they wandered down Bond Street.

Mel could not be bothered to lie. 'Lily's taking me to the opera,' she said.

Thankfully, Pepa was not in the mood for arguments. 'Why don't you wear that red skirt you've got? That really suits you. Especially with heels.'

'Yeah, I thought about that. But I wore that the last time.'

'What do you mean, the last time?'

'When we went to dinner at this journalist's.'

Pepa glanced at her friend and then said neutrally, 'OK, so you can't wear the red skirt. Let's try in here — they had some nice stuff last time I was here. But we'll have to hurry 'cause it's hot and I can smell those fucking rollmops.'

'Two rockets, a Roman candle, a golden fountain and a packet of sparklers. And you call that a firework display!'

'Oh, there's gratitude for you. Have you ever tried to get fireworks at this time of year? They're big rockets anyway.' Jim aimed one of them at Patrick's head.

'Yeah, but we said a display.'

'Good to see that coming off this treatment hasn't reduced your capacity for whinging and moaning,' Pepa said, putting her lighter next to the blue touch-paper and pretending to light it. 'Sparklers are great. We can write our names with them.'

'Oh, you've learned how to do that now, have you?' Patrick muttered.

Mel smiled as she listened to the bickering and squabbling from Jim's bedroom, where she was trying on the new dress that Pepa had persuaded her to buy and which had caused her a few anxious moments as the assistant had swiped her credit card. She looked at herself in the mirror and smiled as she smoothed it over her breasts and down around her hips. It was a simple, elegant, sleeveless dress which Pepa, hanging like Kilroy over the door of the changing room, had instantly told her she must buy.

Mel glanced around her briefly at Jim's possessions. There was a photograph of his grandmother on the chest of drawers, along with a handful of change, a deodorant and a bottle of Clinique perfume. There was a poster of Maradona on the wall, a few books by American authors – Richard Ford, John Updike – at the side of the bed. Some of his shirts were hanging over a chair, a couple of pairs of trainers were discarded by an open cupboard door. He was much more of a label person than Patrick and paid close attention to his clothes. This room was what Jim came home to and sometimes drove him mad with loneliness but there was something new and poignant and pleasingly male about it for Mel.

'Hurry up,' Pepa called as Mel stepped into the living room.

They fell silent for a moment as she stood in the doorway.

'Maybe I'm wrong about the journalist,' Patrick said. 'Maybe you're having some kind of lesbian affair with this Lily Forrester. In which case you *have* to let me watch. Woman-on-woman action doesn't really count as infidelity in my book.'

'Ignore your pig of a boyfriend. You look lovely,' Pepa said. 'I told you you should buy it.'

'Give us a twirl,' Jim said.

'Get back in your box,' Patrick said. 'I may have to smoke my cigar now.'

'Big rockets, cigars . . .' Pepa murmured. 'It's enough to give a girl penis envy.'

'You *would* be envious if you saw mine,' Patrick said.

'That's not what I've heard,' Pepa replied as she busied herself with putting food on plates and opening bottles of wine.

While they were waiting for the sky to darken enough for the firework display, Pepa and Mel stood on the balcony, looking out at the skyline, the trains rolling in and out of the city, the cars streaming south. Mel watched the stretch of motorway down which, only a short time ago, she had headed out of the city to Miranda's garden, Lily's arm on the window, silver bracelets glittering in the sun. She remembered the smell of sage and thyme, the soft grass under her feet, the swallows diving and looping in the sky above their heads. She remembered Lily collapsing to the ground and holding her foot bright red with blood. These images were memories now, like those moments from her childhood so long ago, they were both her and not her, they slid after her like segments of a snake's body. In time, they would be as distant as the small girl who had watched her parents cooking on a paraffin stove at a campsite and been so utterly happy and secure, so protected from any dramas that might have been going on between the two adults. Even when she had woken in the family tent and heard angry muttering followed by the sound of weeping, she had been able to think nothing of it, to ascribe it to some mystery that it was simply not her part to inquire about. And she had sighed and drifted back to sleep, snug in her rose-patterned sleeping bag, her sister sleeping beside her. She had forgotten all about it in the morning. But, of course, she could not have forgotten because it was still there in her mind, it was still there with the smell of paraffin, the fat man with the glass eye, the fox at the door.

Night began to fall and the jokes and banter which sometimes began to tire Mel out were replaced with an easy calm. They lit Cuban cigars on the balcony and talked quietly and drank glasses of red wine – apart from Jim, who sipped peach juice and smoked some grass.

Finally, it was dark enough for the fireworks. Mel and Pepa went and stood in the living room while Jim and Patrick stuck one of the rockets in an empty wine bottle.

'Stand back, girls, and don't be scared,' Jim said as he lit the first of the rockets. They watched with the excitement of children as the paper glowed and then the rocket shuddered and shrieked into the sky. It burst in the sky above them, showering purple and green stars above the railway line.

'Oh . . .' Pepa said. 'That was so beautiful.'

They lit the second rocket and the golden fountain until they were left with the Roman candle. Once again they stood on the edge of the balcony as it began to launch scarlet and turquoise flares into the black sky, globes of light dropping lazily into the darkness, fading and disappearing before the next salvo brightened the sky again.

Why all this beauty, why this sweet feeling of hope?

Mel felt Pepa's small brown arm resting softly on her own, the security of her friends around her. When the last of the fireworks had spluttered and faded away into the darkness they went back on to the balcony to drink more red wine and flourish their names with sparklers on the night air.

the falling woman

Slow and soft the overture began, violins breaking the silence when the coughing had finally quietened. A shudder ran down Mel's spine as she recognised the mournful melody, the melody which Elena and Insarov had heard in Venice, which Gordon Forrester had heard in London, which Turgenev and thousands of other long-dead people had heard all over the world, which thousands of not-yet-born people would continue to hear as the conductor twitched his baton and the curtains opened on a party scene in the Parisian house of a young courtesan.

Mel had met Lily outside the opera house, just as fat drops of summer rain had begun to fall on to the warm street.

'What a wonderful dress,' Lily had said as she kissed her lightly on the cheek.

'I thought I had to celebrate my first night at the opera,' Mel said.

Lily was wearing a simple black dress with a crushed-velvet silver shawl draped lightly over her shoulders. Mel noticed the way that men glanced at them.

'Let's go and order our interval drinks,' Lily had said, taking Mel's arm.

Before they had entered to take their seats, Mel had been unable to resist telling Lily what had happened that day when she had finally met Deep Throat in the café across the road from the office.

She had checked around the café and had taken a table near to the window. It was still early and there were only a few people eating, mostly in couples and none looking like a possible informant from MGL. Mel ordered a coffee and began to daydream, her chin cupped in her hand.

'Hello, Mel.' A voice suddenly startled her from her reverie.

It was Yolanda Munro.

For a moment, Mel was confused and gabbled something about meeting a friend in a moment.

'That's right, Mel.' Yolanda sat down and beckoned the grumpy waitress. 'You're meeting me.'

Mel said, 'But you don't work for MGL.'

'No, I don't, Mel.'

'So?'

Yolanda did not answer for a moment, looking first at the menu which the waitress had discourteously tossed on to the table in front of her and then back at the waitress. The waitress turned her back and slouched off. Yolanda tutted and shook her head.

'Slut,' she muttered, picking up the menu. 'Now, what was I saying? Oh yes . . . Do you have a secretary?'

'Yes.'

'Do you get on well with her, treat her nicely?'

'I suppose so. I try to.' Mel thought about Mary and the speckled eggs from her chickens, the constant supply of cakes. She had told her to take a day off recently because she had stayed late for a few nights, reorganising Mel's filing system.

'You should do. Get on the right side of your secretary and she'll do anything for you. Treat her like shit, Mel, and she'll turn into your worst enemy. Do you know what I mean?'

They were interrupted briefly by the waitress taking their order. Yolanda ordered spaghetti bolognese and a Coke. Mel asked for a sandwich and a Diet Coke. The waitress curled her lip faintly and Mel felt like warning her not to push Yolanda too far.

'So, what does . . .' Mel began as the waitress withdrew.

'What does this have to do with MGL?' Yolanda produced a brown envelope from her bag and slid it across the table. 'This is for you. I'm not going to tell you how I obtained it other than to say that I have a friend who still works for MGL and her boss treats her like slavery's still in fashion. I can't tell you who her boss is 'cause then you'll know who she is. Not that I don't trust you, Mel, but I've got to protect my source. I think you'll find these documents interesting, Mel. MGL know that their new hepatitis drug doesn't work but they delayed the release of the results because they are waiting for some big American company to make a major investment. If news gets out that the drugs don't work, Mel, then down goes the share price and the whole thing falls through. It's all there in black and white. Read it if you don't believe me, Mel.'

'I do believe you. I'll look at them properly when I get back to the office.' Mel put the envelope into her own bag.

'Remember when we were here with Brenda, Mel?' Yolanda started tucking into her spaghetti bolognese.

Mel nodded.

'We had a nice waiter then, better than this moody cow. You'd think I'd just ordered her to dance a jig naked on the table rather than ask for some more Parmesan cheese. Anyway, I've got something else for you. Brenda asked me to give you this.'

She rummaged in her bag and produced a box of After Eights. There was a little card attached. *Dear Mel, Thank you so much for your help. New job going well. Love, B Fletcher.*

'She didn't have to do that,' Mel said, blinking.

'Well . . .' Yolanda fished up a string of spaghetti with her finger. 'You see, Mel, I have this theory. About ninety per cent of all human beings are scum. So when you meet one of the ten per cent who aren't you're pleased. That's why she sent you those.'

'I'm not sure I agree with you about that. I don't think people are so black and white.'

'You're one of these people who think there's good and bad in everybody?'

'Not quite . . .'

'Well, I suppose there's a *bit* of good in most people but it's far outweighed by the bad. Forget that and you're lost. And some people are just pure bad. I lived in a slum on a hill in Caracas when I was little. There were people there who would cut your throat for the price of a rum. More or less the same when I came here, especially in Scotland. If it wasn't like that, Mel, everything would be different, wouldn't it? If it wasn't like that, a good woman like Brenda wouldn't have been treated the way she was . . .' Yolanda said this cheerfully, as if she had come to inner peace through recognition of the fact. 'There are people who will destroy you and they'll enjoy doing it. And don't tell me it's because of their deprived backgrounds, Mel, don't tell me that!'

'OK, I won't tell you that,' Mel grinned as Yolanda shifted into her favoured mode of vehement protestation. *J'accuse* the human race.

'I've had as deprived a background as anybody. I've watched my dad come home and hold my mum's face over the cooker. I've seen a man killed in front of me with a machete – his head split open like a water melon. I've had to take a few knocks in my time, Mel. But I don't use it as an excuse, do I?'

She paused and stared at Mel to underline the fact that this was not a rhetorical question.

'No,' Mel said.

'So you see what I'm saying, Mel. Brenda thinks you're different. Part of the ten per cent. And I agree with her. So you see why she sent you the chocolates now?'

'Yes.'

'Good. It was important for her to be told by you that she wasn't evil, that she hadn't killed that man. God knows, she's suffered for it, she's on sleeping pills and everything. But in your own way you made things better. It was bad luck that the union got too cosy with MGL but she wouldn't have got nothing if you hadn't pushed for it. And to be truthful, Mel, two and a half grand is better than a kick up the arse. She isn't going to get evicted now. Is she?'

'No.'

'OK, now don't tell me you're not having an ice cream, 'cause I'm having one and I'm not eating it on my own. Get moody Maria over, Mel, she's pretending she can't see me.'

'I think I will have an ice cream.' Mel grinned at Yolanda.

'Course you will. And I want to hear about that lunatic who attacked you. Brenda told me all about it.' Yolanda shivered in gleeful anticipation. 'It sounds terrible, chasing you down the stairs and everything. The sound of his feet behind you, breathing down your neck, knowing that he's gaining on you.' She turned her beady eyes on the foot-dragging waitress. 'Yes, darling, would it be too much to ask for you to throw me the menu again? My friend and I are going to have an ice cream.'

Sitting in the darkened auditorium, Mel smiled as she remembered Yolanda. Violetta had just been persuaded by Alfredo's father to abandon his son. Mel heard the music that had played on the radio while they drove back from Miranda's. She had listened to it again at home because Lily had lent her the CD.

I shall be there . . . among the flowers . . . always . . . always . . . love me as I love you.

Mel wriggled her toes as shudders rippled down her spine. She gripped the side of her seat.

In the interval they found their bottle of wine and two glasses waiting for them. Mel poured them both some wine and lit a cigarette.

'So, did the papers prove what Yolanda said?' Lily asked.

'Oh, yes. I've copied them to Paul so that he can do a story with them.'

'Well . . .' Lily clinked her glass to Mel's. 'In some ways that's far worse for them than the negative publicity from an industrial tribunal. And you wouldn't have got those papers if you hadn't been so keen to take the tribunal on. So, there's some justice in that.'

'I suppose so. The court case with the rail company starts soon as well?'

'Yes.' Lily sipped her wine and smiled. 'Although we've got to be prepared for it to drag on a bit. I think it will last for ages. The arguments are very complicated.'

As she spoke, she was bumped by the man in black tie behind her who was expansively offering his opinion on the quality of the duet between Violetta and Alfredo's father. She spilt a little of her wine down her dress. The man did not apologise. A few seconds later, he did it again.

'For Christ's sake,' Lily said. The man carried on holding forth about the performances.

Mel stepped forward and pushed the man's back lightly. He half turned and then ignored her again so Mel gave him a real shove.

'What on earth do you want?' he asked, more in surprise than anger.

For a moment, he became Robert Hislop, Leo Young, Neil Evans and the fat American in Selfridges all rolled into one. But Mel decided that the Pepa approach was probably not the most suitable in the circumstances.

'You keep pushing my friend,' Mel said, 'and then you don't have the courtesy to apologise. So try and be a little more careful.'

'Also, I'd rather not have your opinions shouted in my ear,' Lily added.

The man stared at them for a moment with a crestfallen, almost sorrowful expression. His wife looked away in embarrassment.

'I'm really so sorry,' he said. 'I would have apologised if I had realised. I'm just the clumsiest oaf sometimes. Look at me. I'm so big and you're so . . . well . . . delicate. No wonder I didn't notice. I always shout as well, it's just that I get excited. It's such a bad habit. Let me get you another drink, please.'

'It's OK,' Lily said.

'Come on, Gerald,' his wife hissed. 'There's the bell.' And she dragged him away as he continued to cast apologetic glances over his shoulder.

'Poor man,' Mel said.

Lily laughed. 'You were so hard on him and then you call him a poor man.'

'Well, when I realised that he was upset it was different. I can relate to clumsiness. Besides, it looked like his wife was going to give him a hard time.'

'Poor woman,' Lily said. 'That probably happens to them all the time. Clumsiness can get bloody irritating after a while. Look, it's all over my chest, it looks as if I'm lactating.' She dabbed at her breasts with a napkin.

Mel felt as if she might be about to blush and looked away.

'Anyway,' Lily asked, pulling her shawl more closely around her, 'are you enjoying it?'

'Oh yes.' Mel's eyes lit up. 'It's so different. I get this shivery feeling sometimes. I mean I'm not an expert, I can't tell you about the quality of the singing, unlike Mr Clumsy over there . . .'

'You don't need to be an expert. That's why I don't like noisy opinion-givers at this sort of thing. There might be somebody who is enjoying it and they have to listen to some old snob saying, "Oh, my dear, it really doesn't compare to the performance we saw at La Scala." Why can't they just keep it to themselves?'

Mel said, 'Oh, I don't mind. I wouldn't know what they were talking about anyway. Come on, let's get our seats again.'

During the final act, Mel felt her scalp tingling as the opera drew to its sad conclusion, as a young woman became conscious of her impending death and responded with the most heart-wrenching melodies. Too late, she cried, too late. Mel was aware of her own breathing, the sentimentality and beauty of the music was almost too much to bear. As Alfredo returned to his dying lover and she cried out his name, Mel heard a mixture of gasp and sob beside her and turned to see Lily with tears streaming down her face, trying to control the odd noises always produced by attempts to suppress grief. By the time Violetta had begun to sing of her desperation at dying so young after so much suffering, Lily was openly weeping, as were half the other people around them. When Violetta fell for the last time, with the cry of joy on her lips, Lily took Mel's hand in a hard grip that she did not release until the curtain had fallen.

They did not speak until they were out on the street. Lily looked drained, as if she could not walk straight.

'What do you want to do?' Mel asked.

Lily turned to her with a look of desperate anxiety. 'You don't want to go home straightaway?'

'Oh no, I'm fine. I could murder a drink, actually.'

'Mel, I have to get back for Claudia. We could have a drink at mine. I'd really like that. I know it's out of the way but I'll pay for your cab home. I just don't want to get in a cab on my own now.'

'That sounds perfect,' Mel said. 'Don't be silly about paying for a cab. The pubs round here are horrible and they'll be closing anyway. Quick, get that cab.'

They hailed the cab at almost the same time as another couple emerging from the opera, arriving just fractionally later at the door. The cabbie made a weary Pilate gesture that they would have to sort it out among themselves so Mel turned and noticed to her surprise that their competitor was the man who had spilled Lily's wine in the interval.

'Ah, I see . . .' he said. 'Well, please take the cab. It's really the least I can do . . . Come on, Jean, I'm sure there'll be another one along in a moment.'

Jean seemed unwilling to go along with this and looked challengingly at Mel, inviting her to admit that the cab was not really theirs.

'Thank you very much.' Mel ushered Lily into the back.

'That was outrageous.' Lily was laughing as they slumped back into the comfort of the seats. 'They were there before us.'

'Sometimes in these matters you just have to use every weapon at your disposal. He'll learn not to be so clumsy in future.'

They drove up Shaftesbury Avenue, watching the mass of people passing through Soho at night – the theatre-goers, the young people with broken trainers and sleeping bags, the clubbers, the gangs of drunks, the whores, the tourists, the crack-heads. Lily was quiet and Mel knew that she was still dizzy from the experience; she must be thinking about her husband, times they had spent together after the opera.

Mel said, 'That must have been difficult for you.'

'Yes.' Lily looked out of the cab window, her eyes glistening. 'I had to do it though. I'm glad you were with me. I always thought it would be better if you were there.'

'Why me?' Mel asked.

'Because you're sensitive. I knew you would like it as well. You wouldn't sit pretending to enjoy it or make stupid jokes. I couldn't have gone with somebody who I thought was just going to keep me company. I so wanted you to enjoy it.'

'Sad things are good for the soul,' Mel said quietly. She could see that Lily was trying not to cry again. Lily smiled as her words were quoted back to her.

'I was reading up about it.' Mel continued to chatter, her tone brisk and bright. 'In the bit that came with the CD you lent me. I liked the fact that the first woman to play Violetta was so fat that nobody cried at the end, they all pissed themselves laughing because it was too stupid an idea to think that somebody like her was wasting away with consumption.'

Lily laughed and put her hand on Mel's shoulder.

'Her name was Fanny Salvini-Donatelli. Can you imagine anything more embarrassing than people laughing at this great tragedy? She weighed one hundred and thirty kilos. Poor Verdi was mortified.'

'That's big,' Mel said. 'It must have been hilarious. I love it when people can't stop themselves from laughing in theatres.'

'It's probably the source of all those fat ladies wailing jokes,' Lily answered.

As they approached the house, Mel remembered the first time she had brought a distraught Lily back here, from the Great Northern press conference. Now, she was familiar with Lily's domain, knew how to locate things, understood its patterns and idiosyncracies.

'Hi, Claudia,' Mel said as they opened the front door. 'How's it going?'

'Fine thanks,' the girl dimpled at her. 'Oh, that's a lovely dress, Mel, it really suits you. Lily, whatsisname, Roger from the Families Support Group has phoned a few times. Also, your brother Laurence called. He wants you to call him back tonight.'

'Thanks Claudia. Here's your money. Give my regards to your mum. Mel . . .' she gestured to the bottle of Glenfiddich that stood on the bookshelf – 'would you mind? I'm just going to see Daniel.'

Mel fetched the chunky whisky glasses from the cupboard and glanced, as she always did, into the garden to see if the fox were there. But the garden was empty – only Daniel's ball was being blown about by the soft breeze.

Lily came bouncing down the stairs.

'Fast asleep. I'm sorry to be such a poor hostess but I should also phone my wayward brother, get it out of the way.'

Mel nodded, curious to hear Lily speaking to her brother.

'Hello, *cheri*, guess who? What? That was Claudia. No, she's far too young and sweet for you. Well, far too sweet anyway.' Lily raised her eyebrows at Mel and mimed a person dying of thirst. Mel passed her the drink and Lily smiled in the way that sometimes made Mel feel as if her heart was turning over. She sat down on the sofa, gazing into the glass of whisky. Lily kicked her shoes off and stood with the phone between ear and shoulder, one foot behind her knee, making the shape of a 4.

'I've been to the opera. With a friend of mine. A *woman* friend. What? Oh for God's sake. Mel, he wants to speak to you, he's drunk.'

Mel hated having to speak to people she didn't know on the phone like this. She pulled a face and took the phone.

'Hello?'

'Hi, you're my sister's friend?' The voice was warm and appealing but with an edge of arrogance about it. Lily was also right about him being drunk.

'Yes.'

'Well, try and persuade her to come out here. She's going mad there with all those bloody court cases, I can tell. I know her better than she knows herself. Are you still there?'

'Yes.'

'She can't carry on like this, she's got to start a new life. I can help her here. Actually, put her back on again or I won't get a chance to speak to her, she'll run off to one of her meetings. It's been lovely to speak to you. Come to Paris as well, it's a fantastic city, much better than London with all its self-obsessed people chasing their own tails. What did you say your name was?'

'I didn't. It's Mel.'

'What do you do, Mel?'

'I work for a trade union.'

'Oh. Right. Well, come over here. There's loads of unions. Always on strike over here. See, even the unions are better. Would you mind if I just had another quick word with my sister?'

Mel handed the phone back to Lily and sat down again on the sofa.

'Laurence, I'll talk to you when you're sober. No, I'm not discussing that now. I'll speak to you later. OK.'

She laughed and put the phone down. What a prick, Mel wanted to say but didn't. Laurence was clearly indulged within Lily's family, allowed to get away with playing the lovable rogue, the charming louche.

'He wants you to go to France,' Mel said.

'He keeps nagging me about that. He has a flat in Paris and a house in Provence. Have you ever been to Provence?'

Mel said that she hadn't.

So Lily told her about the pines and olive groves, about forest fires, about the university town of Aix-en-Provence, about making simple salads with fat sun-ripened tomatoes, sitting in the sun and dipping bread in olive oil, fish soup, the mistral. Was there longing in Lily's tone? Mel could not tell.

'Would you like to go out there?' she asked.

'I can't even think about that at the moment,' Lily replied. 'The court case starts next week. Laurence is utterly selfish, he never deals with anything that transcends his immediate wants and desires.'

'But I suppose he's thinking of you.'

'Maybe,' Lily said, 'maybe.' She was obviously not thinking about her brother any longer.

A sudden squall lashed rain hard against the window, a summer storm. Lily peered outside.

'When it rains like this, it always reminds me of those films where the heroine arrives looking drenched but sexy and saying breathlessly, "You bastard, I didn't want to come," before swooning into her lover's arms.'

'Or one of those terrible – usually French – women in films who say, "I lerve the rain. I'm so crazy I jerst go dancing when it rains and per'aps I smerk a leetle marijuana because I am mad."'

They sat silently and watched the rain thumping the window for a moment.

Lily said, 'You know, I do like it when it rains like that.'

'Yeah, well, you're half French. Just don't expect me to go dancing in it with you.'

They sat and drank more whisky and Lily, to Mel's surprise, asked for a cigarette. Only now and again, Lily said, once in a while. She looked strange smoking, as if she were nervous of what she held in her hand but also enjoying her audacity.

Mel told her about the fireworks on Jim's balcony and Lily asked what Patrick would do now.

'I don't know,' Mel said. She truly had no idea but wasn't going to let Patrick get away with playing the invalid now that the treatment was over. Plenty of people with hepatitis C held down full-time jobs and went out of their flats.

'Does he make you happy?' Lily asked.

Mel was startled by the abruptness of the question. 'In what sense?' she stalled.

Lily shrugged. Mel noticed that she was becoming quite drunk.

'In any sense. Well, let's say intellectually. Does he challenge you?'

Don't ask me this, Mel wanted to say, I can manage perfectly OK without asking it of myself. I can get from day to day, week to week, year to year without such questions. And that is not as shabby a compromise as it sounds. I am not unhappy, I have many moments of contentment, satisfaction. Who is to say that this is not happiness?

'I guess . . . sometimes . . . it's difficult to think about in that way.'

'Why?'

'Sometimes in a relationship those questions just don't arise. That question loses relevance.'

'Perhaps you find it too painful to confront?'

'Perhaps,' Mel conceded. 'But I would still say that it is pointless to confront it. We settle into patterns in our lives that are acceptable, agreeable. Sometimes because we know they're not perfect we disrupt them a little and we both enjoy and are scared by that disruption, the consequences it might bring. Some people won't disrupt their lives in that way, perhaps because they can't. Some people disrupt their lives too much, they destroy everything, including other people.'

She suddenly remembered the scene with Mark Thompson in the office, the disarray of her clothes, the almost pornographic frenzy of their movements, stolen pleasure in the half-dark. She would be able to hold that secret, she would enjoy having that secret, a possibility had passed by and she had clutched it to her. Supposing that Mark Thompson foolishly engaged in the typical male quest for absolution or the equally male desire to boast? Supposing he told his wife? Would Mel then be responsible for another person's unhappiness, would she be responsible for disrupting her life? You could do your utmost not to hurt people, you could make it your guiding principle, but sometimes it was a dishonest principle, a piece of wishful thinking which bordered on culpable stupidity. Because pain and dishonesty of one sort or another were implicit in almost all sexual transactions – perhaps indirect, perhaps delayed, perhaps with all the best motives in the world – they were shadows produced by the sun.

'I don't think it's all or nothing,' Mel continued. 'Somebody I work with once said to me that we have to be like Partizans. He was talking politically but maybe it applies to life in general. You have skirmishes and you retreat to rest.'

Lily said, 'It's a rather depressing idea.'

'Is it? I think it's interesting. I don't mean it in a literal sense – adventure and then calm. I don't mean it happens in a sequence like that or that it's planned out. I just mean that there are incidents, encounters, moments that change things and you can choose to embrace them or turn away from them. Perhaps sometimes you have no choice. I'm not only talking about affairs.'

'I know you're not. Although there is usually a sexual element to such things. Who knows what would have happened if Gordon had lived? Perhaps one or other of us would have had affairs. Perhaps we would have made each other miserable.'

Mel shrugged. 'You're right. Who knows? Would Violetta have made a good Mrs Germont? Your relationship would have changed and developed like all relationships. There might have been times when you felt very miserable and times when you felt very happy.'

Lily smiled drunkenly and sloshed more whisky into their glasses.

'You know what Gordon's worst fault was?'

Mel shook her head.

'Well, he did have one of his dad's very bad habits. He would never abandon a plan when it manifestly wasn't working.' She giggled. 'I find those people so irritating. You know, they make you do all kinds of uncomfortable and disagreeable things *because that was what we decided*. Like trying to find a pub with a garden and you walk for bloody miles and you think, Oh for Christ's sake, any half-decent pub that sells alcohol will do, but no, you've got to tramp on, getting more miserable and depressed, because the plan was to go for a drink in a pub with a garden. Like giving up is some kind of statement of character weakness.'

'Right,' Mel said, trying not to giggle at Lily's petulance.

Lily realised that she had been ranting and laughed.

'I just thought I'd share that with you. And we did go to some very nice pub gardens. Put some music on.' She flapped her hand at the stereo.

'Yeah, but you know what? I couldn't take opera right now.'

'I haven't *only* got opera,' Lily said indignantly.

'Or Simon and Garfunkel.'

Lily threw a cushion at her.

'Look in the records. There's stuff there.'

Mel kneeled down on the floor and began to rifle through the record collection, biting her lip at some of the more eccentric or simply tasteless items on display.

'I'm so drunk,' Lily sighed.

'Are you OK? Do you want to crash?'

'Oh no,' Lily said. 'I haven't been drunk like this for ages. You don't want to go home, do you?'

'No.'

'Good, because I wouldn't let you anyway. I would start crying again and if you still wanted to go I would begin to talk darkly about ending it all.'

'I might still go. I might say, "Oh stop whining and get on with it."'

'Ah, but you wouldn't.' Lily sat up and pushed a strand of hair away from her face. 'I know you better than that. You're too . . . I was going to say soft but it's not soft at all . . . you're too full of awkward compassion.'

'Awkward compassion?' Mel felt rather offended.

'I don't mean that you behave in an awkward way. It's very attractive actually. It's like you can't help your good nature, however else you might want to be. No, not good nature, that makes you sound simple and well-meaning. There's a kind of quality in the things you do. The opposite of Laurence.'

Mel couldn't think of anything to say to this. She remembered the girl at school and bending back the nib of her pen, she thought about her lack of concern for the fact that Mark Thompson was married with children, the way in which she had deliberately not invited Patrick to the country with her.

'What do you think of that?' Lily asked.

'I think you're talking bollocks actually,' Mel said. 'And I really don't mean to be rude but your record collection is shocking.'

'I take it all back,' Lily said. She slid off the sofa and on to her knees beside Mel so that they were both flicking through the records.

'Mmm . . . Joan Armatrading . . . Bruce Springsteen . . . Elton John.'

'Stop it!' Lily protested. 'It's too mean to laugh at somebody's record collection. Anyway, this Elton John record is brilliant. I'll still defend it.'

She held up a battered copy of *Goodbye Yellow Brick Road*.

'And to prove it I'm going to put it on.'

'Well, if you insist,' Mel said, filling their glasses almost to the brim with whisky.

After about four attempts, Lily managed to get the needle on to the title track. Mel smiled as she heard the familiar song and had to admit – only to herself – that she rather liked it.

'Ah ah ah . . .' Lily warbled with the chorus. 'Ah ah-ah-ah ahhh . . . ooh ooh ooh . . . ah.'

'You're right, it's quite brilliant,' Mel said when the track had finally finished. 'Especially with you on backing vocals.'

Lily leaned back against the side of the sofa, one leg curled under her, the other outstretched so that her big toe was very faintly touching Mel. It moved with the tiniest of caresses, so tiny that it could be accidental, unintended, just the loose-limbed lack of coordination of the drunk.

'It's true what I said earlier,' she said, staring at Mel. 'You are compassionate.'

Mel's throat tightened. The atmosphere was changing by the second and although she was usually pretty dumb when it came to reading signals, she knew that Lily was openly flirting now. But Lily was also very drunk, perhaps her behaviour just became more exaggerated in these circumstances. Mel felt agonies of indecision, her heart was thumping, she thought she might be visibly shaking.

'Like the way you took me home that time and I had just been so rude to you.'

'Ah well. . .' Mel said.

'Like the time in the orchard when I cut my foot and you took the scrunch out of your hair to stem the blood.'

'Oh yes . . .' Mel laughed through a dry throat.

'Actually, you know what . . .' Lily said, stretching out her bare foot so that it was once again on Mel's thigh as it had been in the orchard. 'Actually, I found it really sexy.'

Mel looked down at the foot as if it were a butterfly which had alighted there. Lily traced a small circle with her toe, looked directly at Mel and did not drop her gaze.

'Did you?' Mel asked foolishly, still paralysed.

'Oh, unbearably so,' Lily said and pulled her foot suddenly away so that she was also kneeling up. They stared at each other for a moment and then they leaned towards each other and their lips touched. Mel could feel how soft Lily's mouth was. She shut her eyes as their tongues met. They moved round – still kissing – until they were both at the foot of the sofa and could lean back on its soft cushions.

'Mel,' Lily whispered as she kissed her ear, as she buried her hands in Mel's hair and pulled her towards her.

'You taste of whisky,' Mel murmured after a few minutes.

'So do you. Whisky and cigarettes.'

Lily ran her finger over Mel's lips. They kissed again and this time Lily took Mel's hand and guided it to her breast. Mel slid her hand inside her dress, felt a strange wonder at the response to the touch of her hand. Lily's hand moved up from where it had been resting on Mel's knee, travelled under the hem of Mel's dress, hesitated, fingers fluttering on the inside of Mel's thigh.

Mel sighed and shifted her position. She bit her lip and slid a little further down the sofa.

'Wouldn't we be more comfortable upstairs?' Lily whispered after a while and Mel nodded.

They stood up and kissed again, clenching each other's hair in their hands. Then Lily led her out of the living room and up the stairs. Mel turned back to switch off the light and saw a nearly empty whisky bottle and a full ashtray on the floor. She flicked the switch and followed Lily up the stairs in the dark.

Mel awoke disoriented, thirsty, her head pounding. She had no idea where she was or what the time was until she turned and saw Lily's curls on the pillow beside her, one arm thrown up above her head. Mel closed her eyes for a second, feeling an intense discomfort that was neither shame nor remorse nor worry but which contained ingredients of all three. The clock said twenty to four and she knew she had to get home. She had not phoned Patrick and he would not be able to sleep in her absence. She knew that she could not stay here until morning, knew how wrong and awkward it would be. It would be a different Lily tomorrow, a very hungover and possibly confused Lily with a small child to care for, a court case to prepare for, not the drunk and aroused Lily whose foot had so delicately alighted on Mel's thigh. Besides, Mel did not want to be here any longer, lying awake with alcohol-induced insomnia in a strange bed.

She got out from under the covers and picked up her clothes from the end of the bed. Then she tiptoed out of the room and down the stairs, dressing as she went. In the living room there was a nearly empty bottle of whisky, an ashtray spilling butts, the sleeve of an Elton John record. Mel winced at the sight of both alcohol and tobacco. Her head throbbed miserably so she shook the remnants of whisky from a glass and filled it with water. The water was cool, pleasurable, but as she brought the glass to her face her fingers still had the lingering capacity to remind her of what had happened. Her head began to throb alarmingly again and she ran her hands under the tap.

'Oh Christ,' she said to the empty room. 'Come on now, Mel, hold it together.'

She found a scrap of paper and a pen and sat down to write on the kitchen table.

Dear Lily,

I had to go because of work today — I'm hardly dressed appropriately. I didn't want to wake you. Thank you for my first trip to the opera, which I loved. I shall have a terrible hangover. I hope you don't feel too bad this morning!

Love,

Mel X

She studied the note for a moment, checking that it gave a breezy and uncomplicated impression, could not be subject to any misinterpretation. The last thing she wanted was for Lily to think that she was resentful or disturbed by what had happened. It wasn't that, but she didn't really know what it was yet and needed some time to think about it. Alone.

PS Phone me.

She got up to leave but stopped suddenly because a familiar cat-like figure was moving in the garden.

'Hi, fox,' Mel said out loud.

And as she spoke, the fox turned and looked at her through the glass door.

'You'd better stay out of the henhouse,' Mel whispered and the fox stared for a moment longer, as if to prove that it was scared of nothing. Then it slipped away. Mel checked she had money and keys before opening the front door and stepping out into the quiet street.

The streets were deserted as Mel walked in the vague direction of the main road where she suspected there would be a cab company. At another time she might have felt trepidation walking alone at this time of night but now she experienced a feeling of liberation, clean air in her face, the sky becoming light towards the east where she lived, where her flat was, her home. She sang to herself as she walked, nobody would do her any harm. And it was as if believing this made it happen because nobody hassled her, nobody made comments to her passing back, even when she stopped at a petrol station to buy juice and ask for directions to a cab company. She felt protected, as if she walked with her prior transgression as a bodyguard, she had crossed too many interesting boundaries to be scared: she was light, she was alone, she was invisible.

As soon as she put the key in her door she knew that Patrick was still awake, even though it was dark. She could feel his resentment.

'That was a long opera,' he said when she came into the bedroom. 'Final act drag a bit, did it?'

She glanced at him. He did not often use so harsh a tone with her.

'I went back to Lily's,' she said, reaching behind her to unzip her dress.

'You could have phoned.'

'Sorry.'

She just wanted to be rid of the clothes she was wearing, rid herself of the new dress, get into bed and pull the duvet round her. She let the dress fall into a heap on the floor and kicked it out of the way.

'So why didn't you?'

'Lily was upset. She had a kind of breakdown afterwards. I was looking after her. Phoning was the last thing on my mind.'

Mel said this half reproachfully, as if it were true.

'Yeah, well, you smell like a distillery. What's going on, Mel?'

'Leave me alone, Patrick.'

'I have a right—'

'LET ME SLEEP. JUST FOR ONCE, LET ME GO TO SLEEP WHEN I WANT TO.'

Patrick turned away from her, hurt and indignant. But Mel's desire for sleep was almost frantic, far too strong to worry about tantrums. Her bed was soft, accommodating, silent. She pulled the pillow to her face so that all she could smell now was soft cotton – not whisky, not cigarettes, not sex – just clean, soft cotton on her cheek.

icebreakers

'Yeah, my name's Melanie Holloway. I'm a regional officer for the GWA in London and what I hope to get from the course is . . .'

Mel paused for a moment. Various phrases were on the tip of her tongue. Fuck all. To get it over with as quickly as possible. Not to be subject to the attention of sad bastards who only see these courses as a chance to get laid.

The circle of faces smiled encouragingly at her.

'Yes?' Bob the course-leader prompted.

Mel gave a faint sigh which might have been a yawn.

She said, 'To develop my leadership skills and to learn from other people's experiences, especially in relation to organising activities.'

'Great,' Bob said, clapping his hands together. 'Now, in our first role-playing exercise we're going to imagine that we're on a plane that has crashed in the mountains. I'm going to divide you into two groups . . .'

Mel groaned. Three more days of this nonsense, this imprisonment, this torture.

She had arrived at the residential conference centre just outside Leeds the previous afternoon, after meeting Paul Flitcroft for coffee opposite her office.

'It's absolutely undeniable,' Paul had said. 'It shows clearly that MGL have been fully aware of the serious limitations of this drug and have deliberately held back from publishing the full results of their clinical trials in order to manipulate the share price.'

'Great. So what are you going to do with it?'

'Me? Nothing.'

'What?' Mel stopped with her cup of coffee halfway to her mouth.

'How about these for words? Spiked, nobbled, leaned-on, blackmailed. My editor won't touch it. The pernicious influence of Dodds, Young and their little drinking club.'

'I can't believe that. It's a fantastic story. An exclusive. What kind of paper wouldn't want to print that?'

'The kind of paper that is scared of the government. The kind of editor who knows that Dodds and his mates have got something on him. Anyway, it made my position untenable. I'm working out my notice.'

'You resigned?'

'Yup. But I hated it anyway, Mel. All the bullshit, all the competitiveness, all the lies, all the careerists. I'm going away for a while. With Miranda.'

'It's a nasty, twisted world so I'm going to travel around it courtesy of my rich girlfriend's money?'

Paul Flitcroft winked at her.

'I'm going to miss your acid tongue, Melanie Holloway, but that's about the long and the short of it. Somebody once said that to be rich is to be able to satisfy the requirements of the imagination. And I have a very large imagination.'

'You do surprise me.'

'I want to write a book, actually. And I need some time to do it.'

'A book? What about?'

'How about a feisty young trade unionist who takes on a drugs company?'

'And loses hands-down,' Mel said, looking down at the spoon she was twirling in her fingers.

'No, you're right, I don't think there'd be much interest in that. I want to do travel books. Miranda's family have a hacienda in Mexico. We're going there for a bit and then we're going to travel about. I've got a commission for some articles – I'm going to meet the Zapatistas, go to this city where women keep vanishing, do Acapulco. I'm doing a scuba-diving course but these bloody kids watching from the balcony keep shouting, "Free Willy!"

whenever I get in the pool, which is rather off-putting. Don't be shocked next time you see Miranda, by the way, she's cut her hair and dyed it black so that she doesn't get so much hassle. I keep assuring her she's as beautiful as always but she isn't. And I've been doing Spanish evening classes. *Yo soy cartero. Pan. Mi casa, tu casa. Como estas?*'

'Fascinating,' Mel said. 'I hope your book is an international best-seller and you're able to live a transcendent life satisfying the requirements of your gigantic imagination, unplagued by charlatans and careerists. But meanwhile, back in the real world, are you saying we're not going to do anything with this story?'

'Who said that? I said *I* wasn't. Which is a shame because the documents mention Dr Margaret Jowell as a key player in all of this. Remember that bitch at the press conference who threatened me with her lawyers? The one who looked at everybody over the top of her glasses. I would love to have been the one to stitch her up. Sadly, I can't. But you know David Finer who does all that stuff on Sunday about why-this-government-is-worse-than-the-Khmer-Rouge? I've always thought he went a bit over the top but it gets up their noses. He's delighted to draw attention to Hislop's position as a special adviser on health and his dodgy business practices.'

'Good,' Mel said. 'There's no way that they can source it back to Yolanda Munro?'

'Not to her, of course. But I would have thought it would be fairly obvious whose office these papers come from. And that limits the candidates. Does that worry you?'

'Not really,' Mel admitted. 'I don't know who the person is and they decided to take the risk. That's their business.'

'Anyway . . .' But Flitcroft's attention was suddenly caught by a couple of pretty girls walking past in the street. 'My God, isn't it incredible in summer when girls just take virtually all their clothes off? It's almost painful . . .' He stared longingly after them.

'Anyway what, you old pervert?' Mel asked.

'Oh . . . yes . . . we now have wonderful new legislation protecting whistleblowers. So, whoever it is has nothing to fear.'

'Right. Which is about as plausible as your interest in those two girls being purely platonic.'

'Probably a little more plausible actually,' Paul said. 'Let's be fair.'

'Fair?' Mel said. 'Who cares about fair?'

'I always thought you did,' Paul said. 'It's what I liked about you. Anyway, I'm off to the gym.'

'How's it going? Do you get to eye up lots of girls in lycra?'

'I do. But, sadly, I think they're all lesbians. They're always in pairs anyway.'

'Oh well . . . case proved.'

'And they have big tattoos on their shoulders and stare at me aggressively.'

'I wonder why. No great surprise that you don't appear to have lost any weight if that's all you get up to.'

'I've lost three pounds actually,' Paul said, sucking in his cheeks. 'I keep feeling rather faint.'

Mel smiled at him, pushed some spilled sugar back and forth across the table.

'I'll miss you as well, Paul, strangely enough.'

'Oh well, I'll be back of course. You can start to hate London but after a year in Mexico I'm sure I'll be longing for it again. And you're one of those funny people whom you meet by chance and never get rid of. I've always known that. You're my friend now, there's nothing you can do about it. We'll meet again. By the way, I'm seeing Lily this afternoon. You know the court case starts this week?'

'Yes.'

'Any message?'

Mel looked down at the sugar on the table.

'Send her my love,' she said.

Paul looked at her and then took something from his pocket. It was a photograph of the three of them on the lawn of Miranda's country house. It seemed like so long ago – Paul in his floppy cricket hat, Lily kneeling with the binoculars.

'I brought this for you.'

Mel could hardly speak as she looked at Lily.

'Take it,' Paul said. 'I'm not going to pry, I know that something has happened between you, I always knew that there was something between you.'

'Please don't . . .' Mel said desperately.

'It's OK,' he said, taking her hand. 'It will be OK. I just don't know which of you I'm jealous of.'

And Mel laughed and rubbed her eyes.

'You're a cheeky bastard,' she said and squeezed his hand.

'Are you going to be in our group, Melanie?'

'What?'

'Our group. We're going next door.'

Mel stared at the woman asking the question. Her name badge said Philippa, she was wearing a corduroy pinafore dress with a lacy-collared shirt. Horrible, misanthropic thoughts bubbled through Mel's mind. *I feel like I am in prison. I wish you would all die. You are an alien, Philippa.*

'I mean, if you want to be in the other group . . . I just thought . . .'

'It's OK.' Mel forced a smile.

'Are you all right, Melanie?' Bob, the course-leader, had appeared by her side. He had a beard and a voice that matched Philippa's pinafore.

'I'm not feeling very well,' Mel said. 'Would you mind if I just went to lie down? I've actually done this exercise before anyway. On another course.' She tried to make a joke. 'I was first off the mountain. I ate everybody else.'

Bob and Philippa stared at her. Why did such people exist? Mel thought desperately. What was their purpose?

'OK,' Bob said. 'Perhaps you should lie down.'

'Good luck,' Mel said to Philippa and gave her an unconvincing, insincere smile.

Upstairs, she stared out of the window at the grounds of the conference centre. A squirrel bounced across the lawn and shot up the side of a tree, birds were singing. Mel was in agony, she could not concentrate, she felt nauseous and, worst of all, trapped, utterly trapped and isolated.

'What the fuck am I doing here?' she said to herself, opening a sachet of coffee and putting it in a cup, switching on the kettle. She tried to open one of the tiny milk cartons, finally jabbing it with her nail so that it spilt everywhere. 'Shit!' She threw it across the room. 'Fucking thing.' Milk dribbled down the wall.

Calm down, she told herself. *Just calm down.* She lay on her back on the bed, breathing deeply, staring at the ceiling.

Mel sends her love.

She winced.

Lily had phoned Mel the evening after the opera. Mel had just about managed to crawl into work late, read her e-mails and go straight home again. She had been desperate for the phone call and dreading it at the same time. Their conversation had been agonisingly polite as they had dodged around the issue. Finally, Mel had told Lily that she was going on this course and that she would call her when she returned. Fine, Lily had said. I'll be busy with the court case starting. You're OK? And Mel had said that she was fine.

Love me as I love you.

It was not that it had been bad, not that it had been unpleasant, not a simple story of sex-ruined-everything. It was just that, even as their bodies had drunkenly collided in the bed that Lily had once shared with her husband, Mel had become aware of the impossibility of it all. There was pleasure but it was the pleasure of proximity, the pleasure of holding Lily in her arms, not the pleasure of real abandonment, not even the pleasure she had felt with Mark – a person about whom she cared very little. There had been release, but it was not what Mel might have expected. At one point – to her dismay – she had become aware that she was going through the motions, that her heart was not really in it. She had enjoyed the tenderness, the kiss, the caress. But they had gone beyond that, and Mel felt a sense of loss, that something critical that had existed between them was gone. If only they could develop a kind of wise knowingness about it, put it to one side and fashion something new out of it, a different kind of friendship, but Mel did not know whether they could. She had slept with men before and stayed friendly with them, although usually even those friendships began to falter. But this was different and she didn't want to just stay friends anyway. She still loved Lily and longed for her and wanted to be with her. Yet it had been Mel who had not called her in the few days before she went away, had retreated to consider these things. Now she was here in this hell and if she were on the mountain now she would take off her clothes and lie down in the snow and viciously attack anybody who tried to rescue her or persuade her to adopt any strategy other than abject surrender to the elements.

Mel had revisited the evening over and over in her mind. Perhaps the alcohol had been the problem, perhaps she had been too drunk. She also wondered whether anything would ever have happened if it had not been for the strange and unique night at the opera. She thought that she might have held her feelings for Lily a secret, might have luxuriated in unconfessed love until that love had the chance to change into something different. But did she wish it had not happened? No, not that either because she still shuddered as she remembered Lily whispering her name, the hand fluttering beneath the hem of her dress. It had had to happen, it had been inevitable. Mel gritted her teeth and clenched her fists. There was no Pepa on her shoulder, no cheerful shameless philosophy that she could appeal to.

And why had she retreated from Lily when she missed her so much, wanted to talk to her so desperately? What would Lily say? What did Lily think?

There was a knock on the door.

'Come in,' Mel called without any enthusiasm.

'Are you OK?' Philippa's head poked around the door. 'Do you mind if I come in?'

Mel rolled her eyes. *Get lost, you corduroy pest.*

'We were a bit worried about you,' Philippa said.

'We?'

'The group. Are you still feeling unwell?'

'To be honest, erm, Philippa, I'm just not in the mood for all this crap.'

'Oh, I don't think you can say it's crap.'

'Why can't I?' Mel demanded with a sudden pugnacity that made Philippa almost hop backwards. Mel relented, although she found something repugnant about this unwanted intruder. 'No, you're right, it's not crap. It's inane, it's a farce, it's money for old rope. I consider it a scandal. People get paid lots of money for this nonsense. Anyway, if you're enjoying it so much how come you're not downstairs getting off the mountain?'

'I just wanted to see how you were.'

'Well, as you can see, I'm fine.'

'You don't look fine to me. Do you want to talk about it?'

With you? Mel stared at her incredulously. She was on the edge of hysteria.

'Perhaps I can help.'

A nasty suspicion started to grow in Mel's mind. There was an evangelist in her room. It was the determination, the refusal to accept the rebuff, the bright-eyed dedication of the woman. Sure enough, she noticed that Philippa was wearing a little fish badge on the strap of her pinafore; she must belong to some fundamentalist group.

'I don't know,' Mel said, 'why the people on the mountain don't just commit mass suicide. Wouldn't you agree that would be the most sensible thing to do? Perhaps preceded by a frenzied bout of group sex to make sure that when they die they at least do it with smiles on their faces?'

Philippa shuddered. 'Absolutely not,' she said. 'Even when we feel real despair, suicide is never the answer. We should remember that, when we feel at our most alone, there is always somebody looking down on us.'

'So, no to suicide but yes to the group-sex part?'

'No to both,' Philippa said firmly.

'OK,' Mel said. 'Listen, Philippa, I would really like to be alone now. You're right that I have a problem and I need to work it out by myself.'

Mel felt transformed, she was cheerful and light-headed. The situation had gone from the terrible to the comic in an instant. She laughed inside as she imagined all the outrageous things she might say to Philippa. She could well imagine Pepa — *You see, Philippa, I'm in a long-term relationship which I can't imagine ever leaving and then the other day I went to bed with a woman with whom I think I'm in love but it's a strange kind of love and I know I could not sustain any kind of real sexual relationship with her. Have you ever experimented with women, Philippa?*

Mel put her hand over her mouth to stop herself from laughing.

'Thanks for coming to talk to me,' she said, opening the door. 'I honestly feel a lot better for our chat. Goodbye.'

'But I haven't . . .'

'No, you've really helped. Perhaps I'll see you down in the bar later.'

She lay down on her bed and hugged the pillow to her before falling asleep. When she awoke, she was starving so she opened the packet of bourbon biscuits by her kettle. They were stale and crumbled into her hand but she stuffed them in her mouth anyway. It was already dark, so she undressed and slept again.

Mel decided that she would not be able to survive the course if she continued to behave as childishly as she had done on the first day. So for the next couple of days, she joined in the role-playing exercises, offered positive suggestions on issues about which she cared not at all, went orienteering and skived off to the pub with Christine and Roger – the two tolerable people she had met on the course but whom she knew she would never meet again.

'Has that bloody fundamentalist been pestering you?' Christine asked when they were drinking wine in the bar after dinner.

'Yeah, on the first day. She came to my room.'

'Me too. She won't leave me alone because she's found out about Sean.'

Sean was Christine's son who was recovering from leukemia.

'She kept on at me about it restoring my faith. I told her I had never had any to restore and that the only thing it gave me some faith in was modern medicine. Anyway, it was a stupid argument because it would mean that if he hadn't recovered then I would be justified in losing my faith.'

'Only if she were consistent,' Roger said. 'Which I'm sure she isn't.'

Mel said happily, 'Well, we'll never have to see her again. It's the last day tomorrow.' She knew it was time to phone Lily and try and sort things out. Perhaps she would phone her from her room later on. She hadn't spoken to Lily about it yet; they would be able to sort something out. It couldn't stay like this.

'Thank God. Do you remember her on the first night, Roger? When we were watching the thing on the news about the rail-crash case. And she started going on about a greater justice. Small comfort to that poor bloody woman who was just standing there crying in the street in front of all the cameras.'

'What?' Mel stared at Christine. She had gone to sleep on the first night, clutching the biscuit wrapper in her hand, unable to go downstairs. She remembered the next morning at breakfast, people sitting around and reading the papers. She had only been able to find the sports page of the *Guardian* which she had scanned for West Ham transfer news.

'Yeah, I mean, greater justice is all very well—'

'What happened? What happened?'

'In the court case? It was thrown out on the first morning. The judge found some legal technicality as to why corporate manslaughter could not be established. And the train driver, I can't remember what happened there, but that was dropped as well.'

Three days ago. And Mel had still not called Lily.

'What woman in the street?' she half shouted. She knew it was Lily. It had to have been Lily.

'What's her name again? That poor woman who's been a kind of spokeswoman and whose husband died in the hospital. It was horrible. She was making a statement to the cameras and then she just broke down completely. Poor soul. What's her name again, Roger? Forest?'

'Forrester, I think.'

'Jesus fucking Christ. Fuck, FUCK.' Mel put her head in her hands.

'Don't let Philippa hear you say that. Mel, are you OK?'

Mel ran to the pay-phone in the lobby and dialled Lily's number. It rang and rang. She almost beat the wall with the receiver in frustration. Nothing, no answer, not even a machine. She called Patrick.

'Patrick, it's Mel.'

'Hi, Melton Mowbray, and speaking of pies, guess what Jim and I have—'

'Patrick, has Lily called?'

'Oh, yeah, yeah she did.'

'What did she say?'

'Nothing really. Sounded a bit weird but what's new? She asked if you were back. She said she'd be in touch.'

'What does that mean?'

'What she says. I suppose she'll call you when you get back. Are you coming back tomorrow morning?'

'Yes. No. I'm coming tonight. Didn't you know the court case had collapsed?'

'What court case?'

'Jesus, Patrick, you watch enough fucking TV, couldn't you have told me about this?'

'Mel, I don't know what you are talking about. But whatever's bugging you, don't take it out on me.'

Patrick said this in a tone of quiet dignity rather than anger.

'I'm sorry, I'm sorry. I'm coming home.'

'Now? It's nearly ten o'clock at night, Mel.'

'If Lily phones, tell her I've only just found out. I'm coming down to London and I'll go and see her.'

'Found out what?'

'It doesn't matter. Just tell her. I'll see you.'

Mel ran upstairs to her room and began throwing clothes into her bag. When she had finished packing, she glared around the room. There was only a dirty coffee cup and a biscuit wrapper on the floor. As she opened the door to leave, she remembered the bathroom, cursed, and swept toothbrush, deodorant, lipstick, perfume, into the open bag.

'Mel, I bought you a glass of wine.' Christine looked at the bag in her hand. 'Where are you going?'

'Home. I can't explain. It's urgent.'

She had not noticed Bob, who was sitting at the adjoining table and who stood up when he heard Mel say this.

'Home? Melanie, you can't.'

Just you watch me, Beardy.

'I'm afraid I have to.'

'But tomorrow is the critical day. We're videoing ourselves in pairs and I've put you with Philippa. It'll be most inconvenient.'

'Sorry, Bob, family crisis. No choice.'

'Could you not at least . . .'

But Mel was out of the door.

She drove fast down the motorway, staying in the outside lane. She had to close her eyes when she imagined Lily breaking down in front of the cameras. Other images of Lily crowded her consciousness – in the car on the way back from the Great Northern, sitting in the garden drinking Kirs, holding up a bag of ice creams on the garage forecourt, collapsing with her bloody foot in the orchard, kneeling in front of Mel, her eyes distorted by alcohol and desire. Mel gripped tight on the steering wheel.

At some point in the journey, she had to stop for food because her driving was becoming erratic and she had drunk two glasses of wine in the bar. If the police were to pull her over, she might fail the breath test and not get back to the one place she wanted above all else to be. She sat in the service station and dipped onion rings in ketchup, drank a cup of tea, studied the spotty teenagers serving the food and tried to imagine their lives. She hardly even knew where she was, somewhere in the Midlands, the heart of the country. There were people playing on the computer games, swivelling with guns, skiing, driving racing cars. There were men and women buying magazines, sweets, fizzy drinks. There was a muzaked version of 'El Condor Pasa' in the background. From her seat, Mel could see a Happy Eater sign. She held on to the edge of the table to steady herself, chewed grimly the harsh food in her mouth.

Lily's house was dark when she arrived at around two in the morning. Mel sat in the car for a moment, composed herself, and then got out and rang the bell. She kept her finger on the bell for almost ten minutes but nobody answered. She called up to the window but there was still no response. Frustrated, she returned to the car and took out her mobile to call on the phone. She rang and rang again – no voice, no machine. Desperately, Mel called Lily's name and somebody in a neighbouring house yelled to her to shut up. Other lights went on in the house across the road and the front door opened.

'Mel?' It was Claudia, the babysitter. She was wearing a dressing-gown over a *South Park* T-shirt, on her feet were slippers shaped like big furry claws. At any other time, Mel might have laughed.

'Claudia, where's Lily?' Mel crossed the road.

'She's not here, Mel.'

'Not here? What do you mean? Where is she?'

'She's gone, Mel. After the court case, Lily was really upset. Her brother came over from France and they went back there the next day. He got her a ticket, they went almost straightaway. On a plane from the City Airport. She's in France. I thought you would know that.'

Exhausted and anguished, Mel sank to the kerb and put her head in her arms, staring down at her feet in the gutter.

'I've been away,' she muttered to herself. 'I didn't know. I've been away. I wasn't here.'

Claudia's mother appeared in the doorway. She had almost exactly the same face as her daughter, only she was frowning at Mel.

'What's going on? Has something happened to Lily? Why are you sitting in the street? It's very late, you know, to be calling out like that.'

Mel looked up at her through her hair.

'Lily's gone?'

'Yes, to France. She was in a terrible state. Her brother had to come and get her.'

'Did she leave a message? Claudia, did she tell you anything? Try and remember.'

Mel looked with such an imploring expression at the young girl that she screwed up her face as if desperate to give Mel the message that she wanted.

'I'm sorry.' Claudia glanced at her mother.

'Now look,' the older woman said, 'I really think you should be getting home. It's far too late for you to be up as well, Claudia. You can't just sit there in the street, young lady.'

'I'm sorry,' Mel said. She was fighting back tears. 'I'm really sorry for disturbing you.'

She made her way to the car and got in, sat staring at the darkened house, the place to which she could gain no access, the place where she had had moments of pure happiness, where she had sat watching a greenfinch in the larch tree, where she had drunk whisky and seen the fox in the garden.

Actually, I found it really sexy.

Did you?

Oh, unbearably so.

Mel clenched the steering wheel then slowly sank her head between her hands, banging her forehead gently on the wheel. Inside, she was howling with misery. It was too late, she had not been here, it was just too late.

love-letters

Mel pressed her face to the window, smelling the familiar sour enamel, watching the passers-by. She had sat by the window most afternoons since calling into work to say that she was on sick leave and had doctors' certificates. It had been three weeks now since she had been in her office. In the late afternoon, she would sometimes see Patrick returning from his new job inputting information on to computers for a magazine. Patrick actually enjoyed the fact that the job was ultra-repetitive and carried zero responsibility. His boredom threshold might be low but in the world of work he liked to be told what to do, do it for the requisite number of hours, and then leave. He did so well at it, robotically punching away at the keyboard, that they had wanted to make him a supervisor but he had refused. Too much hassle, he had said, for virtually no extra money. He also preferred non-career jobs because the people were more interesting. He had even gone out for a drink after work with a couple of South African girls and returned late with a cat-got-the-cream expression that – at any other time – might have made Mel suspicious.

It had taken a little time before Mel found that she could no longer face going to work. After Lily had left, she had gone to the office as usual. It was as if she were in shock, could not face up to Lily's sudden disappearance; she functioned almost normally but with a dull tone in her voice that Patrick had recognised and which clearly alarmed him. He was incapable of breaking through to Mel and decided to retreat rather than confront her or ask her any awkward questions. Jim – who might have asked some awkward questions – was working on the Isle of Wight. Mary did ask Mel whether there was something wrong with her and Mel said that she suspected that she might be going down with a virus. Mary gave her an energy-restoring, druid-blessed herbal remedy which Mel threw away.

'Seen this, Mel?' Graham had tossed her the paper as he came in one morning. Mel had picked it up.

MGL SHARE PRICE TUMBLES AMID FEARS OVER CLINICAL TRIALS.

And Mel had read about the unfolding scandal at MGL after a Sunday newspaper had published allegations relating to clinical trials. This had led to the resignation of Dr Margaret Jowell from the board of the Great Northern and a statement from Robert Hislop that jobs were at risk if MGL's expansion programme were halted. Questions were being asked about Hislop's suitability to remain as a special adviser on the government's health task-force, questions which the government was angrily dismissing.

'Grow up,' the Prime Minister had ordered his critics in Parliament.

'I think we can assume that they'll be looking a little more carefully at the terms of the MGL deal if jobs are under threat,' Graham had said. 'Are you OK, comrade? If you want to have a chat I'm always here.'

And Mel had smiled painfully at this kind and mildly eccentric man who could not help her at all.

That lunchtime, Mel had gone shopping to buy a present for her sister's birthday, wandering into a bookshop to have a look at the books on art. Trance-like, she was drawn to the literature section. She had picked up *First Love* by Turgenev and it was as if she were suddenly paralysed and tears began to drop on to the slim book she was holding in her hand.

'Hey, are you OK?' a voice had said gently beside her. It was one of the sales staff. He was not the usual young bookseller, there were flecks of grey in his beard and he was wearing glasses. Mel had wondered if he were the manager.

'I'm not sure,' she said.

He removed the book from her hand. 'You're making my stock wet,' he said but his tone was not unkind. 'Would you like to come through and have a glass of water?'

Mel nodded without understanding what he was saying to her and allowed herself to be led through to the back of the shop. She sat at a table, surrounded by piles and piles of books, while he went to get her a glass of water.

'Here,' he said when he returned with a finger-smudged glass, 'you'd better take this as well. You've damaged it with your tears.' And he handed Mel the copy of *First Love* that she had been holding. 'Do you like Turgenev?' he asked. 'I think he writes the perfect novel. Beautiful and short.'

Mel shrugged. 'I've only read one. *On the Eve*. A friend gave it to me. But she's gone away now.'

'I see. Is that what you're upset about?'

Was that what she was upset about? She thought about Gordon Forrester and about Brenda Fletcher and about Paul Flitcroft in Mexico with Miranda and about Graham with his stickers and even about Barry Williams with his pomposity and his socks with sleeping cats on them. She thought about her sister Sarah, who had started talking for the first time about giving up her art, who was working as an usher at the cinema. And she thought about Lily, could not rid her mind of the image of her breaking down in front of the cameras, phoning her brother in desperation, Daniel asking her where they were going. *On a plane, darling, we're going on a plane . . . Come and get me, Laurence, please just come and get me, just take me away from here.*

So where were the victories?

Mel knew that she could not return to work and said that she thought she would like to go home.

'I'm sorry you're sad,' the bookseller said. 'Perhaps you'd better not read that until you feel a bit happier.'

'Oh, it will be OK,' Mel said. 'Sad things are good for the soul.'

'Yes,' he laughed. 'But sometimes happy things are even better. Why don't you get a cab? I'll come and wait with you if you like.'

'It's nice here among the books,' Mel said absent-mindedly and then caught his expression and laughed. 'I'm not saying I want to stay here. I think I will just go home.'

Three weeks had passed since then and Mel had not returned to work, had watched the people come and go, had even seen the couple who had kissed so passionately on the street corner walking along in silence, carrying Sainsbury's bags.

Mel frowned suddenly as an unmistakable figure – small, dressed in a bright skirt, T-shirt and trainers – a bottle of wine sticking out of her rucksack – proceeded with familiar determination along the road, almost at a trot, looking up at the window. It was Pepa. What was she doing here at this time in the afternoon? Mel ducked back from the window, unsure whether Pepa had seen her. When the door buzzer rang, Mel did not answer. She was sure that Pepa had not seen her. Go away, she thought, just go away.

The phone rang and Pepa's voice burst on to the answerphone.

'Walk to the window and look out. I know you're there. I *saw* you, moron-features. Come on, hurry up, you silly cow.'

Mel peered out. Pepa was standing with a furious expression on her face, looking up and speaking on a mobile.

'Never, never, do that to me again. Now open the fucking door.'

Mel decided that she had better do as she was told.

'How did you know I was here?' she asked Pepa, who had begun putting some pistachios and figs in bowls and switching the kettle on to boil.

'Patrick called me. He's worried about you, Mel. So was I when I heard that you weren't going to work.'

She turned with her hand on her hip, frowning.

'Have you heard from her?'

Mel blushed. 'I don't . . .'

'Mel, I've known for ages that something was happening there. I think Patrick did as well. Have you heard from her?'

Mel nodded. She could feel a terrible pain in her chest, she was desperate not to start weeping again. One morning, a letter with a French postmark had dropped on to the mat. *My dearest Mel* . . . It was a love-letter, but it was also a letter of farewell. Lily was among the pines of Provence. There were forest fires burning, she said. It was because of global warming. Mel had seen this on the news, a plane over tree-covered hills dropping a curtain of water. It looked a feeble and inadequate response to the ferocity of the flames.

'She didn't put the address,' Mel said and began to cry, her hand in front of her eyes as if trying to stop the flow of tears, as if she were sitting in the back of a taxi and hiding her face from the flash-bulbs of the paparazzi.

Pepa came and put her arm around her friend.

'Oh, darling, please, sweetheart, Mel, please don't cry like that, you're breaking my heart . . .'

'Why didn't she put the address?' Mel looked up at Pepa whose own black eyes were glistening.

'Well, I don't know what happened between you. You slept with her, didn't you?'

Mel nodded. 'But that's not it, that's not why, not just that anyway . . . I can't explain it . . . I loved her. It changed things but I'm not sorry it happened. It had to happen. Then I went away, she must have thought I didn't want to see her, but I missed her and I was coming back to talk to her . . .'

'But Mel, sweetheart, it was impossible. She had just lost her husband as well. You were dealing with a wounded person. I tried to say that to you once. I'm not saying it was your fault, you can't choose who you fall in love with, but maybe you lost track of reality a bit. You didn't see the real person.'

'Who was the real Lily? Who is the real anybody? I don't know what that means.'

'OK, but you have to be careful as well. Her husband dying was real enough. The court case collapsing was obviously real.'

Mel almost groaned at Pepa's last statement. She could imagine how the court case collapsing would have triggered a general collapse in Lily. It was so unfair, so unjust and Lily must have finally had enough.

'You're right,' she said to Pepa. 'I don't know why it happened. And with a woman. You know me, Pep, I've never really . . .'

'I know that. You had a need, there was a space. The fact that she was a woman was irrelevant. No, that's not what I mean because maybe it was highly relevant. But you didn't suddenly change your sexuality because you met her.'

'No, I didn't,' Mel said sadly. 'I've made such a fool of myself.'

'Don't be too hard on yourself. There was obviously something about her. I was jealous, you know. It was like you'd found this soulmate and I was just the person you sometimes got drunk with. We've had such good times together, you're my best friend, I felt left out.'

'I'm really sorry if you felt that.' Mel picked up a fig from the bowl and held it to Pepa's mouth. 'Have a fig,' she said.

Pepa laughed. 'That's more like it,' she said, opening her mouth and letting Mel feed it to her.

'You know that you sometimes appear rather indifferent to people,' Pepa said suddenly. 'It's a very attractive quality, of course . . .'

'But I don't mean to do that,' Mel said. 'I've never thought of myself like that. Quite the opposite.'

'Of course,' Pepa said. 'If you were conscious of it it would be completely different.'

They sat quietly for a moment, Pepa absent-mindedly plaiting Mel's hair.

'I'm thinking of quitting my job,' Mel said.

'Well, there might have been a time when I would have been delighted to hear it. Those men at the top sound like a right bunch of power-tripping old bullies. But it's part of you as well, Mel. You can't just leave the field clear for the creeps. Your job is what you do and you're good at it.'

'I got really stitched up.'

'Yeah, but what are you going to do instead?'

'I don't know. I don't know.'

'Don't make any hasty decisions. Here, have a fig.'

Mel opened her mouth and they sat chewing figs and cracking pistachios for a while.

'So what did she say in the letter?' Pepa asked casually and Mel knew that Pepa was the one person she could show it to, wanted her to read it. She fetched it from the chest of drawers and threw it at Pepa, who took it from the envelope and started to read, her eyebrows lifting and forehead creasing from time to time. When she had finished, she folded the letter carefully and put it back in the envelope.

'Wow,' she sighed. 'You see, Mel, some people will never have a letter like that written to them. I've never had a letter like that.'

'I never will again,' Mel said.

Never again, never again.

'Well, don't get greedy. Anyway, she doesn't put the address, you're right, but it's obvious that she's still very unhappy and she needs to sort herself out. Maybe sometime . . .'

'Don't say that.'

'You're right. You mustn't think like that. I'm just saying that I don't think she's closing all the doors.'

'I'd like to think that was true. Oh, Pepa, I've been so fucking miserable.'

'Mel, I'll do anything to make you happy again. Come away with me, let's go away for a while. I'm not her, I know I can never be her, there was something between you. A right spoiled, precious little pair of lovebirds you were. That's right, laugh, come on, you know you want to laugh. I love you and I'll look after you, stop crying, please don't cry, you've got me, you'll always have me, I'll always be your friend.'

And Mel put her arms around Pepa, hanging on to her as if she were a tree, and Pepa rocked her and murmured endearments and sometimes insults and stroked her hair. After a while, Mel's tears stopped.

'We've eaten all the figs,' she sniffed.

'So we have. Time for the wine then.'

They sat drinking wine and Mel told Pepa about the scene in the bookshop.

Pepa said, 'That reminds me of a scene in a film I saw. This weird guy who really fancied me made me go with him. It was his favourite film, he'd seen it about twenty times. Arty shite, except it wasn't shite. It was Cuban, it had subtitles, you would have loved it, of course. But it was very good, actually. Anyway, this girl, she's unhappy and she goes into this dingy old bookshop in Havana. She's crying like you were and the old bookseller, he's her friend . . .'

'You're not going to tell me the whole plot like you usually do?'

'No. Shut up. I wanted to tell you what he said to her. In Spanish it sounded so nice. He said, *"Descansa, pajarita, descansa . . ."*'

'What does it mean?'

'It means, *Rest, little bird, rest.* But it sounds better, more tender in Spanish. It's funny because the girl also has a lovely granny who sits on the porch with her at night. The granny is from Galicia like me. Lots of Cubans are descendants of *Gallegos*.'

'As you so emphatically told the fat American at Selfridges cigar counter.'

'What? Oh yeah, that fascist pig. Anyway, the granny is from Spain and she sings to her granddaughter to comfort her, she sings an old lullaby from Galicia. It was really pretty. Anyway, I didn't particularly fancy the guy who took me to the film but because I'd liked it so much I let him take me home afterwards.'

Mel started to laugh. 'You went to bed with somebody because they'd taken you to a good film?'

'Yeah. There are worse reasons. We both got a pretty good deal in my opinion. I'll never forget that film and he'll never forget me.'

They both started to laugh, Pepa's head thumping against Mel's shoulder as she did so.

'You're a disgrace,' Mel said. 'Anyway, where are you going to take me away to?'

'Where would you like to go?'

Mel broke away from her. 'Somewhere in the sun. Somewhere near the sea. Somewhere I can put my toes in the sea.'

'Well, we can go anywhere. We can go to Greece, Italy, Portugal, or Spain. We can go to secluded islands or stay on the mainland. We could go further afield, to India or Mexico or Thailand. We can sit on beaches and then go to exotic cities and do cultural things and misbehave in the evenings. In the mornings we'll drink coffee and eat *churros* and laugh at our antics. We can sail away and party with the Wild Things and hang off trees. Threesomes, foursomes, twentysomes – we can do anything you want. And if you don't want to, we'll never come back.'

'I might want to come back for my supper. Patrick might have made a pie.'

'Well, you can decide that when we're there. But you need to get out of this city. And this time I won't take no for an answer.'

'What about Patrick?'

'I've already told him.'

'What did he say?'

'He said OK as long as we videoed any sexual misbehaviour for him. He's been very worried about you. He's an idiot but he's not a bad person. He's frightened of losing you.'

Mel nodded. 'I know,' she said.

'Is he going to lose you?' Pepa looked carefully at her friend.

'I don't know.'

'Oh well.' Pepa continued to plait Mel's hair with her fingers and then she kissed her forehead and murmured, '*Descansa, pajarita, descansa.*'

It was a bright, clear day when Mel went to pick up two tickets for Spain from the travel agents. Pepa had decided on Spain so that they would have the advantage of language.

'But nowhere near my village,' she said. 'Unless you want to get burned at the stake. We'll go to the south. Cadiz would be nice. Then we'll just travel down the coast.'

Mel's doctor had certified that she had been suffering from severe stress and that, while she was fit to return to work, he thought that it was a sensible idea for her to take a holiday. The deal with MGL had been postponed because the company were restructuring in the light of the problems with their clinical-trial results. Hislop was still vice-president and the DTI had announced that no charges were to be brought against any of its directors. Nothing had really changed, Mel thought, except for her. She shivered as she remembered Lily slipping into the seat beside her at the press conference, dropping her pen, looking up at Mel for the first time.

When she had paid for the tickets with her credit card, she went to buy soap and deodorants from the chemist's, to Marks and Spencer to get some new underwear, and a plain black swimming costume because she hated bikinis. She went to the record shop and bought herself some new CDs, including *Rigoletto*. Then she went to the bookshop where she had first broken down and been given a glass of water by the bookseller.

'Hello,' she said when she found him by the shelves. 'Remember me?'

He squinted at her. 'The weeping Turgenev fan? You certainly look a lot happier now.'

'I am. I wanted to say thank you for looking after me that day. I was in a very bad way. I'm going on holiday with my friend.'

'The friend who went away and made you unhappy?'

'No, a different friend.'

'Are you here to look for some sad books for the beach?'

'Maybe something happy and something sad.'

He laughed. 'Ah, the girl who wants everything.'

'Is that so unreasonable?'

'Not as a general aspiration, I suppose. Anyway, I hope you have a nice holiday.'

'I'm sure I will. Thanks. I really appreciate what you did.'

'It was nothing. But don't tell your friends that you can get free books here if you cry enough.'

Mel walked out on to the street with her tickets safe in her bag, hugging her new purchases to her. She was better, she was getting better, but she was not fully recovered. Disruption, she had said to Lily, some people introduce disruption into their lives. Lily had alluded to this in her letter. *I do not regret the disruption that we caused each other* . . .

Mel had arranged to meet Pepa for lunch in the oyster bar of Selfridges. They were going to choose sunglasses for their trip. Mel could feel the sun on her arms, the books she had bought clunking against her bare legs. She knew that Lily had been right to go away, right not to put her address on the letter. Mel would have got straight in her car and driven to Provence and what good would that have done? Now, she was walking through the city to meet her friend, she would look from a plane window at England disappearing behind her, she would hold Pepa's hand because fearless Pepa was terrified of taking off.

Why this sweet feeling of hope?

Mel smiled painfully to herself as she remembered this. She was young, she was flesh and blood, but she was also memory and conscience and desire. A bundle of genetic information, a human being who shivered at the music in a darkened auditorium, at the memory of a woman with sybilline eyes picking up her pen from the floor. Stopping to cross the road, Mel looked up to see a small bird above her head. Angled wings, streamer-tail — a swallow! If she had been close enough, she might have seen its red throat. She paused to watch as it soared above her, taking its flight above the city — so delicate, so fragile. Perhaps it was not a swallow, perhaps it was a swift or a martin, perhaps she just longed for it to be a swallow. It did not matter — today it was a swallow, this little compact miracle of evolution that was rising and falling on currents of air. Mel stood still in the middle of the city, looking up at the clear sky while people streamed around her as if she were a rock in a river. She stood there clutching her bag of books, watching the little empyreal Partizan with its tiny pumping heart, roller-coastering in the blue sky and beating its wings as if sent there by a solitary and guileless impulse of joy.